LUCIFER'S LAIR

THE DEVILS DOMAIN

ANTHONY JOHN HOARE

Authorunit
17130 Van Buren Blvd., Ste. 238,
Riverside, CA 92504
877-826-5888
www.authorunit.com

ISBN 978-1-960075-24-6 (Paperback)
ISBN 978-1-960075-25-3 (Ebook)

Printed in the United States of America

Contents

PROLOGUE

Upon reflection, how different Ian's life might have been if he'd been able to foresee where those initial steps into that sand funnel would lead him. At first, he found it exhilarating to dance close to the fire only to learn how quickly a tiny spark can erupt into a raging inferno.

Compelled by conscience and love, he dedicated himself to forever douse that all-consuming bonfire of evil.

Through necessity, I will tell Ian's story. Barbara, however, used her artistic talent to pen her song of contempt for this corrupt institution of seduction and evil. These are her lyrics.

(Lucifer's Lair)

By foolishness and greed, here I was led. Now I'm trapped by deceit in my own web. I would leave, but there's no place to run. The life I chose is the life of the gun.

So, heed this advice if you will. The dollar's not wealth it's only a bill—a bill to be paid sometimes with your life. The easy way most often brings strife.

There's a place called Lucifer's Lair. Lost dreams lost loves are plentiful there. In this place called Lucifer's Lair: So, avoid this place if you can take heed from one who is dammed.

I didn't think of the pain so hard to bear for loved ones when I entered there. With this life, I can never undo how can I still ask you to be true?

In so deep, there's no turning back. Compassion, for me, is something you'd lack. I'd change the past if I could, but foolish dreams will do me no good.

There's a place called Lucifer's Lair. Lost dreams lost loves are plentiful there. In this place called Lucifer's Lair: So, avoid this place if you can take heed from one who is dammed.

Don't let lust and greed lead you astray. Value life's gifts work hard every day. Love and wealth, you may then find. Be true to yourself; leave sin behind.

Don't be lured by false dreams of fame. Greed most often brings pain. A pain that burns deep inside. A pain from which you cannot hide.

There's a place called Lucifer's Lair. Lost dreams, lost loves are plentiful there. In this place called Lucifer's Lair: So, take the advice of this fool, and do not go where Lucifer rules!

CHAPTER 1

A tenuous meeting

I had visited Seattle's Pike Place Market many times; however, I knew this visit would be a challenging and very different experience. A meeting I'd planned, especially for this visit, would be awkward at best.

I entered the restaurant early: This being all part of the strategy I'd envisioned for this very special rendezvous. I requested seating with a sea view and was escorted to the upper-level balcony. I Chose a seat at my allotted table that put my back towards the balcony's entrance. This also suited my master plan. This chair, overlooking the downstairs bar, also gave a clear view of the main entrance area below. The direction I was now facing bathed my face in the strong sunlight pouring through its windows.

Perhaps when Sylvia was shown to my table, she wouldn't recognize me immediately. Being forced to face the sun's rays should probably blind her momentarily. If my little scheme succeeds, she would be at my table and about to be seated before realizing it was me she was about to meet. I gave the waiter her name, requesting he should escort her to my table the moment she arrived. Looking over my shoulder towards the entrance below assured me it would be easy to see her on her arrival. It wasn't a long wait as she to was early. It was easy to identify her as she walked in. Her blond hair, her immaculately tailored white naval uniform all helped in complimenting those refined looks. Sylvia created a presence that demanded notice.

My little scheme had worked perfectly. She was completely unaware of who she was meeting until she stood before me.

"You bastard, Jason. What are you doing here?"

"Please, Sylvia, please sit down," I begged her. "I've something important to tell you." Her cold glare sent shivers down my spine. Again, I pleaded with her to sit.

"You have every right to walk away, but I wouldn't have arranged this little charade if it hadn't been imperative, we speak." With some reluctance, she perched herself on the corner of her chair. Her legs remained in the aisle. To me, this portrayed her need to accommodate a speedy exit if it was required. The waiter's cheeks became flushed with embarrassment at witnessing this scene. However, he remained motionless at the table, apparently waiting to take our order.

"A large seafood platter for two and coffees, please, and bring the coffee first." I passed him a large denomination bill. "This is for you. After you've served the food, I would appreciate it if we were left alone until we're about to leave. I'll settle my bill at that time." The waiter smiled, apparently more than happy to comply with this request. His voice now reflected a sign of relief at now being able to extract himself from this awkward situation.

"Yes, sir." Money in his hand, he beat a hasty retreat.

"I don't wish to eat with you, Jason. I think you've made it quite clear that there's nothing more to say between us." She rose from her seat, tightly grasping the purse strap she'd never removed from her shoulder. I had to stop her.

"This isn't entirely about us, Silvia." Again, I pleaded. "This predicament we find ourselves in involves circumstances beyond our control, so please listen to what I'm about to tell you. There are things, essential things you must know, and I don't want you hearing them from anyone else but me. You don't have to eat, but this is a restaurant, and we do have to order something if we wish to sit here." Reluctantly, she sat back down, this time committing fully to the chair.

"I'll start the explanation for my behaviour with Ian's story. It's the only way I know to help you understand what I did was:" I paused in mid-sentence and lowered my head. I felt beads of sweat forming on my brow and in my palms. My throat became as dry as parchment paper. I took a sip of coffee; this small sip had become extremely difficult to swallow. I then looked up into those cold gray eyes: Eyes that once portrayed love. I then continued my sentence at the place where I had so abruptly paused it. "As I thought at that time, it was the best choice for both of us."

I took another sip of coffee; perhaps a short pause would help me gather my composure. A deep breath followed this sip. I then experienced a cold shiver down my spine, accompanied by a feeling akin to someone about to jump into fridge water. "However, situations change, and this is why I must now tell you the whole truth. I'll start by explaining how this predicament we find ourselves in today evolved. Ian's story will explain the entire situation that brought us to this place in time. His story starts long before you and I were born."

CHAPTER 2

The place Ian once called home

London in the early sixties was an exciting and vibrant place to live. There were few cities on earth to match its atmosphere and nightlife. Within the Greater London Metropolis is The City of London or The City, as it's known to the local population. Locals often describe the City as the beating heart of commerce and banking.

Specific areas within this Metropolis contain wholesale markets unique to each separate location. These markets are renowned for specializing in particular produce, fish, meat, vegetables, flowers, and clothing. Carnaby Street, situated amid the garment district, was rapidly gaining an international reputation for its trendy clothing styles.

Nightclubs also played to packed houses in this era. The choice of music was as electrifying as it was diverse. The numerous music venues in its vicinity catered to jazz, modern and traditional, the blues, plus the ever-popular rock and roll. Their American music idols influenced many young British musicians. Drawing on personal experiences with other forms of music, they create their unique sounds. London was the city, Ian Shaw, for a period called home. Ian was born in Canada soon after his parents had emigrated there from England. Ian was just fourteen years old when his mother died from cancer. He witnessed the disease destroying her body and seeing her fade away in great pain left young Ian indelibly scarred. This was a life-changing traumatic experience he would never completely recover from.

Lost in his grief and drinking heavily, his father was unable to give young Ian the necessary support he required. Within two years, he had destroyed his health through excessive drinking, which ultimately led to an untimely death. Ian's grandmother journeyed from England to attend the funeral.

On her return to England, she took young Ian with her. In her care, Ian found love and a stable home. She lived in an upper-middle-class neighbourhood and was financially secure. This financial stability enabled her to send Ian to university, where he obtained an honours degree in economics. With this degree, he was able to secure a position in the banking industry.

Five years had passed since Ian joined the bank. In this space of time, he had become very proficient at his job: Efficient and competent enough to be noticed by his superiors at the bank. It was, at this point, Ian received yet another devastating blow with the sudden death of his beloved grandmother, who he adored. She was the only person left in his life with whom he'd had a close relationship. She was his confidante and friend, the center of his world as he was of hers. He'd allowed himself few personal luxuries and even fewer friends at this point in his life. He became so obsessed with work and ambitions they dominated his entire life. The circles in which he moved consisted mainly of superficial acquaintances. People, to be used in one way or another to further his selfish gains. He was never able to cultivate a steady companionship with a woman. He found it extremely hard to commit to any long-term relationship. Perhaps for Ian, the fear of loss prohibited any such attachments.

The passage of time had not quenched his self-absorbed philosophes. Although he was now more relaxed and confident, there remained a need to feed that gnawing quest for power. This new air of confidence, accompanied by a need to indulge himself with some personal pleasures. He could be found at trendy restaurants and cafes that flourished around the city at most lunchtimes. Most nights, he patronized some of London's more exclusive nightclubs.

The bank's hierarchy was about to bestow upon Ian the greatest accomplishment of his career to date. This new promotion would give him the authority to loan substantial amounts of money for commerce.

Early one Monday morning in August of sixty-two, Ian was summoned to Sir John's office. There he was informed of his new promotion to the executive level. He knew this promotion included the many responsibilities that go with such a prestigious position and many perks. Sir John, chairman of the bank's board of directors, welcomed Ian at the door like a conquering hero with vigorous handshakes and back slaps.

"Congratulations, my boy, it's been decided the promotion you've worked so hard to achieve is yours. Now, sit yourself down, and I'll explain some of the privileges and duties accompanying this promotion."

Ian chose a plush dark red leather chair to reside in well receiving his accolades. All these accomplishments had been earned the hard way and not given. The fruits of his labours were about to be served to him on a silver platter.

An invite to sit was a rarity in Sir John's office. It was not usually a friendly place for employees; By design, it intimidated. This office was Sir John's seat of power. Before Ian's promotion, it would have been considered off-limits to people such as himself, people occupying lesser company status. This place subordinate's entered cap in hand with good reason. Ian was well aware of Sr John's sudden mood swings and how he'd heard subordinates berated for minor infringements of company policies in this office.

Sir John continued. "As I am sure you are aware, you'll be joining me as a member of my golf club. I look forward to enjoying a game or two with you there. There will also be a chauffeured limousine at your disposal at all times plus, of course, a hefty increase in your salary.

Another round of congratulation seems in order, as I believe you're the youngest top executive ever in this bank's history." Formalities over, they engaged in small talk before Ian took his leave.

He now felt about as smug as the cat who got the cream. And this was after dining on canary as a first course. Elated, Ian sailed back through the corridors of power to his own office. He could hardly contain his emotions on this short trip. Closing the door to his office, he took a deep breath. Tensions running through his body were released spontaneously by shouting, "YES!" This display of elation was uncharacteristic of Ian. Since the passing of his beloved grandmother, he'd locked all emotions inside a vault deep within his soul. He'd practically forgotten where he'd hidden the key in that place so seldom used. Her death had stripped him of love and robbed him of compassion, emotions he displayed freely to her in her lifetime. However, a skillful facade had kept these characteristics well hidden. He seemed gregarious to people who did not know him well, and few did. Capitalizing on his new club membership Ian arranged a round of golf for that next Sunday morning. Upon arrival, he was given a message by the steward informing him the colleague who he'd intended playing was unavailable through extenuating circumstances.

This news didn't sit well with Ian. His competitive nature dictated a need to beat this man whom he saw as a rival at work. On the golf course, Ian viewed him as an inferior player. To Ian, it was an Achilles heel to be exploited. This attempt at dominance was temporarily held over. Smothering the pangs of discontent, Ian calmly explained to the steward that not having a partner, he would have to cancel his tee-off time.

"There is a member in the lounge, sir, who I believe is looking for a partner if you would be interested?" Ian's morning was beginning to look a little brighter.

"Yes, I'd be very interested." Ian was led through the lobby and into the lounge. From there, the steward escorted him to a table where a man in his early thirties was sitting. Being approximately Ian's age, this seemed to be an excellent matchup for both of them. There was an air of casualness about this man. He was immaculately dressed for the occasion and looked at ease with himself: To Ian, this displayed self-confidence. Ian saw this as an immediate challenge, for he'd always tried to portray these characteristics in his own facade.

The steward introduced Ian. "Mr. Fuller, sir, pardon my intrusion, but I'd like to introduce you to Mr. Ian Shaw." As they shook hands, the steward continued his conversation with James Fuller. "I've taken this liberty as I know you're both in need of a partner for your morning game. I'll take my leave so you gentlemen may make your arraignments."

After Shaking hands, James sat back down to finish his coffee before making an openhand invitation towards another chair. Ian looked at his watch and did not settle.

"I have a tee-off time in five minutes."

"Well, why are we waiting? I had to forfeit my playoff time." Fuller quickly finished his coffee. As he rose to his feet, he patted Ian's shoulder. "Let's get a move on and make our way to the first tee." Ian followed James out onto the fairway. The solitude at the first tee and fairway made it seem like they had the course to themselves. It also gave ample time for some posturing in the guise of practice swings. Being able to tee off at their leisure, without pressure from other players, was relaxing. This time also helped stimulate the pure pleasure both derived from competitive verbal jousting that blossomed quickly between them.

"What a beautiful morning this is. I hope this doesn't distract you from your game, Ian." He inhaled deeply to capture the full aroma of freshly mowed grass.

"It is a beautiful morning, James. I always look forward to spending as much time as possible outdoors when I'm away from the office. I find the outdoors recharges the batteries. And good weather always gives me that extra competitive edge."

"That works for me too. I agree it's healthy to spend as much time as possible in the fresh air. I'm penned up in an office all day myself. I'm an investment broker. Can you tell me what line of work it is you're in, Ian? I hope I'm not seeming too nosey by asking you this question?

"Banking, James, banking," Ian replied pompously. Then, swinging his three-iron, he watched his ball drop and roll close to the flag. A sweeping arm gesture directed James to take his next stroke. Fuller's concentration was focused, and his ball made the green with a good lay that rivalled Ian's ball's position. It was now apparent to Ian that beneath James's laid-back persona lurked a drive equally as competitive as his own.

"How's your putting, James?" Ian's tone conveyed a subtle challenge.

"Not as good as it could be, Ian." He shrugged as if it was of no concern. "I haven't seemed able to find much time for my game of late, but hopefully, that will change."

Eager to intensify what he already perceived as a competitive situation, Ian threw down the gauntlet.

"Perhaps I can entice you into a small wager, James. Say, five pounds, to make the game more interesting." The challenge was readily accepted.

"That would make the game more interesting! Imagine a banker that gambles!"

"Only on a sure thing, James, only on a sure thing," Ian retorted quickly. "Now, let the real game begin!"

They agreed each would keep their scorecards separate. The final tally would be and settled over a drink in the bar. This drink would then be charged to the loser's club account. Ian entered the lounge with a flamboyant attitude, ensuring his entrance did not go unnoticed by several other guests. James guided Ian to stools at the bar in his laid-back style with the help of some subtle body language. Scorecards were now lying on the bar, and the tallying began. Checking was meticulously on each other's cards, in a manner akin to a schoolboy squabble. It wasn't until rechecking their scorecards several times that they agreed; Ian had won by just one point.

"Well, James, it's time to collect on that wager. Drinks to start was the agreement, I believe."

"Correct, Ian, it was a game well played." James dug into his wallet and handed Ian the agreed sum without remorse. Enjoying the rivalry and the company made it easy to accept such a close decision. Ian called the bar steward and then looked at James.

"Right then: I'll start with a tall gin and tonic, please, James. It's an excellent thirst-quencher for a hot summer's day, don't you think?" The cocktail, placed before him, he sipped it appreciatively. James wondered if it was the beverage Ian was savouring or the win. Ian then held the glass at eye level briefly. Hypnotically he gazed at the bubbles dancing inside the glass. This distraction only helped add confusion to this perception before returning his attention to James. "I hear they have an extent dining room upstairs that overlooks the fairways."

"That's correct, Ian. We should book a table for supper. What do you think?"

"That sounds like an enjoyable way to finish the day. We'll book a table for perhaps

an hour or so from now. We can relax here for a while longer before showering and changing for dinner.

Their table provided an excellent view of the now-empty fairways, draped in the last orange glows of sunlight adorning dark skies. Bathed in the reflected half-light, a sense of tranquillity mantled the quiet dining room. After settling comfortably into their chairs, they were each handed a handsomely bound menu. In keeping with the opulence of the surroundings, these handcrafted menus, bound in calfskin leather, were of the highest quality and were embossed with gold block writing and ornamentation. Its gold silk also graced the spine to complete this presentation. In fitting with this establishment, place settings were equally luxurious. Silver flatware, crystal glasses, finely embroidered linen tablecloths and napkins adorned their table.

Ian pondered through the selections before choosing the trout while James ordered a rare thick steak. After taking their orders, the waiter quickly returned to their table, bearing consommé as an entree. Its aroma alone was enough to entice the ficklest of taste buds. There were few words spoken between them over dinner. Both seemed content to indulge in the pleasures of fine dining. The meals were as meticulously prepared and presented as the elegant surroundings suggested they should be. They commented to each other on the meal's excellence. Their stomachs filled and egos slightly tempered; both leaned back in their chairs to continue their conversation. As the evening drew to a close, James suggested a rematch should be planned for the following week. Ian quickly accepted this invitation. He'd enjoyed James's company, a man he now considered a friend. James was the sort of person who was much more outgoing than himself, despite his vain attempts at flamboyance. James's laid-back attitude made Ian feel at ease and lighthearted. Ian enjoyed that feeling.

On leaving the dining room, they went to the reception desk and booked a game for the following week. The two men then exchanged telephone numbers and addresses before saying good night.

CHAPTER 3

Ian moves up the ladder.

Ian's position and salary were affording him all the status and lifestyle he'd hoped it would. Eager to meet every new challenge his career threw at him, he was a man on a mission. With confidence, he treated obstacles as steppingstones in the course he'd set for himself. His chosen course would entrench him as the heir apparent to Sir John. Decisions made in his new position he wielded like weapons. He exploited every opportunity to mingle with rich and powerful clients. Exploitation, by any means, seemed fair game to him.

The next few months proved fruitful for Ian. His golf games with James became a regular thing, and when the weather was unfavourable, they took to playing squash. They also began meeting socially. James would often arrange dates for Ian so that they could go out as a foursome. James never seemed to have trouble attracting women. Unlike Ian, who had never learned the art of flirting as a steppingstone to romance. Perhaps, for this reason, the dates with women James arranged for Ian never evolved into any permanent relationships. It never bothered Ian, consoling himself in the fact that he and James were not attracted to the same type of women. This fact was partly accurate. He also considered most women as not being his intellectual equal. Those Ian deemed his equivalent was perceived as being arrogant and pushy. Ian never realized this was the image he mirrored.

On the golf course one afternoon, James posed a scenario to which he'd given much thought. "Ian, when you loan money to companies, they must have to submit a prospectus as to the intended use of the funds?"

"Naturally, it's the usual procedure for expansions, material acquisitions, takeovers, that sort of thing, James. My job then is to decide if it's a viable enough project to qualify for that loan?"

"If a person were privy to such information, there could be a lot of money to be made; in the stock market, for instance."

"Even with that information, James, which I'm sure would be illegal, you'd need certain skills to profit from this information."

"I have those skills, Ian; if a person like yourself was not intimidated by petty laws, the sky could be the limit. You supply me with the information, and I'd do the investing. All transactions would run through paper companies with Swiss bank accounts. I already have a Swiss bank account. It would be easy to set one up for you. I could attend to all transactions, making it a hands-off operation for you. It would make it virtually impossible for our little enterprise to be traced back to us, or more importantly, in this case, you.

"You've thought this out quite thoroughly, haven't you, James." Ian then stared at him in bewilderment.

"I most certainly have. I'd need you to sign papers for the account and other things occasionally." Despite some misgivings, Ian was intrigued.

"Well, how much money would be an acceptable amount to start such a project, James? I could muster up five hundred pounds; would that be enough?"

"That's just about the amount I can come up with, Ian. I'll get working on the arrangements, so when you're able to feed me the information, we'll be ready."

Well agreeing to James's proposition, Ian still had misgivings about his decision. However, the lure of James's lucrative proposal did seem very attractive to Ian. The sense of risk in this gamble did appeal to his adventurous nature. This concept had crossed Ian's mind before, although he would never have initiated such a venture without that little push from James.

Within a week, Ian had passed on some information to James, and he, in turn, had turned their one thousand pounds into seventeen hundred. The following two months saw Ian and James make the equivalent of two years' salary.

Christmas was approaching and feeling quite affluent, Ian decided to buy himself some new clothes. There were few people with whom to exchange gifts except James, and James was spending the holidays away with family. This self-gift might make a lonely Christmas a little more tolerable. He decided to use Sir John's tailors. One of the most exclusive tailors in London's Saville Row.

* * *

The pampering he received on entering the establishment played to his ego. He was greeted as he entered by a well-groomed gentleman, who gave a slight bow. The man looked every inch the gentleman's gentleman, dress short cutaway black jacket, and gray and black, pinstripe trousers. The shoes he wore had the distinct shine of black patent leather.

"Mr. Shaw, I presume? We've been expecting you."

"That's correct; I'm here for my appointment."

"Could I interest you in perhaps a glass of sherry, or would you prefer a brandy, Sir?"

"A brandy would be fine." After the man had left, Ian postured before a mirror, well acquainting himself with his surroundings.

The man returned, carrying the brandy, and an open box of cigars, on a small silver tray. He presented it to Ian. "I took the liberty of warming your glass, Sir. Now, could I also interest you in a cigar?" Ian took the brandy, and after swirling the golden elixir around the warm glass, he savoured the aroma released by the heat before sipping.

The temptation urged him to take advantage of a Cuban cigar, attractively displayed and presented to him in a colourful box. However, the memory of, what was, an unpleasant encounter with a cigar remained in his mind. He recalled the price he'd once paid for smoking one: A sick stomach and an awful taste in his mouth the following morning. It was the only recollection required to prompt Ian to decline this offer.

"No, thank you, I don't smoke."

"Now, sir, if you would care to follow me, I'll take you to a fitting room where our Mr. Bryant will assist you with the material and pattern selections."

Ian entered the fitting room, where Mr. Bryant stood waiting. Beside him was a beautifully framed swivel mirror. A matching footstool was close at hand. A large table dominated the room's center. They were all made of mahogany, in keeping with the room's decor and extensively used. The mirror itself was strategically placed to one side so as not to interfere with the task of measuring and fitting, yet giving the client a good view of himself at all times. Mr. Bryant then unfettered his neck from the measuring tap that hung there like shackles.

"If we may start, Sir, with your measurements."

While the tailor attended to his task, Ian sipped his brandy. His vanity could not resist the occasional nonchalant glance into the mirror as his posturing accommodated Bryant's work. Measuring completed, he assisted Ian with various pattern selections designed to cover his entire wardrobe. Next came the choice of appropriate materials for the many garments. Ledgers filled with swaths of fabrics were retrieved from built-in cabinets on the back wall and laid upon the table. Ian methodically scrutinized every sample before selecting what he considered to be the appropriate choices. That done, he began the task of matching shirts, ties, and sweaters to his new wardrobe. He approached this in the same meticulous manner that had gone into his other selections. "Now, Sir, I believe I'm correct in assuming you've recently opened an account with us."

"That's correct." Bryant then called for Ian's account to be made current, recording all the particulars of the day's transaction. The gentleman that had first greeted him in the reception delivered the necessary paperwork for Ian's signature, presented on a silver tray.

After receiving the bill, a matching silver pen occupied a place on the table for his use. In a manner befitting a banker, Ian examined the contract thoroughly before signing it. He was awarded a slight bow in a style he'd only imagined reserved for princes and potentates as he retrieved the receipt that was presented back to him on the same tray. Ian relished this treatment as it stroked his ego. After pocketing his copy, he left the store, accompanied by more subservient behaviour from the staff.

CHAPTER 4

A chance encounter.

A morning of self-indulgence had proved to be a rejuvenating experience for Ian. However, his obsession with appearance dictated he should pause to preen himself at least one more time. Utilizing the reflection offered by the store window, he made some personal superficial adjustments to his appearance before continuing his approach to the waiting limousine. Turning abruptly to resume the walk, he collided head-on into a young woman who was also immersed in her own interests. Apparently, sorting through her purse was more crucial than paying attention to where she was walking. This collision caused the Contents to spill over the pavement. Confusion rained as Ian sidestep the objects at his feet, like some highland worrier performing the sword dance. The dance completed, he stooped to help her pick up the contents strewn about them.

"Oh, I'm so terribly sorry," he blurted out. The tone of his voice displayed a complete lack of confidence. The young woman replied in a voice that had the texture of soft velvet. It was soothing and warm to the ear.

"That's alright; it was as much my fought as yours." There was a magnetism about her that immediately sprung the lock to the volt on his inner soul. It was as if she'd owned a matching key to the one he'd purposely lost so many years before. An aura that glowed about her projected a shroud of tranquillity that engulfed Ian. Ian, mesmerized by her beauty, was momentarily lost for words.

She was a woman in her early twenties, petite, with long dark hair. Her fair skin had the quality of porcelain. Her eyes were a sparkling blue, with long dark lashes. It was more than just looks that attracted Ian's attention; that specific chemistry so hard to explain had started to blossom between them the instant their eyes first met. Picking up the last few items, he handed them to her, and she placed them back into her purse.

"May I give you a lift to where you're going?" He couldn't just let this chance encounter pass, and this was an initial, although a clumsy, attempt at striking up an acquaintance.

"No, that's alright, thank you," she replied. Their eyes, still locked in an embrace, gave her time to realize how handsome she found Ian to be. His manly features, slim athletic build, and his polite manner gave him an old-world charm she also found attractive. In his eyes, she perceived tenderness and vulnerability. These were qualities that were hidden so well, few people had ever detected them. This was the part of his makeup he thought had failed him in the past. This was his Achilles heel, which could be exploited and cause pain. He'd endured enough hurt in life. Although, with this woman, that somehow didn't seem to matter. Not wishing to let this encounter slip through his fingers, he became relentlessly in his quest.

"Then, may I suggest you join me for lunch." Ian's persistence paid off. This time she couldn't resist his charm, and she accepted his invitation. The door to the limousine was opened for them. She took a seat and sank into the soft leather upholstery. The fact that this man had the status to command the use of such a vehicle also impressed her. "Now tell me what your favourite foods are, and do you have a preference as to where you would like to dine?"

You realize you've invited me to launch, and you haven't even asked my name."

"Oh, god." He'd been so caught up in this pursuit, he'd completely forgotten the formalities. "How stupid of me, my name's Ian, Ian Shaw."

"Well, Mr. Ian, Ian, Shaw," she replied with a smile, "my name's Barbara." Ian laughed.

"I did sound a bit pompous, didn't I. " Her smile turned to a grin.

"You know, Ian, I'm not really hungry but, if we were to take a walk along the embankment together, I think I'd enjoy that." Ian welcomed the suggestion perceiving she was as interested in him as he was in her.

"I'd be a fool to say anything but yes to a long stroll with a pretty girl," Ian instructed

his driver, Mr. Homes, to drive them to their destination. Once again, their attention focused on each other, and engaging in small talk seemed a pleasurable way of building the foundation for this new relationship.

Homes dropped them off at Westminster bridge, on the understanding, they were to be picked up an hour later.

The skies were overcast, throwing the shadows of its drab gray cloak over the river. However, every cloud has a silver lining for someone. Today it was time for Barbara and Ian to experience this hidden feature. As they began to enjoy the pleasure of this walking together, he took her hand. She gave him a smile and made a comment.

"I like walking here, especially when it's cold and practically deserted. For me, it's a special place on a day like this. It's a place to clear my head and unwind. I find the solitude helps release the stress of the day for a while."

They paused for a moment to lean on the balustrade and view the pleasure boats moored below to ride out the winter months. The wake created by the occasional flow of river traffic caused these boats to undulate slowly. The cold water gently lapping against their side planking was the only sound generated by these river dwellers in hibernation. In the holiday season, brightly painted seats would be packed with sightseers: However, now they looked cold, damp, and uninviting.

Even a cold setting such as this couldn't chill the warm glow Ian felt stemming from deep inside. In that instant, his thoughts were carried back to happier times: A past he'd previously trained his memory not to dwell on.

"I'd forgotten the simple pleasures that can be derived from taking time out to stand back to smell the roses, so to speak. When I was young, my parents would often take me for long walks, mostly on the weekends. I was usually allowed to bring friends along. We would walk along beaches or hike into the mountains. In warm weather, we would often take a picnic with us and make a day of it. I enjoyed those times. There was always time to appreciate the natural beauty around us and enjoy the simpler things in life.

"It sounds like you don't see much of your parents these days, Ian?"

"They died when I was in my early teens, and my grandmother took on the task of raising me. She was a wonderful person. I loved her very much. It's been several years since she passed away. They say time's a great healer, but I still miss her."

Ian hadn't laid himself open to anyone in this manner for many years. James was a close friend, but their relationship was a competitive one. Compassion, he always believed, could be viewed as a weakness. His vulnerability felt safe in Barbara's keeping. These were feelings that had needed expressing for far too long. Never having nurtured a deep connection with anyone since his grandmother's death, it felt good to have a confidante again. The fact that they'd only just met didn't seem to matter. This was a soul mate he was talking to. Barbara, sensing the loneliness he'd endured, also perceived that life was possibly about to change for both of them.

"I think you were fortunate to have had people in your life that love you as much as they did."

"Your absolutely right, Barbara," he felt a tier welling up in his eye. "I'd never looked at it like that before. I've only ever seen it as my loss and never what I'd gained from having people around me who loved me. How short-sighted of me to have thought of it in that way." Until now, Ian had not been able to come to terms with his grief. However, Barbara's few words seemed to have started a healing process.

"I also lost my parents several years ago, Ian, so it's easy for me to relate to where you're coming from. It took me what seemed to be forever to come to terms with my loss, but I had an older brother who was very supportive. He took on much the same role as your grandmother. I'm also lucky to have a group of close friends who stepped in to give me a new and exciting focus in life." Looking at the river, they did not speak. They glanced at each other occasionally to give a reassuring smile. During one of these smiles, Barbara placed her hand on his. He then put his other hand gently on top. Time had run out on this memorable moment in time. Acknowledging that all good things must come to an end, a feeling of sadness now started to prevail.

"I suppose we should be walking back. Homes will be waiting for us by now." They sauntered back to the limousine hand in hand. "I must return to work, Barbara, so where can I drop you off first."

"I live in north London, Ian."

"Right then, north London, it is." Homes stood waiting with a door open as they reached the limo. "Homes, we're taking the young lady home first, please. Now Barbara, if you care to give my driver your address, we'll be on our way." This she did.

Ian didn't wish to sound pushy, but he realized he must again seize the moment. Certain their feelings were mutual, he spoke with a confidence that he'd never experienced with a woman before. "I know this is a little sudden, Barbara, but I'd love to see you again: So, if you're free this evening, what would you say to, going on a date with me? We could go to a show or something of that nature."

"As it so happens, I am free this evening, and I'd enjoy going on a date with you." A feeling of happiness overwhelmed him as she accepted his offer. Perhaps this was love, and if so, he'd fallen head over heels in it. The conversation then explored the pros and cons of theatres and shows that came to mind. In keeping with the moment, it seemed only appropriate the venue they should choose would be a light-hearted one.

"As it's a comedy we seem most interested in, the Whitehall theatre usually has a good show of that nature."

"I've heard good reviews about their latest show, and I do love a good laugh, Ian."

"Give me your phone number, and I'll give you a call when I have the tickets. I'll then arrange a convenient time for me to collect you."

"I'll write it down for you." She foraged through her purse for pen and paper. Unzipping the back pocket inside, she sifted through to the bottom. As much for her own ears as Ian's, she then exclaimed, "so that's where I put my dam keys!" She turned to look at Ian with embarrassment. "I was looking for them when I first bumped into you." She paused to giggle. "Oh shit, now you're going to think I'm stupid. I was walking to my car at the time."

"You've left your car in Saville Roe?" Ian was amused by the way she'd expressed herself regarding the fact she'd forgotten her car. It didn't strike him as being the slightest bit coarse or vulgar. In fact, he thought it cute the way it seemed to be a natural part of her vocabulary.

"Well, you see, Ian, I'd been shopping, but finding nothing that took my fancy, I was returning to my car when we met." Ian couldn't contain the laughter.

"So, your car is still in Saville Roe." She started laughing too.

"Yes, I'm ashamed to say it is. I suppose what I was preaching about taking the time out to relax and clear my thoughts works. Although, apparently, it cleared a few thoughts too many." Ian smiled at the comment, then leaned towards the driver.

"Would you take us back to Saville Roe, please, Homes?"

"Yes, sir." Homes was not wholly oblivious to what was going on, so a silent smirk appeared on his face as he turned the limousine around. On the way back to her car, Ian scribbled down his name and phone number. He then passed it to her. Taking the paper she'd written her address on, he folded it neatly and placed it safely into his wallet.

Homes parked close to Barbara's car, then left the limo to walk around and open the door for her. Ian took advantage of this brief moment of privacy for a few last words.

"I'm looking forward to spending the evening with you. You're the most beautiful, stimulating woman I think I've ever met. Raising his cupped hands to cradle her cheeks, he kissed her softly on the lips. The tenderness in her eyes portrayed a look that expressed new strong feelings welling up inside her.

She left the vehicle, and the door was closed behind her. Ian rolled down the window to wave goodbye. Barbara made a similar gesture, well smiling back at him. "Goodbye, Ian, until this evening." Leaning forward in his seat, he gave Homes new instructions.

"Take me back to the office, please." The car then pulled away. Ian turned towards the back window to catch that last glance. He was trying desperately to prolong every final second of this chance encounter. Fumbling to unlock her car door, she somehow became aware of his action. Feeling compelled to look and share this last fleeting moment, she also acknowledged it with a final sad wave. Ian's limousine turned the corner and disappeared from sight.

CHAPTER 5

Ian makes plans.

The door reserved for staff was Ian's access to the bank's cloistered world. This establishment had become the dipping well from where Ian could elevate this full cup of aspirations to its limit. His comfortable office beckoned to him like the second home it had become. In this place, his burning ambitions could be achieved. Ian's dream was to have total control. Goals set so long ago were falling into place for this pursuit of power. He saw his long-term strategies evolving as planned, and they would be fully achieved on the day he would succeed Sir John as chairman of the board.

His corner office, a status symbol recently acquired with promotion, now felt so comfortable he couldn't picture himself anywhere else. Its inside walls were constructed of luxurious dark wooden lower panels and frosted glass windows topping this arrangement. The outer walls were of aged cream painted plaster, window frames, sills, and baseboards were in matching wood to all other carpentry. It was a clean, tidy, well-maintained office. The dark red leather topped brass studied desk with matching chair, and the bureau delivered opulence without being overly pretentious. Polished wood floors were covered by a quality area carpet, whose age only enhanced its surroundings' character. It was everything you'd expected an executive's office to be in a traditional city bank.

Ian had made a brief stop at his secretary's desk on his way to this office. A new emotion to Ian called Infatuation was rapidly thawing his cold facade. A warm smile at his secretary Jean reflected this change.

"Jean, would you please arrange to have a dozen red roses sent to the young lady at this address." Handing her the paper with Barbara's address, he continued, "and I would like a note attached reading, (Thank you for a delightful lunch, Ian). In my name, I would also like you to purchase two tickets for this evening's early show at the Whitehall Theatre; good seats if possible. Oh! and I'll need that address back when you've done with it."

"I'll attend to that right away for you, sir."

"I'm counting on you, Jean." It was a reply Ian only used in the context of a compliment. He was well aware of her capabilities, abilities he held in high esteem. Jean paged Ian telling him the flowers had been sent and confirmed the tickets had been booked in his name within ten minutes. She explained arrangements were made to acquire them from the box office before the start of the show. These essential details tended to, he settled into his afternoon's work.

Barely little more than an hour had passed before he was again paged by Jean.

"Miss Watson's online one for you, Sir."

"Miss Watson?" There was a querying tone to Ian's reply.

"The young lady you sent the flowers, Sir."

"Oh, of course, Barbara." Not recognizing her sir-name had led to his confusion. "Put her through, please." The connection was made.

"Barbara," although elated, Ian whispered softly, as if perhaps there could be other ears he didn't want sharing their conversation, "I've been waiting for your call."

"Thank you for the roses, Ian. They're beautiful."

"I'm glad you like the flowers."

"Oh, it was so sweet of you; I'd barely arrived home when they were delivered."

"I've also purchased tickets for the early show, so I hope to pick you up at quarter to seven won't prove to be a rush?"

"That won't be a problem. I'll be ready when you arrive, Ian."

"I booked the first show because I thought it would be nice to round out the evening with an intimate supper. So, if that's alright with you, I'll go ahead and book us a table."

"It sounds like you've planned a wonderful evening for us, Ian."

"There's this place; James, a friend of mine, has told me about that sounds very cozy. It has private booths, candlelight, plus exquisite food and service."

"That does sound romantic; I'll have to find something special to wear."

"Until six forty-five then, Barbara."

"Yes, Until six forty-five, Ian."

Time did not pass swiftly for Ian, as his emotions paralleled the pent-up excitement of a child waking before dawn on Christmas day. Eventually, his work was at the stage it could be left for the day. He then tidied up his desktop, as was his custom, every day before leaving. A place for everything and everything in its place was a rule he'd lived by. Completely satisfied, this corner of his world was in order; he could now close the office door. He'd was now able to separate this segment of his life for the first time in many years.

Pursuing social aspects unrelated to business, or competitiveness, until now, had been dismissed as unimportant. Living by this rule for so long had almost made Ian forget the overwhelming pleasure derived from such diverse relationships.

His own parking space at the bank was another privilege of his position. His car was a source of pride, tempered by sentiment; Ian's X.K.120. Jaguar in mint condition was a pale-yellow sports convertible with enough chrome to highlight its classic Jaguar lines. He much preferred this model to the newer X.K. and E types. He always thought the X.K.120 was one of the most classic roadsters produced by Jaguar. It also held special significance because it was his grandmother's car.

This in itself made it a cherished possession, having this sentimental attachment. There was a little ritual to be adhered to when driving this car. It was always done with its top up or down, even in cold weather. His business suit jacket was discarded and stowed behind the back seat; he then donned a white woollen sweater. To match his image; he wore black leather driving gloves, with his university scarf wrapped about his neck; to waft in the breeze. His commute home could now begin. It was an uneventful trip, much the same as most other days.

Home for Ian was a small but upscale townhouse situated in a muse whose cobbled stone courtyard formed the complex's centrepiece. Its main floor consisted of the garage and foyer, whose entrances had architectural designs. These ornamentations matched the other carriage houses, enhancing the courtyard's look. Living space was on to levels above.

It was a religious exercise to immediately garage the car on his arrival home. His gloves and scarf were then neatly stowed in the glove compartment. Only when this ritual had been completed would he enter the house. On this day, it was performed with exceptional hast, spurred on by the anticipation of the evening ahead. His jacket was then retrieved from the car, and his feet made light of the stairs propelling him swiftly to the top floor bedroom. There he disrobed. His sweater was neatly stowed away first before a city banker's uniform took its place on the hangers of his closet. Another part of the ceremony was to go to the bathroom, where he shaved and bathed himself before meticulously choosing appropriate attire for the evening ahead. This spurt of energy used to ready himself would allow ample time for a leisurely drive to Barbara's address.

After reaching the garage, his first order of business was to drive the Jag into the muse. There the canvas top was attached. This operation was performed in keeping with all the consideration given to a treasured possession. Leaving the engine running until this process was completed also gave the car interior time to warm. After locking the garage, it was time to be on his way.

Excitement consumed him on the drive. Although he tried to control his feelings as

best as possible, the tingling sensations created by anticipation continued to torment his body. The seeds he'd sown for the evening's events, events that had occupied his every thought since their conception, were now finally coming into bloom.

CHAPTER 6

Their first date.

Afternoon cloud cover had dissipated, giving winter's crisp, clear evening air a moonlit sparkle. He thought a warm, cozy car would make for a more romantic start to the evening as he increased the heat. Setting the radio's volume low, he then selected some soft music. This he did to create just the right atmosphere. This was attended to in his usual meticulous manner; he was now confident this evening would have a perfect start.

The urgency, and stress, of rush hour volume, had surrendered thoroughfares to the gentler flow of evening traffic. The advantage of favourable driving conditions had allowed Ian to make a good driving time. He circled the block several times to ensure he did not arrive unfashionably early. Deciding the time was now appropriate, he parked his car and glanced towards her apartment. Sweeping aside the curtain of her bedroom window, she waved to him. He rolled down his car window and waved back in acknowledgment.

The moment she emerged from the house, he executed a performance he'd witnessed Homes do many times. Positioning himself at the passenger door and opening it for her, he razed an open hand to offer assistance. "Good evening, Ian. I hope I've not kept you waiting." "Not at all; your right on time." This display of manners had made the impression it was intended to. There was the added bonus of pleasure derived from this doting for Ian.

"I've not been to this theatre before, Barbara, have you?"

"No, but a friend of mine has seen the show and said it was hilarious."

"Let's hope we enjoy the show as much as your friend seemed to have."

"You have a very nice car, Ian." Her fingers explored the wooden dash before stroking the beautiful leather upholstery. "It definitely has that touch of class about it."

"It was my grandmother's car, Barbara, and she was a very classy lady."

"This isn't the sort of car I'd expected to see a grandmother driving." Fond memories made him chuckle.

"Oh, she was no ordinary grandmother Barbara, believe me. She had a vibrant, upbeat personality. There's a story I've heard her friend's tale about the car she owned before this one. It was a two-point-five Bristol. Several weeks after she took delivery of it, she returned it to the dealership complaining of a foul odder that sometimes manifested itself at high speed. One of the garage mechanics agreed to go with her on a speed trial run. Well, it seems they found this long stretch of road, and she put the accelerator to the floor. The man watched as the speedometer climbed, eighty, ninety, one hundred. He then noticed a narrow bridge at the end of the road and a truck coming in the opposite direction. He was horrified that she hadn't attempted to slow down. Gripping the dash with both hands, he watched the speed rise to one-ten. She made the bridge just seconds ahead of the truck. After slowing down, she turned to the man.

"Now, do you smell that awful smell?"

"Smell it, lady, I'm bloody sat in it." Barbara started to laugh.

"Oh, Ian, you took me right in. You had me going right up until the punch line."

"Well, Barbara, it wouldn't have been beyond the realms of possibility for her to have done something of that nature." He would never have spoken to a woman in this manner before, but this self-confidence portrayed how at ease he felt in her company.

Experiencing this blossoming friendship with Barbara and the physical attraction proved to be a fulfilling experience for Ian.

Reaching their destination, he eked out a parking spot near the theatre. On the short walk, Ian felt comfortable creating most of the conversation. A new experience for a man who was unusually like a fish out of water around women.

Displaying aloofness, to mask the shyness he'd felt, had made him seem cold and calculating to most of his dates. This newfound confidence Barbara was nurturing inside of him was proving to be a rebirth towards normality. It was also a process necessary to propel their relationship forward.

The tickets reserved for him at the box office were purchased, and they took their seats. The conversation during the show was sparse. Caressing and cuddling in the dark theatre eliminated the need for words. Towards the finale, their lips moved closer, and they kissed. A disapproving humph, humph, disguised as a cough, came from a man in the seat behind, brought a few sniggers from the two of them. He then leaned forward to give another disapproving cough to emphasize he didn't think it was a laughing matter. This action brought on a bout of sniggering neither of them could suppress. They were enjoying their form of entertainment more than the show they were supposed to be watching.

Discretion being the better part of valour, they vacated their seats to catch the show's remaining minutes. On their way to the exit gave credence to the fact chemistry between them was strong enough to ignore anything other than their own emotions. Returning to the car hand in hand, they were without a care in the world. Ian again took pleasure in opening her door and attend her every need before getting behind the wheel.

It was Barbara who again steered the conversation back towards every detail of Ian's life she could glean from him. She was curious to know more about the man who had somehow managed to sweep her off her feet. Her questions weren't intended to pry but more designed to familiarize herself with him in every way possible.

"Do you have other relatives, Ian?"

"I have a cousin." He paused, remorseful to the fact that this was the total extent of his family." He lives in Seattle, in the United States. He's older than I am; although I've not seen him in quite a few years, we occasionally correspond. I went there to spend a holiday with him once. He's a great guy, commando-type, ex-army intelligence. He has a small boat, and we spent most of my visits salmon fishing on the ocean. I had a great time there. I've always intended to make another trip there, but I never seem able to find the time these days. A city banker's work can be very demanding when you've dedicated yourself to becoming the top in your chosen profession.

Now if you'll give me a minute to park, as we've arrived at the restaurant's car park.

Yes, as I was about to tell you, America's a beautiful country. The scenery in the Pacific Northwest is just spectacular."

As they exited the car, little more was said before Ian escorted her into the restaurant. Once there, they were greeted at the door by the Maitra-d.

"Good evening. Do you have a reservation?"

"I have a table booking for two, in the name of Shaw."

"Ah, yes, Mr. Shaw." He struck a line through Ian's name on his reservation list. "If you'd care to follow me, I'll escort you to your table." They were shown to a secluded booth in the back corner of the room; when comfortably seated menus were presented. "Your waiter will be with you shortly, and I hope your evening with us will be an enjoyable one."

The place had a relaxing atmosphere, plush but comfortable. Every minor detail contributing to the restaurant's ambiance had been fully exploited. Lanterns with flickering candles inside centred every table extending a warm invitation to patrons. A soft music style was playing softly as a backdrop. Ian's choice proved to be the icing on the cake for this perfect intimate rendezvous he'd chosen. At this point, the restaurant was all James had promoted it to be. It was also an ideal setting for Ian to ask Barbara for more personal information. Ian didn't feel he was intrusive about her life as she seemed to be so interested in his life. These questions were fueled by the same curiosity that had sparked Barbara's questions of Ian's past.

"A woman should be mysterious." She gave a coy smile. "Well, let me see, perhaps I'll try to give you a brief history of myself. I have an older brother, his name's John. I have lots of aunts, uncles, and cousins. John's an officer in the military. He's stationed in Aden in the Persian Gulf, so we've not seen much of each other lately. We keep in constant touch by writing. Bridging the gap across the miles helps maintain our close ties." She paused for a moment as if contemplating what to divulge next. "I majored in business and economics. I'm self-employed and run my own company. I've never been in a deeply committed relationship, but I do have lots of friends. I'm a people person. You know, I'm very social; I enjoy the company of lots of friends. At this point, Ian felt a need to speak.

"I too have a degree in economics and business also, like you, I've never found the right person where I felt a need for a committed relationship to develop. I'm sorry to have butted in, but I thought I'd throw that in as we seem to have this shared common ground. Now, please, do continue."

"It seems we do have more in common than meets the eye, doesn't it."

"It would seem so, but your much too pretty to be hidden away in the back office of some musty old bank." She blushed slightly.

"Ian, flattery will get you everywhere." Then she laughed. "Now back to about me. Two of my cousins, Tony, Ron, and some of their school friends, went professional with their band, so I joined them after leaving university. I've always been interested in music."

"So, these two cousins are brothers."

"My mother had three sisters, and they're the sons of two of those aunts. So we're all cousins, and they are not brothers."

"I see; so pop, jazz, classical, what interests you?"

"All music interests me, Ian, but the band concentrates on rock and roll, country, you know, pop music."

"So, you're their songstress, then are you, Barbara?"

"No," she replied with a certain amount of shyness in her voice. She then continued in a more assertive tone. "I have a management company, I manage them, and I also co-wrote some of their songs. I've always been too nervous about performing comfortably on stage; that's not to say I can't sing."

Their conversation was abruptly interrupted by the arrival of the waiter. He was ready to take their order with pen and pad in hand. After they'd selected starters and entrees, Ian took a quick glance through the wine list.

"What type of wine do you think you might prefer, Barbara?"

"I'm not sure, perhaps something bubbly. I feel in a bubbly mood."

"Let me see, a sparkling rose wine would probably foot the bill." He pointed out his selection on the wine list.

"I love that wine. You must be clairvoyant."

"A bottle of Mateus, please, waiter, and you may serve that first." His request was made in a layback manner. The ability to act casual in this type of setting, even with a waiter, had previously eluded him. It was one of James's qualities he'd often attempted to imitate. Unfortunately, Ian's renditions never did equal James's polished style. However, this time, it was no imitation. His casual assurances came from within.

This woman had awakened many facets of his personality that had laid dormant for so long. These traits only needed some form of outside stimulation: stimulation Barbara had now provided to revitalize them.

The wine was promptly delivered to the table. It was then pored, but not before all the correct rituals had been observed. The waiter left, and they were alone again. This romantic moment was enhanced by the warm glow of flickering candlelight. The effervescence of the wine, illuminated by this flickering light, also conjured up the illusion of a fascinating bubble ballet. The quiet relaxing atmosphere encouraged a softer tone in their voices as they continued the conversation.

"You mentioned how nervous you are on stage, Barbara." Toying with her wine glass, she looked almost disappointed she'd been restricted by this inhibition.

"I am, but my forte is the behind-scenes operation. The band's getting quite successful now, so it really is a full-time job." Ian set his wine glass down and eased himself back in his chair.

"So what type of venues do the band play, Barbara?"

"They vary with the seasons. In summer months, we play mostly seaside resorts, well in winter, it's concerts, and dances, mostly in larger cities."

"I take it you enjoy travelling."

"I do, and bookings do come easier now we're established, but arranging accommodation can

be a nightmare sometimes." She paused for a moment to sip her wine, "yummy." This quirky little expression amused Ian, bringing a smile to his face.

"And last but not least, I manage the finances, which believe you me, is not an easy task with those boys."

"They obviously place a lot of trust in you, Barbara."

"That's the main reason they asked me to handle their affairs in the first place. It can be hard finding someone trustworthy in this business."

The waiter delivered the first course and topped up their wine glasses. As with all top-class eateries, the primary considerations must include food quality, presentation, and service. An excellent dining experience reaps its ultimate pleasures only when these criteria are met. This establishment was not lacking creativity in any of these areas.

When the main course was placed before them, the platters displayed a rendition of artistry equaling any culinary Rembrandt.

"This looks almost too good to eat, doesn't it." Ian smiled, well uttering a few words of affection.

"Quite, my darling." He hadn't realized the phrasing he'd used until it was out of his mouth. This should be an endearment reserved for someone in a much longer relationship than one day. However, it felt right, and she did seem to appreciate all the attention he was lavishing upon her.

She paused for another sip of wine before looking him straight in the eye and asking something that had intrigued her since their first meeting.

"Ian, what exactly is your position at the bank? It must be important? You're well educated, have a chauffeur-driven limo, and you shop in Saville Row." Ian usually made a big thing about his job, but his reply was of a modest nature with Barbara.

"It's really not so grand as it sounds; I'm an executive handling large corporate accounts, and I also have specific administrative responsibilities. I oversee a section of the country, in which our branches, and staff, are my responsibility."

"Ah! that would explain the sharp image you try to project sometimes. But it doesn't work on me, you know. I can see right through that shit. I know a warm, caring person is lurking somewhere in those shadows."

"So, you're saying my nicer alter ego lurks in shadows. That doesn't say much for the part of me you think is front and center." She started to laugh, he joined her. "I'm flattered you think of me as warm and caring. Although I'm sure some of my clients may not entirely agree with you."

"Oh, I think I'm a pretty good judge of character, Ian, and I don't care what your snooty clients think; so there." She then accompanied her statement with a giggle.

After finishing their main course, the dishes were promptly cleared from the table. Dessert menus were then presented. Barbara quickly scanned through hers.

"The evening wouldn't be complete without dessert, now would it, Ian?"

"Well, a presentation, with a touch of the theatrical, always adds something to the experience. So may I suggest we share the peach's flame-by. I have it on good authority the server really puts on quite the show in the dessert preparation."

"Good, that sounds exactly like the thing I've been looking forward to. It should be something memorable to round out this wonderful evening." Ian glanced towards the waiter and confirmed their order.

A spirit-fueled burner mounted on a trolley, designed for the precise purpose of preparing such dishes, was wheeled to their table. The waiter lit the small stove.

Various liqueurs and sprites were blended in a pan, then heated over the open flame. When the pan's correct temperature was achieved, the waiter ignited the mixture. This was done with showmanship creating a dramatic and physical effect before the flames were brought under control. The remaining ingredients were then added in the same manner as previously, with a routine befitting a circus juggler. When the small ball of flame that had erupted from the pan had subsided, the dish was quickly served. The dessert was then savoured at leisure. The dining experience now behind them, it was now time to summon the waiter for the bill. Ian showed his gratitude for the excellent service by leaving a generous tip.

Sauntering to the car with hands swinging loosely together, they were in no hurry to end the evening. Within the privacy of Ian's car, she focused her gaze on Ian. In turn, he reached out a hand and gently brushed her cheek with the backs of his fingers. Barbara accepted this show of affection by rubbing her cheek into his hand. He moved towards her and kissed her gently on the lips. She put her arms around him and intensified the embrace. Drawing back from their kiss, they looked into each other's eyes. He then lovingly stroked her hair with his hand and again brushed his fingers over her cheek.

"I think you're the most beautiful woman I've ever met."

"I have strong feelings for you too, Ian. I know we've only just met, but it all feels so right between us. I've never felt like this about anyone before. You don't think I'm silly, do you?"

"How could I think you're silly when I feel the same way. I was serious about what I said; I know you're a wonderful person. I know it's going to be easy to fall in love with you because I think I already have."

"I don't mean to belittle your remarks, but this is all so sudden. Please allow me a little time to adjust."

She put her arms around him and kissed him again. Not wishing to embarrass her or himself, Ian abandoned this line of talk. He was content to immerse himself in the feelings of enjoyment generated by the implications of her kiss.

"Well, young lady, I suppose I should be driving you home now." Having said that, he started the car and drove back to her apartment.

"Thank you for a wonderful evening, Ian. You've been charming. This was an evening I wish could last forever."

"It will last in my memory forever; you can rest assured of that, Barbara. Now, will you be in London for a while, Barbara, or will you be travailing?"

"We'll be working around London until the second week in January, then we start a four-week tour. It kicks off in Swindon and moves on to Bath, Bristol, etc."

"I have a function to attend this coming Friday, a sort of cocktail party thing. I'd love you to accompany me."

"If that's an invitation, my answer's yes. I'll be looking forward to

Friday, Ian, but I'll be working until seven. I hope that's not a problem."

"That'll be fine. I'll pick you up around eight-thirty if that's OK."

"Eight-thirty will be fine. I'll be looking forward to Friday, Ian." She leaned over and gave him a kiss. He put his arms around her and held her in an embrace. She slowly pulled away, with a dreamy look in her eyes,

"Until Friday, then."

"I'll phone you tomorrow," he called as she left the car. Opening her front door, she paused before entering. She then waved to him as he drove away.

CHAPTER 7

A surprising turn of events

It was eight-thirty Friday evening when Ian found himself once more preparing to park outside Barbara's apartment. Phone calls between them in the past few days had become frequent. This helped to stitch the fabric of this new relationship more tightly. Rounding the corner into her street, he caught a glimpse of her silhouette as she peered from the side of a curtained window. It came as no surprise to see her arrive on the sidewalk to greet him the moment his car came to a halt.

In their many phone conversations, she'd described what she had planned to wear to this formal Christmas party. However, he was still taken back by how stunning she looked in her evening gown and wrap. Her long hair swept tightly into a roll at the back gave an unfettered view of her beautiful porcelain features. He could only look in awe, in that brief moment, before stepping out of the car to greet her with a light kiss on the cheek. This was done delicately so as not to disturb her makeup. He then held her hands at arm's length to fully appreciate this beautiful vision of womanhood standing before him.

"You look absolutely stunning this evening, Barbara. You'll be the belle of the ball."

"Why, thank you, Ian; you cut quite the fine figure of a man yourself, all decked out in your best bib and tucker." He had to have a little chuckle at her playful banter as he helped her into the car.

"My best bib and tucker, so that's the designation you've assigned to my formal wear.

"Just trying to say, I think you scrub up well, sweetie." These words, chosen as an affectionate tease, were delivered with an alluring smile.

* * *

Valet parking was in operation, enabling Ian to leave his car at the front of the house. Sir John and his wife -who was hosting the party- were mingling with a group of newly arrived guests gathered inside the main entrance. Entering the house, Barbara found herself in a dubious position. Stopping to deposit her wrap, she could not help overhearing some derogatory remarks Sir John was levelling at the young woman in charge of the coat check. To do such a thing in public, she thought, was in bad taste. This behaviour did not go unnoticed by Ian either as he recalled the many occasions Sr John had unleashed such bouts of uncontrolled rage on subordinates. However, his attitude changed the moment he saw Ian.

"Good evening Ian." His usual boisterous welcome was accompanied by the customary hearty handshake.

"Sir John, I would like you to meet Barbara." Sir John turned his undivided attention towards Barbara as Sir John's wife engaged Ian in conversation. Sir John's persona took on yet another dimension as he began speaking to Barbara. His tone of voice exuded the implications of a seduction.

"And you must be the young lady I've heard so much about. Well, I must say what I've been led to believe about your beauty, I've now had the pleasure of confirming with these old eyes of mine. I'm truly delighted to meet you, my dear, and if I were twenty years younger, I'd be giving young Ian a run for his money. In fact, I could quite easily feel twenty years younger in your company." He reached out to take her hand in a greeting, well placing his other hand around her shoulder to draw her closer. At this point, it wasn't too hard for Barbara to imagine the drool running from his mouth as he placed a kiss on her cheek. Clutching her hand, just a little too tight and too long, he made the moment a trifle more than uncomfortable.

"Why, thank you, Sir John," she replied with a polite but slightly embarrassed smile. Then, with as little force as possible, she graciously slipped from his grasp and passed him her wrap to occupy his hands. Her shall, was then unceremoniously forwarded on to the coat check girl, accompanied by a disdainful glower. His misguided anger was focused on the girl for being slow to intercede in taking the warp from Barbara before it ever reached his hands. Had this happened, he was sure his advances would not have been thwarted in such a manner.

First impressions were important to Barbara. She was seldom wrong about a person. Although presenting himself as very charming and gracious, she could feel it was just camouflage. The actual underlying nature of his attention she perceived to be no more than lust. He struck her as being a strict disciplinarian. She'd also perceived him as being susceptible to volatile mood swings if displeased. Instinct was urging her to use extreme caution with this man.

Ian had been aware of this flaw in Sir John's makeup, assessing it to be a chink in his armour. More crucial to Ian was the possibility it could cause career problems. He perceived that he would fall foul to Sir John's temper one day by the law of averages. With this in mind, he chose to ignore most of Sir John's rude behaviour. Ian was also determined to find a way to exploit this weakness. If Ian could somehow manipulate this behaviour, perhaps it could prove an excellent deterrent to Sir John's wrath. Such a pre-emptive scheme had never been added to the crucible for mixing. Ian had not yet formulated all the ingredients required. If prematurely brought to light, such speculative thoughts would indeed bring about server retribution for such disloyalty to Sir John. Ian was quite unaware; Barbara's uncanny instincts had quickly confirmed the same assumptions about this man.

Entering the ballroom, she commanded the stare of every red-blooded man in the room and glares from some of the younger women. The line of her long blue silk dress showcased the figure of this Aphrodite. Its side slit showed enough leg to be tastefully provocative. Its shimmering dark blue colour complimented her fair skin, black hair, and blue eyes. Ian's chest was swollen with pride at the privilege of escorting such a glamorous woman. He also sensed a strange power had been accredited to him by the more chauvinistic men in the room. They perceived him as displaying this beautiful woman as a highly salt after trophy. This made it all the more pleasurable when introducing her to colleagues and acquaintances. It wasn't long after most introductions were made; they were individually waylaid by people intent on engaging them in conversation separately. Every time Ian tried to get close to her, inevitably, he would be sidetracked by some woman vying for his attention. Ian was fast becoming cock of the walk amongst the ladies, making him all the more desirable to Barbara. The fact he'd never experienced anything approaching popularity with the opposite sex before was now history. This complete metamorphosis had totally transformed his personality, casting aside the shell he'd been encrusted in. It was now easy for him to engage in witty light banter. His shyness had been eradicated and replaced by a new feeling of ease around women. Ian's newfound status as leader of the pack had also negated the urge to compete with other men in mind games.

* * *

Slipping out on the party early was a plan they'd both agreed on. There had been enough sharing for the evening, and it was now time to savour each other's company.

They amused each other with tales of people they'd encountered throughout the evening on the way home. Barbara said nothing to Ian regarding Sir John, not wishing to cause him any embarrassment. Arriving at Barbara's apartment, they soon found themselves embracing, kissing, and petting, for the next half an hour, snuggled down in Ian's car. Feeling their emotions getting the better of them, Barbara suggested she should leave to go inside. Ian reluctantly agreed.

* * *

Christmas had come and gone, with them spending every available hour together. It was Ian's happiest Christmas in many a year. Barbara enjoyed parading around her new beau around to meet aunts, uncles, and cousins. An invitation for Christmas dinner from her favourite uncle, and his family, had been extended to include Ian. He'd made himself a hit with the relatives and had been readily accepted into the family. The relationship had grown so intense in the past month that they were both feeling the stress of restraints they'd put on their emotions. Helping Barbara out of his car after one Friday evening's date, she held on tightly to his hand after he'd given her a final goodnight kiss.

"You know I'm going on tour this coming Monday, and it's going to be so hard not having you close." She paused as if trying to find the right words to say. Taking his other hand, she looked at him in silence for that instant before mustering up the courage to say what she wanted to say.

"Stay the night with me. I want you to be my first and only love." Ian didn't speak as he drew her close and walked her towards her door. Once inside, he gently kissed her on the neck, and she led him to her bedroom. Slowly, carefully, he disrobed her. She pulled back the bed covers and lay down to await his company. After he'd removed his clothes, she held out her hand as an invitation for him to join her. Caressing her cheek with his hand, he kissed her softly on the lips as he slipped in beside her. With his other hand, he started to stimulate her body. She, in turn, ran her hands slowly and softly over his body. Her hand moved nervously ever closer to the most sexually sensitive part of his body. She now felt it pressuring her leg. As he increased her arousal with soft fingers, he placed her trembling hand to the place she'd so nervously avoided. He moved his body over her, and her legs moved aside to accept him. His moves tantalized her. Toying with her at first, he gently caressed himself to her. This simulated the flow of more body lubricants between them, and what started as touching was now developing into a gentle penetration.

Winning her confidence, she freely entrusted her gift into his care. She was now entirely relaxed as he slowly moved inside, going deeper with every gentle movement. He savoured her body as she, in return, savoured his. And as they seethed with each other in the blankets, the sweat from their bodies forced them to cast off the covers. The once gentle movements gave way to an eruption of energy. It could only be quelled by the exhaustion of fuel that drove this engine of love. This expiration did not come easily to two people intent on making the most of this new voyage they'd embarked upon together. Truly a maiden voyage, both could savour as a memory to be treasured in the years to come.

The following morning the manifestation of their love was repeated, again to the point of exhaustion, before showering. Frolicking in the shower was never this pleasurable until fun with water and a bar of soap was discovered. Turning the water off and grabbing some towels, Ian extended that romantic moment by helping her dry off and dress.

Hunger drew them back into reality, and Barbara went to the kitchen to prepare breakfast. As she stood over the range, Ian walked up behind her. Putting his arms around her waist, kissed her softly on the side of her neck. As she leaned her head to one side to accommodate him, he whispered softly in her ear.

"Marry me, Barbara." Surprise compelled her to turn quickly and look him straight in the eye. Was this a joke or an actual proposal, but sincerity was etched deep into his face.

"You're serious, aren't you."

"I've never been more serious about anything in my life, Barbara."

"People will think we're crazy," she replied in a soft voice, "we've known each other such a short time."

"I hope that's not a no, Barbara. I've never been so positive about anything in my life as my feelings for you. I knew we were right for each other from that first moment our eyes met."

"It's not a no," there was a pause in her speech. This was a question that needed much thought. Ian persisted.

"If it's not a no Barbara, what is your answer?

"I suppose it's a yes." His face could have illuminated the darkest of nights.

"I love you so very much Barbara, I know it's right for us, so I see no point waiting." Ian had worked himself into an enthusiastic frenzy that was beginning to overwhelm her. "I'll get a license first thing Monday morning."

"My, you do no how to sweep a girl off her feet, Ian, but let's just slow down a little. There will be all kinds of arraignments to be made. Things will have to be planned, and a hundred and one other things need to be attended to before the day."

"I was hoping for a quiet wedding, Barbara."

"Ha, you and every other man on the planet."

"I'm sorry, Barbara, it's your day. Tell me what I should do, and I'll do it."

"I'll sort out a day I can be back in London, then you can get the license. Give me a minute to think. The band will be in Bristol the weekend after next if I could get back here on that Friday, we could be married then. That's if you wouldn't mind driving to Bristol after the wedding and spending a short honeymoon weekend there, in a nice hotel."

"I like the idea. I'll make all the necessary arrangements this week; just let me know whatever else needs to be done."

"Well, right now, I'd like you to set the table for breakfast." She then gave Ian a soft kiss on the cheek in an attempt to temper his enthusiasm a little.

The remainder of the weekend was spent together, walking in the parks and visiting tourist spots. These were things neither of them had done for some time. People tend to ignore the beauty spots closest to the place where they live, often taking them too much for granted. The evenings were spent at Barbara's apartment quietly enjoying each other's company. Monday morning, Ian kissed her softly as she slept, then left for work. He could hardly remember the last time he felt so contented, happy, and at ease with the world.

She awoke and stretched out her hand for a reassuring touch, only to find his place in bed empty. She was saddened to have missed his departure. Returning to the reality of Monday morning, she packed the things she would need to go on tour and placed them into her car.

A small cafe served as a popular meeting place for the band before such trips, and this trip was no different. The restaurant catered to truck drivers. The large, reasonably priced breakfasts were an excellent incentive for hungry young men on a budget. Tables were set with heavy vinyl, blue, and white checkered tablecloths. The upholstery on the chairs and in the booths had seen better days. However, the service was friendly, and the food quality could always be relied on. The band felt at home here, knowing most of the staff by name and patrons alike. This was a place in which they felt comfortable.

The boys had all arrived and were, awaiting Barbara's company. It was clear they hadn't eaten because their cutlery had not been disturbed. They were suppressing their appetites with cups of coffee. As she joined them at their table, a chorus of good morning greeted her.

"Good morning, boys." Her radiant smile, and perky voice, contrasted sharply to the Monday morning blues that were etched on the band's faces.

"You sound chipper, this morning Barbara."

"I feel on top of the world this morning Jim." Jim was the lead guitarist. He also did most of the singing. With his dominant but likeable personality, he'd established himself as the band's cornerstone. His tall slim build, olive complexion, and dark hair made this handsome young man a valuable asset for a group of entertainers catering to a primarily female fan base. And there was no denying he was definitely a big draw with the ladies.

"We were expecting you to be down in the mouth this morning: Having to leave that young man of yours."

"Well, I have a little surprise for you all on that subject, so brace yourselves. Ian's asked me to marry him." She paused to create some drama before allowing her excited reply to be heard, "and I said yes."

The boys were taken back for the moment, looking at her in silent shock. This made her feel more than a little uneasy. Finally, Jim broke the tension by leaning forward to embrace her. He then kissed her gently on the forehead.

"Ian's a fortunate man Barbara, a fortunate man indeed. I wish you all the happiness in the world." The other three in the group, John, Ron, and Tony, then showered her with a frenzy of well-wishing. Barbara felt at ease again. Their approval meant a lot to her; they were like family. The excitement continued as a barrage of questions was levelled at her.

"Slow down, slow down, your overwhelming me." The commotion slowly died down as she aired her frustrations by frantically flapping her hand. "Please, please, one at a time." Jim tapped his coffee cup with a spoon, signalling he'd appointed himself master of ceremonies.

"OK, lads, you heard the lady, now calm down." The order had been restored. "Now, perhaps, I should go first. If anyone wishes to add something after that, I'm sure Barbara will try to deal with our concerns in an orderly manner. Barbara, have you set a date?"

"Yes, a week after next Friday. Ian will be making most of the arrangements, and after the wedding, we'll be driving straight to Bristol to rejoin the tour."

"Thank you, Barbara. Now let's go around the table, with one question at a time. John, it's your turn next.

"We'll be playing Bath, Friday night, and not Bristol. Is that correct?"

"That's true, but I've booked the hotel in Bristol for you that night. It's only a twelve-mile drive from Bath, and we'll be in Bristol until the following Wednesday." More organized than the others, Tony chose his words a little more carefully for the plans he'd envisioned.

"Early Friday morning, we leave Swindon, where our Thursday night show is, right, Barbs! We could be back in London and ready for the wedding in an hour and a half. If we leave straight after the reception, we could make Bath easily, for the evening show. That's my plan, so what's everyone's thoughts on the matter? Will it work for us?"

"I was hoping you wouldn't mind putting yourselves out a little for me on my wedding day." John was quick to vent his feelings.

"Putting ourselves out a little, we'd forfeit the whole tour if we had to." This was not a commitment given lightly for a band who had always taken pride in the fact they'd never missed an engagement. Ron, as usual, timidly waited until last to ask his question.

"When you're married, will you still look after our interests, Barbara?"

"Ron," John snapped as he shook his head, looking at him in disbelief. "You always worry about inappropriate things."

"It's not a silly question, Ron. John's just being overly critical, so take no notice of him." She mothered Ron just a little more than the other boys. He was less assertive than the other lads, and she saw this as a vulnerability that needed some bolstering from time to time. "I love my career. I could never give it up, and Ian wouldn't expect me to. This is one of the reasons we're getting married on the spur of the moment, so he can join me at the weekends we're on tour." Jim again played the moderator.

"Well, Barbara, now that seems to be all settled, how about we order some breakfast before hitting the road. We've been waiting for you and your purse because we're all flat broke, as you've probably guessed."

"You're lucky I handle the expenses when we're on the road. I think you boys would starve if that was not the case." It was symptomatically devoured; no sooner had breakfast been placed on the table. Their appetites could have shamed a plague of locusts. Barbara, who was accustomed to these young men's cravings, left them to clear any food remaining on any of the plates. She then settled the bill before they hit the road.

CHAPTER 8

An overwhelming situation was happening.

Ian was beginning to realize the magnitude of the task he'd undertaken. Having every detail completed in less than two weeks was proving to be an almost impossible problem. He was having second thoughts that his insistence on an early wedding date had been such a good idea. The type of organizational skills needed was entirely foreign to him, as they would be for any person who had unwittingly thrust themselves headlong into such a task. He often found himself floundering out of his depth, trying to coordinate events to coincide perfectly with existing plans. There was so little time to achieve his goals. He felt like the captain of a leaky ship trying to make port, with no one to man the pumps. His organizational needs would usually be handled by his secretary. How sadly missed was that woman's touch. Unfortunately, she was not available to supervise this particular function. Now more than ever, he began to appreciate Jean's skills and how much he'd taken them for granted.

Organizing the catering for a small reception, he thought, would be a minor detail, but even this proved to be too time-consuming. He'd never considered the difficulties in booking an appropriate size room to hold the reception on such short notice. There were wedding cars to be reserved, floral arraignments to be selected, and the list went on. More things that needed his attention seemed to be cropping up by the hour. Keeping in constant touch with Barbara by phone helped control his sanity. Leaning heavily on her advice when it could be provided and moral support, when needed, gave him the confidence to exceed his own expectations. By the morning of the wedding, he felt he'd achieved a minor miracle. Every last detail now seemed to have fallen neatly into place.

The wedding went off smoothly. A quick registry office ceremony was followed by a champagne brunch at the golf club. The newlyweds then make the rounds, thanking guests before attempting to slip quietly away. However, Barbara's friends had made sure this was not about to happen, having prepared the usual surprises, with their own little twists added. Written all over Ian's car in lipstick were the words, just marred. Tin-cans had also been tied to the back bumper with tie-wire that had been cinched with pliers. There was the usual dowsing of confetti as they left the reception, with several bags emptied directly into the car, ensuring the breeze would distribute a noticeable trail. The piece de-resistance being Jim, John, Ron, and Tony had fitted a speaker to the roof of their van. Their intention was to escort the newlyweds through London's streets, with the wedding march blasting from the speaker.

The bride and groom's first stop was Barbara's apartment. There they change into something more casual. The boys waited outside, with the designated song playing loudly.

Initially, this was found to be amusing, but by the time they'd reached the outskirts of London, this joke was wearing a little thin. Passing motorists tooting their horns, and waving, contributed nothing but aggravation to this predicament. Stopping, when the first opportunity arose, they set about washing the car. The lipstick did not come off quickly when applied thickly. A sympathetic garage mechanic's help was enlisted to cut the wire securing the tin cans. Now they were able to make light of the pranks and start savouring every new moment.

With the stress of the wedding over, adrenalin was now running thin. Ian was now feeling stressed by the day's pressures.

"I don't think I could take another practical joke if my life depended on it.

"Me neither, but I'm sure the rest of our trip to Bristol will be just fine.

The Unicorn Hotel in Bristol's center was the place they chose to spend their honeymoon. The bell boy collected their luggage from the car and escorted them to their room. It was situated on one of the upper floors. This comfortable suit's westerly view overlooked green rolling hills beyond the city. The Quay and docks sprawled out below.

A little honeymoon surprise had been set out on the table to greet them. A chilled bottle of champagne and two glasses displayed a card from the boys in a gift basket presentation. Tipping the bellboy as he left, Ian's attention turned to the task of popping the cork and filling the two glasses. After handing one glass to Barbara, he stroked her face gently and intertwined their arms to engage in a lover's toast. Then taking her by the hand, together, they looked out the window admiring the view, well sipping champagne. The pleasure drawn from this activity fulfilled; they faced each other before embracing and kissing. With her arm's around his neck, she swayed seductively against his body before suggesting they'd be more comfortable on the bed. Sweeping her up in his arms, he set her gently down on the bed. Ian Continued with this show of affection that had stimulated this developing passion. The evening was spent acquainting each other in their diverse preferences for love; new experimentation, in yet untested ways to please made for an evening of epic entertainment.

* * *

Discussing plans for the day over a leisurely late breakfast in bed seemed a fitting way to begin this new union. It was agreed Barbara's business, at the Colston Hall, should be dealt with first. This was the location of the band's next engagement. When this business was completed, the rest of the day would be theirs to explore the city.

* * *

A short walk separated the hotel from the old Victorian auditorium situated on the city center's far side. The picturesque city center, encircled by a ring road, encompassed an immaculately grassed oval, incorporating floral arrangements. At the northeast end of this floral display was a concrete plaza. This area was home to a smattering of shade trees and statues of dignitaries, plus a large Cenotaph. Arterial thoroughfares fed the circular road system. To the southwest, the city docks were showcased beyond a plaza, depicting a statue of Neptune.

John Cabot also began his epic voyage from this old port city to explore the new world. Perhaps he once stood on that very spot. A mixture of buildings utilizing various architectural designs and facades, consisting of stone, brick, and brightly painted stucco, bordered its wide exterior sidewalks. The Colston Hall was one such building, situated just off the center, on one of the feeder roads. Top artists from around the world frequently headlined shows in this theatre. Barbara explained to Ian that the band would perform this evening as an American artist's opening act. The conversation kept pace with the spring in their step as they neared their destination. Reaching the Colston Hall, Barbara attended to business, well Ian explored the venue. Once their business was accomplished, they left the establishment. It was time to enjoy the remainder of their day. Ian offered his guidance. "My grandmother had a friend that lived in Bristol, and we came to visit quite often, so I am somewhat familiar with the city. So what are your priorities, site seeing? Shopping? You name it. If it's shopping, there's a new shopping center just minutes from here."

"There must be some quaint old streets and shops with old-world charm that are just waiting to be explored in a city like this. I love to browse around in places like that, rather than glitzy stores."

"Sounds like an interesting choice to me. Perhaps we can combine a little sightseeing and shopping together." He put his arm around her shoulder and gave a gentle squeeze well, whispering in her ear, attempting to inject a little mystery into his voice. " Well, I know of several streets and markets that might interest you. They're very close to where we are right now, in fact." He nibbled on her ear. She laughed and tried to push his face away,

"Stop being silly in public; people will think you're deprived or something." He nibbled her ear more.

"I'll take you to the Christmas steps first." He guided her through a stone archway into a cobblestone alley with his arm still around her shoulder.

"The Christmas steps, Ian! I thought it was going to be the Casaba you were trying to whisk me off too." He laughed.

"I'm sure you won't be disappointed. It's a very steep street with cobblestone surfaces worked into steps. In fact, we're practically there. It's only just around this corner. Actually, an alley would be a more apt description than a street. It's much the same as the street we're in. This area is an old part of the city. I think it's the sort of place you'd like to visit.

"You seem to have an affection for Bristol, Ian."

"I suppose I have. I had some good times here with my grandmother. You'll probably think it strange for a young man to spend so much time with his grandmother. I found her to be an excellent companion, and she was a fun person to be around. I still miss her."

"I hope I can fill some of that void she left in you, Ian." Ian again squeezed Barbara's shoulder reassuringly.

"How could there be a void in my life when I have a wife like you."

"I love it when you say things like that to me; I think it's so romantic." She rested her head on his shoulder and looked up into his eyes dreamily. "let's skip the shopping, Ian, take me back to bed." There was no need for a second request. Ian, experiencing a surge of hot-blooded anticipation at the mere thought of such an invitation.

"I'll race you back to the hotel, Barbara." In unison, they turned to run back towards the Unicorn. Ian took her hand so as not to outrun her. It would be a hollow victory indeed if the prize he cherished so much were not at the finish for him to appreciate. Laughing, giggling, and tickling each other at every opportunity, they reached the hotel.

Hurrying through the lobby in this playful manner, they were immediately propelled to center stage in this sedate setting. Ian and Barbara had become a center stage spectacle to the audience they'd acquired. It only became apparent to both of them when overhearing a porter's remarks to a guest,

"Newlyweds." The guest's disapproving look changed to a smile, well nodding understandingly, after being enlightened by the knowledge of this little insight.

"Ah."

Returning to the lobby from their room sometime later, they were greeted by other guests with more polite nods and smiles. They'd undoubtedly been thrust back into the limelight. The knowledge of their intimate frolicking had again been exposed. Akin to some pornographic novel characters, embarrassment made them wish the ground would open up and swallow them. Trying to be as inconspicuous as possible, they hastily beat their retreat through the lobby and into the street. The flush that had risen in their faces was now subsiding in the fresh afternoon air. Safely outside, they could appreciate the funny side of the situation and couldn't resist a good laugh.

"I've don't think I've ever felt so embarrassed in my whole life," she said, as the laughter subsided.

"Quite so, and we have to show our faces there again this evening."

"Perhaps we should stay out late this evening, Ian; I mean very, very, late." Ian gave a gentle snigger in reply to this remark. "Now, let's go explore these Christmas Steps you've told me about." The rest of the afternoon was spent browsing through stores, well exploring quaint cobblestone alleyways. Some streets, lacing sidewalks, were so narrow there was barely enough room to allow two-way traffic.

Gray stonework dominated the architecture of buildings. It didn't look drab because of its clean, well-maintained, vibrant appearance.

Exploration and walking feed on energy, so in need of some refreshment, they found a quiet little pub called 'The Assize Courts Tavern.' Entering the lobby, Barbara chose a bar that looked inviting.

Each small bar had its own individual name. The one named 'The pen and wig bar' was in keeping with the pub's Assize court theme. Its warm, inviting look beckoned would-be customers. The bar itself was dimly lit, and its fire burning in the hearth cast flickering reflections into the many bright objects situated around the room.

A mahogany bow window consisting of small thick, bottled glass pains also captured the fire's glowing colours. Barbara seated herself at a table near the window; meanwhile, Ian went to order drinks from the bartender.

"A pint of best bitter and a half, please."

"Coming right up, sir," the man's warm smile accompanied his cheerful reply. Ian's quest for seemingly useless information initiated some light conversation.

"Is there some significance to the name of this pub? Perhaps, for instance, this may have been the spot a courthouse once stood?"

"Yes, sir, there is a reason for the name," replied the barman. "The assize courts are just across the street from this pub."

"Ah, I knew there had to be some connection." Ian's inquiring mind submitted another little bit of trivial information to the memory banks. He paid for the drinks and joined Barbara.

Setting the drinks down, he sat beside her. The conversation then drifted towards all the options available to make this evening a memorable one.

"What would you like to do this evening, Barbara? If you have nothing in mind, perhaps together we can come up with a few ideas."

"Well, I did think, that's if you don't mind, I'd like to go backstage to see the boys; we could stay and watch their show. Perhaps after, you could take me to a nice restaurant for a meal." Ian placed his hand on hers and squeezed it affectionately.

"A show, then supper, that sounds like a lovely way to send the evening. If memory serves me correctly, there's an excellent restaurant quite close to here. We'll go there and book a table for after the show as soon as we leave this pub."

The beer was smooth and appreciatively savoured until both glasses were drained.

"Are you ready for another drink, darling?"

"Yes, please, Ian, but I'd like something different, something that will warm me up. The chill of the day is starting to get to me."

"How about a hot butter rum." The mire name of the drink, he hoped, might be enough to help stimulate warmth into her bones.

"Hot butter rum, yummy; I like the sound of that. I'll give it a try."

The cold night air, radiating through the glass windows, was offset by body heat generated by the crowd filtering into the bar. Most people seemed to be regulars in this establishment, so talk flowed freely between different groups. Lost in the crowd, they sat inconspicuously indulging themselves in each other's company before deciding it was time to leave to secure their evening's reservation. After the restaurant booking had been made, they took a slow straw across the city center to where the Colston Hall stood.

Entering through the stage door, they found the boys engaged in last-minute adjustments. This preening was directly before going on stage. Jim was first to spot the couple and struck up a few bars of the bridal march on his guitar.

"I'm glad that guitar's not plugged into an amplifier," Barbara scoffed. Jim's scolding was accompanied by the pretense of a wagging, disapproving finger. Although she did find It hard to restrain from smiling, well acting out this charade. "I think after that send-off from London, the last thing I want to hear right now is that tune blasted again." Jim gave a little chuckle as Ian nodded slowly in agreement with Barbara. Jim then greeted Barbara with a kiss on the cheek and then Ian with a handshake.

"It's nice to see you both here. Please say you're stopping to see the show. We've added a few new tricks to the act, so I hope you find our new innovations entertaining."

"That's what we're here for; I'd like to check out the improvements for myself. Before the show, there are some arrangements for next week we should discuss."

"Come on, lads, gather around," Jim hustled the boys together. There was a quick scurry to discard instruments, well preening themselves, to tidy up any disarray this may have caused. Barbara then went into a business mod to enlighten them on the meeting she'd attended that morning. Barbara's strategy with the band had always been to keep them wholly informed of their business from a financial perspective. It was just another extension of the strong bond that existed between them. The briefing had barely finished when the band was given their stage call.

Barbara helped with their last-minute readjustments, like some mother hen fussing over her chicks.

Barbara's opinion was their shows had been improving with every outing. However, with this performance, they had made a quantum leap. Perhaps with more promotion, this was the breakthrough they had been working towards. It was a significant step in their quest to headline venues. Barbara's applause from the wings was more than just enthusiasm. It was easy for Ian to appreciate this wasn't only a business connection; they were more like family. She then aired her aspirations to Ian.

"You know, Ian, I think the time's right for the band to make that next step in their career. I know with some behind-the-scenes hard work on my part, they'll get the credit they deserve. I'll make it my goal to have them achieve headline status before the end of this year. Anyone can see they're becoming so much more than just an opening act."

"That was an excellent show, Barbara. I'm sure you're right; in the not-too-distant future, their star will shine on the marque."

As the boys came off stage, John approached them first.

"Would the two of you like to join us for drinks after we've stowed our instruments away?" Ian made their apologies.

"We have a table booked for supper, so I'm afraid we'll have to give that a miss this time around."

"Perhaps tomorrow then." Arraignments were tentatively made for the following evening before leaving the boys to their own devices. They then slipped off to what they hoped would be a romantic meal for two.

The next day had the promise of being bright and sunny. Although it was tempered by the cold air of winter. With these weather conditions in mind, they made plans for the day over a late breakfast. Ian made a suggestion he thought would be an interesting start to the day's outing.

"Have you ever been to Durham Downs at Clifton?"

"No, I haven't."

"It's not far from here if you like; we could take a drive there when we've finished breakfast. It's situated on a Plateau, with a two-hundred-foot cliff face at one end, a perfect lookout spot. The view's quite spectacular."

Looking across the table into her eyes, he reached out his hand, placing it on hers to give a reassuring squeeze. "I love you very much, Barbara. But please excuse me if I'm not always good with words. Quite often, I'm unable to express my feelings with all the correct romantic phrases." Sensing the tender emotion in his voice, she felt he was now as completely open to her as an old, well-read book, its dog-eared corners and worn pages, all unashamedly exposed.

"They say a picture paints a thousand words, Ian; I think it's also true in this case. A look, or a tender touch, can sometimes portray one's every thought and emotion. I think I've always been able to sense how you feel, and I'm sure you feel the same way about me. Just being yourself has always been enough for me. Please don't ever underestimate your ability with words either, because I find the way we relate is very romantic."

"I'm sure I do know you as well as you know me, Barbara, and that's what makes what we have so special."

Breakfast was served, and the conversation, in between eating, centred on ideas that could establish a rough itinerary for the day ahead. The casual stroll to the car was also influenced by the pace they'd set themselves for this lazy Sunday.

Traffic was light, and a road that climbed steadily from the center eventually delivered them to the middle of the Downs. From there, it was just a mile, or two, southwest, across the Downs, open grasslands, to the Sea Walls. These were the steep cliffs given names that abruptly terminated the plateaus south end. Far below, the Port way road accompanied the Avon River through the base of the gorge. The ebbed river slithered its way past cliffs, towards a hazy industrial sky above Avonmouth docks, in the distance. This contrasted sharply to the almost pastoral settings close at hand and to the south. As suggested by its name, Avonmouth is where the Avon River joins the Bristol Channel's saltwater. The channel, in turn, also embraces the estuary of the River Severn in its seaward journey.

Ian parked the car. There was a stiff breeze blowing, so Barbara adjusted her scarf to cover her head before braving the elements. A grass verge bordered the road, separating it from a footpath that meandered along the cliff tops. A perimeter wall edged the path at this point, providing an excellent place to rest and admire the view. To the far side of the gorge, the dense green foliage of Lea Woods dropped steeply to join a rail line that mirrored the path taken by the road on the near bank of the river. The river's high tide that would be contained within high retaining walls now revealed mud flats left by the river's ebb. Watermarks on these walls bore witness to the tremendous variations of tidal conditions.

To the left, upriver, the famed engineer Brunel had constructed his excellent example of a suspension bridge. Its graceful lines straddle the gorge in a picturesque manner. Dominating stone support towers standing like two great sentinels, guarding the approaches to Bristol by water. Separated by the Avon gorge's deep chasm, they were bound tightly to their connection and purpose; by the bridge structure's graceful lines that linked them. Twin straps of gracefully curved riveted steel, supported downward slings, which in turn held the bridge deck firmly in place. The sweeping arcs of the supports reached through from its towers and down to land anchors. This completed the span. Its decking accommodated a narrow two-lane roadway and sidewalks.

Leaving their viewpoint, hand in hand, they walked along the lonely path towards the bridge on this cold winter day. Stopping briefly in this secluded beauty spot, they kissed before again turning to look at the picture-postcard view of the old bridge. She slipped her arm around Ian's waist and gave him a cuddle.

"Do you know where the road leads after it crosses the bridge?" A sense of warmth and well-being lingered as they looked into each other eyes. Another embrace followed before Ian tenderly kissed her forehead. Allowing that moment in time to slip slowly away, he then replied.

"The road would take you through the woods to meet up with a junction. Then depending on your destination, you could make the left turn back to Bristol or the southwest. The right turn will take you through Failand and onto Portishead, or Clevedon if my memory serves me correct."

"Portishead, that sounds an interesting place. Can we go there?"

"Today, your wish is my command, my darling, and I always enjoy a pleasant drive through the countryside."

Continuing their car trip, they stopped briefly at the toll booth on the bridge before passing through the sentinel's archways. Woods bordered the road that took them to the junction, where a right turn sent them west towards their chosen destination. Woodland gave way to open meadows. These meadows were situated atop what once was the same plateau as the Downs. It was now split asunder by eons of erosion.

The Avon river's relentless and forceful trek through the gorge to the open sea is the knife that carved this division.

Following the road straight across the open plateau, its course changed on reaching the slopes to the fare side. At this point, the hedgerow and old stone walls encroached on its verge, confining its width. Channelled through a series of switchbacks by these barriers, they left the plateau, descending into the Gordaineo valley. The valley was full of small farms with lush green pastureland. Farmhouses built of weathered gray stone were complemented by their well-tended gardens.

"How beautiful this all looks, Ian; it must be wonderful when all the flowers are in bloom."

"Yes, I'd almost forgotten how beautiful it is here."

Taking the right fork at the next junction, they continued on to Portishead. Driving past the main street, Ian followed the perimeter road to battery point. There he parked the car at the north end of the seafront.

He remarked that the new open-air swimming pool, built into the hillside at that end of the beach, had been constructed since his last visit. Its southern exposure made it an ideal sun trap. Sun terraces occupying the slope above the pool gave it the appearance of an amphitheatre. Its situation also offered a panoramic view of the foreshore and headlands beyond. This provided an added bonus for those indulging themselves in the rays of summer's sun.

Walking a poolside path that overlooked the estuary, they crested the summit before dropping down to the site of an abandoned gun emplacement. It Stood as a grim reminder of wars long past. Its empty bunker's; cold, damp, foreboding structure now only defied nature. In times of strife, this old empty shell housed a gun with sufficient firepower to bolster the security of the entire expanse of the channel below them.

Ian stooped down to Barbara's height well, resting a reassuring hand against her back. " That's the coastline of Wales we see on the far side of the channel." Ian Pointed across the water. His finger identified the distant shoreline.

"We're playing Cardiff next week; can we see it from here."

"That would be to the far left, I would imagine fifteen to twenty miles, that way." His finger swung to the northwest, giving an indication of the general direction. The bone-chilling wind, now blowing harder up the channel, was extracting a debilitating toll on their bodies. It was one chilly lady who suggested they should return to the car. With joints now stiffening by the cold, the trek back became a chore.

Ian started the car and turned its heating up to full before uttering another word.

"Let's drive to Clevedon and stop for a coffee or hot chocolate." The mere thought of a warm beverage gave comfort to both of them.

"That sounds like a good idea to me. Perhaps after, we could return to the hotel. Maybe I can find time to meet with the boys. I did promise to go over their spending budget with them. And that would be as good a time as any."

"Still keeping a tight rain on the purse strings, I see."

"Yes, but I like to get them involved with the financial end of the business. And as I've probably said many times before, artists are exploited in this industry. They should understand exactly where the money's spent and where if possible, can be saved."

"That's admirable Barbara, I'm sure the boys appreciate your concerns."

It was a short scenic drive to Clevedon, a small seaside town whose promenade had been left unspoiled by the trappings of commercialism. The town center lacked shopping precincts or large grocery outlets. The lack of such amenities helped retain the unique charm of the small rural community it was. Parking the car beside the promenade and close to the pier, they walked to the solitary seafront café open during this offseason. Hot drinks helped to replenish their energy levels that had been depleted by the cold.

The late afternoon air had turned even chillier with the fading glow of the afternoon sun. This half-light also changed the Bristol Channel's previously dark cold blue waters to a muddy grayish brown. Whitecaps whipped up by the prevailing wind and strong tides gave these waters quite an ominous look. This scene would draw pity for any poor sailor in a small boat. It would have to be a compelling need, to be out on these treacherous waters on such an evening,

Reaching the car, he quickly opened the door and hustled her in. He turned the heater to full blast directly after starting the engine. The moment the car started, a burst of warm air increased the cab temperature. This made for a pleasant drive back to the hotel.

With an informal meeting over drinks with the boys, Barbara was able to cover all her objectives. This gave Ian ample time to join them before the evening show. When the boys left to attend their performance, the couple retired to their room. Being able to spend this last evening together before the coming week's separation now became a welcomed gift. Ian had booked a ticket on the morning train to London for the following day. Barbara had agreed to drive him to the railway station to say their goodbyes. This last honeymoon evening made every moment in each other's arms worth savouring. It was like drinking fine wine before finally surrendering to sleep.

CHAPTER 9

Love made work a chore.

Weeks passed into months and living for weekends with his new bride had Ian enthralled with this new lifestyle. Tasting freedom and opportunities available to this gypsy existence made the confinements of his office a lonely, isolated place. Even Ian, who had always savoured the new challenges of his job, could be excused in this instant. He Interpreted time away from her being more than just an annoyance. Focusing his mind, he tried to free it from the distracting thoughts of Barbara. Ian reconciled himself in the knowledge they would be together that following weekend. Because of this radical change in schedules, there was little time for his golf games with James. Ian now regulated their friendship to an evening game of squash and lunch once or twice a week. At one such luncheon, James broached a subject concerning the finances of a man he had recently met.

"There's this man I know, who's chairman of a large company and is contemplating changing banks. To snare that account would surely be a feather your cap, Ian." Ian was casual in his thinking at this point.

"For what reason does this company wish to change banks, James? Can you give me some insight?" James gave a smirk before starting the story.

"All of this must be in complete confidence, of course, Ian." The smile remained on James's face.

"Of course, James, and am I to assume there's some humour involved."

"Let me fill you in. Francis Rudge, a friend of mine, owns a company that does contract work for the aircraft industry. He needs to expand his business, and for that, he needs a substantial amount of money."

"Has he been turned down by his own bank James?"

"Not exactly. Francis had an affair with the bank president's wife, and when it came to light, need I say more." Ian, realizing the opportunity in this situation, was his to exploit now fully appreciated the humour.

"One man's misfortune perhaps could be another man's blessing. Give him my office number and tell him to give me a call."

"I'll do that as soon as I return to my office, Ian." This productive luncheon had boosted Ian's lagging sprites. Feeling quite full of himself, his confidence was high as he received the anticipated phone call later that afternoon. The phone call was from Francis's secretary to set up an appointment. Ian set a time and date for Francis, and his accountant, to bring the company books to his office.

The two businessmen showed up promptly for their prearranged appointment, and Jean's instructions had been to escort them straight into Ian's office. Rudge's uncultured voice, and gruff, dominant personality, overwhelmed the room.

"Pleased to meet you, my son, I'm Frances Rudge, and you must be Ian Shaw, the wonder boy I've heard so much about. This is my accountant Mr. White." Francis made the introductions, well still shaking Ian's hand vigorously. Only after Rudge relinquished the firm grip he'd maintained was Ian able to gesture his clients towards his desk. A place to unladen the company's books.

"Please, gentlemen, pull up a seat and make yourselves comfortable." Ian's calm nature and formal business manner took a slight edge off Rudge's flamboyance. This was a strategy he'd always found successful in depersonalizing any business dealing at hand. The rest of the day was spent going over the company books. Ian kept a close eye on contracts signed for future work and its past performance.

"You'll find nought wrong in those books, the company's as stable as the rock of Gibraltar.

As you see, to comfortably meet the deadlines on these orders, we need to expand. That means new machinery, the expansion of existing buildings, and that's why I'm here, to negotiate a loan to handle these new commitments."

"On the insight gained by what I've seen in your books, I think you can consider the lone approved. On the condition, all of your business will be transferred to this bank." Ian was confident in his analysis and quick to capitalize on the fortunes of the moment.

"If that's part of the deal, and your services, and rates, are comparable, I see no problem with that. All our accounts can then be transferred to your bank as soon as the fine details are smoothed out with Mr. White."

"Quite so," Ian softly replied. "I'll give you the name of our branch manager in your area, and he'll set up your everyday working needs."

"It's been a pleasure doing business with you, my boy." The meeting was concluded with another round of vigorous handshaking.

Meeting James for lunch the next day, Ian waited for an appropriate moment before speaking of something that had weighed heavily on his mind since his marriage.

Barbara's influence had given him a totally different perspective on life, and he was sure she would disapprove of his nefarious dealings with James.

"I've been giving this a lot of thought, and I think this should be our last stock market deal. All good things must come to an end, and I wouldn't want to be overly greedy to be the cause of getting caught with our hands in the cookie jar, so to speak. We've both done exceptionally well out of our little arrangement, and I'd like it to end on an up note." He anticipated a show of indignation from James, but it never came.

"I totally agree. It seems like perfect timing bringing the subject up at this very moment. I have a proposition in mind to invest our capital legitimately, and I'd like to run it past you. It's time we move our money out of those Swiss bank accounts and into a profitable business."

"I'm all ears, James, so what's your plan." The relief in hearing his money was about to be moved into a legitimate enterprise fueled some enthusiasm.

"Set up a property investment company with me; there's good money to be made there legitimately. I'm sure with some creative bookkeeping, our funds could be easily transferred to such a company. Even if anyone was interested in the source of our cash, it would still be virtually untraceable. As the directors of the company, we would be able to draw a good salary."

"I'd like to jump on this, James, but right now, I wouldn't have time to handle a project like that."

"I see no problem there, Ian; I know how busy you are right now. I'll look after all the details. I'll just need your signature occasionally to rubber-stamp the operation." Agreeing to proceed with all the necessary arrangements as soon as possible, they concluded their luncheon. Ian then returned to his office.

One of Ian's priorities was arranging the loan negotiated with Francis to be available immediately and deposited into an account. It was set up expressly to fund a management company to oversee construction to expand his premises. Francis had requested it this way for tax purposes. (The old shell game) as he liked to put it, it was used to form a separate company so the parent company could better write off costs. There was the formality of confirming all Francis's accounts had been transferred into the local branch, for which Ian had not yet received the documentation. A call to the area manager was placed.

"It's Mr. Shaw, Rodney; you've been dragging your heels on the Rudge account. Where's the paperwork?"

"I must apologies that you've not received it, Sir, but it is all in order. I personally guaranty it. Apparently, there was some sort of mix-up in the mailing. I'll make it a priority to have it on your desk as early as possible next week."

"So, I have your word everything is in order, and all the accounts have been set up in your branch as specified."

"Yes, Sir, everything's in order and has been correctly attended to."

"Then, I'll accept your word on this matter and proceed with the transfer of funds."

It was Friday, and Ian's routine, whenever possible, was to leave the office prompt at closing time and drive wherever the band had an engagement to join Barbara. The group's next performance was in Brighton, so it was a close enough drive to enable him the luxury of spending the entire weekend with her. Shortly before leaving, he received a phone call from James, informing him, some documents needed his signature. James also stressed the urgency of the matter. Having an insight into Ian's plans, James suggested meeting at a restaurant where they sometimes dined. He even knew it would be on Ian's chosen route, out of the city. This arrangement did not sit well with Ian. Knowing full well, James was aware of his weekend plans; Ian felt the signing could have been dealt with over launch. The assumption there would be trouble parking in that area at rush hour also agitated him.

Arriving at the restaurant, Ian became frustrated and distraught by the lack of parking. In desperation, finally parking on the double lines directly outside the restaurant, he rushed inside. Hurrying through the door, Ian noticed a meter maid patrolling the street's opposite side from the corner of his eye. Hoping to conclude his business with James before she reached his parking spot, he ventured on.

"Ah! there you are, James." He'd caught sight of him sitting near the back of the restaurant. It was a dimly lit area, and his eyes had a problem adjusting to the light.

"Can we make this quick? I'm in a no parking zone." James pointed to the documents on the table before him. Ian could barely see the wording.

"If you trust me, just sign in the places I've highlighted, then you can be on your way." James sounded uncommonly cold and aloof.

"Fine," Ian snapped. Assuming James was disgruntled with him for such a quick visit. Taking the pen James had provided, he quickly signed without reading, all the while glancing at his illegally parked car outside. "I'll talk to you Monday morning, James, when there's more time," he called back over his shoulder as he hurried out.

Arriving at Barbara's hotel, the afternoon's anxiety had melted into obscurity, as his mind was now fully occupied with thoughts of a relaxing weekend. Greeting him in the lobby, she suggested an early supper before leaving for the theatre. His plans from the time he'd left his office had centred around enjoying her company at supper before the show. If ever a man achieved the ninth cloud's elevation, Ian had, in Barbara's company.

Their hotel was an old building situated across the road from the beach. A wide stone stairway leading up to the front door straddled a concrete well. This well exposed the basement to a modest amount of light through windows set half below ground level, reminiscent of a brownstone. Wrought iron railings topping a low wall surrounded the well before continuing up the stairs to the front door. The old hotel, although clean, was tarnished by time and lacked the charm of its glory days. The dining room, situated on the main floor, was elevated just high enough to overlook road traffic. This offered a limited view of the pebble beach below the promenade. However, it did give a clear picture of the English Channel beyond. Barbara showed Ian to their room, where he unpacked enough of his belongings to freshen up before going back down to the dining room.

The fact they were early for supper meant they had the dining room to themselves. Choosing a table in a bay window they seated themselves. The evening sunlight streaming through the window fell across Barbara's face. Looking into her eyes, he envied the ability of an artist who could capture such an image on canvas for posterity.

"I must be the happiest man alive at this moment. Our weekends together in these seaside resorts make it feel like every day's a holiday when I'm with you." She reached across the table and placed her hand on his, smiled and gave a naughty wink.

"I intend to make you happier than you ever imagined this weekend, darling." He chuckled as she kicked off a shoe and softly stroked his leg with her barefoot.

The waiter interrupted them with a polite cough and asked if they were ready to order. It was a set menu with three choices. Their selection was Dover sole, new boiled potatoes, and peas accompanied by a bottle of Barbara's favourite wine. Ian requested the wine to be served first. The waiter quickly returned and displayed the bottle for approval before uncorking it. Pouring the sparkling rose into two fluted glasses, he left them to enjoy their wine.

This pleasant respite in time together seemed to evaporate as fast as the wine. Supper was soon placed on to the table before them. Large platters, garnished with parsley sprigs, enhanced a food display that looked almost too good to spoil by eating.

Replenishing the wine in their glasses, the waiter inquired if everything was satisfactory before leaving.

Barbara then became fascinated with the effervescence in her glass as it performed its celebration of freedom in dance. Twirling her wine glass, the bright displays of this ballet was high-lighted by shafts of sunlight streaming through a window exposed to a western sun.

"I think a sparkling wine always makes the situation more romantic, Ian, don't you?"

"You may be right; after all, women are supposed to be the romantics." He gave a coy smile.

"Now I think your patronizing me," and again, she rubbed a barefoot up his trouser leg.

Finishing their meal, she continued to stimulate his libido, augmenting her flirting touches with playful banter. Continuing to amuse themselves in this manner until it was time to leave for the theatre, reluctantly, they exited the dining room. Even this exit was accompanied by more veiled promises from Barbara. Ian then drove her to the venue and gave her a peck on the cheek as he dropped her off. He'd also arranged to meet her after the show. Barbara's unpacked cases had been stored in the closet, and the lonely hotel room had a certain hollowness about it. Spending time unpacking the rest of his things, he then set out some of his belonging to give the place that lived-in look. Turning his attention to his briefcase, he then spent some time catching up on paperwork to occupy his mind.

Keeping a weather eye on a clock that seemed to record minutes as hours, it finally displayed the moment in time he'd been waiting for. He'd allowed an adequate amount of time for the return trip before the show's final curtain. He stowed his work back into his briefcase.

Parking in the back streets, he entered via the theatre's stage door. The sight of the boys carefully placing their instruments into cases caught his eye first. Exerting as much authority as possible, Barbara was busy organizing in the storage room. All items were being directed into their own specific place. Those were her strict requirements to ensure nothing would go amiss, a place for everything, and everything in its place.

She emerged from the room to acknowledge Ian; her brow wet with perspiration and cheeks flushed showcased the exertion she'd invested into supervision.

"Hello love, now we've finished here, we'll go for a coffee with the boys if that's OK." The cafe Barbara intended patronizing was used predominantly by people who worked at the theatre and nearby businesses.

"Sounds fine to me." The boys started jostling and pushing each other towards the stage door; these antics continued until reaching the small back street cafe. This boisterous behaviour subsided only after bursting through the front door, well still consumed by tiers of laughter. Although the horseplay had finally finished, an excessive amount of giggling continued as they ordered coffee.

"Are they always like this, Barbara," he whispered in her ear?

"Only on their goodnights. You should see them on bad nights." Her satirical comment brought a grin to his face. With most of their excess energy burned off, attitudes became more laid back. After shows, these relaxing wind-down also served as a business meeting, with everyone contributing their input.

The conversation centred mainly on that night's show. The audience's reaction to each segment of their performance was scrutinized. Analyzing this feedback always proved to be important in the development of their continually evolving act. Although left on the outside of this conversation, Ian was not made to feel like an intruder. Now fully integrated into this small, tightly knit group, his presence had been totally accepted.

Several more coffees were consumed before the talk of the evening's gig slowly evaporated. Walking back to the hotel and retiring to their separate rooms was how the evening was concluded.

Waking from a good night's rest to a sky that promised a beautiful day set the young couple in the mood for a hearty breakfast. Determined to exploit a commitment-free morning and afternoon to the fullest, they arrived exactly on time for breakfast. Occupying a table, they waited patiently for the self-serve buffet to open. The early bird may catch the worm, but being too prompt did have its setbacks. The kitchen staff who provided those worms were running a little behind schedule.

"I suppose there's one thing to be said for being early, there will be no lineup, and the food will be hot. Of course, when the buffet finally opens." She could sense Ian's unappeased appetite was making him a little testy.

"I'm sure it'll be open soon, and when we've finished breakfast, we'll be spending a relaxing day on the beach. But for now, just sit back, chill out, and soak in our beautiful window view. Just keep telling yourself today we don't have a care in the world. We'll let the hustle and bustle of life just pass us by and live for the moment." This conversation was designed as a distraction from what she sensed was fast becoming an annoyance for him. Barbara's talk seemed to have the required effect that she'd hoped for. Ian's attitude mellowed considerably.

"Your absolutely right. I think you've summed up exactly how I perceived the day should be. We'll have to sneak lots of towels out of the hotel though, a pebble beach doesn't make for a comfortable sunbed."

"Jim has an air mattress in his van Ian, I'm sure he'll let us borrow it." At that moment, the boys showed up for breakfast. Barbara waylaid Jim as he came through the door to make her request.

They trundle across the road to set up camp, equipping themselves with everything needed for a day at the beach. Barbara was quite fastidious about which spot would be suitable to settle upon, frustrating her beast of burden, Ian. Walking back, forth, up, down, and sideways, he eventually dropped everything.

"This is the spot, Barbara."

"Your so right, Ian," and giving him a kiss on the cheek, she was totally oblivious to his frustrations. An attempt at landscaping then followed. Shifting pebbles here and there to provide this patch of beach its own identity was her way of staking claim to her nesting area. Ian's assignment; inflate the air mattress. This was only accomplished with a lot of effort, aching cheeks, and a red face, being the price he'd paid. The stage was set to spend the day basking in the sun was complete: Except for a tiny but essential detail. The final touch being, a soothing massage with tanning oil; this was Ian's assignment. He slapped it on unceremoniously and then took much more time than realistically needed with the massage. He made this as intimate as he possibly could well: Constantly checking for preying eyes on this lonely morning.

"Ian!" The inevitable slap on the hand, followed by a smile, re-established the boundaries he'd apparently overstepped. Removing his hands, she then put the cap on the tanning oil.

"Later! There'll be time for that later. This is a public beach, in case you've forgotten." He gave a boyish laugh.

Basking in the sunshine for several hours had warmed the blood and stimulated their need for adventure. Barbara jumped to her feet. Picking her path over pebbles, she slowly moved towards the sea. Ian immediately followed at a painfully awkward trot. With a devilish grin of a plot about to be hatched lighting up his face, he called to her.

"Race you to the water." Throwing caution to the wind, they ran the last remaining steppes, and she dove straight in. After committing to the dive, there was no way to avoid the inevitable shock delivered by frigid waters on warm skin. Standing only up to his knees in water, Ian laughed as he gradually accustomed himself to the temperature.

"Holy shit, it's bloody freezing," she screamed, jumping up and down. Trembling fingers dangled from shaking wrists as she stood shivering in a state of shock. "You bloody ass, you knew it would be this cold. That's why you got me to race you in, wasn't it?" She splashed at him in retaliation, which made him laugh even more.

"Got you. Let's swim; that'll soon warm you up." Utilizing the maximum amount of energy swimming was an attempt at getting their circulation pumping. Their destination of choice was the nearby pier; once there, they paused for a rest. They found a rare type of isolation in this place. The solitude of this spot was disturbed only by the soothing sound of surf slowly scouring a well-scrubbed pebbles beach. None of the people who were sparsely scattered around the foreshore were close, so in this anonymity of the shadows, they'd found their own little sanctuary. Barely touching the bottom on tiptoes, Barbara moved up and down with the gentle action of waves. This motion pushed Ian's body ever closer to her.

"I still feel cold Ian, that swim did nothing for me."

"Perhaps I can warm you up a little." Putting his arms around her, he embraced her with a kiss. Even cold water could not stay the height of passion. Her close undulating body elevated him to arousal. The heaving motion of the waves stimulated his senses as their bodies rubbed together. Making love in the arms of the ocean gave a unique sensation of floating weightlessly, well utilizing the rhythm of the sea that cradled their bodies. Passions simmered slowly in this environment, none the less it did boil and boil well.

With energy drained, a far slower swim returned them to the spot where they'd set up camp than the one that had initially propelled them to the pier. Tony had arrived and was sitting there to greet them. Barbara waved to him as they approached, and a conversation ensued well they quickly towelled dry. Resuming the quest for a tan, they again took up their positions on the air mattress. Basking in the radiation of the afternoon sun, quickly replenished heat surrendered to a cold sea by its comforting warmth. With beads of sweat now starting mingling with tanning oil, Tony had chosen what seemed to be the appropriate moment to propose an offer. "I'm going to get myself an ice-cream cone. Would you, and Ian, like one, Barb's?"

"Yes, please, Tony. How about you, Ian?"

"Yes, I like one. I'll give you some money." Ian started the search for his wallet.

"That's all right," Tony waved off Ian's attempt to offer money. "My treat," he called as he left to fetch the ice-creams.

His tongue had sculptured the ice cream on top of his own cone into a small dome before returning.

"Great tasting ice cream." He presented them with one each. Barbara looked in amazement at her cone.

"What are these things on top of our ice creams." Tony grimaced to stifle his laughter as he made his reply.

"Oysters?" Barbara and Ian looked at Tony in astonishment. "Ousters, Tony, what do you mean, ousters?"

"I here they're supposed to enhance your," he paused for a while, being dramatic, then smiled and said in a questioning tone, "swimming?"

"You little bugger, you've been spying on us." Throwing her ouster at Tony, It hit him square in the back as he ran down the beach laughing. Ian then followed suit and tossed his in the same direction. Looking at each other with surprise, which then turned to embarrassment, they realized they'd become the butt end of one of Tony's twisted humorous pranks. In unison, they burst into laughter, unable to control the tiers that rolled down their cheeks.

Tony cautiously returned to take up a position on his towel sometime later. Obviously, he'd been waiting for things to cool down and the arrival of the other boys. Their presence would make any attempt at continuing the little feud impossible without exposing his little scam in its entirety, causing embarrassment to both Ian and Barbara.

The remainder of the afternoon was spent playing with a beach ball. Finishing their game, they decided to pack things up and return to the hotel for an early supper before preparing for the evening show.

The next morning, they strolled the promenade before meeting the boys for their traditional Sunday lunchtime drink. Barbara found a stool to perch herself on at the end of the bar. Well, Ian and the boys were content to just stand. After ordering drinks, John poked a fresh wound with a sharp sick.

"So, did you two go for a swim this morning?" The four boys turn their heads away to snigger in the pretense of anonymity.

"I can see you're not going to let us forget about our dip in the sea any time soon," Ian quipped in a humorous tone. It was plain to see he was as much amused at the pun as the boys.

"Perhaps from now on, you should confine your," ---Jim stopped and looked around to grandstand for his audience before continuing, "Swimming to the privacy of your own bedroom." This brought more howls of laughter, accompanied by some foot-stomping. When the laughter finally subsided, Jim quickly changed the subject, not wishing to go for overkill.

"Will you be able to meet us in Weston in two weeks, Ian?"

"Yes," he took a sip of beer before continuing. "I'm counting on being able to be there."

"That's good. We always have a good time at Weston. It's a favourite stop on our tour. We'll give you a tour of the local pubs."

"I don't think so." In an assertive tone of voice, Barbara put her foot down in a way that equalled the authority of a Sargent major. These boundaries, now set; they stayed to talk and drinking until the 2:00 P.M. Sunday afternoon closing time. Leaving the boys to go their separate ways, Ian and Barbara intended to spend all remaining time before his departure for London by themselves.

With warm sunshine radiating from a cloudless sky, and the smell of fresh sea air stimulating their senses, the remaining afternoon revolved around enjoying a promenade straw. Stopping to rest occasionally, they found relaxation just sitting quietly, looking out to sea. Words weren't needed to express the feelings of contentment that engulfed them on this pleasant afternoon.

Reluctantly they made their way back to the hotel for supper, knowing their holiday weekend would soon conclude. The band's following engagements would take them along the south coast and into Cornwall. Being too long a drive for a weekend meant there would be a two-week separation before their reunion in Weston. For them, savouring these last precious moments was the equivalent of the appreciation given a fine wine before the final swallow. There were more than a few tears shed as Ian kissed her goodbye and closed the door of his car.

CHAPTER 10

From the ashes.

Monday found him once more engaged in the lonely life of a bachelor banker. His first day proved boring and uneventful, but Sir John's ominous message awaited his arrival the next morning. Jean passed him a sealed envelope, which he opened, and read immediately. It was short and to the point, a very cold, unfriendly summons, reading (My office directly). Hurrying to Sir John's office, he gingerly tapped at the door.

"Is that you Shaw," Thundered Sir. John's voice.

"Yes, Sir." Ian now felt the anger of Sr John's uncontrollable temper seeking out him as its next victim.

"Get your ass in here and close the door behind you." From behind the desk where he sat, Sir John glared at Ian. He was not invited to take a seat but directed by an angry pointing of his finger, and a frozen stare, as to where he should stand.

"It appears you've authorized a small loan to Allied Electronic Controls."

"It was rather a large loan, actually."

"Yes," replied Sir John abruptly, with ever-increasing vocal tones. "Don't interrupt me when I'm talking, Shaw. The president of Allied is a close friend." Confused thoughts flooded Ian's head. Recalling Francis' affair with the banker's wife, why would Francis go through James and him if Sir John was such a good friend. Why had Francis not approached Sir John directly?

"Are you aware of what I'm saying, Shaw? You're mined seems to be somewhere else."

"Yes, I'm sorry, Sir John, I was listening."

"Heaven knows what your explanation for all of this is going to be. No one seems to have any knowledge of this loan you've underwritten. It would never have come to light this soon had it not been for the diligent work of one of our branch managers."

"But that's impossible, and yes, the loan was channelled through one of our local branches. The manager there has all the signed paperwork regarding the transaction. When I meet with Mr. Rudge and his accountant." Sir John interrupted Ian with a voice that moved several decibels above the loud volume he'd already been using.

"Who the hell is this Rudge you're talking about?" Ian's speech turned more submissive each time Sir John's words became harsher.

"The president of Allied, Sir."

"Rubbish," Sir John shouted. His anger had now turned to rage as his hands smashed down on his desk with a resounding crash. The sound made a now cringing Ian physically shuddered. "Captain Ronald Hunt is the president, has been for years. I will be calling our accountants to sort out your bookkeeping immediately. I will also have to consider involving the police of this matter. Consider yourself on leave as of this very moment. You're to leave these premises immediately. You are not to return until we've got to the bottom of this matter." His tone was slightly more subdued on his following statement, "I sincerely hope this mess will end favourably for you. Now get out of my sight."

Ian, without ceremony, immediately left, returning to his apartment, and still reeling in shock. Once there, he phoned James, only to have the operator inform him, James's number had been disconnected. Now frantic at not being able to trace James anywhere, Ian phone his bank in Switzerland. After giving his personal account number, he then asked for its status, intending to scrutinize all recent transactions. Listening to the information coming over the phone, he quickly scribbled it down in the hope of understanding what James had done on his behalf.

Comparing dates and the amounts of money involved, he came to a chilling conclusion regarding the contracts he had so hurriedly signed in the restaurant for James. The loan he had made to Rudge had gone to a paper company set up in Rodney's branch. From there, it was transferred to Ian's own account in Switzerland. From there, most of the money had been converted into negotiable bonds. A small portion, approximately the amount Ian himself had in the account, had been invested in an English company.

Contacting Rodney proved fruitless. At first, Rodney tried to be noncommittal. When pressured by Ian, he flatly denied any knowledge of the transactions. He then claimed Ian himself had set up the paper company that received the transferred funds. Circumstances were spinning out of control. His life was crumbling around him. The very first thing the following morning, he ran a title search of the English company. It was no surprise to find the only name to show as the company's principal was his, in which his money had been invested. Panic and fear were now influencing his every decision.

His thoughts were, how could a man with his knowledge of banking have allowed this to happen. How could he have been duped so easily? He was now fully aware that signing those papers for James without reading them on Friday afternoon had been his downfall. That whole signing scenario had been the climax of a masterfully engineered sting operation that revolved around Rudge and James.

Clinging to the faint hope of finding James, perhaps in a favourite haunt, Ian scoured the city like a drowning man, vainly grasping at anything resembling a stroll. Aware the police would now be looking into his affairs, he could do nothing but wait for the enviable. His ties to the investment company would be a fuse wire they'd trace back to the explosive evidence planted in his Swiss account. The scenario had been so well set up; it would be virtually impossible to convince anyone of the truth. Even if the truth were known, he was still guilty of insider trading.

Arriving back at his apartment, the fraud squad was waiting there to arrest him, having followed the trail he knew they would. The officer in charge informed him of his rights. He was then handcuffed and taken to a waiting car. Driven to a nearby police station, he was fingerprinted and taken to a cell.

The turmoil of the past two days had occupied his every thought. Only now, sitting in the lonely cell, did he have time to contemplate that glorious problem-free weekend he'd so recently enjoyed. Oblivion had concealed the facts that were changing his life. In past times, greed and arrogance supplied the fuel used to drive this vehicle that had propelled him to this predicament. Although his life since then had changed dramatically, it had been too late to avert this unforeseen destiny. He was finding it hard to perceive his predicament when he didn't have a care in the world only a few days ago.

This bleak Wednesday evening could definitely be counted as the lowest of lows at this point in his life.

His philosophizing was abruptly interrupted by an officer entering the cell to inform him he would be taken to another location and formally charged. Ian requested a lawyer. He was then advised to wait until he was at this new location and phone his lawyer from there. Within the hour, two officers had arrived to escort Ian.

He was surprised and most definitely ill at ease when he was driven out of the city. Surprise turned to fear when the car was driven to an airfield, and he was requested to board a commercial jet.

"Where are you taking me?" his protest was accompanied by physical resistance.

Frog marched to his seat on the aircraft; he was forced to sit and then buckled in. Again, he repeated his question, this time shouting. "Where are you taking me?" He got the only reply he would get; it was cold and to the point.

"You'll know as soon as we get there. Now be quiet, and don't force us to restrain you further." It was pretty obvious he would get no more information from his guards. Trying to rationally assess the situation, he estimated that they'd been in the air for at least ninety minutes. Ian was perplexed as to where their destination would be. Also, what was the purpose of this journey? It was beyond his speculation.

Deprived of a day's good toiletry, accumulated grim in this time of upheaval had reached the point of intolerance for a man who took pride in his appearance. He made a comment regarding his concerns to the older officer.

"Officer Johnson will escort you to the washroom. The flight attendant will supply you with a razor." Ian found solace in the fact his remark had not fallen on deaf ears, even though the reply itself was so cold. Finishing his grooming, he felt a little better, although the thought of his predicament still weighed heavily on his mind. A light snack served before landing was a welcomed gift of manna to a man who had not been able to take sustenance that day. On arrival, Ian was taken off the plane first to a waiting car. The other passengers on the aircraft started their short trek to the terminal building in the opposite direction. Ian thought it strange some seemed to be juggling passports along with hand luggage. It was dark, and there were no readable signs for Ian to establish his bearings by. Ian was equally as sure his guards would not tell him. Bundled into a car, he was driven through an unfamiliar city, then up to a large office complex, where it stopped outside the main entrance. Officer Johnson removed Ian's handcuffs and asked him to accompany him into the building. Johnson escorted Ian to the reception desk, where he showed the on-duty security guard some identification. They were then both issued identification passes for the building. Loosely supervised, Ian was led up the broad stairway in the main floor's central lobby. All the while, Ian surveyed his surroundings with nervous apprehension. Directed into a large office, Ian was ordered to sit on a chair, fronting the large desk that dominated the room.

"Lord Simpson will be with you soon, Mr. Shaw." With those words, Johnson made an abrupt departure. If this plot was thickening, Ian had no idea what its consistency would end up being. In total confusion, he sat and tried to analyze a situation that seemed to be about as clear as mud.

An elderly Goliath of a man with a grim persona entered the room from a door directly behind the desk. This was a man whose very presence commanded respect. Perhaps he would shed some light on Ian's predicament.

"I am Lord Simpson," he announced in a commanding voice. "I am an associate of the world's oldest company. I am also chairman of the world bank," Ian spoke softly with anxiety in his voice.

"Where am I, and what is this place?"

"Zurich Switzerland, Mr. Shaw, and for the present, that is all you need to know."

"The charges concerning the crimes I've been accused of are surely no concern to the world bank."

"Not exactly, Mr. Shaw, but we've had an interest in you as a potential recruit for our organization for quite some time. You seem to have the necessary skills needed to assist in the finance department of our organization. A business, I must say, that requires a person not fettered by the restrictions of morality." It was starting to sink into Ian's mind, who had manipulated his demise, and for what purpose.

"What of the charges against me in England? Would that be of no concern to you?"

"Once you decide to join us, the whole matter will be forgotten, just as if it had never happened. No police file, no bank misappropriation, all a misunderstanding."

"How can that be." Ian could not hold back his skepticism.

"You'll soon come to understand the extent of our influence. It's also easier to recruit a man with a questionable past and no apparent future, wouldn't you agree.?"

"You do seem to have me over a barrel, Lord Simpson." His business demeanour returning, Ian was ready to deal. Although with no apparent way out, the situation he'd got himself into made him extremely nervous and skeptical. "What becomes of the money moved from my Swiss account?"

"It's still in England, secure in your investment company to do with as you please. It's your money. The whole matter will be nullified the minute you make your commitment to join us." Ian shuddered at the consequences of not committing fully to the invitation.

"The company you wish me to work for, may I ask its name, Lord Simpson?"

"It has no name Mr. Shaw, and it has many names, but that's no concern of yours."

"Then, exactly what will my duties and salary be?"

"Your duties will be on a need-to-know basis when you are assigned a project. As long as the project remains profitable, you will be entitled to some of that profit. There will also be an expense account set up in your name." This was a much more lucrative arrangement than Ian would ever have expected from a legitimate company.

"I'll also enlighten you on the companies main goals: power and control. Money is merely a tool that helps control commodities and people. We've been challenged on this concept many times, but we always win out. You see, the greed of man is on our side."

"Then, being a mere man, I have no option but to accept your offer, Lord Simpson." Ian stretched out his hand to seal the deal, now feeling in a lighter frame of mind. Lord Simpson acted aloof, then hesitant, before shaking it. His hand was chilled like a body from the morgue with frigidity strong enough to drain all heat from the very depths of Ian's soul. His eyes, dull and glazed, projected this same cold persona. This brief touch of hands left Ian hollow and drained for an instant. It was as though he'd just had a close encounter with death.

"There's an office assigned to you, and an expense account has been set up in your name. You will be working under the supervision of Mr. Peterson. Starting time, nine tomorrow morning, sharp. Everything you need to know at present has been dealt with; therefore, this meeting is adjourned. On your way out, visit security at the front desk; they'll attend to your immediate needs."

Lord Simpson left the room as unceremoniously and quietly as he'd arrived. Now alone and still bewildered, Ian made his way back down to the front desk. It was apparent he was expected. Before Ian could speak, a set of keys were handed to him and a list of instructions. Ian was then talked through the arrangements set out for him.

"These are the keys to your apartment. I hope you will find everything there to your satisfaction. A chauffeured car is waiting at the main entrance to take you there. It will also pick you up tomorrow morning at eight-thirty sharp and return you here. On arrival, you will check-in at this desk. The person on duty will be expecting you. Have you any questions."

"I don't think so. Everything seems to have been covered quite thoroughly." He left the building a free man. But what was the price he'd paid for that freedom? This conglomerate could defiantly not be deemed a charitable organization.

Arriving at his apartment, he was duly impressed. It was stocked with all the things he required to satisfy his every whim. The fridge's food and wine, all personal favourites, plus a well-stocked liquor cabinet, graced the dining area. It felt comfortable. The surroundings had an air of familiarity. Ian was not much of a drinking man, but he occasionally enjoyed a gin and tonic. It felt like a significant reprieve for Ian from the last few harrowing days. A weight had been lifted from his shoulders. This was not the time to analyze a situation beyond his control. Now more relaxed, he then poured himself a tall one to steady his nerves. It was a favoured brand. Ice, a small bottle of tonic and a slice of fresh lime, was obtained from the fridge, then added. Perfect, he thought as he took the sip that helped subdue the trauma inflicted on him of late. Feeling more at ease and with his drink in hand, he made his way to the bedroom. Pyjamas were laid out on the bed for him. The closet and dresser contained an array of new clothes. Trying on some jackets, he held some of the other garments to himself. He knew all had been tailored to his fit. Checking labels in the clothing, he could see why. They'd been made by his own tailor. Posturing to the mirror with vanity befitting a peacock, it was plain to see whoever picked these clothes knew his taste well.

Sipping his drink, he sat and relaxed for a while to familiarize himself with his new surroundings. Deciding it was now time to rest, Ian set the alarm for the morning and made himself ready for bed. Laying in bed, his body felt exhausted, drained by the toll of events of the last few days. In contrast, his mind was pumped with the high of the dark horse who had just won the Derby but was fully aware this win was at a significant loss to something else: His own integrity. However, he also couldn't help feeling a little lonely. He was missing his bride.

In the last two days, he'd not been able to contact her due to the turmoil of events. The arrangement had been for her to phone him at his apartment in London each evening. Ian knew she would worry over the fact he'd not been answering his phone.

He made up his mind to try and reach her the following day, all the while hoping she'd not attempted to contact him through the bank.

His first priority the following day was to trace the phone number of Barbara's hotel. His call was then transferred to her room.

"Barbara, it's me." He'd Intended to explain everything possible about his new job without involving her in the details of his recruitment. Hoping to slowly ease her into the reality that the new job was also in another country. Ian was then interrupted by her anxious reply.

"Ian, where are you? I've been unable to reach you. Are you alright?"

"I'm fine. It's been quite hectic for me in the last few days. I've taken a new job, a significant step up, but it's in Zurich." The subtle approach had just been blown out the window.

"Ian, that's Switzerland! don't you think we should have talked about this first?" Apparently, he couldn't calm her down by trying to talk his way out of this one. She'd never been this angry with him before.

"There were certain factors beyond my control. It was quite an aggressive recruitment. A one-time offer I couldn't refuse."

"I hope you're doing the right thing." She paused. There was remorse in her voice with the following sentence. "How will this affect our time together?"

"There are still a few things to iron out. I promise from now on I'll keep you fully informed. Really it's a great opportunity I've been given. I want to tell you all about it when I see you next. Phone me collect tomorrow evening. I have to leave for work soon; I can't be late on the first day." He then gave her the phone number of his new apartment.

"I'll phone you tomorrow, and I won't forget the time difference, as you did."

"Oh, I didn't give it a thought; I'm so sorry. No wonder you sounded so tired." He gave a kiss into the phone's mouthpiece, "I love you very much."

"I love you too, Ian. Please take care." Her voice then changed to an authoritative tone, "and keep me in the loop."

A jump start of coffee, accompanied by breakfast cereal, preceded some meticulous grooming tasks for his first day at the office. At eight-thirty sharp, the phone rang to say his limousine had arrived. With his usual eye for precise detail, he arrived at the waiting limousine. After being driven directly to the complex, he entered and presented himself forthwith, as per instructions. On signing in, he was given the keys to his office and directed to its location. An open reception area fronted his new abode, and he was greeted by a woman seated behind a desk.

"Good morning, Sir, may I help you."

"Yes, I'm Mr. Shaw; I was told this would be my office."

"I'm pleased to meet you, Mr. Shaw, my name is Ingrid, I'll be your secretary. The first thing on your agenda this morning is a meeting with Mr. Peterson at ten, and until then, your time is your own. When you've settled into your office, perhaps you'd like me to introduce you to some of the people you'll be working with."

"That sounds like a grand idea Ingrid, I'd appreciate that."

After familiarizing himself with his office, he returned to Ingrid's desk to be paraded around the building, like some new trophy, to meet his co-workers. Last on the list was Mr. Peterson's office, where she introduced them before taking her leave.

"Call me Pete; Mr. Peterson is far too stuffed-shirt for this office." Peterson's accent was American, and he was by far less formal than people Ian had been used to working with in banking. Ian found this casual attitude very refreshing, although there was something about Pete that bothered Ian. Brushing this feeling aside, he dismissed it as his own insecurity in such unfamiliar circumstances.

As Pete was assigning him work, Ian took the opportunity to inquire about personal commitments and freedoms.

"I had some leisure time planned for the weekend after next. Will those plans now have to be scrub?"

"We don't punch the clock in this office. Complete your work to my satisfaction, and your time is your own," was Pet's reply.

With his nose to the grindstone, Ian buckled down in days preceding his planned weekend with Barbara. As luck would have it, his next assignment would require him to be in London on Tuesday of the following week. This would give him the much-coveted long weekend he'd been so looking forward to. Working himself unmercifully, even spare time was utilized, with small details such as acquiring his much-needed passport.

Friday arrived, and with it, a whole different perspective on life since his ordeal. He handed his report to Pete, anticipating the equivalent of an excellent passing grade. He waited for a reaction. Pete quickly glanced through it.

"This seems to be thorough and to the point. I can see why you were hired. Excellent work, Ian. Now, I know you're anxious to leave, so I won't keep you; enjoy your weekend." He then shook Ian's hand.

"Thanks, Pete, I intend to." Ian's spirits were high. School was out. His first stop was the apartment, to pick up luggage, then on to the airport. He arrived there very early, caught up in the intensity of his own enthusiasm. Not before the plane was airborne did he allow himself to unwind and indulge in the pleasures of forty winks.

CHAPTER 11

A new lease on life

Zurich being many hours behind him and far removed from Barbara's world, Ian stepped off the connecting flight he'd taken to Bristol. He rented a car and followed her directions to the Winter Gardens Pavilion at Weston Super Mare, a seaside resort.

Some thirty minutes later, he found himself driving the seafront, searching for his final destination. The completion of this journey and the person awaiting his arrival had been foremost in his thoughts since leaving Switzerland.

Expecting show rehearsals to be taking place inside the pavilion, he parked close by, in a side street. Discarding his tie, it joined the jacket he'd previously removed and tossed unceremoniously onto the back seat. Loosening his shirt collar, he then rolled up the sleeves. This casual look felt more environmentally in keeping with the seaside resort's ambiance that surrounded him. Sweeping his hair back with both hands, he was now ready to hang loose, to coin a phrase from Barbara's book.

Beads of sweat were now forming on his brow as this beautiful hot sunny afternoon worked its magic on his body. Rounding the corner to reach the pavilion's front entrance, he was confronted by a throng of holidaymakers jostling their way along an overflowing sidewalk.

The pavilion dominated all surrounding buildings on the town side of the promenade's adjacent road. Built of white sandstone block, it dazzled the gaze, with reflected glare from bright afternoon sunshine. A large half circular bay window adorned with exterior fluted stone columns that reached high to support a flat roof, covering this feature, graced its frontage—Weston's own little White House.

The promenade paralleled the beach opposite in its entirety; destinations lost in a haze of people and heat only emphasized its length. A granite block wall edged this walkway. The other side dropped to a golden sandy beach, some ten feet below. This rampart also supplied ampul protection from gales and high tides. At various intervals, stairs and ramps ran from the promenade to the beach, affording public access.

Hoards of people occupying every bit of available promenade space in this area created sounds that intermingled with noises made by children at play on the beach. Added to all this commotion was the unmistakable din drifting through the air from the amusement arcade at piers end. This conglomeration of melodious pollution was more than adequate to overpower the drone of road traffic. Augmenting sight and sound are other senses, those sympathetic to atmospheric vibrations and smell. Brine laded fresh sea air mingling with essences of cotton candy, fish, chips, and freshly made doughnuts are not unusual to this environment. Fuse these elements with seasonal hysteria, and it provides an experience unique to a seaside resort. This place definitely vibrated to the chorus of jubilant energy.

Ian entered through the main entrance to access the ballroom, where he'd been given to understand rehearsals would be in progress. Walking into this sanctuary away from the sunny seafront was quite dramatic. The room was tranquil, instilling a sense of calm to its every corner. The band was on stage about to start another number. Barbara was seated at a table in the corner, mulling over some papers, almost as if doodling, perhaps composing. Glancing up to see Ian's approach gave her face a glow that illuminated that small corner of the room. She flew from her seat to greet him. Flinging her arms around his neck, she smothered him with kisses.

"I've missed you so much, Ian."

"Not half as much as I've missed you, my darling." Combing through her hair with loving fingers, he then cradled her head in his hands and drew her body closer. He then kissed her passionately.

A devilish grin came over his face as he slipped his hand into a pocket to retrieve an expensive gold watch. Dangling like a carrot before her, it swung from his fingers with the motion of a pendulum. This became too great a temptation for her to contain. Barbara attempted to snatch it from his grasp was made. Quickly raising it beyond her reach, he grasped her around the waist and kissed her once more. Relinquishing his hold, he held out the watch. "Give me your hand." Fitting this small timepiece proved difficult for Ian. He fumbled with the dainty strap on such a delicate wrist. "I seem to be all fingers and thumbs. There that's got it." She giggled as she waved her wrist in jubilation.

"It's beautiful, Ian, thank you." Kissing again, they were momentarily distracted as the band started to play. She was the center of his universe at that moment, a position she was not about to relinquish to any more distractions from friends.

"I think the band can do without me for a while. Let's go for a walk. The weather outside's gorgeous. It's far too nice to be inside."

Walking out through the back door and into the gardens, they faced its centrepiece, an ornamental fishpond. Italian in style, yet also reflecting its Victorian origins, the garden blended perfectly with the rest of the pavilion.

Pausing to talk, they sat on the edge of the stone wall that surrounded the rectangular pool. Shaded by the pavilion, this portion of the garden was serene and relaxing. Vines weaved their way through white boxed trellises and overhead beams to form the pathway's portals. Large coy gliding beneath water lilies in the pool, creating an atmosphere perfect for meditation. It was a place perhaps to spend time with a good book. It provided an ideal setting for Ian to reveal all the details concerning his new job. Ashamed of the circumstances leading up to his recruitment, he downplayed that segment of the saga.

"Now that you're based in Zurich, will this make it more difficult for us to see each other, Ian?"

"Perhaps for a while,---I'm not sure." Ian's voice had a slow sullen tone to it. Wishing to make the most of this last, long summer weekend, he chose not to dwell on the negative.

"I don't have to return to work until Tuesday, so I plan on making this a memorable long weekend for both of us. Fortunately, my next assignment's in London, and that'll take me a few days to complete, so I'll be staying at our apartment there."

"That's great, Ian, we finish here on Monday, and the band's playing Bristol on Wednesday. I've already made the necessary arrangements for that show, so we could be together for the few days you're in London. We'll also be able to travel there together."

"I was hoping that might be the case. Let's walk." Rising to his feet, he offered her his hand.

Heading out of the gardens, they crossed the main road and stepped onto the promenade. There appeared to be fewer people than when he'd first arrived. This seaside walkway seemed to run on forever in either direction. It now seemed devoid of people in its far reaches. Walking to the wall that overlooked the beach, they sat for a while to take in the view. The tide had receded so far; the water was now only visible as a shimmering mirage in the distance.

"I don't think I've ever seen a beach where the tide goes out so far." Ian's hands shielded his eye's from the sun, well gazing South.

The Victorian leisure pier, who's expanded far end housed an amusement arcade in a castle-like building, imposed its structure on the seascape. It was well maintained, with an abundance of ornate cast iron and steel structural work painted black. All woodwork, in contrast, was white with reds and blues used to highlight trims.

Pennants flying from its numerous high pinnacles were augmented by bunting strung from every possible vantage point. Together these flags crackled in a dance orchestrated by the breeze. Proudly standing as a cherished gem from the age of leisure pier building, it indeed remained a jewel in the crown of Weston's promenade.

On the sands below the pier were donkey rides for children and brightly painted wagons drawn by horses for all to enjoy. Brilliantly coloured wooden-sided structures with canvas roofs and awnings shaded tables and benches from the sun. These serve as makeshift restaurants. The specialties of these cafes were cold seafood, such as cockles, mussels, winkles, whelks, and gelid eels, tea and lemonade, which were also provided for liquid refreshment.

Crowds of children gathered around a Punch and Judy tent, where the show was about to begin. Barbara envisioned spending quality time with Ian in a more intimate setting.

Looking north, the promenade being notable less crowded, seemed to offer that choice.

"Let's take a walk this way, Ian." Taking his hands, she pulled him to his feet. Luring him towards her desired direction. Her sparkling eye's promised a seduction equaling that envisioned by the wails of a siren's song.

After walking for about thirty minutes, they came to the end of the promenade. An old pier that had fallen into disrepair lay beyond. Turning to retrace their steps, they passed a hotel on a point. Its entrance advertised a lounge bar. This cool shaded room beckoned them inside. Tugging at his hand, she guided him towards the door.

"Let's go in for a sandwich and a cool glass of beer. I feel like some refreshment: how about you?" He put his arm around her waist and playfully pulled her through the door. An aroma of beer filled the air. They chose a table near a window, and she made herself comfortable. Ian went to the bar and ordered two small glasses of best bitter, plus some cheese and tomato sandwiches, to appease their appetites. His order was handed to him on a tin tray, decoratively displaying colourful ads of brewery products.

Bathed in sunlight, pouring through its southwest window exposure, her table gave an excellent view of the beach. Directly below them was a small bay whose farthest side outcrop housed several large structures. The beach ended at the rocky headland. At that point, it spawned birth to the hotel's foundations, whose bar they took refuge in. Their high vantage point laid out before them a panoramic view. On this hazy, hot summer evening, the main beach's golden sands blended into the grassy headlands' fussy greens many miles away. In the small cove below, a retaining wall had been built to unite the two capes. Capturing the waters of retreating tides, it formed a marine lake with its own sandy beach. Small children were still playing in the sand at the water's edge on this pleasant evening. They made themselves busy with a variety of tasks. These tasks included designing and constructing sandcastles, digging motes, excavating canals. It was accomplished meticulously enough to pass inspection by the most fastidious construction foreman.

"I've been thinking; you won't need the car you rented, Ian. We can use my car to drive to London and for driving around here."

"Yes, that's true. I'll return it tomorrow. I'm sure the rental company will have an office in a town of this size." Finishing her sandwich, Barbara's following statement was delivered with reluctance in her voice.

"Well, I suppose we should be taking a stroll back when you're ready, Ian. The band's opening for Ronny and the Bones this evening."

"I can't say I've heard of them. Are they popular?"

"Oh, I can't believe you said that Ian, they're great. You really must stop going to those snobby clubs of yours; get out and meet some real people. Most people you associate with there must have broomsticks stuck up their asses to be as upright and uptight as they seem to be." This comment made him laugh well, swallowing his last mouthful of beer. The result of this misdirection of air and beer caused an eruption of a magnitude ten. Putting his hand to his mouth, Ian tried to stem the flow of beer that had started spurting over the table. Ian's attempt had about as much success as a finger plugging water from a fast-flowing facet. Speech eluded him until he'd cleared his airways.

"Barbara sometimes you say the most outrageous things. Come along; we'd best leave before we wear out our welcome here."

"Well, I've done nothing wrong. It's you that's made a mess of the table."

Ian returned their glasses to the bar on the way out. They took a leisurely stroll back to the pavilion along the promenade. Time lingered on their side, prolonging those precious moments on that peaceful, warm summer evening, so far from the madding crowd.

It was easy to see crowds forming lines outside a still distant pavilion, intent on purchasing tickets for a forecast-ed sellout performance.

"Are they waiting to see Avebury Barbara?"

"I wish! They're waiting to see the Bones. Tickets are worth their weight in gold for their shows." Bypassing the crowd, they entered through the back door. Once inside, they made their way backstage. From this vantage point, they were able to see the audience starting to filter in. Some couples had started dancing to records being played.

The band was making final preparations, behind the curtain, for their stage introduction. Barbara took Ian by the hand.

"Come, let's watch the show out front with the audience tonight."

Sitting at a table reserved for band member friends, well awaiting the show's start, she made a modest confession. Whispering shyly into Ian's ear, she gave signs of embarrassment. Perhaps aware that some of her most inner thoughts were about to be exposed. This is the constant plight of anyone writing with passion.

"The first song the band will perform this evening contains lyrics I penned for one of Jim's melodies."

The M.C. came on to the stage with much fanfare, tipping a hand to the crowd with appreciative bows. The introduction then began with all the flair of the circus ringmaster.

"Ladies, and gentlemen, to open our show this evening, let me introduce to you Avebury. The band's leader is Mr. James Evens, lead guitarist and singer. Ladies and gentlemen, let's hear a big round of applause for Avebury."

Introductions complete, he made his exit as the curtain behind him rose to showcase their performance in all its glory. In conjunction with neatly tailored suits, excellent grooming was a design the band had nurtured to depict their clean-cut image. Jim stepped up to the microphone, and with colourful verbal commentary, announced the list of songs they were about to perform.

Speaking in a quiet, subdued manner, he'd set the stage for his resounding dramatic start. Turning his back to the audience, he unbuttoned his jacket and slipped his right arm out of its sleeve. Spinning back around and holding one side of the coat at arm's length, it opened like a Matador's Cape. The audience was his bull, and he was about to take it by its horns. The jacket's red silk lining shimmering in spotlights glare exploited this effect to the maximum. He strummed his guitar and broke into their first song. By the time they'd started their third song, no one was dancing. The crowd had gathered around the stage, clapping and swaying to the music. A standing ovation, followed by calls for more, erupted after they'd finished their last number.

After Avebury had taken their final bows and left the stage, the M.C. came running out to subdue an audience whose unquenchable thirst had left them hysterical. The microphone in his hand, he spoke loudly. He utilized as much gesturing and posturing as possible to emphasize his message.

"I'm sorry, ladies and gentlemen, much as your enthusiasm is appreciated by Avebury, we must move on. We are on a tight schedule this evening, and we must press on with the show. I'm sure you've all been waiting in anticipation for our main attraction this evening. I am pleased to present Ronny and the Bones." The crowd irrupted into a frenzy as they sauntered on stage. After waving in response to the cheers from the audience, they went straight into their performance.

Their reputation was well-founded, exceeding the expectations of most. Even Ian had been converted. He insisted they stay until the show's end to fully appreciate the entire act.

"They're a great group, Barbara."

"I knew you'd like them, Ian. I think you've been converted, but we do need to work a lot harder on getting you to lighten up more." Conspicuous in silence, he was determined to sidestep this hornet's nest that had just been kicked into his path.

The ballroom and pavilion now behind them, they joined the throng of people filtering across the beach road to access a now illuminated promenade. From this point, their hotel lay due south. Passing the Grand pier, Barbara pointed to a narrow strip of parkland they were approaching. "Our hotel's that way, Ian, just across the green." This parkland east of the beach Thorofare paralleled it on its entire southern route; another road on its town side isolated this island of green. The two Thorofare's, however, were intermittently joined at strategic points for traffic. Fronting the town were several hotels, maintained to a standard that reflected its illustrious Victorian past.

A full moon reflected its image in the high tide's calm waters on this beautiful clear night. The evening's silence was broken only by the gentle lap of channel waters planting soft kisses on the sea wall. Barbara moved closer to Ian. As they put their arms around each other, they continued their walk with bodies entwined.

"We have a fourth-floor room overlooking the Bristol channel. It should give us a good view of Wales from our balcony tomorrow morning." Before speaking, he kissed her brow.

"My luggage is still in that hire car. I suppose I should fetch it when I've walked you to the hotel."

"Where did you park the car?"

"Near the Winter Gardens." Walking Barbara to the lobby, he left her in the company of boys, who had also just arrived. "Meet you all in the bar in fifteen." He shouted as he left the hotel. Perhaps not one of his better ideas. This would be the equivalent of leaving her with Tweedle

Dumb and Tweedle Dee and relying on them to act responsibly. The party was in full swing by the time he'd returned.

The Bones had arrived to elevate the festivities to a whole new level. Keeping such company, it was inevitable the mornings wee small hours had arrived long before bedtime.

Sleeping late the following day and waking to overcast skies was a situation Ian's slightly under the weather demeanour found depressing. Seeing little promise of a brighter day ahead with no sign of a break in cloud cover did not help these feelings. Looking from the balcony, he called over his shoulder to Barbara, who was still in bed.

"I don't think we'll be able to see Wales from here this morning, my darling. In fact, we haven't even got a decent beach view with the limited visibility this weather's providing."

Pondered her thoughts, she determined a drop of rain wasn't about to drown out her parade.

"Let's return that rental car after breakfast, and we'll take a drive in my car."

"Where will we go?" Ian's voice echoed the melancholy feeling this drab morning had instilled in him. "It's hardly the weather for a drive ether."

Focusing on the window's rain patterns, he was intrigued, perceiving it as a blueprint for an ecological system. Rain spots united to form small streams. These would be streams then flowed together to form small rivers. Propelled by gravity, these torrents running ever downwards converged in one large puddle at the sill. In Ian's mind, it represented an ocean. Imagination mirrored mood.

"I have just the place in mind for a day like this." The optimistic tone of her voice gave Ian's spirit a lift. "I read a pamphlet in the lobby promoting a gorge about forty-five minutes drive from here. Photographs displayed the rouged beauty there, along with a picturesque village. Even on a rainy day such as this, I'm sure it has something to offer.

It also said there are several caves in the gorge offering guided tours." Ian was receptive to this idea. Thoughts of propping up some bar to say out of the rain would not be his first choice of entertainment. Engaging in the previous night's drinking session had instilled enough misgivings to deter him from a possible repeat performance.

Breakfast over, the address of the nearest rental car company office was retrieved from the phone book. Returning his rental car to this office proved to be a marathon undertaking, as paperwork bogged down what should have been a simple transaction.

Customer impatience only seemed to serve as a source of entertainment for this clerk. Ian's face, now slowly turning red, indicated the rise in stress levels. Fully aware of the grief being inflicted, Ian's tormentor became more meticulous. It was apparent he intentionally slowed the process down even more. He then insisted on making a second thorough check of the car. Perhaps this was intentionally done to further annoy Ian; who would know. This was a man who derived twisted pleasure from injecting a little misery into someone else's life.

After an excessive amount of scrutiny, he finally found a small scratch. This insignificance he'd developed into a significant event. Ian, now red at the gills, with steam spouting from his ears, protested quite vocally. Snatching back the rental agreement, he pointed vigorously at the relevant paragraph. "Here's the verification right here in black and white (small scratch on right side back door). I don't think you bothered to read the bloody thing at all, did you?. So don't screw me around anymore."

However, this did not speed the process along; this annoying little man's ego had been deflated with the exposure of his little rues. It was several more long minutes before Ian emerged, exhibiting every trait of an impending coronary victim.

Jumping into Barbara's car, he didn't utter a single word but just sat there fuming with anger. Barbara had driven a considerable distance before a curse targeting the clerk spewed from his lips. Her touch, and a gentle smile, was all the medication needed to pacify this savage soul. A long pause followed, allowing him to regain his composure before she spoke.

"Don't let a silly thing like that spoil your day. You're better than that." Smiling back at her, he'd not intended relinquishing his wrath so quickly, but her smile, and the sound of her voice, quelled all those negative emotions. By accessing his actions and analyzing the words (lighten up), he resolved, they should be portals to his new outlook on life.

"I'd truly be as big an ass as that troubled little man if I allowed that to happen, wouldn't I?" She gave his hand a reassuring squeeze.

Driving back to the seafront, she turned south, following the beach road for a mile or two. The beach drive ended in an abrupt left turn to head inland. The southwestern sky was clearing, with occasional shafts of sunlight illuminating the high grassy downs of a peninsula far south. Could this be the promise of a brighter afternoon, despite a light drizzle that was still falling?

"Before we turned, I noticed the beach continued on into the distance. This whole coastline seems to be one huge sandy beach " It was characteristic for Ian to notice such trivial things and commit them to memory. Barbara, not being quite so obsessed, acknowledged his remark with a smile and a nod.

"Where are we heading now?"

"There's a map in the glove compartment, Ian. Look for the town of Cheddar, as in Cheddar cheeses."

"Ah, yes, I see the map. I hope finding Cheddar will be as easy." Coming to a road junction, their destination was well signed.

"It's posted Ian, we probably won't need the map after all." These words came as a welcomed relief to Ian, who had minimal success at best accessing the desired area. It was turning into an actual wrestling match, with the map acquiring the upper hand. Finally, folding it back to its original form, it was returned to its designated spot in the glove box.

"I'm glad our map's no longer required. I sometimes get a little queasy reading in moving vehicles. Now all I have to do is reach that plain where I can just chill out and enjoy the scenery." Coining Barbara's phraseology was an amusing veiled attempt to indicate he was pursuing the attitude change she'd suggested he should work on.

Before delivering them to their destination, Cheddar, Barbara's chosen route, meandered through the rolling Mendip Hills, passing farms and small hamlets.

The rain had stopped, and warm sunshine turned wet roads into caldrons of steam, surrendering moisture skywards from whence it came.

Signposted car parks at the edge of the town just south of the main road proved adequate parking. They parked the car as close as possible to the mouth of the gorge. Ian checked his bearings before joining Barbara in a short stroll to the junction giving car, foot and traffic, gorge access.

The entry point to this geographical phenomenon had sufficient width to accommodate a small segment that catered mainly to tourism. This hamlet was isolated from the main town by its geographical location. Some of its buildings clung like moss to cliff walls. Every inch of available space had been utilized. Village structures mostly accommodated small cafes, gift shops, and specialty outlets that produced their own merchandise.

These operations spawned thriving cottage industries, such as candy factories, handmade clothing, leather goods, and more. One factory outlet, open to public tours, professed to be the only Cheddar cheesemaker still producing that product in Cheddar.

A few pubs displayed luncheon menus outside on colourful Sandwich boards. This was to entice would-be customers through their doorways. The lower village centred itself around several manmade connecting ponds. A culvert channelled fresh spring water from the opposite side of the road to feed these small reservoirs. A crevasse in the cliff face had created the portal from where this elixir of life was erupting. Crystal clear water gushing from the cliff's base had filtered through several hundred feet of limestone rock to reach this point of exit. Through irrigation, waters from the uppermost pool supplied the lower ponds with a constant supply of the earth's lifeblood. Low-level brick retaining walls topped with wrought iron railings constrained this water systems boundary.

Water lilies lent tranquillity to these calm oases. Old London Plain, and Chestnut Trees, dotted among small plazas, provided shade for hot summer days. Just north of the spring were two cave entrances, which grabbed the couple's attention.

"Which one do you think we should explore, Barbara."

"Well, the rain's holding off. Let's take a walk up through the gorge."

"Sounds fine by me." Passing through the village, they followed the narrow gorge road that wound its way upwards, constricted now by steep cliffs encroaching on its shoulders. The Cliff face occasionally relinquished enough space to allow small car parks to flourish. The village soon despaired into obscurity as they proceeded on, veiled by the road's many twists and turns. The gorge was now a wild and isolated place.

Pausing to view mountain sheep grazing on cliff face ledges, they were awestruck by their agility, jumping from ledge to ledge scouring for spars vegetation. The road continued its steep rise as cliffs melted into surrounding hills. Eventually, the gorge had become no more than a valley. The bleak cliffs had now surrendered their gray demeanour to green moorland. Livestock, grazing in lush pastures, replaced mountain Sheep. Drawing inspiration from the surroundings they stop, to absorb the rugged beauty of this place. It was also an appropriate time to contemplate their return.

"Perhaps we should start back towards the village, Barbara." Feeling rejuvenated and the morning's brief encounter with anguish left far behind, Ian felt at peace with himself.

Stretching her arms, well closing her skyward gazing eyes, Barbara took a deep breath as though she was experiencing some profound spiritual enlightenment.

"If we must." The moment had passed. Emotions can be duplicated, but events can only be relived through memory.

"This place reminds me of something someone once told me. I'm sure it must be this place they were referring to."

"I thought you told me you never heard of Cheddar."

"That's true, but I couldn't help but notice the effect the place seems to have on you, and the story was about a gorge. A man was caught in a terrible storm, and I believe it must have been here. He found shelter in a rock face cleft. Remembering that storm and the solace found in that shelter inspired him to write the hymn 'Rock of Ages.'

My grandmother's friend told me that story after we'd sang that very hymn in church one Sunday morning. She also told me she'd visited the gorge that had inspired its composer."

"Ian, the extent of your knowledge never ceases to amaze me. I'm sure we'll find a constructive use for it someday."

"Was that a compliment or a putdown?" She laughed.

Arriving back at the village, she wrapped both arms lovingly around his left arm and snuggled close.

"I'm in the mood to go exploring caves now." Ian pointed to the nearest one.

"Then shall we explore that one?" She nodded approval, and he escorted her to the entrance. A middle-aged woman was sat in the admissions booth. Her persona seemed as drab as the clothes she was wearing. Adjoining the pay station was an old turnstile that resembled a revolving door. Intertwining iron bars were now tarnished and pitted by time. However, the ongoing activities of eager hands had polished a fresh sheen into the patina. This gate, along with a wood hoarding displaying scenic reproductions of the wonders that awaited visitors inside, secured the entrance. He moved his face towards a small opening in the booth's window.

"Admission of two please," he shouted, allowing his voice to echo through the booth, as he was sure the woman's thoughts were elsewhere.

"That'll be five shillings, please, love." She made the request sound as dull as the way she looked. Ian could not help thinking to himself as he passed her the money, how precious time is. It seemed such a waste to be squandering it in this way, doing a job that held little to no interest for this person. With all the enthusiasm of a vegetarian at a steak barbecue. Glancing at the booth's clock, she passed Ian the tickets. "There will be a guided tour starting in five minutes." Picking up her book, she started to read. In trading reality for the world of fiction, Ian could only hope she'd find solace in that choice of escapism.

A group of people had congregated in a chamber near the cave's mouth. As they joined the group, a man with a buoyant personality arrived to address the gathering. Good afternoon, ladies and gentlemen, my name is Ted, and I'll be your guide today. I'll be happy to answer any questions about the cave you may have during the tour."

Ted continued his spill as to why the cave entrance was the lowest point of the cave. "The caves themselves were formed by rain gathered on the hills atop the cliff face. This accumulation of water then filtered down through its limestone deposits. Eventually, the water gouged out convenient pathways. Pathways, through eons of erosion, formed vast caverns. All this was spurred on by the filtration of water on its journey to the bottom of the gorge. So, this explains why these caves run uphill.

Some experts believe the Cheddar Gorge itself was formed in much the same manner. The theory being one such cavern grew so large it was unable to support its roof. After it collapsed, it was transformed into the gorge we see today.

Ian and Barbara had paid little attention to his commentary, indulging themselves in intimate small talk. Ted became momentarily distracted by Ian whispering sweet nothings into Barbara's ear. This slight annoyance was not something he was about to let pass unchallenged. This situation could rival his status as the star attraction, which was a definite slight to his ego. Calling Ian out had caught the couple entirely off guard. The anonymity they'd found in the crowd's numbers had now been stripped away. All eyes were now on them. Strangers were now sharing their intimate moments.

"I believe you have something to say on the matter, sir?" This query had been Ted's little ploy to inflict embarrassment.

"Hmm, hmm," grasping at strolls and trying to stave off total embarrassment, Ian instinctively posed a question.

"How far does this cave run." Ted had made his point, content in the fact he'd drawn them back into his fold.

"Good question, sir." Ian breathed a sigh of relief, sensing he had been let off the hook.

The crowd's attention had again returned to Ted. Ian looked at Barbara, and they sniggered like two small mischievous children who had been reprimanded but had avoided detention.

Still, in serious mode, Ted explained how many years before a small dog had been lost in a cave known as Wokyhole. The entrance to this cavern lay some fifteen miles away by road and to the far side of this range of hills. His story continued, telling how some ten days later, the dog turned up in this very cave, but his passageway through this subterranean maze was never discovered. "So, in response to your question, sir, the entire cave system has never been fully explored."

Such an elaborate story afforded ample opportunity for an ambush by a would-be heckler:

"Did you make him pay admission?" Ted, an expert at dogging bullets, wasn't about to be shot in the back that easily.

"No, sir, we understood he'd paid his admission at the far side."

This being Ted's arena, he more than outmatched the young bull that had just locked horns with him. The crowd's laughter was the stamp of approval on Ted's swift reply. Moving on through the cave, they paused in a cathedral-like chamber. It contained crystal clear rock pools formed by water dripping from above. Stalactite and stalagmite formations had their natural beauty and colour enhanced with spotlight illumination.

"This is awesome," Ian remarked quietly to Barbara, not wishing to disturb the cathedral-like serenity of this chamber.

"Isn't it just."

After progressing a little further, their trail terminated on a small beach. Its lake waters flooded the remaining chamber. On accompanying sides, this chamber had steep, smooth walls that dropped sharply to below the waterline.

Ted illuminated a subterranean cavern under the far side of the lake with a flick of a switch. Then came his grand finally to his well-rehearsed spill.

"To continue on from here, as you see, would require scuba gear, so this concludes our walking tour. I thank you for being such a good audience, and if anyone has more questions, I will be pleased to try to answer them for you."

Slowly they made their way back to the cave entrance, stopping along the way to take in the many unnoticed wonders in the first passing.

The sun had banished the cloud cover entirely, and it was now a pleasant summer afternoon. This prompted Barbara to point to a tea garden directly opposite.

"let's have some tea in that place, Ian."

"Yes, I'd enjoy a cup of tea right now and perhaps a snack." The garden in question was bordered by black wrought iron fencing with a matching gate open to welcome business. Brick pillars integrated into the fence at regular intervals provided rugged support. The same brick, as used as pillars, formed a path around the patio's fringe.

A grass lawn provided the bed from which brightly coloured umbrellas blossom like flowers, offering shade to tables and chairs. In keeping with the setting, lawn furniture constructed of ornately scrolled cast iron was also painted black. The garden was adorned with colourful flowering hanging baskets. The restaurant's eves supported more of these kaleidoscopes of nature.

The single-story structure had been constructed to resemble an Elizabethan building. More hanging baskets that were in abundance were suspended from black-coloured wrought iron bracketed poles. These poles sprouted from large planters that, in turn, were filled with flowers that cascaded over their rims like waterfalls.

Choosing a table on the sunniest part of the patio, they made themselves comfortable. A waitress soon made her presence known and broke into her well-rehearsed sales pitch, enlightening them on the restaurant's list of afternoon delights.

"I would like to recommend the freshly made scones, clotted cream, and strawberry jam. These are products are locally sourced. Even the strawberry's themselves are grown in fields on the cliff tops. Barbara's mouth was beginning to water as she imagined fresh cream melting into freshly sliced warm scones, topped with colourful crowns of sweet strawberry jam.

The sale had been made, as Barbara placated to her desires.

"It sounds totally illegal, so I don't know about you, Ian, but I'm going to pig out now and diet tomorrow." He reached out, touching her hand, as his grin affectionately, to acknowledge her humour.

She gave a confident laugh, taking pride in the knowledge she had, a figure most women strive to achieve.

"The works, for both of us, then please."

The long walk and the cave tour helped provide an appetite to fully appreciate the flavours about to explode on their tongues. After mentally licking their plates and sipping the last of the tea, they settled their bill before strolling back to the car, hand in hand.

"When we get back to Weston, I have a meeting with the pavilion's manager before tonight's show. I'll need to freshen up at the hotel before I'm off to work. She had a detached tone to her voice in her last sentence.

"It looks like it's going to be a lovely evening. I think I'll buy a book, sit on the beach and enjoy a read; well, you're working."

"I only wish I could join you. That sounds like a perfect way to spend a pleasant summer evening. As soon as our opening act is through, I'll leave and join you. We'll meet at the pier entrance around Nine o'clock."

"I'll be there waiting."

Reaching the car, he placed his hand on her shoulder as she reached for the door handle. He then gently turned her around. Leaning her against the door, he kissed her. He was becoming aroused as he held her close. Her breasts pushed into him as their hips slowly moved in unison to the dance of love. Sensing his arousal, she looked lovingly into his eyes and touched his face.

"This a public place, Ian. Let's save it for later." Intoxicated by the moment, he'd become utterly oblivious to their surroundings. He smiled and kissed her lightly on the forehead.

"I was getting carried away there, wasn't I." He took the keys from her hand. "Perhaps I should drive. That'll give you a chance to rest on the way back."

"If you don't mind." He opened the passenger door for her and helped her in, before returning to the driver's side.

A warm breeze from Ian's open window flowed through his hair, well his elbow rested casually on the window seal throughout the drive. Soft music, quietly resonating from the radio, provided a lullaby that soon lured her into dreams. With little traffic on the road, and the sun's orange glow dancing through hedgerow leaves, he thought how pleasant a drive this was. Pressures of past weeks seemed very distant. They were like a passed from another life. His new reality gave him time to enjoy the moment.

"We're at the hotel Barbara," he said softly as he switched off the engine. Shaking her gently by the shoulder, he then stroked her cheek with the back of his finger. She awoke to check her surroundings.

"Oh, I still feel so tired." Stretching her arms and yawning, she ran her fingers through her hair. "I'll just have time to walk to the pavilion after I've freshened up."

"Is that all there's time for, a wash and brush up." She smiled and pushed him on the shoulder in a playful manner.

"Yes. We'll have the rest of the evening for that, and I promise you it will be worth waiting for." He put his hand on her shoulder to kiss her on the cheek. She turned and gave him a peck on the lips.

"Later then, although the anticipation's already driving me wild. Waa woo!" He threw his head back well, giving the wolf howl.

"Easy boy, or you'll have the neighbours throwing cold water on you." He laughed.

Returning to the hotel room, a new book in hand, he walked out onto the balcony. A comfortable chair and a small table beckoned to him. The panoramic view of the channel shimmered in the dwindling light of a now watery setting sun. This easily persuaded him that it was a relaxing a place as any for a quiet read. He'd also be able to enjoy a drink in the privacy of his own company. This appealed to him more than the reality of clothing and shoes filled with sand if the beach were his choice on this warm evening. The seashore also couldn't afford him the luxury of that gin and tonic; he was about to go down to the bar and fetch himself.

The book he'd chosen was a new spy novel; action-filled, plus intrigue, he'd once perceived such stories as being totally detached from reality. However, after the recent turns of events in his own life, perhaps those perceptions of fantasy should be re-evaluated.

Lost in the concepts of the author's imagination, time slipped quickly by. Looking up from his book, he could see the incoming tied, lapping gently forwards over the sandy beach to form shallows. Inching towards the promenade wall slowly, relentlessly, it was recapturing the coast relinquished in its ebb so many hours before.

It would soon be time to meet with Barbara, he thought. Checking his watch for confirmation, he walked into the room and placed his book on the night table. The stir stick from the drink savoured much earlier that evening now found a new vocation as his bookmarker.

He wasted most of the allotted time for a spruce-up by meticulously grooming his hair. Every brushstroke was painstakingly patted into place; each wave then precisely eased into its exact spot before it received his stamp of approval.

Once more, a mirror became the sounding board that mesmerized him, and narcissism became the thief that stole his perception of time. Now running late, he was determined to make up the time with a brisk walk.

The harsh sting of his aftershave, now just a refreshing tingle, was stimulated by a salty breeze. It redefined its smell, making him more aware of the aroma.

Engaged in a good stride, he soon reached the main road's junction that ran through town. Lights from the many amusement arcades there gave an eerie glow to a dusky light created by the sun's futile struggle with approaching night. Some signs flashed, others illuminating arcade names lit up the area around their entrance like so many magical grottoes and the lights from machines inside added to this psychedelic display. The street was a busy place. Every corner reflected the hustle and bustle of people out for an evening's entertainment.

Turning away from this crowded area, he crossed the green and headed towards the beach. The pier was not to be outshone, with a display of lights that dominated the coastline. The Grand pier's bright gift of light reflected off the dark waters below.

The smells of popcorn, cotton candy, freshly made doughnuts, fish and chips blended perfectly with fresh sea air to simulate Ian's appetite. He sat on the sea wall with his back to the sea and waited.

Fortunately, Barbara was also late. The promenade lights switched on in a cascade, illuminating it from end to end. The distinct notes of the pier's calliope could be faintly heard over the sound collage that formed this seaside night music.

Barbara skipped lightly across the road to join him. That well-defined spring in her step reflected her mood.

"Have you been waiting long?" Putting her hands on his shoulder, she raised herself up ballerina fashion to kiss him quickly on the cheek.

"Not long." Taking her hands in his, he drew back to enjoy the entire portrait her form had painted before him. She looked towards a stall at the pier entrance.

"That food smells so good. I always seem to be eating when I'm at the seaside."

"Yes, but it's only small portions, so would you like some fish and chips?" There was a playful sarcasm in his tone, being fully aware of her weaknesses.

"I eat fish and chips far too often." Her concerns gave Ian cause to snigger. "Oh, what the heck, yes."

"That looks as good a place as any to buy them." His nod directed a path to the stall that had captivated her sense of smell. Walking entwined together, they approached the counter, and Ian placed their orders.

"Can we go for a walk on the pier when we get our supper? It's the best way to enjoy fish and chips, you know, eating them wrapped in newspaper as you walk."

"Planning on walking off the calories as you consume them, are you?" She delivered a playful slap on the shoulder for that remark.

"I'm serious; there's something about the environment that enhances the experience." This speech was delivered with comedic body language befitting that of a mime.

Their orders were placed on the counter. She meticulously unfolded hers, creating a display equaling the most elegant bouquet, then proceeded to douse it in salt and vinegar. Ian looked on with a grin on his face, saying nothing. Discretion, he thought, was the better part of valour. He then used the salt and vinegar himself, but in moderation, unlike Barbara.

The pier turnstile proved to be a juggling match, so he handed his fish and chips to Barbara. After retrieving money from his pocket, he fed it awkwardly into the slot, having greasy hands, for Barbara's entrance fee. Barbara did a balancing act with the fish and chips held high as she passed through the gate. She ran ahead as he fumbled more money into the turnstile before being able to give chase. Stopping suddenly, she turned to hold his fish and chips out in presentation style, conceding to his victory in the race. He graciously accepted his prize with a bow. She touched him on each shoulder with her meal.

"I dub thee Sir Ian, Knight to the grand order of greasy spoons."

"I promise to protect the public against overcooked food and lousy service to the best of my ability."

"Arise, Sir Ian, and enjoy your fish and chips." She fed a chip to his mouth, after which he sucked her fingers well, looking lustfully into her eyes. She withdrew her hand, slowly well feigning a look of indignation.

"Why, Sir Ian, your shameless." They both laughed, and the moment passed. This moment ended abruptly as their privacy was interrupted. This intrusion came in the form of a group of children running in the opposite direction.

Continuing their walk, they gazed into the distance far beyond the pier's end, witnessing the coastline of Wales biding good night in the ever-failing light. Finishing their meals, Ian took the empty wrappings and formed a projectile to toss basketball-style into a waste bin.

"I must admit you were right; the salty night air, as we walked, did seem to add something to the fish and chips."

Walking into the funfair building, they initially found the noise overwhelming. A Ferris wheel, bumper cars, and several other rides, including a carousel with its calliope, seemed to be vying for the title of chief noisemaker. Sideshows lined the outside walls; target shooting, darts, coconut shies, slot machines, and other such games contributed their fair share of sound. Barker's voices barely heard over the din were hustling would-be customers. Constant jostling from a seething crowd induced them to stop at one such stall, dedicated to archery, for a break. Kewpie dolls in various sizes covered the side walls.

"Oh, win one of those for me, please, Ian." She was bouncing up and down like an excited child hidden deep inside had just been released.

"For you, I'll do anything. I bow to your command." A smirk came to his face as she raised an eyebrow in a look of disbelief at this lousy pun. He paid his money and was given a bow and three arrows by the Barker, who then pointed to the back wall.

"Pop three balloons on the wall and win a doll." The bow felt comfortable in Ian's hand, and he made all three arrows count. He was a natural.

"Would you like to try again for a larger doll, Sir?" The barker's shout was aimed at titillating the crowd's appetite. After laying his money down, more arrows then flew rapidly at their mark. His aim was steady, confident, and sure. Balloons were bursting with a sound similar to the crack of gunfire. This commotion was starting to attract attention. The third successful performance has begun to draw a large crowd. The barker held the biggest doll from the wall high, displaying it as a would-be prize.

"Two more perfect scores will get him this, ladies and gents. Does he go for it? Just six more arrows come on, give him some encouragement." The crowd clapped, whistled, and cheered their approval. Six arrows were placed before him, but Ian hesitated with his money. Should he take a lesser-sized doll or go for broke. The barker whispered to Ian," on the house, sir, this is the busiest I've been all day." It was a good bet for the barker. Ian stood to gain the large doll at no extra charge or lose any chance of a prize with one miss. He was no longer alone; the crowd was with him. People were lining up to try their luck. Some were even able to hit a balloon or two, but Ian's aim never faltered. This was his night; he had the magic, the doll, and the girl. The barker handed him the largest doll.

"Congratulations, sir." His shout commanded attention. His following words were for Ian's ears only. "You've been good for business. I've never seen anyone do what you just did. It's the first large doll I've ever had to part with." Ian handed the doll straight to Barbara.

"Your prize, my lady." Ian's reward, a very appreciative kiss.

"I've always wanted someone to win me one of these. It's the sort of gift that has no meaning if it's bought; it has to be won."

"You're a strange girl. You have such quaint ideas. I think that's all part of what I love about you so much." Putting his arm around her shoulder, he gave her a hug. She held the doll close to her chest, her new baby. With Ian's arm still around her shoulder, they walked in solitude back along the pier. The promenade quite now was rejuvenating itself in slumber, awaiting its cleaning to start a new day as they headed for their hotel.

The lobby was awash with people spilling from the bar. Crown prince, Jim, led his entourage straight towards Ian and Barbara.

"We're going to a party. You two must come with us." A glance into Ian's eyes from his seductress foretold the promise he'd been savouring all day.

"We're going to bed Jim; we intend to have our own private party there." Jim doffed a would-be hat and bowed in the direction of the stairs. He conceded the decline of his offer. Jim watched their assent, like a court witnessing the departure of their king and queen. The gang then trooped off to their party.

Looking at each other brought a grin of anticipation to their faces, she started to run. Ian chased her to their room. They dove onto the bed, hastily removing each other's clothing. Layer by layer, the clothing was rapidly removed, occasionally pausing to soothe and caress each other's bodies.

The course of lovemaking moved slowly at first. It then steadily accelerated until the fulfillment of love was achieved in unison with their bodies and emotions' final eruptions.

The sound of Sunday church bells greeted the morning. Ian dressed and left to buy Sunday papers. Barbara was enjoying her morning sitting on the balcony when he returned. A freshly made pot of tea, accompanied by toast, and marmalade, richly displayed on the hotel's most elegant silver wear, had just been delivered. He couldn't conceive a better way to spend a pleasant Sunday morning. Sitting, relaxing, beautiful setting, the smell of fresh sea air in his lungs, his papers, a cup of tea. Yes, he thought, life is good.

After reading all the articles that interested her, Barbara dropped her paper by her chair. She then slipped into the room and called over her shoulder to Ian.

"I'm going for a shower." Ian glanced up from his paper to see his vision of beauty walking away. Her long black hair was flowing over her white rob, her shapely legs and well-contoured body rekindled memories of passions unleashed the previous evening. Enslaved by emotion, he could no more ignore his instincts than those same irresistible forces that beckon birds north in spring. Following her into the room, he watched as she slipped off her robe. Placing his hands on her bare shoulders, he started to gently massage her body and kiss her softly on the neck. She turned round to embrace him. They fell gently on the bed to revisit the euphoric achievement experienced in that magical moment of the previous night. He could always make her feel sex was the fulfillment of their love. There was never a sign of lust in his lovemaking; he only portrayed gentleness and affection, even in the height of passion. He was her perfect lover. Bathing in the glow of this fresh experience, they returned to the mundane tasks of making themselves ready for the day.

This Sunday, like so many other Sundays, was intended to be a slow lazy day. It was a day that gives the toil of the week meaning. In keeping with this philosophy, it was near noon before they ventured from the hotel.

"The boys will be going to the pub about now."

"How can you be so sure?"

"Does salmon swim upstream? Sunday afternoon in the pub, it's a ritual with those boys." The authority in her tone told him she knew she wouldn't be wrong. "Let's join them for a quick one before we go out for the afternoon."

"That sounds fine with me, as long as it doesn't turn into a pub crawl to find them."

"I think it'll be a safe bet they'll be in the nearest one. That one there, most likely." The boys had used the noon-opening pub doors slightly ahead of them and had taken a position at the bar. Jim, being the most charismatic, was the standard-bearer at the group's center. John, the drummer, was first to spot them.

"Over here, you two." He shouted, well waving a hand of recognition in the air. "What would you like to drink?" Ian looked at Barbara for approval.

"Half of bitter?" She smiled and nodded. "That'll be two halves of bitter then, please, John."

Ron's shy and timid nature lacked the illusion of confidence he could portray in his stage performance. In a reserved, soft-spoken manner, he looked to Barbara for some reassurance.

"You've written down all the arrangements you've made for us in Bristol, haven't you? I know you're not going to be there, and I would like to make sure everything is straight." John, overhearing, butted in.

"Of cores, it's all straight, Ron. You know Jim has all the particulars.

Barbara wrote them down and gave them to him. You worry way too much that's your trouble, Ron."

"No, I don't. I just want to make sure everything's straight, that's all."

"Ron, forget about business; just shut up and drink your beer. It's your round. You always drag out calling in the drinks. I think your hopping someone will forget it's your turn and get them in for you." John grind, well passing his empty glass to Ron. "Are they always like this, Barbara?" Ian's soft reply was for her ears only. She touched his hand and leaned closer to give her answer in a whisper.

"You should be here when they've had a few more beers."

Acting as if it was some kind of drinking competition, they all guzzled down the freshly drawn pints. Ian could only look on in amazement, hoping he was not expected to compete. Tony slammed his glass down on the bar first. Looking at everyone with a sense of pride and accomplishment, he smacked his lips.

"Does everyone want the same again?"

"Let me buy this round." Ian seized an opportunity to exit this beer fest. "Barbara and I are leaving now, and I would like to buy you all a drink before we go." He called to the bartender. "Same again for the lads and one for yourself. Will this cover it?" A ten-shilling note folded neatly along its middle was stood on the bar to ensure it wouldn't dampen on a wet countertop.

"More than enough, sir, thank you."

"We'll see you, boys, later."

"You don't really have to go, do you? You can stay for just one more, surely!" Knowing full well one leads to another, Tony manipulatively pleaded his case. Using every tool in his shed, he played out this scenario to the hilt. Looking at Barbara with sheepish eyes, he already perceived her to be the weakest link.

"Well." She looked at Ian for courage. "It's too beautiful outside to spend the whole afternoon in the bar, but."

"How true." The speed of his retort emphasized his wish to leave. He then herded her towards the door with skills befitting a border collie. He saw her usual will of iron becoming pliable as Tony increased heat to this performance by the minute. "See you later, lads." Holding their pints in a salute of gratitude, they toasted Ian's round in a raged chorus.

"Cheers."

"Let's get our swim things and go to that large open-air swimming pool on the promenade."

"The one with the big white wall all around it."

"Yes."

"That sounds fine to me." An afternoon basking in the sun appealed to Ian's lazy Sunday philosophy.

The pool's patio was begging to accommodate the deck chairs, and beach towels, of would-be sun worshipers. The pool also looked inviting. Its wedged shallows starting at nothing tapered very slowly into deeper water. The depth at the far end reached fifteen feet to accommodate an international standard diving stage. It imposed its dominance over the center, shallow's. The shallows accommodated a large three-tier fountain.

Toddlers were playing in its large lower pool. Barbara chose to spread her towel on the part of the patio most suitable for sunbathing. Ian left his things with her and walked down the side of the pool. Reaching a point that was deep enough to accommodate a dive. He took the plunge. Within a minute, he was back at Barbara's side and reaching for his towel.

"That was a quick swim." She looked up at Ian's pale, shivering form.

"That water's cold enough to fu-freeze a p-penguin's chuff." He combined towelling off with a vigorous massage in an attempt to restore life to frozen flesh. The rest of his day was spent working on a tan. Even sweat generated by the sun's warm rays could not induce the temptation of another dip. That water, he thought, was best suited to arctic creatures. Early evening was heralded in by shadows cast from high walls, stealing sunshine from their chosen spot. This artificial sundial had indicated it was time for them to leave and ready themselves for an evening's entertainment. Ian suggested booking a table at a restaurant for a late evening meal. This would allow them time to drive north and explore that part of the coast.

* * *

Passing the marine lake and old pier, their chosen course narrowed as it approached a toll road. The scenic route that awaited them was described by an informative booth attendant. He explained how it ran through picturesque Kewstoke woods before terminating at Sand Bay. This coast road initially climbed into a wooded bluff overlooking the channel. Cruising this scenic drive for several miles, the tree line thinned as it descended from its lofty heights to join sand dunes that initially divided the road from the sea. Dissipating dunes then blended softly into a golden sanded crescent beach. The base of a far headland brought the beach drive to an abrupt end. The road itself terminated at a large car park that nestled into its grassy slopes.

Isolation had claimed the spot where Ian was about to park. Back down the road, behind them were small quiet dwellings, clustering around a solitary pub. This small community seemed to be the only link to civilization.

"It's early still. Shall we take a walk up the headland?" Barbara kissed him on the cheek and soothed his thigh with her hand. She did not have walking in mind. He turned to embrace her in a passionate kiss as her hand filtered through his clothing to expose the prize she was seeking. Sliding his hand between her thighs, he tantalized her with his fingers before removing all obstacles to their desires. Allowing her to slide down and rest on the seats, he slipped off his jacket to serve as a pillow for her head. As he moved over her, she availed herself to him in every way possible. He massaged his hands up her back and onto her shoulders. Gripping tightly, he eased himself into her, assisted by guiding hands. Ian was cautious at first as he slowly rotated his hips. The moist heat of her body enticed him to delve deeper with each movement. She could feel the entire heat of his body emulating from that one spot, now deep inside her. Motions became more intense and furious. Euphoria now held the baton conducting the symphony of nature, performed by these participants. Summits of extreme pleasure reached, and passions quenched, the chains of enslavement to these base instincts could now be relinquished.

* * *

Taking a leisurely drive back to Weston, the fading sunlight was dancing with the shadows of tree foliage. From open windows, Breeze swept through their hair as they bathed themselves in the comforting glow of passion spent.

"I can understand why you enjoy your job so much, Barbara. The whole summer's like one long holiday when we're together."

"Yes, I do get a lot of free time on the road, but it's only fun when I have you to spend it with. Looking to the future, eventually, I'd just like to look after the business's financial end. I'd like to set up shop in one place, somewhere we can call home. I would have to represent several groups to make that happen. However, I have some ideas I'm working on. My dream would be to have my own studio one day. It would be a place where the artists I represent could record their work. I could rent to anyone wishing to make use of its recording facilities to help pay the bills. Hopefully, it would still leave enough time to allow me to follow another love of mine, song writing. The band must make that all-important brake through with a recording for that to happen, and I'm sure that will happen soon. I'm working on a record deal for the boys right now that hopefully will materialize within the foreseeable future."

"Things really do seem to be happening for you. I had no idea. Will this mean you'll be spending more time in London?"

"I could set up an office anywhere. Really, the location wouldn't matter. I thought perhaps we could buy a house, and I could have an office at home to start."

"I like that idea. When I have time off, I won't be running all over the countryside looking for you. Where would you like us to buy this house, or haven't you thought that out? Although you do seem to have given much thought to this plan."

"That depends on you, Ian, with all the travelling you'll be doing. I suppose we will have to live close to an airport." She laughed at what she intended to be a sarcastic remark; however, Ian saw merit in the humour.

"That's not a bad idea at that, Barbara. Personally, I find the pace in this part of the country much more relaxing than the hustle, and bustle, of London, don't you?" Griped with enthusiasm, he didn't wait for her reply. "There's an airport to the south of Bristol, and the countryside's dotted with small villages. I know this valley that I'm sure you'll just fall in love with. When we drive to London, Tuesday, let's start early and give ourselves some time to check out that general area."

"You've got me so excited about it. I'd like to skip the beach tomorrow and drive to the countryside instead."

"We could spend what's left of the long weekend in the country. If we check out of our hotel first thing tomorrow, I'm sure we could find some small country inn in that area to stay the night."

As if prearranged, Weston's promenade lights lit up to greet them as they entered the town. Driving to a small restaurant on the main beach road, they were right on time for their previously booked reservation. The restaurant's thatched roof, and walls constructed of large pebbles, pointed with cement, gave it a cottage-like charm. Two large bow windows sectioned into lesser pains radiated the flicker of candlelight that illuminated tables inside. The performance of this delicate swirling fire dance brought the warmth of life into this establishment. It was a place that welcomed guests with its old-world charm and comfort. The head waiter met them at the door.

"Good evening, sir, do you have reservations?"

"Yes, my name is Shaw."

"Shaw, yes, and that would be a table for two, Sir? Please follow me. "Menus in hand, he escorted them to a table and assisted with their seating. The menus were then presented. Ian immediately ordered drinks, allowing them time to talk, well browsing through the list of culinary experiences.

"How much do you think we could afford to spend on a house, Ian? I've already put my apartment in London up for sale; that should give us a good down payment."

"We probably won't need your money, Barbara. I have a considerable amount of money sitting in an account doing nothing. It's the fruits of some investments that recently matured. What better use could there be for that money than to buy a house? If it's possible to set up your office and studio there, it could be a decent tax write-off for us. We may as well take advantage of all the opportunities.

"Wow! you're certainly full of surprises. I won't be able to sleep tonight; I'm too excited."

"We may as well enjoy the money I've been making. That's something else that was missing in my life before I met you. I'd forgotten how to enjoy myself." Stretching his hand across the table and placing it on hers, he gave a gentle, reassuring squeeze.

"I love you, Ian. You always know how to make me happy."

The waiter returned to the table to take their order, providing a brief interlude from their aspirations. The conversation soon returned after his departure, to the same theme but with fresh ideas.

"Perhaps we should look for an old house that we could renovate to suit our needs. The charms in some older houses are hard to duplicate, don't you think?"

"I agree; a mature garden can also enhance a property."

"I don't think there are too many houses out there with studios already in them. We could completely refurbish and upgrade before we move in."

"You seem to be talking about a very large house, Ian? How much can we afford."

"We'll have to see the price of the market before we commit ourselves, but I'm confident we'll find something within our budget."

"Let's go back to the hotel after supper and pack, so we can make an early start tomorrow." The thought of their own home had now totally consumed her.

"Don't you think we should tell the boys we'll be leaving tomorrow instead of Tuesday?" Totally absorbed in the excitement of house hunting had relegated other agendas to second place.

"We'll call in the pub on the way back to the hotel. I'm sure they'll be spending time there, propping up the bar." Their habits were entirely predictable.

Supper was placed before them with all the gracious bows and rituals befitting a formal dinner. The waiter then departed.

"They seem to spend a lot of time in the pub, those young men." There was the tone of a disapproving father figure in Ian's voice.

"Well, at least I know where they are, and they never get into trouble, except perhaps for the minor squabbles amongst themselves. And I'm sure you could analyze that behaviour and give me a full rundown on all the why's and wherefores."

This jab was delivered with a cute smile. Ian knew a put down when he heard one, but he could see she was right. His attitude had changed so much since they met, and he knew it was for the better. Ian then paraphrased one of her favourite saying, a philosophy he was now trying to live by.

"You're right, but I think I am learning to lighten up, although, for me, it's perhaps a slow process."

"You just need to hang in there. The real you is so different from your banker's image." His reply was a grind.

After finishing supper, they left the restaurant. Barbara drove her car back to the hotel to park it for the night before they took a starlit stroll to the pub in search of the boys. They were easily found, polishing that same spot on the bar with their elbows, as if they had never left.

"Good evening, boys, and how did tonight's show go." Barbara slung her purse onto a bar stool.

"It went well. Would you two like the usual." Tony reached for his money after tipping back his glass.

"Yes, two halves will be fine." Two small sparkling mugs of bitter ale were soon placed in their hands.

"Knock them back quickly; it's Ron's round next. He'll try to get them in before your ready, so he won't have to buy you one." This cheeky comment was accompanied by a wink.

"We've decided on a change of plans. We'll be checking out of the hotel first thing tomorrow." Jim's slow, soft-spoken voice always commanded the attention of the boys.

"I'm assuming you two are planning something exciting to warrant this sudden decision."

"We've decided to do a little house hunting and spend some time in the countryside." Two more drinks from Ron were thrust upon them. The process was quickly repeated by Jim and then John. Barbara kissed Ian on the cheek, allowing her to whisper discreetly in his ear.

"It's lucky the bartender has to call time, or we might not be leaving here! Before early tomorrow morning." Ian nibbled on her ear, well affectionately stroking her lower back. Tony was not about to let this behaviour go unnoticed.

"For god's sake, Ian put her down. Can't you two keep your hands off each other for more than a minute?" This brought cries of laughter from the others. Time was eventually called, and empty glasses were whisked from the bar. Leaving the pub and feeling no pain, they all walked together back to the hotel. The boys were still in a party mood. An iron will was needed to resist their attempts to prolong the evening. Plans that had been set in motion were not about to be jeopardized by a late morning check-out.

CHAPTER 12

A change for the better.

Passing the airport and delving deeper into the countryside, a sense of timelessness overwhelmed them. Old stone walls and foliage sheltered fields from the country roads they were driving on. These roads snaked their way through the area to no apparent destination. These meandering lanes together formed a gigantic maze that hadn't seen change in eons. Entering this enchanted valley was like taking a step into the Mendip's hills own Brigadoon. These country highways didn't afford the width for a comfortable pass by oncoming traffic in many stretches. Ian stopped the car on a grassy verge near a lake. Barbara stepped out of the car and walked up to a wooden railing. It bordered the lake at this point, so she looked out across its waters.

"You're right Ian, I do love it here." Taking the map from the car's glove compartment, he spread it over the hood.

"Perhaps we can find a large village nearby that would have a real estate office in it. They probably won't be open today because it's a holiday, but they may have listings in the window that we could check out ourselves." Finding several villages on the map, Ian chose one closest to what he loosely referred to as a main road. Let's try the community we passed through on the way here. According to the map, it's called Winford, it's marked as having a hospital, so I think it should have a real estate office." They drove back to Chew Valley's metropolis.

"You know, Ian, pubs or churches are usually the hubs of activity in small communities like this. As it's not Sunday, and we don't know the vicar, I suggest we make some inquiries in a pub." He had to laugh at her sense of reasoning even though he thought it to be sound.

"You're probably right, the bars should be open now, but perhaps we could have just a coffee this time, though." Ian drove slowly into Winford, accessing his surroundings. A pub with a hand-painted sign depicting a military man caught his eye: It seemed to be from the Napoleonic era. The name (Prince of Waterloo) was printed into its bottom surround. Empty livestock pens across the road gave a good indication that this was a market town. Farmers from the area would congregate here on market days to buy and sell livestock. This pub would probably be a beehive of activity on such days.

"This seems as good a place as any to start." He parked the car.

The old country pub had thick stone walls and small windows. Its floor, of large gray flagstones, had been worn unevenly through time. The furniture and fittings were made of large dark well-polished wood. A low beamed ceiling projected a feeling of intimacy and comfort on the decor. An ample amount of brass, and well-polished glasses, hanging above the bar glistened in the minimal amount of rays of sunlight filtering through small windows. This same light source, reflecting from the bar's large mirror, helped supplement poor visibility in this inadequately lit area.

Walking up to the counter, they occupied two bar stools, attracting a barmaid's attention who was busy cleaning.

"What may I get you both."

"Would it be possible to get two coffees?"

"I'll put a pot on for you if you don't mind waiting."

"That'll be fine; we're in no hurry," Barbara spoke to the woman as she filled the pot with water.

"Is there a real-estate office in the village?"

"There is, but it's closed today. However, Mike's the man you'll be looking for, and he's sat over there by himself. It's his office. "She looked around them to get a full view of the realtor. "Hey, Mike, this couple would like to talk business with you." Mike smiled and beckoned them to his table.

His round face, and stocky build, gave him the appearance of being a jolly sort of person. Dressed in a shirt, tie, tweed jacket, matching waistcoat, and hat, which had found a temporary resting place on the table, he looked every inch the county gentleman. He stood up to shake their hands as they reached where he was sitting. After Introductions, Ian started to outline what they had in mind.

"We're interested in buying property, a large house. Preferably near one of the many lakes in the area, or even with a lake view. We were wondering if you had a list of properties we could do a drive-by today. We realize this is a holiday, but we have to be in London tomorrow."

"We're not that formal down here. This is a farming community, one day's much like another. Animals have to be tended to come rain or shine. I'll drive you around myself that way; you won't get lost. It can be a bit difficult if you're not familiar with the Chew Valley. So you're looking for a large house. Most houses in the area are small." Barbara aired her thoughts.

"We were thinking of something on the lines of an old farmhouse that we could renovate."

"Then you're looking for land because farmhouses go with farms." He could see a disappointed look on her face.

"However, do you know the lakes are reservoirs? The valley was flooded several years ago to form them." Ian looked puzzled.

"We didn't but is there a reason we should know this." His usual inquiring mind was showing little interest.

"Well, I'm about to get to that. You see, when the valley was flooded, the old manner house was left on some high ground near the lake, with the rest of its lands underwater. It's been empty for years, too big for most people to manage the upkeep, so it's in a sad state of repair. "Mike reached for his briefcase. "I have a picture of it here, with the asking price." Barbara took a quick glimpse at the price, and her jaw fell.

"I think that's entirely out of our league. A manor house, I don't think my husband and I are looking for something that grand." She looked at Ian, expecting him to be smiling at her indignation, but he was saying nothing. She could see the wheels turning. "It's well beyond our reach, Ian!"

"This price, it's not written in stone, is it Mike?" Barbara could only look on, dumbfounded at Ian's apparent interest. "You see, it may just be what we're looking for. I have a good feeling about this place. I know it's right for us."

"Ian, look at the price again; you can't have seen it correctly?"

"It's alright, Barbara; it's well within our budget." It was her turn to say nothing. For a woman that always had the quick retort and the last word, this shock had muted her entirely. It took a while for her to regain her composure.

"Ian, you can't be serious, there's obviously still some confusion with the price, and that's before renovations, plus upkeep. We don't have that kind of money, do we?"

"It's alright, Barbara. As I told you, my investments have been very profitable for us."

"Well, if you think we can afford it, let's go for broke, I say."

"Well then, you two, now that's settled, when you've finished your coffee, I'll drive you over there."

Every minute of driving through narrow lanes was charged with anticipation of what awaited them. Could this house be the realization of their latest dream? When they eventually arrived at the gated driveway, all Barbara's wildest fantasies materialized before her eyes. The mansion in front of them looked magnificent, still holding on to much of its former glory. This grand oblong Georgian-style house was built of a smooth gray sandstone block. It featured large windows divided into small panes, of which several were broken. This gave the place a sad, abandoned look. Several round stone pillars supported a balcony that gave cover to the front entrance.

The deck of this picturesque half-round canopy had a stone balustrade surrounding it. Access to this veranda was through French doors. However, neglect through time had taken its toll. Wood rot was evident in the framework and around doors and windows.

Mike opened the door, and they entered a large lobby. Confronting them was an impressive sweeping staircase that led to the upper floor. An archway opened into a large reception area to the right. A half-opened door to the left gave a limited view of the library's book shelving. Behind these rooms, a corridor running lengthways gave access to numerous other ground floor locations.

"Let me show you the rest of the downstairs before we go to the second floor." Mike then started quoting from papers he'd retrieved from his briefcase. "To our right, there are several rooms, the largest of which has a beautiful lake view. It's listed as the music room. Apparently, it's large enough to hold a ball."

Windows at both ends of the wide corridor produced an adequate amount of light. Ambling through the west wing, they viewed smaller rooms in passing. Eventually, Mike swung open the door to the music room. Barbara stood in awe.

"Ian, look at this room!" Drawn to French doors at the back, she walked over to look outside. "What a view, it's gorgeous. Can we go out onto the patio?" Mike fumbled with the keys.

"Let me see, I think this must be the one. The old door creaked and groaned as it was opened for what must have been the first time in many years. The patio, green with moss, had a surrounding stone balustrade identical to the front's half-round front porch embellishment. It also accompanied a stone staircase that descended from the patio center to the garden below. This garden, temporarily reclaimed by nature, ran gently down to meet an uninvited lake. It was now intruding on its privacy. Barbara's attention was drawn to matching doors at the other end of the house.

"What's behind those doors, Mike?"

"I believe that must be the main lounge. The dining room, and kitchen windows, are the two that lay beyond. Mike opened another reluctant door with a bit of persuasion from some willing hands.

A spacious room awaited their company. The marble fireplace, oak floors, and cornices, although hidden under dirt and grime from time, still retained echoes of its once regal splendour. Exploring the remainder of the downstairs, they'd gone full circle, arriving back at the entrance lobby.

"I can't wait to explore upstairs, Ian." Mike again referred to the oracle that was his briefcase. "It seems there are ten bedrooms, a games room, and a reception area above us, with French doors leading onto the front balcony. Several of the rooms have on-sweets. There are also two main bathrooms." Barbara swept through the upstairs. Ian followed, meticulously checking details, and making notes.

"Ian, it's a palace; I love it. You're certain we can afford it?"

"If you love it, it's yours. I've always imagined I would someday own a place like this. It's always been a dream of mine too."

"I don't believe this, I'm sure someone will pinch me, and I'll wake up." Her gratitude produced a comforting warmth in Ian, the kind obtained from giving.

"There's so much to be done; when will we be able to start?"

"Well, Mike, it looks like you've got an interested party for the place. Now I'm sure we can shave a little off the price."

"I'm sure we can come to an amicable arraignment because of the state of disrepair. It's been a bit of a white elephant for me. I thought it would end up being torn down and sold for land value. That would have been such a shame. It really is a beautiful house. So! as soon as we iron out the final details, we can get all the papers made up and signed, then the place is yours."

"We'll be looking for a local contractor to undertake the restoration. Is there anyone you could recommend, Mike?"

"Perhaps I can. There is a man that works in the area; he's reliable and an excellent craftsman. I can personally recommend his work; because he's my brother." Mike's grin turned to a laugh.

"We look forward to meeting him."

"If we're through here, I'll lock up and take you back to the village."

"We'll take another look around; well, you're locking up. We'll meet you back in the lobby. I'm sure my wife will want another look at the music room."

A low stage at one end could comfortably accommodate a grand piano. In more elegant times, it was possibly home also to a string quartet on formal occasions.

"I could have my own recording studio in this room." She turned to Ian for approval.

"I thought you would like to do that. I think it's a fantastic start to our plans for the house. I can't wait to see the place come to life with all the trappings of a home. I'll be looking after all the construction costs, so you'll have money from the sale of your apartment to equip the studio you've always dreamed of." She put her arms around Ian's neck and kissed him. Looking into his eyes, she then stroked his face.

"This really is a dream come true." She gave him another quick kiss and ran to the lobby laughing. For Ian, the sound of her voice, as she called to him to join her, seemed to breathe life back into the old house. An element that had obviously been missing for many years.

"You'll need someone to help you run a house this size Barbara. "Mike, who was standing close behind, stepped in with a good suggestion.

"The basement has an apartment and storage rooms. It was probably used as servant quarters years ago. If you let it out to a married couple, that might work out well for you. The woman could work in the house. The husband could look after the gardening and any heavy work that needs to be done, on a part-time basis. In this area, a lot of men are willing to take on another job."

"That sounds like a good idea Mike. If you hear of anyone who might be interested, perhaps you could let us know."

"I'll certainly do that; I'm pleased to sell this place to someone who'll make a home for themselves here. It's a lovely property. I'm sure you'll both be extremely happy here. As I said before, it would have been a shame to have seen the old place torn down and sold for land value. Well, if the two of you have finished here, I'll drive you back to your car."

Mike locked the front door; well, the soon-to-be property owners took a last quick walk around the grounds. He then drove them back to Winford, where they stopped at The Prince of Waterloo for a late lunch. Close to afternoon closing time, the only food available was cold cuts, cheese, and fresh bread. This proved to be more than acceptable when digestion was aided by the introduction of draft ale.

"We'll have to find somewhere to stay the night. Have you any suggestions, Mike?"

"They do take in guests here sometimes, Ian, but it may not be up to your standards."

"If it's clean, I'm sure it will suit us just fine, Mike." He looked at Barbara with a grin.

"We're not snobs, are we dear." She smiled back.

"I wouldn't recommend it if I thought it wasn't suitable."

Ian went to the bar to arrange lodgings before going upstairs to inspect the room. The room had white sloping ceilings and exposed wood beams. Two small dormer windows set the tone for its decor. The bed's oak headboard, footboard, matching night tables, dressing table, chair, and wardrobe, were all from the twenties circa. This ensemble only served to enforce that lost-in-time sensation. Well, lace curtains, backed by bright floral drapes, with matching bedspread, brought life to the room's clean, fresh country style. He glanced out of one of the windows. It overlooked the pub's back area.

Narrow cobbled streets lined with rows of small cottages and a few shops gave this area the appearance of a pedestrian precinct.

This quiet backroom tucked away from the village's main road would surely accommodate a comfortable night's rest. Satisfied with the room, he signed the register and took their luggage upstairs.

Mike took them to his office, where all the necessary documents were signed. The only thing left was transferring funds and registration of deeds to make the property legally theirs. The remaining afternoon, and early evening, was spent familiarizing themselves with the area. Returning to the room at the pub, they rested before going out for the evening.

After dining, they returned to the bar at about eight-thirty. Mike and his wife, Marge, were seated at what seemed to be their usual table. Ian and Barbara asked if they wouldn't mind sharing their company. Mike immediately made them welcome and introduced his wife before ordering a round of drinks. Mike raised his glass to Ian.

"Cheers. I'm glad we ran into you two this evening. I spoke to my brother after I left you this afternoon. He said he would be in the Old Mill pub this evening if you'd like a word with him."

"Yes, I would, but exactly where is the Old Mill?"

"I'll take you both in my car if you don't mind us tagging along, that is."

"You're the company we imposed ourselves on this evening, and the ladies seem to be hitting it off well, judging by their conversation."

"Right then, we'll finish these drinks and leave, if that's OK with you two?"

Leaving, The Prince of Waterloo, they piled into Mike's car. Ian rode upfront with Mike while Marge and Barbara made themselves comfortable in the back. Ian accessed their speed to be a little excessive for narrow winding lanes but resisted a comment.

The car's headlight glare, highlighting tall bordering hedgerows, exaggerated this effect, producing a feeling of claustrophobia in Ian. Picking up even more speed, Ian's hands now grasped the dashboard as he sampled this luge racing experience firsthand. The only vehicle he'd ever experienced this kind of gut-churning feeling in before was a roller coaster. Ian could no longer stifle his fear.

"My! this is a lot faster than you were driving earlier today, Mike." The veiled attempt at making a light comment was overshadowed by the fear in his voice. Mike, totally oblivious to Ian's plight, made a nonchalant reply.

"You couldn't drive this fast in daylight. You wouldn't be able to see anything coming towards you."

"Mike, we can barely see a hundred yards in front of us now with all the twists and turns these lanes are taking."

"Well! headlights are the key; on a clear night like this. You can see on-coming traffic light up the sky a mile away." Only slightly reassured, his following comment was for Barbara's ears.

"I'm starting to realize how grandmother's mechanic must have felt."

"You can start breathing again, Ian; we're here."

"I think I'll be having something a little stronger than beer to start. That drive was rather exhilarating, to say the least."

Walking into the pub, they were greeted with a look of recognition by a man standing at the bar. Mike waved, then turned to Ian, and Barbara, for their attention.

"It's my brother Tom." They joined him at the bar, and Mike made the introduction.

"This is the couple I spoke to you about."

"Now, what would everyone like to drink? I think I'm ready for that large scotch myself." After drinks were served, Ian queried Tom regarding essential renovations that were needed at the house.

"I'll give the house the once over as soon as possible, and I'll give you an estimate that'll be broken down into each segment of work. I'll put in a few price options, depending on which alternatives you choose. I've heard, through the grapevine, you'll be looking for some help around the place when you move in."

Ian tipped back his scotch as Mike pointed to the glasses indicating another round.

"I'm pleased to see Mike's been spreading the word, have you someone in mind?"

"My wife's nephew, who works for me. He's getting married in a couple of months. He and his bride will be looking for a place to live, and that's not easy to find around here, you know. He's a good lad. You'll be able to meet him when we're working on the house.

Perhaps you'll be able to come to some arrangement with him and his bride to be, I'm sure they'd be interested."

"That'll be a good opportunity for Barbara and me to meet them." Now the ice had been broken, and business talk set aside, a social evening followed with their newfound friends. Ian thinking how late it seemed, glanced at his watch.

"Good grief, It's past twelve o'clock. Time should have been called hours ago."

"Oh, they're not that fussy about time this far out, Ian. Tom went straight to work from here one morning." Tom rubbed his head and smiled.

"I think those days are long past. I'll not be doing something like that again in a hurry."

"Don't the police ever come around this area?"

"Only if they want a late-night drink. They have been known to do that." Ian shook his head in disbelief. "Well, I suppose we should drink up and go. It is getting late."

"Come on, let's take you two back to, The Prince of Waterloo."

Before being dropped at the pub, they arranged to meet at Mike's office the following morning to pick up a set of house keys. Their plans were to spend some time there before driving on to London.

The morning was spent planning changes and making notes. Methodically starting at ground level, they'd progressed to the upper floor. Some time had passed when they heard Tom's voice calling from the hall below.

"We're up here."

"I'm on my way up." They met him on the landing. He was a much fitter man than his brother, making lite of the stairs. "I was on my way to do a spot of fishing when I saw a car in the driveway. Thinking it would have to be you two, I stopped by. And It looks like you've made a start by taking notes. That good."

"We've listed some of the changes we'd like."

"May I." Tom held out his hand. Barbara, who had been the scribe, handed Tom the list.

"This all seems very straightforward. I recommend you have the whole inside re-plastered, but we would try to restore all ornamental plasterwork. Also, you might consider having the outside stonework sandblasted. It would bring the place up like brand new. The electrical wiring is up to standard; the health ministry used it as a convalescent home for children in the fifties. There was a lot of work done on the house at that time. The roof's also sound. After you left the pub last night, I spoke to a roofing contractor in the bar. He told me he'd completely renovated the roof at that point in time. He then added that it was good for another hundred years, but I will give it the once over. So structurally, the place is sound. Anything needing to be done will be cosmetic."

"Your list seems pretty thorough. The heating system is something I'll have to get a plumber to inspect, but outside of that, I can work out a rough estimate for you right now."

Tom left for his van's solitude to work on his estimate: Well, Ian and Barbara continued their planning. He returned with his written estimate within a half-hour. One or two items were discussed before Ian accepted the quote. A time frame for work was then set out and agreed upon before the deal was sealed with a handshake.

"Well, the fish have been waiting for me long enough. I best be on my way." Ian walked him to the front door.

"Good-by then Tom, I appreciate you calling by so soon." Returning to the back of the house, he joined Barbara. She was looking out across the lake, well, trying to visualize her garden restoration. "Why don't I drive to a store and pick up something for a picnic. We could have it right here on the patio."

"I think that's a lovely idea. There are a few remaining details I'd like to re-check in the music room; well, you're gone. We won't have much time after we've finished our picnic because then we really should be thinking of leaving for London."

"I agree, so I'm off for the groceries?"

"A sandwich and a bottle of beer would be fine for me."

"I think this is an occasion, Barbara, so it's going to be champagne and the best picnic lunch I can find. For now, I'll leave you to your thoughts, but I'll return as quickly as possible."

Returning with a French loaf, cheese, patty, crackers, and numerous other items, plus the all-important bottle of bubbly, he set his banquet down. Allocating a section of patio between them for their table. Garden steps were utilized as seats.

From this vantage point, they could fully appreciate the lake's serenity as it unselfishly spilled its tranquillity onto their presents. Anglers fishing for trout from small rowboats occasionally grazed this silence by whipping the air with rod and line.

"We'll have to get a boat for fishing when we move in." Ian gave a surprised look.

"I didn't know you liked fishing Barbara."

"You'd have to teach me, but it just looks such a peaceful and relaxing way to spend a lazy day."

"When you mentioned getting a boat, I was more thinking along the lines of you teaching me." They both laughed. "Although that idea does appeal to me. Perhaps we should build a retaining wall along the bottom of the garden where it drops away.

Razing that lower section with fill, we could then incorporate a jetty. Dreams dissipated as time again became their master. Reluctantly they locked up the house and packed the car for their trip to London.

CHAPTER 13

A working vacation.

As time passed, it became apparent to Ian how this clandestine company inflicted misery worldwide. One such scheme was rich countries were pressured for resources to aid poor nations. These same supplies were then diverted to fuel black-market trading. Cash from such nefarious deals would then be used to support dictatorships' lifestyles who squandered much of the money buying arms. Sometimes these arms were acquired from the very countries that had supplied aid initially. So, in effect, they'd provided this military hardware free of charge. It was the ultimate elaborate shale game that was being played out at the expense of world poverty.

Weeks passed quickly into months, and the months eased into a year. Ian became more involved in troubleshooting for the company. With people he perceived as highly dangerous, this involvement gave him reservations regarding his personal safety. Voicing his concerns, he found a sympathetic ear in Pete.

"At times, I feel quite venerable in work I am now required to do. Visiting dangerous parts of the world and meeting with sometimes unsavoury individuals is not exactly my idea of a company junket."

"We should have had this conversation long before now. I'm sorry I've been sorely lacking in this department. We'll have a bodyguard assigned to you. It must be someone with a military background. He'll be put on the payroll."

"Then, there's no one actually available for the job?"

"Not at this point in time."

"Would it be possible for me to choose someone myself?"

"Is there someone You have in mind?

"Yes, my cousin, he lives in Seattle. Ex green beret, army intelligence, I think he'd be interested."

"You're off to England for a few days Ian, why don't you fly to the States and meet with him when you've concluded your businesses."

"That would be great. It could almost be like a holiday."

"So why don't you take your wife with you." Ian was on a high; his concerns had been placated, plus the added bonus of seeing Robert again.

Flying to Bristol the following Friday, he was elated with thoughts of the world being his oyster. Working primarily out of their newly renovated home enabled Barbara to meet him at Lusgate airport on his arrival.

The house, fully refurbished and again bathing in all its former glory, was a credit to local craftsmen's meticulously work. Settling in is always a long process. They were still accumulating small intimate items that make a house a home. Mementos can only be collected over a period of time. They're usually accompanied by cherished memories that enhance their personal value.

Content in this country lifestyle, Ian looked forward to when his office at home could be used to thoroughly analyze and plan his reports. Barbara's record deal for the band had materialized, giving them a measure of success in their industry's segment. This success had afforded the luxury of hiring a full-time road manager: Which in turn allowed her personal ambitions to mature into more writing and studio work.

On the drive home, Ian nonchalantly sprung his surprise on her.

"Would you be able to take a few days off next week? If you can, and only if you're not too busy, that is, you could join me on a visit to say America for a couple of days?" The question was delivered with a devilish grin. Her jaw dropped as she turned to look at him in pleasurable surprise.

"Are you kidding? I've always wanted to visit there. I'll have to get some new clothes. When are we leaving?"

"Can I take that as a yes then?" She kissed her fingers and placed them on his face.

"You bet your sweet bippy. We can drive to Bath tomorrow, and I can shop for clothes. I've not got a thing to wear, you know. I love the stores there. It's such a lovely city, don't you think?"

The very tone of her voice, bubbling over with enthusiasm, made it clear he'd be hearing little else but talk of America until they were actually on their way.

"Yes, Bath is a lovely city."

In the short drive home, she quizzed him continuously for details of their destination. He listed differences she would expect to encounter. This only fueled more questions with little time given to answer one before being inundated by more.

"Where in the states are we going, and what will the weather be like there?"

"Seattle and the weather will be much like here. I'm going to see my cousin there."

"Seattle's the place you've told me about. It's on the ocean, and there are mountains all around it, correct?"

"Yes, that's correct. This time of year, there should be snow in the mountains. We may be able to go skiing. Do you think you might like that?"

"That sounds fantastic. I've always fancied giving it a whirl; it seems like lots of fun."

Ian was hustled out early the following morning to shop at Bath. By early afternoon he was all shopped out, not having Barbara's stamina, or passion, for this activity. With some reluctance, she curtailed her indulgences and surrendered to his thirst for city exploration.

Tongue in cheek, he add-lib-ed from a city guidebook he'd purchase, giving his own attempted humerus slant to the rendition. "A city renowned for its Georgian architecture. I think I saw his sign as we entered the city (For good architecture, see George)." That remark earned him a punch on the shoulder. Rubbing his shoulder, he feigned injury.

"Steady on, that hurt. That's husband abuse, you know. I don't know if I should read to you anymore." To emphasize his point, he again rubbed his shoulder. "It's also a renowned spa city. The pump rooms seem to be the spot to be. An area where it's all happening. Apparently, this tearoom overlooks the Georgian baths. I quote (Its hot mineral waters, flowing from an underground source, offer therapeutic spa treatments to bathers).

There's something that interests me on a lower level. It's a Roman bath's complex built nearly two thousand years ago. That sounds like an interesting place for a visit when we have a little more time than today."

Picking a few places of interest, they spent time sightseeing before deciding to go for late afternoon tea. A tea house, situated in a row of shops built atop an old stone bridge to form an integral part of its structure, attracted their attention. Its rear windows offered a picturesque view of a weir one hundred yards downstream. Swans gliding graciously around this pond vied for handouts from passers-by. Many ducks also congregated in this area. A footpath accompanied the river's west side, with a small park sitting high above this embankment. This river setting made the perfect peaceful backdrop to enjoy an English-style high tea.

Barbara managed to persuade Ian to do a little more window shopping before rounding out their evening's entertainment, which included attending live theatre.

Silhouetted by car headlights, their home exhibited its welcome as they entered its driveway.

Ian placed his hand gently on Barbara's shoulder and kissed the side of her neck as they entered the front door.

"I feel tired; I think I'll have an early night."

"I'll be joining you; it's been a tiring day." She kissed him on the cheek before making a hasty retreat up the stairs. She called back over her shoulder. "I hope you're not really that tired, though."

"I think I'm just getting my second wind." Mustering up some untapped energy, he bounded up the stairs after her.

Allocating work time to mornings and evenings, in the following days, afforded them leisurely afternoons of antique store browsing in Bath and Bristol. There were always areas of such a large house to accommodate furnishings.

Tom proved to be a man of many talents, one such flair being furniture refinishing, so they used his skills again. Acquiring furniture quickly became an obsession preceding their trip to America. This left Tom with a sizable amount of work.

Departing from London's Heathrow airport on an early morning flight, their destination was Canada's west coast. From Vancouver, Ian intended to drive south, by car, to Seattle.

Because of time differences, arrival at Vancouver International airport was slightly after the noon hour that same day. Nostalgia had drawn Ian to British Columbia. It was a place he'd spent a happy childhood with his parents.

Planning a leisurely Seattle excursion the following morning for a prearranged meeting with Robert justified this diversionary trip.

Hiring a car on arrival, they drove to the Bayshore inn, where Ian had made reservations. Situated adjacent to picturesque Coal Harbor, a small bay in the Burrard inlet, their room commanded a spectacular view of this body of water and its surroundings. Stanley Park, Vancouver's crown jewel, was situated on the opposite shoreline of Coal Harbor. This small cove, home to numerous small pleasure craft littering its waters, also played host to many other facilities.

The forested peninsula, on which Stanley Park had been created, projected its dominance across the inlet. It provided a sanctuary to these sheltered waters of Coal Harbour. It also isolates this large natural harbour from the waters of English bay beyond. This channel applied a tight stranglehold on the fiord's mouth. These same water bodies provided sanctuary and protection that offered ideal accommodation for Vancouver's major harbour amenities.

From the park's high forest bluffs emerges the engineering feet of a time long past. The Lions Gate suspension bridge's Span united the south and north shores. Majestically silhouetted against a backdrop of snow-capped mountains, it bends art with structural form. Ian accessed the distance from the hotel to the park entrance.

"Although it would be a pleasant walk if weather conditions were more favourable, I think today may prove to be too inclement for that exercise. So, I'll take you for the two-bit park tour, by car. That's if you're not feeling tired from our flight?"

"I feel fine, Ian. A drive in the fresh air will blow the cobwebs out. I think I'll enjoy playing the tourist."

Entering the park, Ian's memory was jogged by old familiarities as he followed its one-way system, exterior road. Whenever conditions permitted, this route paralleled the sea wall.

Stopping at a Totem Poles group, displayed as tourist features, they left the car to take snapshots.

"Vancouver's beautiful. Is this where you were born, Ian?"

"I was born in Langley, and that's where I spent my childhood. It's about twenty miles east, up the Fraser Valley." He pointed in the general direction. "It's just a small town. What say you, we take a drive this evening and find a nice restaurant in that area. I still own my parent's property there. I'd like to drive by and see the old place again.

Grandmother always maintained it as a nest egg for my future, and when she passed away, I never could bring myself to part with it." There was often a melancholy tone to his voice when reminiscing about those happy days. Barbara sensed old memories had been stirred. Similar emotions, mirroring those she was sure Ian was now experiencing, gave her comfort occasionally. Those were happy times for Ian, and he was now able to appreciate that fact.

"Take me around the rest of the park." Her perky voice was an attempt at sparking a more upbeat mood.

"Yes, of course." Their next stop, the miniature railway, supplying more nostalgia, offered rides to tourists most of the year. The station area in these seasons teemed with wildlife looking for handouts. Squirrels, raccoons, many verities of birds native to North America, plus peacocks roaming freely, called this spot home.

A paddock adjacent to the miniature railway's station gave Ian's memory another jog. "I have a vague recollection of being put into the saddle of a pony in that enclosure. I couldn't have been more than a toddler at the time."

Walking paths accompanying the train tracks through wooded areas, animal enclosures en-route were still a big draw for adults and children alike. Exhibits were strategically placed to create the illusion that animals native to North America resided in their natural habitat. Truly a great tourist destination even in this winter season.

Trekking the path, full circle, they arrive back at the station. Ian pointed to a petting zoo, now closed for the season, close to the railway station.

"I remember that place; it was the highlight of my day to visit and play with all the young animals. As I recall, one time, I was having great fun chasing chickens around the place until a small bill goat joined in behind and started chasing me. That did dampen the enthusiasm for a while." Barbara gave a snigger.

"What a little rascal, chasing those poor chickens. You deserved getting your comeuppance like that. I would love to have been there to have witnessed that one."

Walking east, they headed for one of the park's main attractions, the zoo area. It was a small zoo boasting a large assortment of animals and birds, free for public viewing.

This area was also home to Vancouver's aquarium. Barbara was more interested in the bandits, disguised as cute squirrels, who were preparing to mug her for handouts.

"Oh, Ian, get the camera: Well, they're running all over my arms. They're so cute. I've never seen squirrels so friendly."

"Say cheese." He snapped several pictures.

"I'm starting to feel chilly. Can we go back to the car now?" She gave a little shiver as she pulled her coat collar up.

Ian replied. "This visit would be incomplete without a stop for hot chocolate at concessions stand."

Slightly fortified by a warm drink, the bone-chilling damp was staved off momentarily when accompanied by a brisk walk back to where they'd parked the car.

"Is America as scenic as Canada, Ian?"

"It's only one hundred and thirty miles from Vancouver to Seattle, so mountains, and forests, are much the same.

I'll phone Robert when we get back to the hotel and tell him that we've arrived safely. We'll drive down to see him tomorrow. With an early start, we can take the scenic route."

New plans were being hatched well in conversation with Robert. One hand over the mouthpiece, Ian turned to Barbara. "Robert suggested we go skiing tomorrow." She nodded enthusiastically. He made more arraignments before hanging up.

"He said he'll meet us at mount Baker; that's about halfway for both of us. He told me we'll be able to rent ski equipment on the mountain. Robert's an excellent skier. He's volunteered to give us some lessons."

She put her arms around Ian's neck and kissed him. "We should have an early night if we intend to be up early tomorrow morning, Ian."

"Is that an early night or one of our famous early nights you're talking about?" She giggled.

"Any way you want it, but I can only hope the flight hasn't tired you that much."

"I think we'd get more rest if we did have a late-night; that would probably make us too tired for anything else but sleep." She feigned a sad look. He gave her a hug and returned the kiss.

"Oh, you know I'm always up for an early night Barbara."

"Yes, Ian, I think up being the operative word for you." He gave a chuckle.

"I'm going to book this restaurant in Langley for an early supper." He pointed to an ad in the telephone book. "I hope Bavarian cuisine will meet with your approval?"

"Yummy, that's sounds different. It'll make a pleasant change, and yes, I'm sure I'll enjoy the whole experience. It'll be nice to visit your hometown. I'm sure you're looking forward to that."

They took a short rest before supper. After a quick nap, they were unable to resist indulging themselves in activities that had been carefully planned for after returning from an evening out on the town.

Visiting Ian's old neighbourhood, they made a brief stop at his property before supper. Although it was rented, a glimpse from across the street was more than adequate for his nostalgic needs. This house held many happy memories for Ian, treasures ignored by time and left to tarnish in that vault he had used often in sadder times. However, adhering to Barbara's outlook on life, a bright polish had recently been put back on the old silver, and it was now ready for display.

As Barbara held his hand, he remembered her words (Celebrate the love, not the loss.) Reminiscing then produced simple pleasures from memories stored in every nook and cranny of the old place.

Nostalgia also demanded a slow drive down Main Street, seeking out familiar landmarks; it felt good returning home. Ian parked outside the restaurant. He was now looking forward to enjoying a pleasurable evening with the woman who had turned his life around. Many ghosts had been laid to rest, as an abundance of beautiful memories far outweighed any bad ones he still possessed.

Skipping breakfast facilitated an early arrival on the mountain via a scenic drive. After reaching the picturesque scenic coast road to Bellingham, the early dawn light reflected its colourful display. The bright sun's rays dancing off the Straights of Juan de Facia's waters highlighted the gulf islands' silhouettes beyond. Mount Baker's perfect volcanic cone dominated the Cascade mountains profile to the east.

"What an awesome morning, Ian; this drive alone is worth the trip." Turning inland, the road past low-lying farmland before winding its way upwards through mountain forests. As their progress took them higher, it entered the snow line. Trees now displayed their winter coats of snow. And the forest floor became a carpet of untrodden white.

Arriving at the ski area, Robert was waiting for them near the lodge. He was a large, barrel-chested man with full facile hair. Robert was not a man to be overlooked, even in a crowd. Substitute the skies for an axe, and he would have looked right at home in the woods. His whole persona was made prevalent by the plaid shirt toque and suspenders supporting his black ski pants. This attire only added to the allusion he was Paul Bunion.

He threw his arms around Ian's shoulders, giving him a bear hug that practically lifted him off his feet. His lips were tight, his eyes watery with emotion. He then slowly turned his attention to Barbara. He gave her the same bear hug greeting, well planting a kiss on her cheek.

"It's a pleasure to meet you at last. Ian's told me so much about you, Barbara, in our phone conversations." Stepping back, he held her hands out at arm's length.

"Now, let me get a good look at you." She smiled and did a little pirouette.

"Do I get your seal of approval, Robert?"

"Barbara, you're a beautiful young woman. Now let's get you two some skies. There will be time to talk later." That said, they went inside and rented equipment.

"To start off, we'll do some bunny slopping behind the lodge." The next hour or so was spent honing some rudimentary skills before progressing to a chair lift.

Disembarking at the ride's top, they remembered Robert's instructions to the letter. Unfortunately, they weren't able to put theory into practice. Barbara caught her ski pole in the chair, triggering a series of events with Ian trying to help. Stepping on her skies, chaos then ensued. Rolling down the off-ramp entwined, a vigilant operator was forced to immediately stop the lift. Completely blocking the ramp with their entanglement, Robert gingerly offloaded directly behind and started untying this human knot.

Overwhelmed by laughter, tiers were now forming in his eyes, to the point he almost lost his own balance. Once on her feet, Barbara tried to maintain some dignity by brushing unwanted snow from her clothing. Eventually, seeing the situation from Robert's point of view, she started laughing also. Ian, with his ego slightly dented, was unable to see anything humorous transpiring from this disaster. However, the sight of Robert's tiers did coax him into a grin.

"We'll ski down this way first." Robert, who was barely audible, between wiping watery eyes, and giggling, pointed the way. "Follow me, and do exactly as I do." Snowplowing along well-groomed trails, they were able to accomplish their objectives without any major misshapes.

"Now, before we attempt our next chair ride, I'm going to review the process with you one more time." Meticulously he showed them how poles should be held correctly, stances well, offloading, and other rudimentary practices required for smooth chair disembarkation.

"Right, I think we're ready to try again."

Once more, they readied themselves to exit the lift. Barbara wriggled off the chair ahead of Ian. This was accomplished with a reasonable amount of dignity. On the other hand, Ian busily engrossed shepherding Barbara completely disregarded every scrap of tutoring Robert had laboured so hard to instill. When good coaching has not been adhered to, results are usually less than satisfactory. Going much too fast, he lost control and rammed Barbara from behind. Although spectacular, this wipe-out perhaps didn't warrant as high a mark in ineptness as their first performance. Again, the lift operator shut the operation down, allowing them time to clear the ramp.

As Robert joined them, Ian was looking rather glum, being quite embarrassed by his dismal performance.

"Do you think we'll ever get the hang of this?"

"Ian, tomorrow, I'll have you skiing like the pros." Again, they made their trek down the mountain under Robert's watchful eye.

Their third attempt was planned as a maximum effort in concentration and skill. Psyched up and ready to go, the off-ramp lay beneath their skis. Failure was no longer a word in their vocabulary. However, just as they were about to disembark, an attentive operator stopped the lift.

"There you go, the two of you, take your time. Everything's under control." Obviously, this little accommodation caused further embarrassment when accompanied by a chorus of discrete chuckles and loud applause from other skiers. Clearing the ramp without incident was a poor consolation. It's hard to maintain the pretense of cool when everyone around you knows your not. Robert's tongue-in-cheek comment on joining them was no pump for deflated egos.

"He must have been worried about your safety. I've never seen them stop the lift for no reason before."

"Well, that's a confidence booster." Barbara was still quite indignant about the whole ramp thing.

"The second time was not my fault either, so there. I think I'm doing quite well." She threw her nose in the air to stress the point. Robert, just grind.

"A few more runs, and we'll break for lunch. It's important not to get overtired. Let me treat you both to a good American hamburger with all the works, fries and a coke."

"Sounds good to me, Robert."

"Me too. By then, I'll need something warm." Barbara put her ski polls under one arm and rubbed her cold hands.

The cafeteria was crowded, and people jostled for space. Barbara was sent to find a table as Ian and Robert waited in line to order lunch. Food orders were pumped out promptly by the kitchen's production line. It wasn't a long wait. Joining Barbara at the table. Hunger, fired by exercise and fresh air, made lunch much more enjoyable.

Clearing empty food rappers from the table, there was now time to sit back, sip coke and enjoy some conversation. Robert broached the job offer.

"I've been talking to some friends of mine about your proposition Ian."

"And?"

"Well, one of my friends is very keen for me to take the job. He's an old army friend with whom I did some special forces training in England. We trained a lot with the British commandos then, and we based most of our own training programs on those experiences. I've not seen Colonel Johnny Watson for several years now, but we still keep in touch."

"Johnny Watson." Barbara blurted, loud enough to turn several heads in the vicinity, "Johnny Watson, you know my brother Johnny?" Robert was grinning like a Cheshire cat.

"That's right, it's a small world, isn't it, Barbara?"

"I can't believe this. You actually know my brother." Repeating herself, half expecting to be told it was a joke.

"That surprises me to Robert. You'd not mentioned that."

"Well, Ian, when do I start looking after you?"

"As of when you were looking after us on the ski hill, as far as I'm concerned." Ian placed his hand on Roberts's shoulder and gave a reassuring squeeze. "I even have a company credit card made out in your name." He reached in his pocket and handed it to Robert.

"What's the cash limit on this card, Ian?"

"There is no limit for company business."

"Who decides what's company business?"

"You decide that Robert."

"Wow, with a card like this, I'll not bother to ask about the salary." Gripping the card with finger and thumb, he fanned himself.

"Any bank in the world will honour this card for a cash advance without question.

"This gets better and better. I'm starting to think millionaire." Finishing his coke, he placed the empty cup on the table. "What say you we hit the slopes now?" Barbara had been mingling with the locals sitting behind her. Well, Ian and Robert were talking business. Unaware they were leaving, Ian tapped her on the shoulder to get her attention.

"We're going to torment that poor lift operator now, Barbara."

"I'll be right with you." Taking some time to say goodbye to her newfound friends, she joined Ian and Robert at the ski racks.

Engrossed in this newfound sport of skiing, they were among the last diehards to call it a day.

"Did the two of you intend to return to Vancouver this evening?"

"We had intended to. Why did you have something else in mind?"

"Yes, say with me. I've rented a cabin at the bottom of the mountain. There's lots of room. They have a lodge where we can spend the evening.

Picture a large stone hearth, a roaring fire, people sitting around singing songs, telling stories. It's all part of the skiing experience. This is what it's all about."

"That sounds great, can we, Ian? Although we didn't bring a change of clothes."

"I'm sure the two of you can buy something at the lodge's gift shop to tie you over for one night."

"Well, I'm up for it, Barbara. I think it'll be a fun evening."

Unplanned events in the past always seemed to create problems for Ian. He'd possessed an uncontrollable need for total control up to this point in time. A rekindled attitude towards life, initiated by a wonderful woman, had become intense in him, especially after revisiting his old home. The veil he'd shrouded himself in that had only been glimpsed through by Barbara to this point was falling fast. He was now able to fully enjoy many aspects of life he'd always denied himself.

Arriving at the lodge just before its shop closed, they were disappointed in its limited merchandise supply. It mainly specialized in ski clothing and only the bare essentials for an overnight stay. Treating themselves to two hand-knitted sweaters, they settled on woolly long johns as a close trade for pyjamas. Toothbrushes and paste were supplied at the front desk.

Robert then led the way to his cabin, nestled snugly in the woods. After showering, they made themselves ready for an evening at the lodge. Securing the cabin door, they headed out for their evening entertainment. Snow in the trees and on the ground reflected moonlight like a mirror, providing natural illumination to an otherwise dark night.

"I fancy a beer before supper. How about you two?"

"Barbara and I are not that hungry yet, so I think that would be fine by us." He glanced at her for approval, making sure she'd not changed her mind. A smile and quick nod confirmed her intentions.

The lounge was exactly how Robert had described it. A large wood-burning fireplace on its eastern wall was fronted by a sizeable lower floor area. Seats built into this lower area's perimeter were fronted with tables and chairs. A wood railing separated this conversation pit from the main bar. Selecting a spot most beneficial for warmth, the lower level became an obvious choice on this cold evening. Several large logs roaring in the hearth personified every expectation related to this experience.

"Where's the bar? I'll go fetch some drinks." Ian was about to stand.

"Relax, we can order them from our waitress. I'm sure she'll be with us soon."

"They have waitress service here." Robert turned towards Barbara.

"Oh yes, it's not an English pub. This is America, and we don't serve warm lifeless beer like you're used to either. Just good cold American draft, with a healthy froth on it. Although I must admit here in the northwest, some of us prefer the stronger bite of a Canadian brew."

The waitress arrived with a full tray of draft beers and set them down before them. Robert covered the tab, plus the standard tip.

"Do people always tip for service in North America, Robert?"

"Only if you're satisfied, Barbara. For an attentive server, it's just a recognized way of saying thank you. It's also an incentive to keep up the good work. People rely on tips to supplement wages."

"I see. Now, this table full of beer, are we expected to drink it all ourselves?" Robert took one of the glasses and tipped it back in one swallow, then gave a laugh.

"I don't see a problem with that. I'm sure we'll be ordering several more trays before the evening's over." He winked at Ian and gave another smile.

Prices here seem very reasonable, compared to England. Are the wages low?"

"People I know make two or three times as much as their British counterparts."

"People must live like kings here, Robert. That would explain all the new cars I've seen on the roads." Ian, who had been shaking his head in disbelief at the line of conversation, started to laugh.

"Barbara likes to look at things from what she perceives as a practical point of view, Robert. You'll have to excuse her." She scoffed at them.

"I like to interpret that as a woman's perspective on life in general. I fined men are the ones who are totally impractical. Most men I know seem to be more interested in women, cars, and beer. Not necessarily in that order."

"I think we've just been politely insulted, Ian, don't you?"

"Yes, I think we have." They both had a little chuckle, much to her indignation.

"Is anyone feeling hungry yet?" Her light-hearted tone totally differed from her previously put-down, levelled at men in general.

"Yes, I think I'm ready for a bite to eat." Ian patted his tummy.

"I'm feeling a little hungry now. Perhaps we should order some food."

"The place is starting to fill up if we leave our seats to visit the dining room; I don't think they'll be vacant when we return."

"Dinning doesn't have to be formal. We can have food brought to this table."

"I was hoping that might be possible, Robert. Will that be OK with you, Ian?"

"Fine with me." Robert maneuvered himself out from where he was sitting.

"I'll go fetch some menus."

"I like Robert. You described him perfectly in every detail. He's such a nice man."

Returning with menus, he passed them around. Barbara browsed through the selections.

"I'm not sure what I would like. Have you any suggestions, Robert?"

"Have you ever tried southern fried chicken? If you haven't, it's a must."

"That sounds interesting: I always like trying different foods. Before I give it a whirl, what is it exactly?" Robert replied.

"It's Chicken coated in batter, then deep-fried, and it's usually served with French fries."

"I'll definitely order that; it sounds like farmyard fish and chips to me." Ian could not control his broad smile as he slid his menu casually onto the table.

"A thick juicy steak will work for me just fine."

"I'll have a double hamburger with all the works." Menus were re-stacked. Robert passed them to the waitress after she'd finished writing down their orders.

A man with a group at another table, started strumming his guitar in an attempt to initiate a sing-along. Robert became immediately involved, electing himself the leader of this impromptu choir. Going from table to table, he encouraged everyone to join in, including Ian. Even the delivery of supper did not deter Robert's enthusiasm for his newfound vocation. Usually, a reserved man, somehow the atmosphere of the place, had fired him into a state of intoxication, although it wasn't through alcohol. As much as he seemed to be enjoying his hamburger, bites were only taken in the short instances when music had abated. However, in between singing a few more bars, swilling beer seemed to come naturally to him.

This sense of comradeship had become contagious. It wasn't long before people started mingling and introducing themselves in between songs. The man playing guitar stopped and held his instrument high over his head with one hand, which induced a sudden silence.

"Hunger and fatigue were starting to take their toll on him. Would anyone like spelling me, so I can take a refreshment break." Tensions abated as Barbara walked over to speak to him.

"Well, we have a pretty young lady here from England, her name's Barbara, and she would like to give it a try." Barbara gave a cute curtsy as an acknowledgment to hand clapping and cheers. First, she played a guitar solo to get the instrument's feel: it was a complicated piece. Robert was dumbstruck, finally venting admiration with more cheers, handclaps and whistles. The crowd also showed their appreciation.

" Ian, she's phenomenal."

"I knew she played well but playing something that difficult so proficiently even surprises me. She is phenomenal, isn't she."

After playing a few more songs for people to sing along with, she tried to hand the guitar back to its owner. Neither he nor the crowd would allow that to happen, chanting more repeatedly.

"OK, OK." She made a calming motion with her hand. "There's a song I'd like to try out. It's a song I wrote myself. After you've heard it, you'll probably beg me to stop." She'd won the crowd; there was laughter mixed with shouts of (NO WAY).

Singing a heart-wrenching performance of a sad ballad, the songs' personification mesmerized her audience, initiating more than just a few watery eyes. The place was cloaked in silence long after her rendition had concluded. The silence was now becoming an embarrassment. "Will someone please say something?" Ian broke the crowd's fixation by shouting at the top of his lungs.

"You're bloody fantastic. I love you." Applause then erupted from every corner of the room. "I've never heard her sing like that before. I had no idea she has such a beautiful voice."

"She's a very talented lady, your Barbara. You should be proud of her, Ian. You're a fortunate man."

"Oh, I'm fully aware of just how lucky I am."

Party time was eventually brought to its inevitable end. Cold, crisp night air filled their lungs as they strolled back to their cabin, accompanied by melodious sounds of feet crunching untrodden frosty ground.

"Barbara!" a voice broke the verbal silence. They stopped and turned to see a man running towards them.

"Hi, my name's Jeff Morgan." Surprised at this late introduction, she shook the hand he'd extended. This is my husband, Ian Shaw, and our friend Robert." They, too, shook hands.

"I'm in the music business, and I know talent when I see it."

"That's a nice compliment, thank you. I'm also in the industry Jeff."

"Are you under contract, then?"

"No, I'm in the management end of the business."

"Perhaps we could talk about this over breakfast tomorrow." Is eight o'clock good for you, People? It'll be my treat." Barbara looked at Ian; he nodded approval.

"Eight tomorrow will be fine, Jeff." They said good night and retired to their cabin.

"Well, that was unexpected." Bathing in her night of glory, a relaxed aura of confidence seemed to emanate from her.

"I don't think you would be surprised if you sang like that in public more often. You really do have a great talent. I had no idea you could sing and play guitar that well."

"I was fortunate, being taught guitar, and coached in singing by the best. I do regard Jim as being in that category. Quite the perfectionist when it comes to his music, you know. Accepting anything less from an associate would be out of the question for him. Plus, I also told you I'd studied music from childhood."

"Well, I think Jim was playing a stacked deck, working with your talent."

"I wholeheartedly agree. You're wasting a true gift on folks like us. You should be entertaining large audiences." She looked at Robert and gave a little giggle of embarrassment at his compliment. He joked when perceiving her shyness to further embarrass her. "Your giggling, is that meant to insinuate I'm a large audience? Because that's not the kind of large audience, I meant." Robert was delivered a hard shove to the shoulder for that comment. Rumbling chuckles from his deep voice reverberated off the cabin walls.

Robert allotted them the bedroom, well preparing the lounge's bed Chesterfield for himself. The woolly long johns bought as a substitute for pyjamas turned out to be not such a great idea. An almost intolerable irritation to tender skin was created by course wool. A night of tossing, turning, and scratching ensued, with cold temperatures ruling out an unthinkable alternative of sleeping nude.

Reveille was sounded by Robert's knock on their bedroom door. Eventually, they emerged, looking like something the cat would not even bother to drag in.

"I don't know how you two do it. Skiing all day, late evening, and you still managed to keep that bed creaking all night." Barbara's face flushed with embarrassment.

"It's not at all what you think, Robert." He cut her short by lowering his head slightly and holding out a hand big enough to stop a Mac truck.

"You don't have to explain yourself to me. After all, you two are married, and I'm not your father." Ian could see Robert was just yanking her chain, and she was biting.

Without seeing through Robert's teasing, Barbara was still a little miffed as she opened the cabin door. Her suggestion was delivered more like an order.

"We should go for breakfast, Jeff will be waiting for us, and I'm interested in what he might have to say."

"I didn't think you were interested in performing." Ian's calm tones attempted to smooth troubled waters.

"I'm not, but I'm always interested in making new contacts. You never know what doors they can open."

"That's a good point of view. You never know where things may lead." They made their way across to the restaurant. It was eight o'clock sharp, and Jeff was in the reception area, waiting to be seated.

"Good morning to you all, It seems everyone's on time."

"Yes," Barbara said, "Robert was our alarm clock this morning. Without him, we may have slept in."

The hostess arrived to escort them to a table. They were then handed menus, and coffee was promptly served.

Jeff was a man in his mid thirty's, and judging by his vocabulary, well educated. He got straight down to business in a forthright no-nonsense manner.

"So you say you're not under contract Barbara."

"No, I'm not Jeff, but as I told you last night, my interests lie in management and song writing."

"Exactly who do you represent?"

"A group of young lads who just got their first big break with a record at number three on the English charts."

"The songs you sang last night were written for a woman. Am I correct?"

"Yes, but I've had success writing many songs with the band as a group. Although I do feel the need to write my own material. It's a therapeutic outlet that gives me pleasure."

"Then, I couldn't convince you to record some of your own work Barbara."

"Not at this point in time, Jeff."

"So, would you consider another woman recording your work?"

"I hadn't given it serious thought, Jeff, but yes, it would be nice to hear my songs being sung."

"Get them published, send them to me, and I'll shop them around to my contacts. I'm sure there will be several lady singers who would give their eye teeth for material like yours, Barbara. I'd also appreciate the opportunity to represent your interests here in America."

After finishing breakfast, they exchanged addresses, and phone numbers, before Jeff made his farewells, having to fly out that morning.

After breakfast, they immediately hit the slopes to take maximum advantage of the remaining time, and skiing became a significant element of that leisure time.

Recapping rudimentary skills, Robert attempted to instill knowledge acquired the previous day. An hour or so had passed before attempting something more challenging.

This time there were no problems in offloading. Rendezvousing with Robert, who was first to disembark, they hovered on a crest overlooking several runs.

"Follow me. I'll take you down this run." He pointed to a run left of the chair. Ian peered over the edge of what he perceived to be a precipice.

"You can't be serious, Robert."

"Just bend your knees, and let your skies run straight. You'll be fine." Barbara had discovered new challenges for herself in this sport.

"Come on, Ian, don't be chicken. The worst you can do is fall down. Heaven knows we should both be good at that, with all the practice we had yesterday." Ian's soft laughter belied his attempted bravado. Robert and Barbara skied off together, leaving Ian to gingerly follow. Picking up speed and abandoning all previous fears, he started gaining on them. He turned his head on passing, calling to rub their noses in the fact that speed had accompanied his newfound confidence.

"I find this invigorating." However, his ego had become more significant than his skill. Losing concentration, his ski tips crossed, causing him to fall sideways into a snowbank.

Barbara sped by, unable to stop on the steep slope. Finally, finding a safe haven in a lower ball, she waited. Robert stopped to help. Assisting an uncoordinated and indignant Ian to his feet, well coping with his own bouts of laughter, proved more complicated than it should have been.

"I'm deaf in my left ear." Ian's winning only made Robert laugh louder.

"It's nothing to laugh at. I can't hear a bloody thing on my left side."

"That's because snow impacted your ear as you fell on it." Robert's big hands were no match for Ian's tiny ear. His uncontrollable giggling didn't help. "I can't clear it. You'll have to do it yourself." Having no more luck than Robert, he finally decided to ski down to Barbara for a bobby pin to remove this cold intolerance that had begun to induce pain. She was led out in the snow waiting for them.

"What took you so long?"

"I've snow packed so tight into my ear, and I can't get it out. Can you give me a hair grip, quickly it's starting to freeze my ear?" She obliged him with her assistance, and the snow was removed.

The rest of the day was sunshine, blue skies, and fresh powder conditions. It was a skier's dream. All good things must come to an end, but a reluctance to leave was counterbalanced by fatigue. Ian arranged his meeting with Robert in Switzerland before driving back to the cabin. Gathering up the few things left there and saying goodbye to Robert, they left to go their separate way.

Arriving at their hotel in Vancouver, Canada, by early evening gave them time to shower and change before visiting the lounge for cocktails. Ian soon found it wasn't just fatigue that was a problem. Barbara was quick to pick up on his sluggish movements.

"What's wrong with you? You look like an old man moving around."

"I feel like one. I've never had so many aches and pains in my whole life, plus my legs feel like jelly."

"Now you mention it, I'm starting to feel a little sore myself

"I'm going to enjoy relaxing with my backside parked in that chair, with a drink in my hand. I don't think I'm fit for much else this evening." Sitting with a view of a sleepy harbour bathed in moonlight seemed an inviting spot to unwind. "Besides, with your company, what more could I want anyway." She pulled her chair closer and put her hand in his. Looking across the water, neither felt the need for words. Perhaps it was a time to just enjoy each other's company and not be concerned about the rest of the world.

They left the hotel late the following morning and drove to the airport to catch their flight to England. Arriving in England, Ian boarded a connecting flight to Zurich, and Barbara went to their home in the west country.

CHAPTER 14

Ian, you drank way too much

Clearing the decks of outstanding work, Ian had allotted himself time to accompany Robert, through company orientation, before their first assignment. Familiarization started with a trip to Pete's office, where introductions were made. Some small talk ensued before getting down to business. Pete then handed Robert a hefty folder containing details of their next deployment.

"This will be Ian's next assignment. You'll find all the necessary information required on the leading players and detailed information concerning locations. We have an extensive library of intelligence information that will also be at your disposal. I've arranged a meeting for you with our head of security. Although by the very nature of your job, you will be acting independently on most projects. I suggest you return to your office, settle in, and study your brief before that meeting. Ian and I have things to discuss."

With cordiality befitting a military man, Robert took leave of his new bosses, substituting salutes for handshakes.

"You're next assignment's in Africa, Ian. It's in a particularly hazardous area, so I'm sure that Robert's skills will be fully utilized on this assignment. Joseph Amir is seeking a large amount of capital. This would presumably be to buy arms. We're prepared to supply financial assistance, but there will be strings attached to this loan. He will have only one year to repay it." Ian was a little taken back by these stringent demands.

"Even selling foreign aid goods on the back market, he couldn't accumulate funds equaling these figures you've handed me."

Ian had become anesthetized to company involvement in dark activities. Reluctantly he'd been coerced into regard such unacceptable clandestine behaviour as standard company policy. Having no control over this aspect of his life, this predicament bothered him. It would be enough to foster depression if such thoughts were dwelled on.

Merely a pawn in someone's grandiose chess game of life was his rationalization for his company affiliation. These thoughts enabled him to maintain some sort of sanity: Nonetheless, a very well-paid pawn.

"That's correct, Ian, but his neighbouring country Comare, is very rich in oil, and they've not been as cooperative with certain people as we would have liked them to be. This has caused instability in our oil pricing policies, a matter we would like to see corrected. Therefore, you will impress upon him his need to take control of the oil fields in question."

"The United Nations would never allow him to take over another nation's resources, would they?"

"No, but by the time the dust settles, Amir should have obtained a sufficient amount of funds to service his debts, and I'm sure Comare will also have received our message."

"And these loan conditions are the ones you wish emphasized, unofficially, of course."

"That's correct, Ian. Needless to say, this information is of a sensitive nature. At no time is this information to be put down in writing. And needless to say, related to anyone outside this office."

"I fully understand." Pete stood up, indicating the briefing had finished.

"If there are no more questions, I think we can say this meeting's concluded. I suggest you leave for Africa as soon as possible. Amir has a reputation of being quite ruthless and given to uncontrollable rages, so be very careful in your dealings with him. The name Bloody Joseph was well earned.

Does Robert own a gun? If not, arrangements will be made. I'll make sure the two of you acquire diplomatic passports. That way, you'll be able to carry weapons legally."

"I'll speak with him about it, Pete, and he can make himself useful in his area of expertise."

Ingrid was charged with flight arrangements. Robert designated task was the acquisition of weapons. An armoury for law enforcement, made available for company use, incorporated a firing range. Robert gave Ian a much-needed crash course in the use of small arms. He was a quick learner with excellent hand-eye coordination. Ian also achieved a good perception of the gun's mechanics. By the end of the afternoon, Robert had taught Ian to be very proficient with the weapon he'd chosen.

* * *

Africa did not exactly welcome them with open arms. Sticking out like two white sore thumbs amongst dozens of black fingers, they became the objects of inquiring stares in this small airport. The driver, who had been sent to collect them, picked up their bags and carried them to a waiting Land Rover without uttering a word.

"Not exactly Zurich, is it Robert?"

"You either love Africa or hate it; there is no in-between. For me, there's a primitive beauty here that you'll find no were else on earth."

"There's also squalor, disease and the dust." They climbed into the vehicle. It unceremoniously pulled away the moment they were in, with one door swing open.

"Can you give me some idea regarding the duration of this trip, driver?" Ian was feeling the discomfort of heat.

"General Amir will be expecting you to be on time. I won't be late." Not quite the reply Ian was looking for. Now in a depressed mood, he viewed the barren county side surrounding them.

"It would take a while for me to get accustomed to a place like this, bad roads, heat, dirt, and poverty."

"The poverty's caused by men like us, Ian, as for the rest, you were always an outdoors enthusiast. What happened? Have you become so pampered by good living you've forgotten your roots?" A hearty slap on the shoulder was meant as a morale booster.

An abrupt stop at the gates of a fortified compound engulfed the vehicle in its own dust storm. Two armed guards approached them, and after a quick check, they were waved through. Two more guards met them at the inner bastion's front steps. Its foreboding white concrete walls reminded Ian of a prison, not a palace. One guard stepped forward and greeted them, exhibiting impeccable English.

"Gentlemen, welcome to the presidential palace. I will escort you to your quarters. If you will follow me, please." He led them inside. It was opulence in access: marble floors, fluted columns, grand archways, and an abundance of gold fixtures. There was an abundance of exquisite artwork adorning walls. Attempts to impose grandeur on this would be sanctum could not alleviate the eerie death-drenched atmosphere that possessed this cold silent Mausoleum. The mere sound of their footsteps breaking this morgue-like silence sent shivers down Ian's spine.

Escorted to a second-floor corridor, they were directed to their assigned suite. After opening the door for Ian and Robert, their escort then related Amir's wishes concerning Ian's meeting.

"Let me know when you are ready, and I will inform general Amir. He will then notify me if it's a convenient time for him." He then took up sentry duty at their door.

Robert closed the door of the apartment. It was as opulent and spacious as the rest of the palace. Their every need had been anticipated, right down to favourite drinks in a well-stocked bar. In their suite were several bedrooms to choose from. They decided on two adjoining bedrooms. This was on Robert's suggestion, for security reasons.

"Is this more like what you're accustomed to, Ian."

"Yes but driving past the poverty to get here makes me feel a bit guilty now." Ian poured himself a drink from the bar, "Will you join me, Robert."

"I'll have a club soda, please. I never touch alcohol, or women, when I'm working. I make that a strict rule." They finished their drinks before discarding dust and grime accumulated on their journey.

Making their readiness known to the sentry, Ian's preparedness was relayed by phone. It was a brief conversation.

"You are in luck gentlemen; general Amir will see you right now."

They were escorted to an office on the main floor. After Robert had made a security sweep of the area, Ian suggested he should wait outside. Ian then made himself comfortable in a chair.

Amir made a grand entrance. Such a show of theatrics made it evident to Ian he'd be dealing with a man who possessed an enormous ego. Taking up a position behind his desk that had been subtly elevated to impose dominance. For privacy, he then ordered his entourage to leave.

"You understand, General, there will be some stringent terms attached to this loan."

From what was perceived as usurping power, Vibes of anger emanated from Amir as his face reddened, although he said nothing. Trying to ignore evident tensions, Ian soldered on. He outlined terms set down in his own verbal briefing. Finding these terms favourable to his psychopathic tendencies, Amir's animosity subsided, with a rapid mood swing.

"These are excellent terms, even better than I had wished for. I love a good war."

Thinking discretion is the better part of valour, Ian showed no emotion or reply to this comment. Instead, he followed it with a simple statement.

"Funds will be made available to you as soon as they're required. Arrangements have been made for advisers to help in arms selection and instruction and training in their use. I think I've covered every aspect of our deal, so if you have any questions, this would be the time to ask."

"Conditions seem to have been laid out quite clearly, so now perhaps we can celebrate."

Ian declined not to sample the General's infamous reputation for hospitality, which most often would end in violence.

"I think I should be returning to head office as soon as possible there is still much work to be done on this deal."

"Nonsense, you can't leave without experiencing all the pleasures of my palace."

Sensing a decline to this insistence might trigger another mood swing, Ian capitulated.

"Of course, General, it was impolite of me to refuse. I wasn't thinking. Most times, my line of work deigns me access to life's simple pleasures."

"Come to the dining room in one hour. I have a marvellous evening planned."

"Until this evening, then."

Ian beat a hasty retreat from the room. Joining Robert outside, they went straight to their suite. Ian spoke softly as they walked.

"I believe he's mentally unstable, Robert; we'll have to be very careful what we say. He's invited us to his dining room in one hour for food and entertainment. I couldn't refuse."

"You did the right thing, Ian. It would have been unwise to refuse his hospitality. My job's to handle situations of this nature. That's what you're paying me for."

Reaching their quarters, Robert cautiously opened the door. They were greeted by a room full of half-naked women. Several were lying around in various provocative poses. Two approached Ian, while two more tried working their seductive charms on Robert. Robert was quick with an appropriate retort as he pealed one from around his neck.

"I'm sorry, ladies, much as we appreciate your offers, we're both still in love with our wives." He opened the door, and with a flirtatious grin, ushered them out with a slap to the backside of a girl that dallied a little too long.

"The man offends very easily, Robert. I hope this won't offend him." Ian was ill at ease with the situation.

"I don't think those girls will say we weren't interested in them. Let me worry about security. I'll pour you a drink; you look like you could use one." His usual grin was now embroidered into the fabric of his face. He walked to the bar slowly, meticulously, he selected a large tumbler. Pouring a large gin with enough tonic to give an adequate amount of flavour, plus a good slice of lime, he topped it off with vodka before handing it to Ian. He poured himself a club soda and tipped it back. Ian tried to follow suit.

"Wow, this seems a little strong." Ian sucked the alcohol from his tongue.

"It's just your usual, but it's probably a higher prof than your used to." He finished his club soda with a smack of the lips. "This heat makes a man thirsty. Drink up and give me your glass; you look like you could use a refill. I'll do the honours. I need to freshen up mine anyway."

"I'm nowhere near finished."

"Knock it back, Ian, quinine in tonic's good for you in hot climates." Spurred on by Robert's persistence, he tipped back the remaining portion. He then blindly hand over his glass. An identical concoction was then discreetly poured and handed back to him.

Looking at his watch, Robert again urged Ian to make haste with his drink, using the excuse it would be unwise to keep Amir waiting. Robert kept Ian active by insisting he had not dressed appropriately for the occasion. Robert then declared a change of clothes might be in order. This, he hoped, would speed up intoxication by increasing his metabolism.

Alcohol was now influencing Ian's equilibrium; stumbling on the stairs was a first reliable indication. Robert played the good shepherd. Trying to laugh it off, his best efforts at speech were riddled with drunken slurs and uncontrolled giggling.

"I feel a little woozy Robert, it must be fatigue from the trip." Even this vein attempt to rationalize the situation was overwhelmed by the rantings of his alcoholic stupor.

"It's probably an empty stomach Ian, and you're not used to this heat. You'll feel fine when you've had something to eat."

As they entered the dining room, Amir greeted them with applause. Everyone placated the general by joining him in a standing ovation. Ian gave a somewhat drunken wave of recognition. This amusement of guests.

Amir, centred on the head table, was flanked by his chiefs of staff. Two side tables accommodated the lesser echelon, who were predominantly army officers. He unceremoniously pushed several of his staff from their chairs.

"Make way for our guests." The tables were a virtual cornucopia of food and drink. He gestured to a waiter to pour Ian a large glass of wine. Nude dancers performed sensual activities on tables, all of which seemed to eventually evolve into a grand finale of various sex acts. "Drink up, Ian," Amir called. Reluctantly taking several gulps of wine, Ian raised a somewhat shaky glass to his host. Robert placed a leg of greasy lamb on Ian's plate.

"Eat something, Ian; you're drinking far too much on an empty stomach. You'll make yourself ill." As Ian stared down at the lamb, his stomach heaved. Robert grasped the meat and forced it into Ian's hand. "This will do you a world of good." Assisting a somewhat shaky hand towards his mouth, the grease-laden haunch left its residue around Ian's lips.

Meanwhile, some of the audience were joining the floor show. All this whirling and gyrating of participants had a dizzying effect on Ian, whose head was now pinning faster than the dancers. He needed the washroom badly. In a futile attempt at leaving, he turned and threw up over the floor behind himself. Stumbling from his chair, he fell in a state of drunken stupor into his own vomit. Ian's demise became a new form of entertainment for Amir. This initiated a bout of uncontrollable laughter.

"I must apologize, General; he never could drink wine." Robert, throwing a limp Ian over his shoulder, like so much dead meat, and left the room smiling.

Morning's rude awakening came with a shoulder tap from the butt of Robert's handgun.

"Time we flew the coup, Ian." Robert had planned to utilize the palace's early morning slumber time as a window of opportunity to make their discreet departure. Hurrying down to the compound, they commandeered a vehicle for their airport journey. Boarding the first flight available, Ian's head was able to throb in perfect time to the drone of the engines

"How much did I have to drink last night?"

"Just enough, Ian, just enough," Robert ordered him a large glass of water. "It may seem difficult but drinking water will help your hangover."

This hastily arranged flight had transported them to Egypt, with no connecting flights available until the next day. A pleasant respite for an embattled Ian. Being still somewhat inebriated, he needed some assistance from Robert to disembark an aircraft he perceived was still in motion. With its windows down, a taxi ride to a nearby hotel did not alleviate his predicament. Arranging to meet in the dining room later for supper, Ian was a no-show. Robert's appetite wasn't about to wait for the possibility of an appearance from Ian. Indulging himself in the hotel's kitchen's many culinary delights, which predominantly catered to Egyptian cuisine, he satisfied his hunger before phoning Ian's room.

"Good evening, Ian, I hope I'm not disturbing you. I went ahead and dinned alone, thinking food might be the last thing on your mind right now. You were looking pretty ill when I saw you last."

"Yes, you did disturb me. I was sleeping before your phone call woke me. I'm still feeling under the weather, and why do you have to sound so bloody loud and cheerful. You shouldn't have bothered to phone. I really don't feel hungry."

"You must eat something, Ian. It will help settle your stomach."

"I believe I've heard you tell me that once before." Robert gave a chuckle.

"Get room service to bring you something light."

"Why on earth did you allow me to drink that much anyway? After all, you were sober." His disgruntled manor echoed his pain.

"It was my master plan to get you into that state. I thought it an excellent ploy to excuse ourselves. I spiked your drinks in our room before we went downstairs. I have to admit the throwing up was the perfect touch to the performance. The icing on to the cake, so to speak. It made you a real hit with the General." Ian's patience was wearing thin.

"You did what? You're supposed to protect me, not cause me bodily harm."

"We were in a perilous situation. There were two options, defuse or extradite. The first option proving impossible, I chose the latter. There was gunfire after we left, and I saw three bodies taken out. You slept through the whole thing. I, on the other hand, took sentry duty. Although I didn't expect anyone to bother us, we had given no cause for any form of displeasure. Best avoid a confrontation before it happens than dealing with one after the fact. I really don't think you would have agreed to my plan if you had known what it was."

"No, I would not have. But I suppose you did the right thing; after all, we did get out of there in one peace. Your lucky I'm an amiable drunk." This sign of appeasement towards Robert showed all was forgiven. "I must admit I was a bit nervous being in that situation."

"You'd have been a fool not to have."

"Now, get some food inside of you to settle your stomach. I'm going out for the evening. I'll see you tomorrow morning if that's OK."

"Yes, that's fine with me Robert, have a good time." He ordered some very bland food and a glass of milk, thinking it was probably best for what ailed him. Bland may have been good, but it definitely wasn't appealing. He picked through the food unenthusiastically until he decided to sidestep the issue of eating by phoning Barbara. Her voice was like music to his ears, so Ian expressed his joy with an outpouring of sweet nothings. Keeping the seedier side of his businesses under raps, he skirted around his latest exploits. No amount of prompting could pry the true nature of his role in world affairs. Diverting conversation to happiness found in his life with her was always his way to avoid this issue.

"It's been hell without you these last few days, but we'll be together soon."

"I've missed you to Ian. When will you be home?"

"I'm not sure, but it will be as soon as possible; you can be sure of that."

"I've been to Bristol with Marge, shopping for groceries."

"Welcome to the mundane life of a housewife."

"Yes, and I love every minute of it." She blew him a kiss over the phone. "I'll be counting the minutes down until you're here." Her last statement was purposely delivered with all the wailing and sighing of a siren in heat bent on luring some poor sailor to his doom. His sex drive momentarily crushed his hangover.

"You make me want to forget everything and come home to you right now." She laughed; having felt she'd made her point.

"I'll be waiting for the moment you arrive, until then." she blew another kiss, and he reciprocated with the purr of a randy ally cat before dropping the phone down. He returned to his bland meal that was full of no surprises.

CHAPTER 15

Barbara makes a new friend

The front door vibrated with a series of loud bangs.

"I'm coming, I'm coming." Opening the door, Barbara was confronted by a man whose features looked familiar. Although she was unable to put a name to the face of this man standing before her.

"Good evening. My name is Bill Ackerman."

"I knew I recognized your face. I have several of your records. I'm pleased to meet you. My name's Barbara Shaw, Bill." She held out a hand for a welcoming shake. "How can I help you?"

"My band and I were given to understand you have a recording studio." He pointed at two cars loaded with people parked in the driveway. As she peered towards them, there were some reciprocal waves and smiles from open windows.

"Yes, I have, but it's barely up and running. My groups coming here tomorrow to do some recording and check out how things sound. There's sure to be some fine-tuning to be done, and I'm relying on one of the boys, who's a good sound engineer, to iron out any rough spots.

"Then, I would like to know if it would be possible to rent your studio for the night. I don't think that some fine-tuning should pose a problem; we have our own sound engineer. You see, we were working on a new album when we had an electrical fire in the recording equipment. To retain the magic of the moment, we feel it's essential to keep recording. This is well we're still hot, so to speak." Barbara gave a polite giggle.

"If you'd care to call your band over, I'll show you the studio. How did you hear about me, Bill?" He beckoned to the group.

"Oh, it's a tight-knit community in these parts; there's not too much happening around here that goes unnoticed. I don't live far from here, you know. I have my own home recording studio, and after the fire, it was only a short drive here, so we came straight over, hoping you'd be home. I would have phoned, but I didn't know your name at that time." With his entourage in tow, Bill followed her into the studio, well his sound engineer checked out the control room. He spoke into the microphone.

"This is a very nice setup you have here, Barbara." Bill ran his hand lightly over the control panels with a caressing touch. He exhibited the kind of appreciation given a finely tuned piano. Barbara stood by as the band set up their instruments.

"Would you mind if I joined your engineer in the control booth for a while, Bill?"

"Not at all, It'll be good to have an audience, especially one as pretty as yourself." Bill was an old smoothy; she gave a gracious smile at his charming style. All the while, their engineer worked his brand of magic; well, the band tuned their instruments.

"OK, boys, let's try to settle in and re-establish our grove before recording some fine music. They were hot and on a roll. It only took a few hours to get most of the material they'd been working on, on tape. Barbara noticed fatigue had started to take its toll on quality.

"Would you people like to take a break for a cup of tea?"

"Beer would be appreciated if you have some." There was a cheeky grin on the band member's faces.

"I think I can accommodate you there if you drift along to the kitchen when you are ready. I'm sure I can rustle you up some sandwiches also."

Sitting around the kitchen table, the conversation flowed.

"How long have you lived in this area, Bill."

"I was born and razed here and wouldn't want it any other way.

I'm just an old homebody at heart. Where better a place to live. This is God's country, don't you agree."

"Yes, my husband and I love it here, Bill. Now, this is a surprise for me; I thought you only played Dixie land jazz. Those solos you played on the clarinet were so soulful. I really enjoyed them."

"We're trying to appeal to a broader audience. It's more commercial, but this is also the way our music's taking us."

"It has success written all over it as far as I'm concerned, Bill."

"Why, thank you, Barbara, flattery will get you everywhere." He laughed. "And what exactly are you involved in to have a setup like this?"

"At present, I manage Avebury. You may have heard of them."

"I believe so; they have a song in the top twenty right now, haven't they?"

"Yes, they have. I'm also in the process of having some of my own work published for the American market."

"So you're a songwriter with connections in the states."

"Budding writer Bill, although I co-wrote the chart single Avebury's having some success with at present."

"If Avbury's song is anything to go by, I can foresee a great future for you." She laughed.

"Now who's shovelling out flattery." It was Bill's turn to have a chuckle. His crew slowly started making their way back to the recording studio.

"Well, I suppose we should finish up what we've started, and then we can be on our way." Rapping up all loose ends within the hour, they were ready to leave.

"I really appreciate you helping us out like this, Barbara. If I can return the favour at any time, you only have to ask; you have my number. Maybe I can put some business your way if you're interested, renting out studio time, arranging gigs, and such, who knows."

"I'd appreciate that after all; that's what I'm in business for."

The band unceremoniously piled back into their vehicles. Bill being the true showman, made his exit with flair and style. Doffing his bowler with a sweeping bow as he slipped into his ride.

CHAPTER 16

Disappointment turns to joy.

Pandemonium erupted throughout the house at nine-thirty sharp that morning. The boys had arrived. Barbara seemed ill-prepared, having been so rudely awakened from a well-earned slumber. Appearing in her dressing gown, she was badgered into preparing breakfast for four hungry, demanding mouths. Complying with that obligation, she left the boys to pig out at the trough, well she showered and dressed.

As it was their first visit to her new home. After clearing breakfast, they were given the grand tour before settling in. Allotting each one his own room, they were invited to make themselves comfortable and regard the place as they would their own for the next few days. Tony related his impression of Barbara's home with his typical form of wit.

"So, what did you do to afford a place like this, Barbs? Perhaps Ian wone the football pools, or did he rob a bank?" Many a true word spoke in jest if the truth of Ian's business ventures were known.

"Whoops, bad choice of words seeing as how Ian works for a bank." She slapped him on the shoulder lightly and laughed at his pun.

"You cheeky little beggar."

"Joking aside, you've done a really nice job of turning this place into a lovely home, Barbs."

"Now," John asserted his presence, "down to the important things, are there any good pubs nearby, Barbara." She looked at him with a frown.

"I wondered when that subject would come up. With your way of thinking, I didn't realize there was such a thing as bad pubs. I'll take you on a pub crawl this evening, if you're good boys, and get all of your work done." This teasing brought a few disgruntled laughs.

"So, if you're mindset is a pub crawl this evening, I suggest we get started. There's a lot of ground to cover, with those new songs Jim, and Ron, have written: Plus, I have a few of my own I would like you boys to try out."

"She won't let us out until she figures were through, so let's get to it." Tony had a solemn look about him as he lightly tapped his hand on the top of the piano several times for attention. He then gestured with his hands for quiet.

"Before we start."

"Hay, hay, what's this all about." Ron's voice boomed. Not wanting to be upstaged, Tony paused, then repeated himself.

"Before we start, and well everyone is here, I have an announcement to make. This is something I've thought long and hard about. I've decided to leave the band." You could have heard a pin drop with the bombshell Tony had just laid in their laps. Insecurity razed its ugly head; anger, frustration and confusion then ensued as everyone started speaking at once. Jim's voice rose above the chorus.

"You can't do this to us, Tony." John endorsed the feelings vented by Jim.

"No, this is foolish. We're so near to success. This could blow the whole deal." Ron's face betrayed his thoughts. Portraying a puzzled look but quite out of character, his rationalization had a calming effect.

"He must have a good reason. Let's all calm down and hear him out." A morbid silence now rained.

"Thank you, Ron. I didn't want to do anything until we'd achieved a measure of success. We've all put so much hard work into getting where we are. I felt it might jeopardize Avebury's future if you're compelled to find a replacement when hovering so near our goal. Now we're well-known, people will be lining up to audition for my spot. Jim's solemn voice aired the close nit camaraderie of Avebury.

"We may be able to find a replacement Tony, but we'll never find someone to take your place. Is there no chance you might reconsider your decision?

"No, Jim, as I said, I have given this much thought. This was my reason. I wish to explore a music path that will take me away from what we are now doing. From my perspective, it would be wrong to keep going with the band when my musical interests are elsewhere. On the brighter side, I hope we will see a lot of each other because I would like Barbara to continue managing my interests."

"Well, for me, this is good news, Tony. Every cloud has a silver lining. I'm looking for new talent to represent, and you certainly have talent." Tony, in his best attempt to chair this impromptu meeting, took a paper from his pocket.

"I've also taken the liberty of making a shortlist of possible replacements and contacting them. You could hold auditions here in the next few days if you're comfortable with that." He looked at Barbara. "If that's alright with you, of course." She nodded her approval.

"Whatever you boys decide will be fine with me." Jim was still trying to comprehend the situation's full ramifications.

"This is all rather sudden, Tony; give everyone a little while for it all to sink in. As you say, you've given it a lot of thought, but it's still new to the rest of us. Perhaps if we sleep on it, we can discuss it more rationally first thing tomorrow." Barbara could see there was no point dwelling on the subject any longer.

"I think that's a sensible idea; now, how about we get to work."

Finishing their studio work late that evening, they pressured Barbara into making good on her promise of a pub evening for beer and sandwiches.

* * *

Ron played doorman for Barbara as she entered the old pub with her entourage in tow. Its substantial ruff gray stone walls, small windows, and large hearth with roaring fire was reminiscent of the typical County Inn, it was. The old furnishings, constructed of heavy-looking dark wood that had been well polished by time. There was also the required amount of gleaming brass fittings and glass, befitting such a watering hole.

"This is a cozy little place, Barbara. If you care to take that table near the fire, we'll order victuals and ale."

"Fine, I'll have a ham roll and a small beer if you're buying." Barbara had visited The Carpenter's Arms before, knowing the bar, purposely rigged with practical jokes, sat quietly back to enjoy the fun. Walking up to the bar, they were distracted by the fast-talking barman who captured their attention with jokes and eye contact. John was the first fish to be netted.

"Ah!" His screams, and flaying arms, brought attention to his plight. A giant spider vanished back into ceiling beams from where it came. The boys quickly exploited John's misfortune, but only Barbara could see another barman in a dark corner, manipulating strings and playing puppeteer. Their server then unceremoniously deposited their food and drinks on the brightly polished copper-topped bar. Without saying a word, he then slapped down their change in the same manner and walked away. Coins were rolling all over the counter between glasses, beneath food trays, and coins were even seen further down the bar, although no one saw them go that far. Jim tried calling him back, but ignoring protests, he proceeded to serve another customer. Jim was stunned.

"What a jerk, do you believe that." Portraying his indignation, Jim proceeded to gather up his change. Most coins were easily retrieved. Others proved to be more difficult. It took a while before it dawned on him; these coins were glued to the bar. Barman one simply turned to grin at Jim without a word being said: Fish number two had just been fried.

Taking the brunt of laughter in good stride, Jim knew he was tagged as the second banana in practical joke central. Picking up their food and drinks, they joined Barbara at the table. It nestled snugly against the fire's right-hand wall. John did the honours, passing around food and drinks, well everyone settled in.

"Quite the pranksters in this bar, don't you think? I thought you'd get a kick out of it." John took his seat.

"You must have seen all these gags pulled before Barbara."

"I have, but it's always fun to see someone new fall for these playful cons. Show time's so spontaneous. I still find it hilarious to see your past predicament re-enacted by another patsy. It's also a nice cozy place to spend an evening".

There were horse brasses attached to their leather display strap dangling out of plum on the wall, close to Tony; this seemed to disturb him. Reaching over, he corrected this annoyance. Continuing his conversation, he then noticed from the corner of his eye the decoration he had found so irritating slowly moved back out of the perpendicular. Reaching over again, he adjusted it back into plumb and was surprised when the offending ornament pushed back.

"Wow, did anyone see that?" Barbara, unbeknown to Tony, had pointed out to everyone else the puppet master pulling another string. The fish were biting tonight. Even the grand pooh bar of pranks had been gaffed in this time, taking the bait, hook, line, and sinker. Being a good sport, Tony was first to laugh at himself when he realized he fell for another house prank.

"OK, now I've been had. Are there any more tricks we should know about, Barbara?"

"I don't know. Maybe I'll be the next victim?" A few more drinks and a lot more conversation rounded out an evening's entertainment before Barbara drove everyone back to her home.

The following morning, the light early breakfast for guests consisted of scrambled eggs, toast, and a hot coffee pot. At first, there was little said. Ron played mom, clearing away dishes before pouring another round of coffee. Jim slapped his hand softly on the table, checking to see if all eyes were on him.

"Well, I suppose I'm elected spokesman then. I've had time to mull over what Tony's said. In my opinion, he is correct, we should find a new band member as soon as possible. Starting our tour in five days, we'll be playing small towns at first. It'll be an excellent opportunity to incorporate a new band member into our group. Venues of that size will be a perfect sounding board for ourselves and our new associate. It'll also give everyone time to adapt and polish a new act before any major engagements." John voiced his agreement.

"Your logic makes sense, Jim. How do you feel about it, Ron?"

"I'll go along with the two of you, I suppose." Jim knowing Ron's reluctance to air a strong opinion, interceded.

"This is not our decision alone. You're a member of this group, and we value your opinion, Ron."

"I've always left the decision-making to you people, and that's been fine with me. However, I will use my vote to take in a new member how I see fit because that will be important to me."

"We wouldn't have it any other way." Jim and John nodded in agreement. Tony again checked his list before placing it on the table.

"Right, now that's sorted out, check out this shortlist I've compiled." Mulling over Tony's list, most names were familiar. It mainly consisted of people that had at one time or another shared venues with Avebury. Tony pointed to a name topping his list.

"In my opinion, Jack Redmond's creativity as a musician far outshines anyone else I've selected, although he has no sing voice.

That shouldn't prove to be a problem. I've always wanted John to do more of the vocals than he does. I know Barbara's written some songs more suitable to his style than mine."

"I suppose it's only fair I take some pressure off you, Jim. As you've said, it gives us a chance to diversify more, using Barbara's music."

"You know Tony; this could work well for us. Perhaps you should have decided to leave long ago. They then patted him on the back and ruffled his hair with affection. I'll make some phone calls if you all go to the studio and get things set up there. I'll set auditions up for Thursday if that suits you, people." Barbara took on the role of a spokesperson.

"That seems fine, Tony. You can hold auditions in the games room upstairs." He joined the band in the studio within the hour.

"It's all set. I have six people coming at ten-thirty Thursday morning." Barbara saw flaws in Tony's organizational skills.

"All at the same time? Perhaps you should have let me organize it? Oh well, they'll just have to wait their turn. At least it won't matter if someone's late."

The next few days proved to be long and hard for Barbara, but being busy is helpful, especially when attempting to keep your mind off other things. Ian's latest phone call told her his homecoming would coincide with auditions. Keeping her fingers crossed, she hoped auditions would be over, and the house would be empty before his arrival. She had a plan in motion for the boys to be out for an evening's entertainment, giving her time alone with Ian. An intimate dinner for two, candles, wine, and soft music, is what she'd envisioned.

The cheery on the cake for later would be to flaunt herself in a new red silk negligee to tantalize his sexual appetite. Wanting this night to be a memorable occasion, she'd planned for every alternative down to the last detail in case Murphy's Law prevailed. And this being their first night in their new home together since the renovation completion, she wanted everything to be perfect.

* * *

Barbara was pleased when the first person to audition arrived half an hour early. Ushered upstairs to the games room, she asked him to set up. She then fetched Jim and company from the kitchen, where they'd been taking a coffee break.

"Your first audition has arrived."

"Who's the keen one?" John asked. Barbara, preoccupied with her perfect evening, gave a blank look.

"I didn't think to ask." Jim shook his head in disbelief and grind. Tony, however, wasn't about to let oversight pass unchallenged.

"You had the nerve to tell me I'm not organized." Jim cast some wisdom towards her shortcomings.

"Ian's due home this evening, isn't he?"

"That he is Jim." Tony saw an opening for another jab.

"Well, we all know what your minded is going to be centred on all day, sex, sex, and more sex."

"You've got a dirty little mind, Tony." Grabbing a dishcloth from the sink, she targeted his fleeing form as he made a swift exit.

"Ha, take that, you pig." As Tony disappeared through the door, a well-aimed dishcloth breezed the side of his head as he beat his hasty retreat upstairs to find sanctuary. His laughter from the higher floor reverberated throughout the house. As the boy trooped out to join Tony, Jim reflected on the moment.

"Life's going to dull without him around; he's always there spicing things up." John put in his two-pence worth.

"They defiantly broke the mould when they made him." Ron could only giggle. Jim then called back to Barbara, who had remained in the kitchen.

"Will you play hostess for us, please, Barbara."

"Of course." Picking up the cloth from where it had landed and feeling kind of smug, she juggled it in her hands before dunking it into the dirty laundry basket.

Five more applicants arrived for auditions. Barbara was surprised to see one of them was a young woman. She did not think Tony to be so liberal. As each applicant finished, Barbara would usher in the next prospect. Then came the young woman's turn. Barbara introduced her as Ann Gibbs. Tony immediately rose from his chair.

"Who the hell are you."

"I believe you were just told my name, but for the hard of hearing," and she shouted, "it's Ann Gibbs."

"That's not exactly what I meant." Tony's frustration was showing. His well-orchestrated little show was starting to play some disconcerting notes.

"I only invited people whose music or reputation I'm familiar with to this audition."

"Well, Jerry Simon was not available, so I'm taking his place. Is there a problem with that?" Tony's anger was showing.

"We're not looking for a girl replacement, so I think you'll just be wasting everyone's valuable time."

"Please just give me a chance. I've come a long way to be here." Her good looks did not hinder her cause. Barbara intervened on Ann's behalf.

"Tony, don't be such a chauvinists pig; give the girl a chance." Ron tried to calm the waters.

"You did say you valued my opinion in these auditions, and I say let her do her showcase. Anyone with that much spunk deserves a shot. Besides, it should no longer concern you, Tony; you've resigned, remember." It had just been hammered home to Tony; he was no longer a member of Avebury. And no longer a party to any decision-making.

"I suppose it's not up to me anyway, so carry on." Realizing he'd been a control freak from the outset of auditions, he now understood it was time to bow out gracefully. Ann gave an impressive performance with flawless vocals. Barbara then escorted Ann back down the stairs. She then asked her if she would wait while she accompanied the last applicant. It was Jack Redmond, the front runner in the selected group for auditions.

Returning immediately to Ann, she gestured towards the kitchen.

"Would you care to join me for a cup of tea Ann?" She could see Ann's veneer of bravado was wearing thin.

"Yes, please, I'd like that." Following Barbara to the kitchen, the kettle was set to boil.

When tea was made, all the condiments, plus a plate of biscuits, were placed on a tray. Barbara showed Ann to the lounge overlooking the lake.

"I feel I should tell you, the last person I took in for his audition is the front runner for the job."

"I suppose auditions were just a formality, then, is that what you're saying." It's hard to find a place to start in this industry, doubly so if you're a woman. I was hoping this would be a big break for me, but you also have to be able to take rejection and brush yourself down and try again." Up to this point in my career's best achievement was playing in an orchestra part-time. I only got that job because I have a degree in music. And that's not where my interests lay." Barbara passed on a few words of comfort.

"Don't be discouraged Ann, I know it does take time, but I'm sure you've got what it takes to make it." Ann was now feeling at ease with Barbara and wished to know more about her.

"I hope you don't mind me asking, but what's your connection to the band? I imagine you as a girlfriend or something of that nature. Am I correct?" Barbara laughed at that assumption.

"Good lord, no. I'm their manager."

"Wow! I'm impressed. Then you do understand what I'm saying is true; it is harder for a woman.

" I do Ann, it took a lot of hard work and persistence to get Avebury to the point we're at today. Hopefully, this is only a beginning for me, a first step in the many goals I've set myself. Perhaps I'll tell you about that sometime soon."

Ann, checking out her surroundings, wondered who could afford such a stately manor.

"This is a beautiful home Barbara, who does it belong to?"

"It belongs to my husband Ian and me. Come, I'll show you around." Barbara, well showing Ann the ground floor, purposely left her studio until last. Ann was in awe as she entered.

"You have your own recording studio. This would be every artist's dream. Are you a singer Barbara?"

"Only for my own pleasure, the studio is to record the work of people I manage, And anyone wishing to rent time here. That doesn't come cheap.

"Ann, I'd like you to look at some songs I've written. I'd like your opinion if you wouldn't mind."

"It would be my pleasure." Ann had seated herself at the grand piano and was getting a feel for its tones. Barbara soon returned with her music sheets. Browsing through Barbara's work, Ann found one song she was particularly drawn to. She played piano softly, well working her own rendition into the song's fabric. After humming it over several times, she fused music and words together. Together they flowed from her very soul. Such passionate emotion was inconceivable. It sounded like it had come from someone who had lived the experience portrayed in lyrics and melody. As Ann finished the song, Barbara wiped a tier from her eye before applauding vigorously.

"Your interpretation was how I imagined that song could be portrayed by the right singer." She placed her hand on Ann's shoulder and gave it a squeeze. You're going places, girl. Would you consider me tagging along for the ride as your manager? I may have something to offer. I have a contact in the states interested in these songs for a singer he has in mind. If we do a demo tape and send it to him, perhaps I can persuade him to go with you on one or two of my songs. After all, it would be more beneficial for me to manage the person singing my songs."

"I'm flattered by your confidence in me. If you give me a chance at the same measure of success Avbury's achieved, I'd be a fool to say no."

The boy's swaggered through the door, with Jack in tow. His deadpan vacant expression belied the emotion he was capable of extracting from a few guitar strings.

Jim's high spirits took a dive seeing Ann in the room. Dropping his head gave a good indication he was embarrassed, but putting on a brave face, he acted as spokesman for the band.

"I'm sorry, Ann, it was a difficult decision, but we've decided to go with Jack. Taking on a woman would have meant changing so much of our act at such a crucial time in Avebury's development. Although, with your talent, I must admit it was a temptation. Strange as it might sound, even Tony voiced support for you."

"This is great news." The boys looked at Barbara in disbelief, thinking she was definitely on a different wavelength to make what sounded like such a callous statement. Ann could only snigger quietly to herself, being the only person in the room with an insight into Barbara's understanding of the situation. Tony picked up on Ann's reaction and jumped straight in, never missing an opportunity for a tease.

"The thought of sex or the lack of it lately must be eroding your brain. Do you realize what you just said? You've devastated this poor girl's ambitions." Seeing Ann now in full-blown laughter, everyone realized they'd been on the outside looking in. "Now, let's hear you dig your way out of this one." Barbara started laughing at what had been perceived by her words.

"OK, I should have been more informative before I said what I said. I've persuaded Ann to join our stable as a solo artist. So you see, it's all worked out for the best. Now to business, and I'll try to be more coherent in future." A sarcastic smile directed towards Tony accompanied a protruding tongue.

"I'd like Ann to do a demo tape for me. I've envisioned some string accompaniment for that showcase. Ann, could you give it to us one more time, please." Wringing every ounce of emotion from her body, she bared her soul once more. She even eclipsed her first performance. Her audience stood in awe before applauding.

Barbara let the moment pass before speaking. "Anyone! any ideas to contribute?" Tony lifted his hand.

"I see your point about strings. The music avenues I've been travelling in lately have brought me into contact with the type of musicians I believe you have in mind. So why not leave it with me, and I'll see what I can come up with."

"Avebury, you'll be leaving tomorrow to start touring. Ann, I would like you to stay here next week to work on this demo. Tony, you'd better also stop over. I know you can find work in the studio to amuse yourself. And we can utilize your expertise on Ann's demo. I think that wraps everything up. Now I'd like to congratulate Jack and welcome him and Ann into our little family. Now, what say you, we go grab a coffee. "As everyone started to leave the room, Barbara turned to Tony as an afterthought.

"Oh! I think it should be your job to inform the other candidates who auditioned for Avebury of their decision, Tony. There's also one more thing I'd like to request of everyone; it's a personal favour. Could you all make yourselves scarce this evening?" Tony sang out his reply.

"Barbara's got a red hot date tonight; her husband's coming home, now don't be playing gooseberry, or you may hear her moan." There were more than a few jeers and whistles to the chorus. Then Jim put his ore in the water.

"Heaven forbid we should be the ones to pour cold water over a horny pair of alley cats. I think we know the very place to take Jack, and Ann, this evening, The Carpenters Arms. I'm sure you two love birds will be in bed before we hit the bar." Barbara slapped Jim lightly on the shoulder.

" You've been around Tony far too long. Now I have work to do, and so have you, so let's get on with it."

Barbara showed Jack, and Ann, to their respective rooms, before going to the kitchen. There she made preparations for a romantic supper she'd been planning for Ian. When she'd finished all the cooking preparations, she joined the group in the studio. She was surprised at how well things were going. She then joined Tony in the control booth.

"I've had some luck with those strings you wanted. It seems they've been working on a recording for a local band, and they were hoping to use their studio. Now that work's finished, that studio is no longer available due to a fire. So, they're out of luck and at a loose end. I think they'll do the gig in exchange for studio time.

"Sounds like a good deal all around, Tony."

"That's what I thought, so I told them to head on over tomorrow."

Several hours had passed, and fatigue was setting in. Barbara haled the group over the intercom. "Why don't we call it a day and wrap this up first thing tomorrow when we're fresh." Looking for a reaction from other band members to confirm their intentions, John walked up to the mike.

"I think we would like to keep going a little longer if that's alright with you. We'll try to be out of your hair before you get back. We know this evening means a lot to you." She waved through the control booth windows.

"OK, I'll leave you to it then, see you all tomorrow. Help yourselves to breakfast; Ian and I may have a lie-in." She left with a grin on her face befitting the Cheshire Cat.

Arriving at the airport before Ian's flight landing, she went to the lounge to try to catch a glimpse of his aircraft coming in. His flight was on time, so there was no long wait, as he'd flown first class and was first through customs. An attendant called a porter to assist him.

Fetcher, give this gentleman a hand with his luggage." After walking a short distance, Ian's curiosity aroused he posed a question.

"Fetcher! that's an unusual name, or is it a nickname?"

"I guess you'd say it's a nickname. My real name's Fletcher, and it used to be Fletcher, fetch this, Fletcher, fetch that, then it became just Fetcher." His jolly belly laugh suited his stocky build.

"Ah, then Fetcher is a nickname."

Barbara joined Ian, greeting him with a peck on the cheek. They then walked together, arm in arm, with Fetcher tagging along behind toting Ian's luggage. After Ian tipped Fetcher, Fetcher touched the peak of his cap with finger and thumb in gratitude.

"Thank you kindly, sir."

Isolated in the privacy of Barbara's car, some passionate embracing occurred.

"It's good to be home. I've missed you so much." She drew closer and whispered in his ear.

"Having the house to ourselves, I've arranged an intimate dinner for two. I know this will be a special event for us. We will be completely alone in our home since its completion. No building, and decorating paraphernalia, no guests, the whole evening to do whatever we wish.

"Then, I have a gift for you that's appropriate for such an occasion."

"Oh, what have you got for me?" He kept her dangling, milking her curiosity for all it was worth.

"Not now, later when the mood's right. It's a special gift, you'll see." He threw in this statement to intensify her curiosity.

"You must tell me, you know, I'll just keep on until you let it slip." Ian laughed and shook his head.

"Never, now, what have you planned for dinner?"

"That's going to be my surprise then, so there, but I'd like it to be a formal affair. We'll dress as we would for any formal occasion. I want everything to be just right. The dining room's table has been set, and there's candelabra soft stereo music, wine, you name it.

"It sounds like you'll be trying to seduce me."

"That comes before supper, fool; I can't wait that long." He reached out and soothed her thigh.

"In that case, I'd like you to drive a little faster."

She sped into the driveway, stopping abruptly in front of the house. Jumping out, he raced to her door and swept her up in his arms. Carrying his prize into the house, he rushed her upstairs to the bedroom. It became a frantic race of who could disrobe who first. After falling onto the bed, two naked bodies seethed and boiled in this broth of love. Rest came only with exhaustion, slowly as a more sensual requirement of their needs emerged, an aspen leave like quivering manifested itself, only this trembling was euphoria. Laying still, side by side, they held hands savouring moments past, well-regaining energy so willingly lavished upon one another. Now, rejuvenated in the warmth of their marriage bed, it seemed an appropriate time to shower and dress for dinner.

Entering the dining room, Ian could fully appreciate the elaborate preparation made by Barbara. Set on a side table was an arrangement of flowers. A bottle of champagne with two glasses and a note were also placed close by. Barbara picked up the message.

"It's from the gang. Here is a little gift that we hope will add to your special evening." She went on to read signatures as Ian popped the champagne's cork. Handing her a glass, he looked tenderly into her eyes.

"A toast to us, Barbara. May every year of our marriage be as happy as our first years and may there be many more to follow.

"To us." After touching glasses, their arms entwined well-sipping champagne in a lovers toast.

An oven timer signalled her kitchen call. Removing the casserole dish, and parading it through, in a manner befitting a new year's haggis piping ceremony, it was placed center stage. This complete meal contained chicken breasts basted in honey, surrounded by an array of vegetables seasoned with herbs, and garlic, simmering in chicken bouillon. Crackling and bubbling, this stew was enhanced by sweet aromas. This simple to prepare but tasty supper exhibited a golden glaze, which provided a look of elegance to their meal. Timing being all-important for a perfect evening, her schedule was running like a Swiss watch. Ian, who had made himself busy lighting candles for table illumination, then topped off the Champagne glasses. The first course, previously cooled shrimp cocktails, waited to grace their table. This dish was savoured slowly, over a pleasant conversation and sips of wine.

The first course now finished; the entree followed. Culinary paint was applied to platters, emulating a recipe book presentation, with garnishing created by her own artistic flair. Truly a composition to savour, so Ian prepared to enjoy this Rembrandt set before him. Tasting a morsel, its flavours erupted over his tongue.

"Ah! This taste's fantastic. I think you've excelled yourself this time Barbara."

"Thank you, Ian, I'm pleased you appreciate my efforts, but it was surprisingly easy to prepare."

"You never cease to amaze me. I'm sure it must have taken a great amount of skill to put together." She smiled modestly. Supper was then rounded off with sherry trifle dessert, prepared in stemmed glasses. Savouring this final course, again, they brought each other up to speed on current events over some light conversation.

Ian topped up their champagne; well, Barbara went to the lounge and selected a window seat. He joined her there. Mirrored moonlight from a tranquil dark lake's water made the perfect romantic backdrop for sipping champagne. Words weren't needed to appreciate the moment. Sitting close, enjoying soft music was the only requirement needed to capture this perfect setting. He took empty glasses to set aside, gently took her by her hands, and looked into her eyes.

"I think it's time for my gift to you." He reached into his inside jacket pocket and pulled out a large envelope bound with a red ribbon. "I never did buy you a wedding gift Barbara, so this is my wedding gift to you." She carefully slipped off the ribbon and removed a document from the envelope. She glanced through it, occasionally turning her gaze at Ian in what seemed to be bewilderment.

"Aren't these the deeds to the house, Ian?"

"Yes, they are. I've transferred the deeds over into your name. The house is yours."

"I don't know what to say. Ian, this is the best evening of my life. I love you so much. Tiers of joy flowed from her eyes as she put her arms around Ian's neck and kissed him. It was a wonderful gesture making the house legally mine, but it will always be our home." Taking her by the hand, he led her upstairs without saying a word.

* * *

Leaving Ian to a little more sweet slumber, she slipped on her robe and made her way quietly down to clear away the evening dining room aftermath. It was a pleasant surprise to find everything had already been tidied away. In her excitement, it had slipped her mind Roger, Tom, the builder's nephew, and his bride Brenda were about to move into the basement apartment. Brenda, as of this day, would be taking over housekeeping duties for Barbara. Brenda greeted her from the kitchen door.

"There's a pot of coffee made. I've been expecting you down. Would you like breakfast?"

"Coffee and toast will be fine, thank you." A slightly bedraggled Ian showed his face next. "Good morning, sleepyhead. You look a little worse for wear this morning."

"Oh, I'm fine. Just not quite come to myself yet. A cup of coffee should do the trick; it'll give me the caffeine jolt needed to jump-start my engine. I have a mountain of work to do in the next two weeks, so I'll drink my coffee, toddle off to my office, and make a start on it. Agendas for the summit meeting before Christmas will be due on Pet's desk by then. I'm just grateful this work can be done at home. Robert should be joining us within the next few days. At present, he's working with Lord Simpson's security team preparing for the conference."

"It'll be nice seeing Robert again. When we've finished coffee, and before you retreat to the seclusion of your office, I'll introduce you to the two new people I'll be representing."

"I'll top my coffee up and take it with me in that case. After you've made the introductions, I really must go to my study to make a start on that work."

"You don't intend working all day looking like that, do you?"

"If I'm good enough to meet these people you've been telling me about, then I'm sure I'll pass for working in the privacy of my own study. After all, isn't that what working in the comfort of your own home is all about."

"When I said finished coffee, and before, retreating to your study: in the (and, and, before, bit), I expected you to wash shave and make yourself presentable. Now off you go and tidy yourself up." Muttering and grumbling to himself, Ian headed for the shower.

Returning sometime later, casually dressed but looking smart, he got her nod of approval.

"Now that's the Ian, I know." Walking to the studio control room, they looked in on Tony first. "How are things going."

"Oh! Hi, Barb's, Ian. Things are going well, so we're about due for a break." He answered into the studio intercom. "OK, people, what do you say we take a break." As instruments were discarded, Tony, Barbara, and Ian entered the studio. Barbara introduced Ian.

"Ann, Jack, I would like you to meet my husband, Ian. "Jack's Avebury's new band member, and Ann's the beautiful, talented singer you've heard so much about." Ann blushed.

"Your embarrassing, the girl, Barbara." Slipping his arm around Barbara's waist, Ian drew her close. "On behalf of both of us, I'd like to thank you all for the flowers and champagne. It was a nice gesture and was much appreciated. That being said, I'll leave you to enjoy your break." He squeezed Barbara reassuringly, accompanied by a kiss to her forehead, before making his exit.

"OK, back to business. How's that demo tape progressing?" Tony looked to Ann for confirmation before replying. Ann acknowledged with a nod.

"Very well, I'd say. I still have some overlaying to play around with, but by Friday, or early Saturday, we should have it all wrapped up."

"That's what I was hoping to hear. I contact Jeff Morgan in Los Angeles to fill him in on what I have in mind. I'll leave you to it. If you need me, I'll be in my office."

A busy Los Angeles morning coincided with a fruitful late afternoons wrap-up in England.

"Hi Jeff, it's Barbara Shaw."

"Barbara, great to hear from you. You've phoned at an opportune moment. How can I help you?"

"I have a demo tape I'd like to send you. I'd appreciate you promoting it for me. I'll also enclose the material you were so keen on for your own singer, plus more."

"As I said, an opportune moment Barbara. I've started my own label, so your work and the tape you're sending will be most welcome. After I've heard the tape, I'll see what I can come up with for you."

"The girl I have is good, so I've had Avbury do back up, with string overlays. It'll be geared to impress."

"The only one you'll have to impress is me, and your songs have already done that. I'll sign you to contract in a New York minute. All you have to do is say the word." She laughed.

"You're an old flatterer, Jeff, but I do appreciate the thought."

"It's not flattery; I know hot when I hear it, but if I can't sign you, I'll take all the songs you can send me. And it's an open offer on that contract."

"Thanks, Jeff, but I'm a little too busy for anything like that right now. Please let me know what you think of that tape when you hear it."

"Will do. I will call you soon." Putting down the phone, Barbara smiled to herself, well rubbing her hands smugly. Confident there would be a deal in the works for Ann. Long hard workdays served to enhance limited personal time. Evenings became moments of cherished memories.

CHAPTER 17

A day trip to Bath.

Bill Ackerman's association slowly developed into a close friendship. He was making good on his promise, directing studio time Barbara's way. However, this much-appreciated business only served to make workdays longer. Hard work has its rewards, so she and Ian were fare enough ahead of the eight-ball to afford a day off by the following week. A day they decided should be spent on an outing to Bath. Ann was leaving the next day after wrapping up her demo. Robert was at a loose end, and Tony's schedule seemed extremely flexible when Ann was around. So, they were invited along on this jaunt.

Barbara's plans didn't include dragging three men kicking, and screaming, around clothing stores, so she suggested they visit the hot baths to enjoy an afternoon spa treatment. The two women, now unfettered, could let themselves loose on the cities boutiques.

"Time to shop until we drop Ann. We'll meet up with you boys at the baths in two or three hours." Tony's fabricated tease was explicitly aimed at Barbara.

"That's alright if you're late; I'll take Ian and Robert to the nearest pub. It won't be hard to find us; we'll be propping up the bar."

"No, your not." Barbara's reply was sharp and humourless. I'm not having you goading Ian into getting drunk this afternoon. Besides, I know Robert would never allow something like that to happen." Robert looked sheepishly at Ian as the two bust into laughter.

"Come on, Ann, this is obviously some kind of inside joke, and they're just going to tease me if I stay longer. Let's leave them to stew in their hot bathwater."

Ian, Robert, and Tony, intent on indulging themselves in every spa pleasure offered, visited the masseuse first. Neglected fitness ethics, coupled to a small frame, ill-prepared Tony's beer diet body to absorb the pummeling Robert's rock-solid form, or Ian's athletic build could accept. An embattled Tony quickly found sanctuary in hot tubs, cold pools, and the relaxing effects of warm mineral swimming pool waters. Several hours of self-indulgence signalled an end to these extended pleasures.

After showering and dressing, they became embroiled in a race upstairs to the pump room with newly invigorated bodies with excess energy to burn. The pump room's tearoom was a Georgian-style tea room overlooking the Georgian baths, where they'd arranged to meet Barbara and Ann. Obviously, the girls had dallied longer than anticipated in the stores, and boutiques, of Bath. This gave Ian and co; ample time to participate in the ritual of English high tea. It was a pump room specialty.

The girls arrived with a bounty of bargains and must-haves. Tony was quick to assist Ann set down her shopping. This conspicuous hovering continued until the girls were finally allowed to be seated. Some of the afternoon's spoils were enthusiastically displayed.

"I see you ladies weren't only satisfied with window shopping." Ian's little jab raised one of Barbara's eyebrows."

"Ian! Half the fun of shopping as a twosome is to see something you must have and then, being talked into buying it, against your better judgment. So now you know why women always like to shop in pairs. For a married man Ian, you seem to know very little about the more logical thoughts of women when compared to those illogical thoughts of men, like yourself." Robert looked at Ian and shook his head.

"When will you learn? You're not going to win these verbal sparring matches you always seem to maneuver yourself into. You've just been put firmly in your place, and I think it was done exceptionally well. Why don't you try to redeem yourself by fetching the girls a pot of tea." Ian trotted off, tail between legs, well trying to maintain as much dignity as possible.

"I've brought a large pot and another platter of cakes, so if anyone would like more, there's plenty. While waiting for you girls, we contemplated how a visit to the Roman baths might prove interesting. They're located in the lower level of this building."

"What do you think, Ann? I think we might find it interesting."

"Sounds good to me, Barbara. That hot cup of tea's making me feel less like a pop-sickle, but staying inside for a while longer would suit me fine."

"Well, it's unanimous then; we take the tour. Robert, and I'll take your shopping to the car, well the rest of you finish your tea. It was apparent Tony's attentiveness to Ann was a little more than just good manners. Thinking it might be cruel and unusual punishment to drag him away from her company, he was not invited to help with that particular task.

"We'll meet you in the main lobby."

When they arrived, a small group of early birds congregating in the lower level were conversing with the tour guide. As the crowd grew, she escorted them into the main baths to begin the tour.

"I'm Mrs. Brown, your tour guide for today. I'll be accompanying you on a journey back in time to when Bath was a Roman city. This place was, at that time, probably a central focal point of the community. Casting your minds back two thousand years when these baths were a place to socialize, relax, and perhaps network much the same as people today would. Imagine crowds of people dressed in garments similar to those you probably noticed depicted in lobby murals as you entered.

As Roman citizens, we would expect entitlement to all amenities and pleasures our wealth could afford us. Opulence can be seen in marble fixtures such as fluted columns, statues, and tiled floors throughout this complex. This display of wealth undoubtedly was due to an exceedingly prosperous population. These features can still be appreciated today because of structural integrity that has resisted the ravages of time." As with all experienced guides, she was an excellent storyteller whose spill was polished and well-rehearsed. After more reminiscing, she moved on to explain its recent history.

"Today, these baths are still fully functional, showing building methods used by Roman engineers were built to last. However, over the years, the River Avon, which runs nearby, flooded this area frequently. Silt deposits, accumulated over centuries, completely buried the structures we see here today. These columns that stand approximately fifteen feet in height were hidden entirely. Where we now stand is thirty feet below today's ground level. When the Georgian baths were built, no one knew the Roman baths existed below. Workmen discovered Roman coins in an old well. This prompted an archeological excavation. When the main pool, you see before you, had been cleared of silt, it filled itself with hot spring water. This flow happened automatically through the original plumbing system, and it does not leak. This system is a fantastic testament to Roman plumbing and the six-inch sheet of lead that lines the pool's bottom. Now allow me to point out the smaller pool at this end of the main pool; this is the cold-water pool. It is fully functional. In a horseshoe around the cold pool, there are hot tubs. They are Individually carved from solid marble and stand on a subfloor. Each tub has a fire hearth underneath this subfloor to heat the hot tub's waters above. We will now go below to view the hearths. After that, your tour will conclude."

Reaching the hearths, she gave her final lecture, and then before leaving, pointed out more things of interest.

"On this level, there's also a museum you can independently browse through. If anyone has questions, now would be the time to ask, and I'll be pleased to answer them, so thank you for being such a good audience."

Small museums, however fascinating, can only hold the attention of a group for a short while. Even Ian's thirst for trivia knowledge soon waned.

"Let's take a drive around the city, then later we'll find a country pub where we can have supper." As they neared the exit, Ann pulled up the collar of her coat.

"I don't know about anyone else, but just the thought of going outside makes me shiver. So, a drive in a warm car's fine by me." No one else voiced an opinion, so Ian assumed it to be a unanimous decision.

Driving through a park, situated on one of Bath's seven hills, a similarity it shares with Rome, the shadows of dusks shadows had now arrived. Low light was obscuring the visual beauty of their surroundings, so Ian drove on. They passe and on through an avenue of London plane trees, towards Bath's Georgian Crescent. This well-illuminated example of multi-storey terraced Georgian homes, built of bath stone, formed the famed crescent. Bath stone is a light-coloured natural sandstone cut into large square bricks and utilized as blockwork in construction. Black painted wrought iron guard railings fronted inward opening upper floor French doors. This matched the guard railings fronting the houses. All remaining trim, and doors, also painted black, made for a perfect colour contrast to the light-coloured sandstone. Steeps leading down from the above street level main floor embraced its flagstone sidewalk. This sidewalk, in turn, was fronted by a cobblestone street. A small park arcing in tune to match the crescent also accommodated an exterior walkway. A low stone wall with an iron railing painted black, in keeping with balustrades in front of the houses, separated the park's sidewalk. From this same direction, floodlights illuminate the homes in the crescent's exteriors. On such a dark evening, the highlighted building's architecture exhibited all its glory. Ian stopped the car for a moment.

"You can see why Bath has the reputation of being one of the best examples of Georgian architecture." He paused in silence for a while, allowing everyone to appreciate this spectacle.

"I'll head towards home now if there are no objections. If we make a slight detour, there's a pub that has a good menu."

"What pub's that, Ian? Do I know it?"

"You might, it's called The Waldegrave. It is just past Pensford on the Wells Road."

Cold driving rain, beating down hard made roads resemble rivers. Paddling would have been mandatory to reach the pub's front door. So, Ian let everyone out at the main entrance. Using his umbrella, he ushered the gang in, and if he'd had a cloak like sir Walter Raleigh, he would have most surely laid it on the ground for Barbara.

Parking in the back car park, he then made a quick dash for the rear door. On entering, he shook the excess rain from his coat and discarded the umbrella. He then joined Robert at the bar, where he'd ordered their drinks. Together they ferried trays of refreshments to the fireside table, where everyone had settled. Tony had snuggled his chair close to Ann's: although she seemed oblivious to the attention, he poured her way.

The pub's evening opening hours had not long begun, so Ian's party were its first patrons. The Waldegrave was a typical English country pub, cozy, charming; with an atmosphere that welcomed guests. Its food menu proved extensive, ranging from trout almondine to rack of lamb, stakes, curries, seafood, chicken, and so much more. They ordered a wide selection of food. When they'd finished eating, Robert pushed his plate to one side and washed down the last morsels with a swig of beer.

"I could get used to pub grub, as you Brit's like to call it. It equals the cuisine of a fine restaurant at pub pricing."

"Well, I'm glad everyone seems to have enjoyed dinner. What I would like to suggest for the remainder of the evening is we return home, and if willing, Barbara entertains us with her singing." Ann offered assistance.

"Tony and I can help with the entertaining. Hot chocolate, sitting around a fire in the lounge, will make it seem Christmassy, especially if we all join in with some carol singing." Tony stood up and drained the last dredges from his glass.

"Let's settle the bill and leave." Ian took out his wallet.

"Let this be my treat." Well, he was paying the tab; he asked for the use of the phone.

Placing a quick call to Roger and Brenda in the basement suite, he inquired if they knew where he might buy a Christmas tree that evening. Roger came through with an offer Ian couldn't refuse.

"Well, Ian, Brenda and I were going out tomorrow evening to buy one ourselves. It wouldn't be a problem for me to take my truck and go right now, and I could pick one up for you at the same time."

"Thank you, Roger; I'd like to take you up on the offer."

"It would be my pleasure, Ian."

Ian hung up the phone and joined everyone in the bar. After donning their coats, they went outside to brave the elements.

Roger, and Brenda's logging expedition completed, they returned with trees shortly after Ian drove into the driveway. It then became a communal activity setting up both trees. When final adjustments had been made, with no doubting Thomas's disputing if trees were set up correctly or not, they invited Roger and Brenda to join the sing-along. It was a memorable evening, with more than a few snapshots taken as a record to ponder over in some distant future. As with most happy times, they pass all too quickly. The singing and storytelling around a roaring fire came to an end in the wee small hours of the morning. A weary group of revellers had succumbed to the beckoning of some cozy beds.

Over donuts and coffee, a business meeting with Ann was the first order of Barbara's day.

"I know I've given you all the details for your upcoming schedule, but I've written down your itinerary on this sheet." She passed Ann the information, which Ann flipped through. "The shows I've booked for you, Ann, I've kept near as possible to where Avebury will be working.

That way, their road manager will be able to look after you also. If you have any problems, I'm only a phone call away, so good luck, and I'll try to come to see you next week."

"Thanks, Barbara. I'll look forward to your visit." Ann fairly bounded out of the office, barely able to contain her excitement. She was going on tour with a paycheck to look forward to.

In the coming week, Barbara's intentions were clear; to help Tony record music he'd been working on. His newfound musician friends made frequent stops at the house, and she foresaw a new group forming. A group honing their skills through trial and error and feeling each other out before recording Tony's work together.

Two days after Ann's departure, Barbara drove Ian to the airport. Having to return to Zurich to prepare for the conference, Ian rediscovered enthusiasm for the job. This was something that had alluded him of late. Fetcher was on hand to help Ian and Robert with their luggage as Ian said his fond farewells to Barbara.

He caught the last glimpse of her waving to him from the lounge as his aircraft taxied for take-off. His return wave probably went unnoticed as aircraft engines roared and the plane soared skyward.

CHAPTER 18

And on the world stage.

Ian sifted through the backlog of correspondence that had accumulated on his desk. In the process of doing this chore, he was interrupted by a call from Ingrid.

"Pete Peterson requires your presence immediately." Promptly trotting along to Pete's office door, he gave it a light tap, tap.

"Come in. Ah, Ian, when I said as soon as possible, you really took me at my word. You must have flown here. Sit yourself down. We have a lot to discuss. Plans you've been instrumental in drawing up for the upcoming summit meeting will set the stage for our real goals. I am about to fill you in on the big picture. It's a plan far too sensitive to be committed to paper. We intend the policing action in Vietnam to become a full-scale war. This will fire world economies, especially in industrialized nations. Increased gross national products in these countries will mean higher wages, higher prices, and tax increases. Higher taxation will sustain economic growth for several years. Arms manufacturers and petrochemical companies will stand to increase their profits considerably. They, in turn, will be seeking funds for expansion. With spiralling inflation, interest rates will rise, and countries will be forced into debt."

Ian made a quick analysis of what he thought the outcome of this would be and voiced his opinion.

"This would surely mean an economic depression within a few years."

"We feel this boom could be maintained for ten to twelve years. We will have achieved our objective, with better economic control over every major world power by that time. There will be no country capable of paying off their loans to us."

"Western nations would not allow themselves to be drawn into such a situation surely, Pete."

"Ian, it's imperative heads of state at this meeting be convinced the free world is losing ground to communism. They must also be confident that the expansion of communism in Southeast Asia will mean a loss in their oil assets. Subsequently, if communism is allowed to expand at this rate, it would mean a gradual end to western economic dominance and the total collapse of their own economies." Ian questioned the strategies of this plan.

"Then this would mean communism will prevail either way. Unless they're coerced into a parallel situation.

"Correct on the second count Ian, they too will be forced to do the exact same thing to protect their foothold on power. Also, with their weaker economies, they will be more susceptible to a balance of payments deficit. Our long-term goal will make it easier for future control of oil, food, and raw materials. And your proposal for easy credit to every person through a credit card system will work well with this plan. A credit line of this nature will serve to increase the national debt of each nation. It was well-received by our head, Mr. Luke Desate. He liked the concept. Eventually, cash could be eliminated, and all transactions would be channelled through the banking system. No one could perform transactions without our knowledge, and everyone would have their own bank number." There was an element of surprise in this statement for Ian.

"I thought Lord Simpson was the head of the company. That he intern would be answerable to a board of directors. I assumed this board would be the representatives of the major banks of the world." Pete Laughed.

"That's a naive thought, Ian. I would have expected more from you. Lord Simpson never makes policies. He takes his orders direct from

Mr. Desate. Mr. Desate takes orders from no one. Let me put it this way; in every system, there's always a dominant figure. Every board of directors has its chairman. In the banking industry, Mr. Desate's word is absolute. Lord Simpson is chairman of the board of directors of The World Bank, and there's no one on the board that would oppose his decision." Ian was amazed at what he was hearing.

"This implies one man controls all world commerce. He could virtually start or stop wars, famine, crate prosperity, or rescission, at will."

"Now you're getting the picture. To some extent, this is true, but control is not always absolute. Although I imagine that to be his ultimate goal."

"That's pretty scary when I think about it, Pete. Perhaps it is as well for me that I am just a tiny cog in this vast mechanism."

"You underestimate your position in the company Ian. In banking, I am directly responsible to Lord Simpson and no one else. I have three people besides yourself answerable to me. We also have security teams that handle covert operations. Now you know your status in this company, you can fully appreciate the importance of your work. Work that in your time with us has proved invaluable."

"You make it sound like I am sitting on the right-hand side of god, Pete." Pete flashed a sombre glance.

"I sometimes think of it more like the left-hand side of the devil." Ian laughed at Pete's play on words. But Pete's poker face did not crack. Ian found this strange, never having pictured Pete as a cynical person. The moment passed as Pete continued the briefing. "Your job at the conference will be to lobby heads of state from the free world. This you'll do through the delegations they'll be bringing to analyze talks. These delegations, in turn, will advise their heads of state on appropriate policies to endorse. You can best make our policies clear by the use of graphs compiled from reports you've formulated. From these reports and charts, you will prove to them the only way to maintain a strong economy is protectionism. Enforcement must be maintained even at the price of full-scale war. You can then point out the negative side of events if your recommendations are not followed to the letter. All your meetings will take place before the main summit meeting, which will merely serve as a public endorsement of policies."

"Pete, If some member countries will not endorse recommendations for full-scale war, how would you suggest I handle it?"

"We don't anticipate everyone committing their countries to war, Ian. We just need the United States to make further commitments with little opposition from other western nations."

"I see. Then I can assume I'll have been assigned a conference room for my presentation."

"Conference room three, I believe. Robert will be able to give you more information on that than I can. After all, he helped coordinate security for you on these meetings."

"Fair enough. I'll consult Robert."

"You'll also be required to host several receptions for heads of state and their delegations. Again, Robert can enlighten you on arraignments for these functions. He has a detailed report of your itinerary for the next three days. I know this is short notice, but it was an oversight on my part. We would like your wife at your side, hosting these social functions. Heads of state, and delegates, will be accompanied by their wives, so it's only fitting your wife should attend."

"I'll get in touch with her immediately Pete, she'll be here tomorrow."

"Well, Ian, I think I've covered everything; if anything crops up that I've missed, don't hesitate to get right back to me."

"I won't, Pete, thanks." Leaving Pete's office, he prepared for some fancy footwork to convince Barbara she should drop everything and join him at a moment's notice. He was apprehensive as he picked up the phone.

"Barbara, there's something extremely important I need you to do for me. It's a big favour."

"It must be urgent to hear from you so soon, nothing serious, I hope, Ian."

"No, it's nothing like that, Barbara. I know this is a lot to ask, but I need you to drop everything for a few days and join me in Zurich. I'm hosting several receptions, and I need you as hostess." Barbara's own work agenda, and ambition, would never allow her to play second fiddle to Ian's carer, so her reply was abrupt.

"The answer is no, Ian. I'm too busy right now."

"Please, Barbara, at least consider it."

"What kind of reception is so important that I should drop everything at such short notice to play hostess."

"OH! we'll be hosting functions attended by the President of the United States, prime ministers of Great Britain, Commonwealth countries and other superpowers. " There was silence after Ian finished talking. "Hello, are you still there."

"Yes, Ian, I'm still here; you had me going there for a moment. I suppose I deserved a smart-ass comeback like that for being so abrupt with you. I'm sorry."

"It's not a joke. I really need you here."

"You've got to be still kidding me, right, Ian?"

"Barbara, can you just be here?" The anxiety in his voice told the story.

"Oh! Yes, of course, I'll be there for you. I just need time to take this all in. You never told me your work was this important. In fact, you've never told me much about your work at all."

"Yes, I realize that, but most work I do is on a need-to-know basis. As a banker, I've never been in the habit of discussing my work with anyone, as most transactions are confidential and boring. You've been instrumental in helping me separate my private life from business, and I like it that way. After my grandmother died, and before I met you, I had no private life to speak of. My work was my life. Work to me now is a chore I must do, and time shared with you is my reality. It was never my intention to be secretive about my work, but you've never asked, and I've never found the need to mention it."

"I'm sorry, Ian, I didn't intend you should explain yourself to me. It's just that I am so surprised at what you've told me. I'm still in shock."

"Just pack a bag and go to the airport. Your flight arrangements will be made by the time you get there. Just go to the VIP lounge, and they'll look after you. I'll meet you at the airport this end. Until this evening, Barbara. Love you." Her mind, a buzz with what had just transpired, induced a quiver in her reply.

"Love you too, Ian."

A heavy hand slapped the door as Ian hung up the phone.

"Ian, it's Robert."

"Come in." The door opened to a flamboyant-looking Robert. "My God, who dressed you today?"

"I'm trying to change my image. What do you think?"

"I like the old Robert better."

"The old Robert isn't attracting the ladies, Ian. So, I thought, with this upcoming function, it was time for a wardrobe change." Ian shook his head in disbelief.

"I thought this function was going to be a twenty-four-hour-a-day job for you, not a social event."

"Well, you never know, and I think I look rather, Sheik."

"When are you going to have the chance to wear those clothes. When you're on duty, you're supposed to blend in, not stick out like a sore thumb."

"I plan on looking more like one of the guests than security. I'll be mingling in the crowd. How do you like the mike in my lapel and my earpiece."

"I'm sure they prove essential for picking up women. Anyway, Robert, what are you here for, other than to give me eye strain." Robert sniggered at Ian's friendly sarcasm.

"Well, there are a few things I need to go over with you, Ian. Is now a good time?"

"Now's fine, but first, I must make some travel arrangements for Barbara."

"So, you managed to sweet-talk her into coming then. You old silver-tongued devil you." Ian phoned Barbara's travel requirements through to Ingrid for her to deal with. His slate was now clear.

"OK, Robert, now you've got my undivided attention."

"Well then, Ian, how about we take a tour of where you'll be holding your upcoming meetings and functions. I suggest we start with the conference rooms." He ushered Ian in through the back door. "Your meetings will be private, so the front doors will not be used. Tight security will ensure a press blackout of all happenings. The main summit will also have high-level security, but news media will be in attendance. They'll be allowed to photograph heads of state, coming and going, plus access to the press gallery. A room will be set aside for you to address the media with prepared statements at appropriate times. For absolute secrecy, your briefings with delegations will start at three-thirty A.M. preceding all summit talks. This will allow your delegates to formulate their recommendations and present them to their respective heads of state. This can be done before the summit debates commence. A ruff schedule for you, I'm afraid. Now let's take a drive to the hotel where receptions, and banquets, are to be held."

Robert, like a kid with a new toy, put his concealed radio to use. He called for a car to meet them at the front door.

"Does that thing work in the car, Robert?"

"I've been assured it will, providing we're not out of range, and it does have an extensive range, or so I've been led to believe. Neat gadget, don't you think." Ian just gave a smile. "All Lord Simpson's security is equipped with them, it's little things like this that give a team the edge, and they're the best men you'll find anywhere. I find them very professional and easy to work with." Their car came to a halt.

"So, this is the hotel, Robert."

"This is it. Many heads of state will be staying here, and that's why it was chosen for banquets." Robert again took Ian step, by step, through security arrangements.

"That'll be my most challenging job, keeping tight security on what's perceived to be a social event. There will also be celebrities from the press and television attending these events.

Armed security guards will be covering all entrances and exits, naturally, under our team's direct control. I think that's all you need to know. Now, is there anything you're not clear on, Ian?"

"As you say, security's your baby, so I think you've clued me in on everything I need to know. How about lunch before we head back to the office. It'll give us a chance to sample the food here."

"Lunch sounds good to me about now."

* * *

Walking to the car, Robert's appetite satisfied; he looked at ease with himself.

"Now, I can afford to relax for a while. I'll be able to get a little R and R before delegates start arriving tomorrow."

"Speaking of relaxation, I've been meaning to ask, have you made plans for Christmas, Robert?"

"You're the only family I have, Ian, so Christmas has always been a lonely time for me."

"Then you've answered my question, you'll spend Christmas at home with Barbara and me. Who knows, maybe Barbara's brother will be able to join us."

"I'd like that very much, Ian, and it would be the icing on the cake to see Johnny again."

Returning to the office, his first priority was to check Barbara's flight arrival time. Embroiling himself in work was the best way he knew of blocking the anticipation of seeing her soon. This anticipation, he knew, would only cause the time to drag.

It was late evening when she stepped off the plane. Ian took great pleasure in the emotions that constantly stirred within him on their first kiss. Bubbling with excitement, she returned the kiss, over and over again. A porter quickly joined them, pushing a trolley load of luggage.

"Good grief, is this all yours? When I said to pack a bag, I wasn't expecting you to bring your whole wardrobe." He was perturbed that his next surprise would seem to have been scuttled. "I've arranged a shopping expedition for you tomorrow, as part of my way of saying thank you for coming at such short notice. I thought you'd enjoy buying new clothes for this occasion." That bought him another rain of kisses before she snuggled her arms around him to walk together to the waiting limo.

"Well, you didn't tell me that, and I didn't know what I would be expected to wear, so I brought everything. Anyway, you really know the way to a girl's heart by giving me a shopping spree for clothes. I can always make room for more clothes.

You're so thoughtful. I'm so going to enjoy myself, even the flight you booked me on was great. People were falling over themselves to serve me. I could quickly get used to this VIP treatment." She continued to bask in all the attention as her luggage was delivered to a waiting limousine. She was suitably impressed with Ian's apartment building when they arrived. On entering, he gave her the grand tour of her temporary home while the driver delivered her luggage.

"So this is your home away from home, Ian. It's very plush."

"This is not my home, and it never could be. Without you, it's just a place I stay when I'm working in Zurich."

"Then, for the few days I'm here, I intend making it our home."

She hugged him around the waist and kissed him. The Driver returned with the remainder of her luggage before leaving.

"Let me make you some hot chocolate. We can sit in bed and drink it well we talk."

"That sounds like a good plan, Ian. I'll be wearing something special for you tonight." She gave a sassy wink as she left the room. Ian set the hot chocolate on the side tables and slipped into bed to wait for her. She emerged from the bathroom and strutted towards the bed in a sultry manner. Her curvaceous body, skimpily clad in silk and lace, fired Ian's blood temperature far higher that of his hot chocolate. He threw back the covers inviting her in. Straddling his loins, she tantalized him with body movements. His hips undulated with the motion that was reminiscent of an ocean's swells. She then suckled his body into hers. Gentle ocean swells making landfall often becomes turbulent, blanketing the shore in heavy surf. A surf that pounds, recedes, and pounds back relentlessly until the tide's zenith is reached, then in its ebb, tranquillity once more returns to the beach. Drenched in exhaustion, it was time to sit back in bed and relax, in a way Ian had first envisioned. Barbara glowed with satisfaction: Well, his stallion's blood, pulsing through veins, negated the necessity of talking, so it came slowly.

"I've invited Robert home for Christmas," was the slow introductory to the conversation.

"I was hoping you would, Ian."

"It would be nice if John could join us, then I could finally meet him. I feel like I already know him after hearing so much about him from yourself and Robert."

"That would make my Christmas if he could be with us. I'll phone and ask if he'll be able to make it. I'm sure he must have some leave due. He's not been to England for two years or more." Barbara finished her chocolate and snuggled in. It was the first time his apartment in Zurich did not feel like a hotel room.

The following morning Ian left for the office early before Barbara had awoken. He waited until nine o'clock before phoning her.

"Barbara, I hope I didn't wake you."

"No, I've been awake a little while."

"I've arranged for a car to pick you up at ten-thirty and take you shopping. Robert's invited a few delegate's wives to join you. The chauffeur has a company credit card for you, issued in your name, so enjoy, and I'll see you this evening. We must be at the reception by seven-thirty, so I'll see you at the apartment prior too."

"How much can I spend on this card, Ian."

"Spend what you like on this occasion. It would be a good time to do your Christmas shopping."

"How much is what I like Ian, I have no idea."

"There is no limit on the card. This is your fee to the company for coming here at such short notice."

"That's a girl's dream come true. But don't you think I might break the bank?" Ian laughed.

"If anyone could, it would defiantly be a woman. I'll see you this evening, and I know whatever you choose to wear, you'll look like a million. But don't get carried away and forget I'll be picking you up at seven sharp."

Lateness being a woman's prerogative, she was still making last-minute adjustments to her appearance when Ian arrived at the apartment. Visiting the salon for the entire treatment after shopping gave her a gracious yet sexy look. She'd chosen to wear the same blue dress that suited her so well at the first formal affair they'd attended together. As she entered the living room, he was stunned by her breathtaking beauty.

The short wait had been worth his while. Words that followed came from deep within his heart, a place Barbara had easy access to.

"You look stunningly beautiful, my darling. I'll be the proudest man at the reception this evening."

" Thank you for saying that, Ian. You've given my confidence a boost. I'm so nervous knowing I'll be escorted by the most charmingly handsome man there, so I'm sure a lot of eyes will be on me. I still can't believe this is all happening. Today I went shopping with the wife of Britain's prime minister. This evening I'll meet the president of the United States. This is so unbelievable I can't stop shaking."

"You'll be the toast of the ball. You look lovely; you have nothing to be nervous about. Now it's really time to leave."

Arriving at the reception, they were ushered to the foyer to greet visiting guests.

"Now, I'm the nervous one." He took her hand and looked to her for confidence. She gave his hand a reassuring squeeze.

"You'll do just fine, Ian."

As dignitaries and their wives arrived, they were greeted, then entertained with cocktails. Socializing became an easy adaptation for two people who had always shunned this formal element of society. Ian made a brief speech before dinner, welcoming everyone, and when dinner was over, the guests were invited to join the host and hostess in the adjacent ballroom. Taking the led, the orchestra's playing preceded their entrance. It was a successful event with time spent dancing and mingling.

Rounding out the evening with a final speech. Ian then set about finding Barbara in the crowded room. Unbeknown to him, she'd struck up a friendship with the U.S. president's wife. This was good PR for Ian. And by the time he'd located her, the president had also joined them. It was an excellent opportunity for Ian to become acquainted and talk one-on-one socially with the president. Shortly after which the first lady and the president were whisked away by security.

"I think that went rather well, darling: Don't you? I'll have Robert arrange for our limo now."

Returning with Barbara to the apartment, he stayed for a short time. She was sound asleep before he was about to leave for his first early morning meeting, scheduled for three-thirty A.M. Leaving a note on the night table, outlining arrangements for a sightseeing tour the next day. He kissed her softly on the cheek and slipped out quietly.

The following two days for Ian were all work and no play. They became akin to star-crossed lovers as these ships passed all too swiftly in the night. She was content to play the role required of her. The last day of Ian's gruelling summit schedule had arrived. An afternoon luncheon with a few speeches rounded out proceedings.

Socializing after lunch was now a chore, except for Barbara's brief visit by the first lady. In this new acquaintance, Barbara found more common interests than she expected to see in such a famous person. They talked as close friends would until it was time to leave. Joining Ian after saying farewell to her new friend together, they returned to Ian's apartment.

"I hate to kiss and run, Ian, but there are things at home left on the back burner that need my attention."

"I understand and don't think I haven't appreciated that sacrifice. I'll book a flight for this evening. I'll be home myself in two days, and I'll not be required back here until after New Year's Day."

"Good, then we can look forward to the Christmas holidays. Book my flight, then come to bed, and we can enjoy what's left of the afternoon. I intend making the most of it."

Making a quick phone call, he then followed the trail of discarded clothing designed to entice him. Barbara would be flying that evening, but he knew they'd both be soaring long before that time arrived.

CHAPTER 19

Good news for Ann

Fetcher, working the late shift, greeted her as she disembarked. Quick to continue the VIP treatment, he catered to her every need. He felt he knew her well enough to strike up a conversation on the way to her car. His broad west county accent gave colour to his vocabulary. This brogue, heavily entwined in ancient Saxon, emphasized vowel usage.

"I hear you live in the old manor house."

"Yes, we fell in love with the area, so we bought the house."

"The misses, and I, live down in Winford village. There are carol singers in the square on Christmas eve, you know. The whole village turns out for that occasion. The singers dress up to look like something out of an old Charles Dickens novel. When they've about done, they'll walk to church, behind the village, still singing their heads off. Everybody then goes in for midnight mass service."

"What a wonderful way to start Christmas. I think my husband and I may join you."

Reaching the car, Fetcher loaded her luggage. He gave his usual solute, a slight bow of the head as he touched fingers and thumb to cap peak, as she tipped him. After arriving home bushed, she left her luggage in the lobby and went straight to bed.

The following morning Brenda carried her bags upstairs. Knocking softly at the bedroom door so as not to disturb her if she was still sleeping, she whispered there was a fresh pot of coffee waiting in the kitchen. Barbara was awake and answered to say she would be right down.

Tony sauntered into the kitchen to join Barbara for breakfast.

"Good morning, Barbs. Your phone's been buzzing off the wall since you've been away. Jeff's, been trying to contact you from practically the moment you left, and on his last call, he said you needed to phone him."

"Thanks, Tony. I'll make that a priority as soon as I've finished my breakfast."

"Now, how did you enjoy your trip." Exuberant hand gestures embellished her colourful reply.

"You wouldn't believe who I've been hobnobbing with. I've been shopping with the prime minister's wife. I met the president of The United States, and I've made friends with the first lady. She's given me her personal phone number and told me I must say in touch."

"Wow! I'm impressed, Barbs."

"It was an experience of a lifetime Tony, something I'll never forget. Now it's back to work. Apparently, there's a lot of catching up to do. First off, I must phone Jeff and find out what's so urgent."

She topped up her coffee and toddled off down the hall to her office. Setting her fresh poured coffee down near the phone, she placed the call.

"Hello Jeff, it's Barbara, so what's the drift."

"Am I glad to get hold of you at last?"

"Is there a problem, Jeff?"

"No, it's just that things are happening a lot faster than I'd anticipated. I thought your demo tape was good enough to record, so I cut some discs and sent them out to radio stations. At that time, I tried to contact you to sign some contracts. People loved it: The record's been playing on stations right across the country. It's a hit. It'll be on the charts this week for sure. Congratulations, Barbara, you've got my label its first hit record. You should have contracts arriving in your mail by now. Get them back to me as soon as possible."

"Yes, naturally, I will, Jeff, thank you, and I be talking to you again soon." Her calm business demeanour deteriorated into euphoria as she ran out of her office, clapping her hands and yelling.

"Tony, Tony, Tony, it's a hit, it a hit." The commotion brought Tony from the kitchen.

"What are you talking about. What's a hit?"

"Ann's record, your demo tape, it's a hit." Tony's jumped up and down in unison with Barbara. Then his handclapping stopped abruptly. He hadn't totally comprehended what Barbara had said. He then questioned what exactly it was he'd been celebrating.

"Ann has a hit. How did it happen? She hasn't cut the record yet."

"I'll explain later; first, I must tell Ann. I'm supposed to drive up and see her tomorrow, but I can't keep it to myself that long. I'm going today. Keep me company on the trip. We could be there in two or three hours."

"Sounds great. I'll get my jacket and be right with you."

"Meet me at the car in five. I'll fill you in on all the details driving there."

Driving north, they passed through Bristol, then on to Gloucester before reaching Birmingham. Ann had been booked into a small hotel on the outskirts of the city. It was a hotel the band had used before. Barbara was able to drive there without a problem. They found Ann sitting in the restaurant having lunch.

"Hello Ann, may we join you." Ann face beamed at the sight of friendly faces. The road can be a lonely place. She stood up to greet them with an embrace. Tony would have walked there for that welcome.

"This is a pleasant surprise; sit yourselves down. I wasn't expecting you until tomorrow, Barbara, and an added bonus, Tony too. What brings you here today ahead of schedule."

"I've great news for you, Ann. It was too much to keep to myself until tomorrow. The demo we made is going over big in America." Ann interrupted.

"Does someone want me to record your songs?" Barbara's uncontrollable excitement was getting the better of her as she bounced up and down in her chair.

"A record's been cut from our demo, and they expect it to be in the U. S. charts next week."

Ann, overcome with emotion, dropped her knife and fork and stood up. Slowly pushing palms to cheeks, her face paled under pressure. It was now her turn to lose control and jump up and down in hysterics. Racing around the table, she threw her arms around Barbara. There wasn't a dry eye as tiers of joy flowed freely.

"I don't know what to say; it's like my Christmas gift from you, Barbara. I want you to know how much I appreciate you taking me under your wing. Having someone looking after my interests and giving me the moral support, I've so needed has made a world of difference to my life." Tony moved closer to Ann and whispered softly in her ear, putting his arm around her shoulder.

"You'll always have my support, Ann. We're like a family to each other, Barbara, Jim, the boys, myself and now you. We all look out for each other." His voice changed to a more upbeat tone. "This calls for a celebration. I'm phoning the boys and asking them to come over. We'll all go out and buy you a gift, so you always remember this day."

The boys arrived within the hour, and piling into Jim's van, they set off shopping. Jewelry stores were the favoured places where that special gift might be found to mark such an occasion. An hour later, all shopped out and frustrated by the lack of inspiration, a small pin caught John's eye.

"Hey, this might be appropriate." Gathering around the showcase like athletes in a huddle, John pointed out his find. It was a small gold pin, fashioned after a music note and highlighted with diamonds. Barbara shared her opinion regarding the choice.

"I think that'll fit the bill perfectly." As she paid for the pin, Tony fastened it to Ann's jacket. Ann's emotions, still in flux, once more brought her to tears as she hugged and kissed everyone. Tony received an unforgettable kiss.

"This really tops a great day. Thank you, everyone, for helping to make it that much more special."

"It's been our pleasure, Ann. Unfortunately, Tony and I can't dally too much longer. The drive home will be a long one. Before I leave, I'd like to extend an invitation to everyone; you'll be welcome at my home for the Christmas holidays." John, Jack, and Ron said they would be spending the holiday with family but thank Barbara for the invitation. "Well, then Jim, Ann, I'll be expecting you early Christmas eve. Tony will also be there. As you know, he's lodging with me, for the time being anyway. Many hugs and kisses preceded their departure, with farewells dragged out to excess by Tony and Ann.

Barbara turned the car radio down low so they could talk on the drive home.

"Well, Tony, you've not said too much about your project, so now we have time; how about you fill me in."

"Well, you know it's a musical, more of a rock opera, actually. It's developing into a cross between a Wagner opera and West Side Story." He gave a little chuckle.

"I've heard most of the music, and as you say, it's a far cry from where you were. It's top-notch but very different, so how would you like me to market it?"

"I've given it a lot of thought, and this is what I've come up with, Barb's. First off, book some engagements for me, and I'll work the material into an act. I plan on christening my group, The Blue Boys. I'll wear a blue velvet outfit. I even thought of dying my hair from its blond ringlets to black. Then it wouldn't take an Einstein to associate me with Gainsborough's painting. I'm hoping this flamboyant act will draw some attention, giving the songs some recognition.

Remember that actor that had the hots for you a few years ago."

"Oh yes, how could I forget Richard? He wasn't a bad chap, really. The trouble was he had the hots for everything in a skirt. What about him, anyway? How does he fit into all this?"

"With one of those songs I wrote, I did an arrangement to accommodate his voice."

"Tony! you've got to be joking; he can't sing; I've heard him try."

"This can work. I'll have him talk his way through the song. If I can persuade him to record it, people will listen and buy it, just because of who he is. Who knows, it could be a hit; stranger things have happened. If my plan works, and there's interest in my music, I'd like you to market the project as a west end show."

"There seems to be a lot of ifs in this equation, Tony. And there will be a lot of unfamiliar ground I'll be treading."

"It is a dream Barb's, but It's my dream."

"It takes work to make most dreams come true, so let's get our noses to the grindstone and become dream makers. Now there's a plan for this project; how about you fill me in on the storyline."

"It center's around a Saxon nobleman, banished by his father to France, before the Norman invasion. Returning to England, to stand with his king in battle. He arrives too late. The Battle of Hastings is over, and Norman's rule the land. Overwhelmed by remorse for his reckless ways being instrumental in banishment, he returns to his father's castle for forgiveness. He's confronted by his father and young brother's heads at the castle entrance, mounted on pikes. In a rage, he enters the castle, finding twenty Norman knights sleeping in the main hall. He draws his sword and shouts a battle cry to sleeping Norman's. Awake! Awake! His rage draws a lion's strength from deep within. He jumps on the table, and running down it, he attacks without mercy. He slays each and every one of them to a man. Becoming outlawed by ruling Norman's, Saxon peasants look to him as their champion. They refer to him as Hieraward, The Wake. This was his battle cry that rang through the hall that night. The story then follows his exploits up to his capture and execution."

"You have a song that I helped you with about Lady Godiva. Where does that fit into this saga?"

"This is how I imagine the opening scene to be if ever it becomes a show. I picture a nude woman riding a white horse across the stage. I would have the entire cast stood behind her with their backs to the audience and singing that song."

"But how does this fit into your show?"

"Well, Barb's, Lady Godiva was Hieraward's mother, so I thought the nude scene would be a good hook to start the show."

"That's an intriguing plot for a musical. Did you make this story up, or is it a story you read somewhere?"

"It's a true story Barb's, a part of English history."

"I've never heard the story before, Tony. Are you sure?"

"Yes, but most of it was handed down as folklore. Some of his exploits were probably woven into the Robin Hood story if truth be known. Remember Norman's won and the Saxon's lost. The heroic exploits of someone they considered an outlaw would have been played down in their history, don't you think?"

"I must say you have an excellent creative imagination. There's lots of passion and a good storyline, all the necessary ingredients for success. I'd say it has enormous potential, and I like your marketing ideas. I'll ask Ian if he knows anyone that produces or does financial backing for that type of show. As for bookings for yourself, I can get road work for you whenever you're ready."

Reaching Bristol, Barbara was starting to feel a little hungry.

"Would you like to stop for supper, Tony?"

"Make you a deal drive on until we reach the Chew valley, stop in a pub there for supper, and I'll drive home after, Barb's."

"Fine by me, I just didn't know how hungry you were." Stopping for supper in one of the many country pubs that double as fine eateries was a pleasant end to an eventful day.

CHAPTER 20

A memorable holiday season

The airport drive had become a familiar trek. Within two days, Barbara was once again making that journey to collect Ian. Awaiting her arrival, he walked from the main terminal to greet her as she parked. Fetcher trailed behind, pushing a luggage cart laden with Christmas gifts.

"Look's like your lot will be in for a fine Christmas with all the gifts you've bought sir." Fetcher's friendly comments in his slow, broad dialect gave Ian a sense of knowing he was home. As Fetcher loaded Barbara's car, Ian foraged between packages to retrieve one in particular.

"Well, I hope I've not forgotten anyone, Fetcher, and here's a little gift for you and your family."

"That's thoughtful of you, sir. Thank you ever so much." With his gift tucked safely under his arm, he watched and waved as they drove away.

"This evening, I've envisioned finishing up the Christmas decorations. I've bought another tree for the lobby and lots of lights; we must have lots of lights. Everyone will arrive on Christmas eve except John. He'll be arriving on the twenty-third."

"That'll be fine. Robert's arriving the same day. I'm sure they'll have a lot of catching up to do."

"I've also made plans for Christmas eve. Apparently, carol singers gather in Winford village square, dressed in nineteenth-century costume. I think that'll be a picture-perfect start to festivities. When carolling in the square finishes, they led a procession to church well still in song. Once there, midnight mass will be held, celebrating Christmas. We'll then return home and exchange one gift before bed. Christmas morning, I've arranged a Buffy breakfast, well opening our remaining gifts. Finger food will be set out for afternoon snacking, and to round off our day, a traditional turkey dinner."

"It sounds like you've left no stone unturned to create a memorable Christmas for everyone. It'll be good to spend this holiday in our own home with family and friends." She took her eyes off the road just for a moment to give a smile of acknowledgment. He stroked her shoulder. She, in turn, rubbed her cheek against his hand.

"It will, won't it. John will be flying into a military airfield, so he'll be arriving from there by train. I told him we'd meet him at the station. I hope that's all right with you?"

"What time's he due to arrive? I've told Robert I would meet him at Lusgate airport that evening."

"John's due to arrive late afternoon. So, we should be able to pick Robert up after John, with time to spare. I'm meeting the boys and Ann tomorrow. I'd enjoy your company on the long drive."

"Yes, that'll work well for me. I've got a few small gifts for people who won't be spending Christmas with us." She slid her hand onto his leg and slowly massaged his inside thigh.

"We'll have the next few days to ourselves, and I won't have to share you with anyone else."

"I think I've started enjoying Christmas already." He pulled her hand onto his groin.

"Ian! I'm driving." She smiled and gave the family jewels a gentle squeeze before pulling her hand quickly away. "Down, boy, or you'll be needing a cold shower when we get home." He gave a disappointed sigh.

Ian's first job, after unpacking his luggage, was to pour two sherries. He carried the drinks to Barbara and assisted in finalizing Christmas decorations. Orchestrating Ian's every move, his body became an extension of her will to accomplish tasks beyond her physical ability. His impute was only solicited as an ego booster, then masterfully disregarded in favour of her own grand plan. It was a tired and somewhat frustrated Ian that sank into a comfortable chair beside the lounge hearth's warm glow. Still running on adrenalin, Barbara placed her sherry glass on the piano top and sat down to play. This was her way to unwind in the relaxation of this warm, dimly lit room. Soothing tones from mellow songs put him at ease as he watched her play. Silhouetted in the backdrop of a window full of stars in the clear night sky, her form produced a cameo on the glass. Tranquillity subdued the day's stress; as exhaustion commanded, he sat and listened in contentment.

For a brief moment, his thoughts turned to the conference he'd just left. Decisions made there would no doubt put many people's lives in turmoil. Quickly he turned his attention away from those dark despising thoughts of company policies that inflict dire consequences on world affairs. Perhaps Pete was right. Was Desate some kind of devil who had no regard for human suffering. Ian was fully aware; resignation was not an option. The recruitment methods used on him had made that painfully clear. But this was Christmas, a time of peace, and love, a far cry from his work world. A world, in past times, he'd easily disassociate himself from had now become harder to separate from present reality. That unique atmosphere engulfing this peaceful valley again prevailed in his mind. And the comfort of his favourite chair and exhaustion lured him into sleep. Barbara fetched blankets from the closet, and after carefully placing his feet on a foot stole, covered him before retiring to bed.

Time has a way of curtailing pleasant moments in life with its all too quick passage, well granting torturous moments the duration they ill deserve. Reflecting this philosophy in the next few days, including a brief visit with the boys, sped quickly by. On the twenty-third, preparations were in full swing for John and Robert's arrival. Nervous anticipation and excitement mounted within Barbara throughout the morning. Thoughts of seeing John exerted stress that would only be liberated with that reassuring hug and kiss she knew would be her greeting. Three o'clock had taken its own sweet time coming. Ian checked his watch.

"It's time we drove to Temple Meads railway station Barbara." For a woman who had been waiting all morning for that announcement, her reply was no surprise to Ian.

"Just give me five minutes, and I'll be with you." Five minutes became fifteen, so it was no surprise to Ian that their railway station's arrival was a late one. Barbara spotted John waiting outside the main entrance. Barely giving Ian the chance to stop, she jumped from the car.

"It's John." She pointed and ran to him. John was her complete opposite physically. He was tall, robust and fair-haired. No one would suspect they were siblings; there was no family resemblance whatsoever.

Ian inched the car to where John stood before getting out to meet him. Barbara was still draped around John's neck, the position where her flying leap had ended. He supported her body in two powerful arms as both her feet dangled in midair. Tears of joy ran down her cheeks as she rained kisses on him. Finally, letting go and wiping the tiers from her eyes, she turned to Ian.

"Ian, this is my brother John. John, I'd like you to meet my husband, Ian." The introduction was cemented with handshakes.

"I'm pleased to meet you at long last, John. Barbara continuously talks of you, so I feel we're already well acquainted."

"Your no stranger to me either, Ian. Barbara writes wonderful letters filled with stories of your lives together."

"Let's get your things loaded into the car. On our way home, we'll be picking Robert up at the airport." John placed his baggage into the car.

"It's been a long time since I've seen Robert. You'd best prepare yourselves for some tall stories and some taller glasses of beer if he's still the same Robert I remember."

Forty-five minutes awaiting Robert's flight arrival was not enough to catch up on the time of two entire years of separation. However, strong bonds were reinforced over coffee in Lusgate's lounge. Time flew as quickly as Robert's flight, and he was soon standing before them. Robert usually travailed light, but he appreciated some helping hands, being overburdened with Christmas gifts this time.

Driving home, the car's headlights illuminated a landscape that had been recently blanketed with light snow. Glistening hedge row merged with narrow snow carpeted narrow lanes perfectly, giving the illusion of experiencing one enormous bobsled luge ride. Arriving home safely, they unpacked their luggage before meeting up in the lounge, where Ian made himself busy playing bartender.

"Take a seat around the fire, and we'll do some socializing as soon I've poured everyone's drinks." John decided to look out the window before settling.

"Are you a fisherman, Ian?"

"No, but we've talked about building a jetty, and Robert's already picked out a rowboat. Thank goodness power boats aren't allowed on the lake. I'm sure it would spoil its tranquillity. When we have a jetty, I know there will be plenty of willing hands to teach Barbara and myself the finer points of fly fishing."

"That would be my pleasure Ian, I'm a fisherman myself and drag out my rod-and-real whenever the opportunity arises. I'd enjoy teaching both of you all I know about the art of fly fishing. After all, it would be a shame to live beside a lake like this and not take full advantage of it.

"I'll be looking forward to taking you up on that offer. You must visit us often, from here on. I'm sure when the fishing season begins, we'll all be able to spend some memorable hours on the lake." John, practically drooling at the mouth, remained standing to envision that concept. Garden spotlights shed an incandescent glow upon a snowy blanket to contrast sharply with the lake's inky blackness beyond. This landscape held John's imagination captive.

Tony walked into the lounge, cradling a crate of beer like some cherished possession.

"Good evening, everyone."

"John, I'm sure you'll remember to be wary of our resident practical joker, cousin Tony."

"Oh, I'm sure we've not forgotten one another." Shaking hands, they said, (Oh yes) in unison. Tony's eyes singled out Robert.

"I've brought you a case of lager. I know how you prefer your beer cold."

"Well, that's very thoughtful of you, Tony. Only a real beer connoisseur could begin to understand how important preferences in brew choices are. And a nice glass of cold beer would go down well right about now."

Tony walked to the piano, and sitting down, ran his fingers over the keyboard.

"Come on, Barbs, get the old six-string, and join me." It was never easier to persuade a person. She'd already started to fetch a guitar.

"Let me freshen up everyone's drink before the two of you start to entertain us." Robert held up his beer bottle.

"I'm fine for the moment, thanks, Ian." Barbara made herself comfortable on a stool by the piano, well Ian, again played host. Songs then began flowing as freely as the drinks. This small select audience proved an excellent sounding board for some melodies Tony had written for his musical. These were songs never before heard outside the studio. Confidence in the material appealing to a broader audience was reinforced when scrutinizing Ian, John, and Robert's, reactions to his work. Stopping to sip his drink, he then, with arms outstretched, bowed his head to his audience.

"Well, do you like my latest renditions." That brought the round of applause he'd been angling for. Ian elaborated with what he thought was everyone's view of the project.

"If you weave these melodies successfully into the storyline's fabric, which I'm sure you have, success finding a backer should not prove a problem." It was an opportune moment for Barbara to solicit Ian's expertise.

"Would any of your old contacts know anyone who's been involved in that type of financing, Ian?"

"There was an acquaintance, a club member, but I only knew him by name. I couldn't give you a phone number or address."

"All I need is a lead to work with, and the name of a club member may be enough."

Tony continued singing beer hall songs to encourage a sing-along. It wasn't hard to motivate a group whose spirits were higher than those inside their glasses. When singing finally abated, they returned to their seats around the fire. The talk continued until silhouetted hills across the lake became distinguishable once again in a predawn glow.

Late morning brought the arrival of Jim and Ann. Pub lunch at The Prince of Waterloo was favoured rather than someone sweating over the kitchen oven. As in most small communities, the pub was the leading social spot for villagers and local farmers alike. On this early Christmas eve afternoon, it was crowded. Most people had started their holiday celebrating with friends and colleagues before heading home. Christmas decorations adorned the bar creating a festive awareness. A sense of merriment and well-being bathed the pub in this unique Christmas atmosphere. Jim perceived this more than most.

"There's nothing quite like a pub on Christmas eve. There's just something different about it." Jim's philosophizing left the door wide open for a ribbing. Walking through that door, Barbara's quick retort capitalized on the invitation.

"If anyone wanted an expert opinion on the pub atmosphere, there would be no better person to ask than you, Jim."

"A catty remark like that should cost you the first round, Barbara." This tongue-in-cheek return salvo, he figured, was a good defence against more ridicule. Tony was quick to side with Jim, endorsing his request.

"You set yourself up for that one, Barb's. I'll have a pint of bitter." Tony gave Jim a little nudge to the ribs, and they giggled like schoolgirls.

"You're my brother John. Stick up for me."

"Don't look at me; you got yourself into the situation. Buy the round and be done with it."

"You're as bad as they are. You men always stick together." Her purse strings were opened with feigned indignation. There were more than a few sniggers at her muted muttering while paying for drinks.

"What a bunch of cheapskates, inviting me out for drinks and then making me pay." These remarks, aimed at the men in general, were just a wined up to emphasize her hard done by act. There were no seats available, so it was standing room only. Drinks were then ferried to where everyone stood.

Ann was attracting the attention of several young men, which was obviously annoying Tony. Barbara whispered in Ian's ear.

"How sweet, he's in love." This message, discreetly conveyed, left Tony, and Ann, from the loop. Intrigue concerning Tony made him the victim of scrutiny, then sniggers. Feeling bewildered and self-conscious, he checked himself over, trying to establish a reason for the source of humour centred about him. Things were allowed to die down before Barbara's whisper gave him insight into the joke.

"When are you going pluck up the courage and tell her how you feel?"

"What are you talking about, Barb's?" Although feigning ignorance, his red-faced demeanour told a different story than his spoken word.

"You know what I'm talking about; you can't keep a secret like that from me. I know you too well. This could be payback time for all the pranks you've pulled on everyone else."

"Please, Barb's, don't say a word. You'll embarrass me no end."

"All right, Tony, just as long as you talk to her and tell her how you feel."

"Barb's, she may not think of me in that way."

"Don't be such a little chicken shit; there's only one way to find out, and that to talk to her."

John eyed everyone's empty glasses and eased his way towards the bar.

"Would someone give me a hand with the next round of drinks?" Tony quickly took the coward's way out and bailed to forestall the inevitable.

"I will, and I'll get some sandwiches this time." Barbara headed off his procrastination at the pass.

"You're not getting out of it that easy, Tony. You stay here; Ian can give John a hand."

Knowing he had been painted into a corner, he looked at Ann. Not knowing how to broach the subject, he looked to her for some inspirational input.

"Ann." No words followed; his well of creativity thought had run dry.

"Yes, Tony." His open mouth catching flies was accompanied by a stupid vacant look.

"I didn't think I'd see the day you'd be lost for words. Oh, Barbara was right about you; it's all a front. You're shy." She put her arms around him and kissed him as Barbara led a group cheer.

"Well, I see my little talk did have some effect. You really seemed to have swept her off her feet, Tony." A good pun, after seeing Ann nearly ball a surprised Tony over. In an attempt to restore some dignity, he whisked Ann into his arms and returned the kiss. Again, losing composure, he blurted out words that had eluded him earlier.

"Ann, I love you." She put her arms around his waist, and he held her tight to his chest.

"I think you'll have to put each other down for a while; no one's about to feed you both beer and sandwiches." This statement flowed off them like water from a duck's back. With no fresh fuel for the fire, this playful ribbing had run its course. Socializing continued until lunchtime opening hours finished. Tony chose to ride back to the house in Ann's car. He'd initially rode in Jim's car, perhaps hoping things would turn out the way they had. It was several hours after everyone else had returned home that Ann and Tony showed their faces. Joining everyone in the lounge, they sat around talking, well enjoying Christmas treats. Barbara had set out savouries, cakes, a pot of tea, and such like.

Seasons festivities were carried into the evening with Barbara's planned return trip to Winford village for carol singing. Fetcher, and his wife, who lived across the village square, brought pitchers of hot spiced cider. This helped maintain the reveller's warmth and high spirits. This whole scenario had been well organized. Carol singers started their walk from the old church in Dickensian style dress, led by a standard-bearer carrying an old-fashioned candle lantern on a pole. The procession's rear guard carried a similar torch. The choir's distant voices were heard as little more than a muffled chant until emerging into the village center. Songs then pierced a crisp cold night air's silent void. With clarity and tone that out glowed any aura spread by lanterns light. Light snow engulfed performers in this picturesque setting, forming a semicircle in The Prince of Waterloo's car park. Barbara captured this Christmas card scene for posterity with many camera shots.

An hour of singing was concluded with the assembly slowly making its way behind a choir back to the church, still in full voice. Pews were soon occupied by parishioners filing in. Solemn silence rained as individuals meditated in preparation for midnight mass. The old stone church had been given a cosmetic facelift to create warmth and well-being for the special event to follow. The service concluded with a feeling of a profoundly emotional experience fulfilled before returning home.

Hot chocolate was served as Barbara directed everyone into the lounge.

"It's past twelve o'clock, so it's officially Christmas day. Ian and I have bought everyone a present to open now. All other presents must wait until tomorrow morning." Tony objected like a small, tired child, who had just been told its bedtime.

"That's not fair." Jim joined the protest.

"Yes, Barbara, after all, you said yourself it's Christmas day."

"You boys are like children. Half the fun of Christmas is opening presents around a warm fire, Christmas morning. If you open them all now, there will be nothing to do tomorrow morning. For this reason, you have one presents now to circumvent any fuss." Robert and John sported grins a mile wide, viewing the charade being played out before them. Finally, Robert could no longer contain his thoughts on the situation.

"Barbara! You seem to have acquired the mother's role because you're treating them like they're your little boys. And I must say, their portrayal of two adolescents is worthy of an Oscar nomination." John's grin turned into full-blown laughter as a chorus was created by Ann and Ian's accompaniment. Ridicule gave the trio a rude awakening to how ludicrous their antics had sounded. Barbara tried talking her way out of her predicament, embarrassed by what could only be perceived as childish bickering.

"We were just joking around. It was a send-up, you know, a leg-pull. I really had everybody going there, right." Tony wasn't about to blow her cover.

"We were aware of your game, so we worked it with you, Barb's. It was easy playing along to entertain, wasn't it, Jim?"

"Absolutely, we really had them going, didn't we." John's laughter subsided to a grin as he mimicked Barbara ridiculing of the boys as a rebuff to their transparent explanation.

"Remember, you're not allowed to touch any of the other presents until tomorrow morning." She banged her empty mug down on the table and glared at John.

"Well, I've finished my hot chocolate, and I'm going to pour myself a scotch and ginger. Does anyone wish to join me? Scotch sounds really good to me right now. So, she poured herself an exceptionally large one. "John, if you want anything, you can pour your own." He could see this was a payback joke, as she gave him a quirky smile. Ian jumped in, although on whose side it wasn't clear.

"I can see we've ticked off the waitress, so I suppose everyone had better get their own drink from here on." There was a group cluster at the liqueur cabinet. However, Robert found his poison, which was a stash of cold lager nestled in the refrigerator. Armed with drinks, everyone made their way to the fire, where they sat quietly in thought. This moment of mental solitude was enhanced by surrounding friends and loved ones. Each individual stared into glowing embers through crystal glasses, content to sit and sip away the remaining time before bed. Ann snuggled into Tony, and Barbara draped herself around Ian, portraying their inevitable fatigue. It was time for tired people to drift off to their respective resting places.

Barbara's speech about nothing to do on Christmas morning if there weren't presents to open did not apply to her. The thing she wanted most was to stay in bed and nurse a hangover. However, quiet was not in the boy's vocabulary, especially when considering someone with self-inflicted injuries. Excessive noise from their antics was designed to arouse everyone, especially one particular everyone nursing that hangover. Resigned to the fact there would be no peaceful lay-in for her this morning, she reluctantly came downstairs to a round of cheers. Ian handed her a coffee; still ailing, she groped for the cup.

"Everyone's eager to open their Christmas gifts, Barbara." Ian sounded nonchalant to her plight. Cradling a ruffled head of hair with her other sympathetic hand and eyes half shut, she holed up in a chair and sipped her coffee.

"Please! does everyone have to shout? Just give me a minute to come to myself, will you." A minute was defiantly an understatement; her hangover was not one about to pass that quickly. The boys made themselves the unofficial distributors of gifts. A roll Barbara was pleased to relinquish, being self-indulged in pain. Her indisposition contributed to a complete lack of interest in events. This gave rise to more satirical remarks concerning her predicament. Ann eventually took pity on her and volunteered to start preparations for Christmas supper. Tony was quick to render his services. Being close to Ann was his idea of a great Christmas, even if it meant there was work involved. However, he continued to overplay the noise game when he included pots, pans, and anything else that came to hand.

Noon couldn't come soon enough for Barbara, knowing one of the men was sure to suggest a pub visit for a launch time beer. Leaving Ann to handle supper, they were barely out the door before Barbara was back in bed to sleep off what ailed her.

Returning from the pub, it wasn't only Barbara thinking bed rest was a good idea. A few others were also in need of a quick nap. Ian, still being of able body, decided to spell Ann in the kitchen. This gave Barbara a chance to freshen up before supper.

Six o'clock rolled around before anyone showed their face downstairs to join Ian in a glass of sherry. The kitchen became a focal point for helping hands, and only when all the preparations were complete were the dining room chairs occupied. The Turkey was placed before Ian, at the head of the table, for carving. A somewhat wobbly John rose to his feet.

"Before we start, I'd like to propose a toast. Let's give thanks for this meal we're about to enjoy and those who worked so hard to make it possible. I think a special thanks should also be extended to our hosts and." There was a pause in his speech as though he was lost for words. He then quickly rambled through his next sentence. "A merry Christmas and a happy new year to you all, and thanks to our hosts. Ah, I believe I'm repeating myself. Time for me to shut up." Glasses were raised, and the toast was made.

A feast fit for royalty was ferried around the table, turkey, potatoes, vegetables, stuffing, cranberry sauce, and gravy. For dessert, only brandy flambe plumb pudding, served with Devon-shire Cream, was good enough for the occasion. After finishing supper, the favoured choice of drinks was brandy or coffee. They then all retire to the lounge.

Curious to find if Avebury's chart position had altered, Tony, and Jim, decided to take their coffee into another room and listen to the radio for confirmation. They knew a pirate radio station anchored in international waters would be playing current hit parade standings: So they tuned in. Listening intently until their song had been categorized, they then decided to listen on. The weather played havoc with reception as the disc jockey raped up his final spill with an announcement.

"Before I finish, we have a few minutes of show time left, so I'd like to play a new release from a fresh on the scene American artist. Her song's just broken onto the American charts, and I'm sure we will be hearing her in our top twenty next week. My prediction is this young lady is heading for stardom, and remember you heard it from me first." Tony immediately recognized his instrumental arraignment leading into the vocals. He's playing our song; he's playing Ann's recording. Tony could hardly contain himself as he ran to the lounge.

"Ann, Barbara, everyone quickly, you must come to listen. They're playing Ann song on pirate radio." Turning the radio's volume too high, silence rained until Ann's song had finished. The silence that fell in the room could have been cut with a knife. Tears well up in Tony's eyes as he placed his hands on Ann's shoulders. A soft kiss to the back of her neck preceded his quiet words of praise.

"What a wonderful surprise Christmas gift, congratulations, Ann."

His very next comment was intended for everyone else in the room. "They must think Ann's an American girl because the record was released Stateside." This statement definitely annoyed Barbara.

"I'm going to phone that radio station right now and put them straight on her nationality." Jim looked up at Barbara from where he was sitting.

"I don't think you'll be able to do that, Barbara. Those pirate stations broadcast without a license in international waters. They probably wouldn't have phone access."

"Then I'll jolly well write them a letter tomorrow so there." She quelled her ruffled feathers somewhat with that thought.

Everyone filtered back into the lounge, except Jim, who stayed for a while longer, hoping to hear another of Avbury's resent releases, before deciding to join the others.

Caught up in the moment, Tony had forgotten what they'd been listening to the radio for. Jim's solemn tones reminded him.

"I suppose Avebury dropping a spot in the standings was to be expected, " Jim's sad tones indicated he needed pepping up.

"You've got so much more good material coming online. Your next songs can only build on your first success. Trust me, I just know it." Barbara had now wholly joined the land of the living.

"Tony's right, Jim; you should be proud. Things are going so well for Avebury. Your record company doesn't know which song to promote as the A-side on your upcoming release; both sides are exhalant. You'll be reuniting with Avbury the day after boxing day, which should give ample time to put a final polish to your act, before that all-important first TV appearance, on New Year's Eve." She looked at Ann. "Speaking of New Year's Eve, I had a phone call yesterday regarding a local booking. It's for a New Year's Eve dance. It's just a small jig, but it's only a twenty-five-minute drive from here. Tony, I also took the liberty of booking you to accompany her on that new synthesizer you've acquired. It'll be an all-nighter with just the two of you performing. I've tickets for the rest of us, so we'll all be able to spend New Year's Eve together."

"Sounds like a fun job. I'll be pleased to accompany Ann Barb's, but how about joining us? We can make it an improved group." She was a little taken back at Tony's suggestion, but her expression showed intrigued. "Come on, Barb's, it'll be great having you on stage with us." Ann was also warm to the suggestion.

"Tony's right, it'll be great. I know you're also trying to get me some extra pocket money, but why don't you join us? We can make it a real party night."

"Why not? I can play rhythm guitar and spell you vocally, giving your larynx a break."

"How did you come by this booking anyway, Barb's."

"I took it as a favour for a friend. When an act that had been booked was cancelled, they needed a replacement. The dance organizer is a friend of Bill Ackerman. So, Bill referred him to me, hoping to rustle up an act to accommodate their needs.

Putting an act together in the next few days is beginning to sound like fun. What better way for close friends to pass away time than by doing the thing they love most, jamming." The next few days playing around with songs for their new act became almost therapeutic. It was a time that allowed creativity artistry to run wild, unfettered by deadline pressures.

The early New Year's Eve crowd had congregated at the bar as Barbara and the crew finished setting up their equipment on stage. There were more than a few disappointed looks from faces expecting to see a favourite local band. Barbara did not want disappointment to overshadow their opening. Playing frontman, she quickly stepped up to the microphone.

"Good evening, ladies and gentlemen." At least, maximizing her sensual soft velvet tones ensured the attention of every male in hearing distance. "I'm sorry to announce the band scheduled to play this evening is indisposed." Heckling calls broke the background silence, with one particular voice overwhelming everyone else.

"To much Christmas cheer on doubt." This brought a few laughs but many more boos. (Refund) was heard whispered before it became a chant that echoed around the hall. Trying to keep order, she waved her hands in a calming motion. Thinking on her feet, she aimed her vocal charms at appeasing a hostile crowd.

"However, I'm sure you will be pleased to hear we have a few surprises for you this evening. I would like to introduce your band for this evening. On the keyboard, we have Mr. Tony Bishop; some of you may remember him as an ex-member of Avebury." This brought some encouraging whistles from Barbara's family and friends as Tony took a bow. I'm sure you'll be hearing from him soon in the charts. He'll be fronting for a new group, The Blue Boys. On lead guitar, we have the gorgeous Miss Ann Gibbs." Ann gave a strum on her guitar, well curtseying in her tight jeans. This drew more than a few wolf whistles. "Ann's first hit single has entered the American top twenty this week, and it's destined to be a chart-topper. I'm sure you'll all become familiar with her work in the near future. As for myself, I am Barbara Shaw. Tonight, I'll be playing rhythm guitar and singing back up. We've also acquired the skills of Jerry James on drums for this evening. Let's hear a big hand for Jerry, people. I also wrote and co-wrote some of the songs we will be performing for you this evening, plus one currently in the charts. So, you see, I think you can safely say you've been upgraded." She pointed to Ann. "Hit it." Ann stepped forward and laid into a hard fast rock number. This was geared to grab a now susceptible audience. Overwhelming sounds obliterated any heckling that remained. And within five minutes, they owned the stage, palm feeding an appreciative audience to a feast of exquisite ruthenium and song.

A commotion at the main entrance briefly took center stage for revellers close at hand. A group of about twenty teddy boys were trying to gate crash the dance. Reluctantly they were let in after buying tickets, even though it was apparent some were intoxicated. These rabble-rousers seemed hell-bent on intimidating anyone who crossed their path. They obnoxiously mingled with other partygoers.

The band took a ten-minute refreshment break, and Barbara walked down to join Ian. Tony and Ann stayed on stage talking. The leader of the gang made a grab at Barbara as she passed him by.

"Come with me outside, and I'll show you the meaning of a good time." He manhandled her into a kiss. Ian, her knight in shining armour, rushed to her defence. An opportunity several teddy boys had been hoping for. A fight ensued. John, being close at hand, went straight to Ian's aid. His unarmed combat expertise would soon demonstrate anyone invoking his displeasure was destined to be nothing more than floor litter.

Thug one was grabbed by the scruff of his neck, raised slightly, then tripped, and introduced to the floor, face first. Thug two was pulled off Ian by John's sturdy left-hand grip on Teddy's collar. After forcing teddy to the ground, John used his foot, placed firmly on Teddy's rear thigh, to hold him down. His clenched hand then twisted Teddy's collar, strangling him into submission. And another face was introduced to Mr. polished floor. Teddies were now swarming like flies, and another came at John's right side. Raising his right elbow to shoulder height, John sighted it at a conspicuous jaw with his clenched fist to his chest. A quick snap extended his arm sideways with a bull whip's power and speed, and it connected squarely on number three teddy's jaw. It dropped him like so much dead meat. Turning his attention to another annoyance, he gabbed this teddies pants seat and collar. Lifting his rear slightly well, forcing him off balance by pushing his head down, an invitation to the bums rush was then extended. This rush targeted a converging mob. John's release was perfect; they were taken down like balling ball pins. He'd scored a strike. It was clear this raucous was over as he stared down any survivors; one riot, one ranger.

Meanwhile, Robert had fought through to Barbara, accounting for several more gang members along the way. Tony had been immediately involved, mixing it up with one thug who had waylaid him as he'd rushed off the stage to aid Barbara. Ann was also doing her bit, punching and kicking Tony's assailant. Big Boy, who had started the fracas by grabbing Barbara, released her and faced Robert.

"Be careful, Robert; he has a cutthroat razor." The thug brandished his cutthroat razor high above his head. Robert gave his usual grin as he reassured Barbara.

"It's just a temporary arrangement." Big Boy gave some threatening slashes towards Robert. Stepping out of range, Robert played it cool, taking time to size up an opponent with a lethal advantage. When Big Boy finally made his move, Robert was more than ready. For a large man, Robert moved like a cat. Swiftly, smoothly, he met his attacker with outstretched hands crossed at the wrists, forming a butterfly. Big boy's wrist was intercepted in mid-swing, lodging firmly in Robert's cross palmed butterfly's V. Robert gave his hands a skillful roll, and the butterfly became a Venus Flytrap. One of Robert's large hands held the Bug's wrist firmly in a twisting lock. His other palm delivered a devastating arm-breaking swat to the back of Big Boy's elbow to resounding screams from the recipient of the blow. There was no stomach for fight left in Big Boy's gang as they hustled themselves through every available exit. It was an exodus of rats scurrying to leave a sinking ship.

With feathers only slightly ruffled, Barbara and Co. were back on stage and ready to play. The audience showed their appreciation with a round of applause, accompanied by whistles and cheers.

"Just like the bar fights of old, Johnny boy." John slapped Robert's shoulder, then checked out Ian, who was dusting himself off.

"Thanks for your help. I don't know what I'd have done without you." Robert, in turn, slapped Ian's back and laughed.

"That's my job. I'm your bodyguard remember."

"I almost felt sympathy for that fellow when you broke his arm after hearing his screams of pain. Don't you think it was a bit severe?"

"No one died, Ian, and they won't be waiting for us outside when we leave. It could have been us going to the hospital and not them. I think just enough force was used. Wouldn't you agree, John?"

"Absolutely, Robert. I don't think he was going to ask if you'd like to borrow his razor for a shave. After all, he was the one with the weapon, trying to use deadly force."

A silence descended on the hall as Barbara took center stage to sing solo. Her debut as a stage performing solo artist. Her soft voice had been indiscernible, singing backup behind Ann's powerful vocals. The audience was soon aware of how talented this singer, pouring out her heart in this poignant love song, realy was. She was not just another rising star in the heavens; this audience was witnessing a supernova. They showered their appreciation on the young women that had entertained them so well as she took her bow. There was little applause, just a steady chant of more, more, more, more. Two more songs were sung accompanied by Ann before the count down to twelve o'clock began.

Twelve o'clock was greeted by balloons released from ceiling netting, and noisemakers replaced band acoustics: Time for lovers and loved ones to embrace and welcome a new year with new hope. Ian went on stage to be with Barbara. Tony and Ann were already closely entwined. Robert and John lucked out as they were ensnared by two women from the crowd. Everyone in the hall joined hands and sang Au-Lang-sine as more balloons were released and popped, making more noise.

The show was over; it was time for the circus to leave town. The hall started to clear as crowds gathered up their belongings and drifted towards home. Ian and company set about packing up band equipment before their exit.

New years day was spent quietly winding down a successful holiday. It took Ian a few days to conclude his work at home before returning to Zurich. John spent another week with Barbara before his return to Aden.

CHAPTER 21

Ian forms a drug cartel.

The now-familiar landscape below them drifted from view as the aircraft entered a cloud bank. Ian's eyes focused on mist outside the aircraft's window, well philosophizing with Robert.

"Do you ever think about the jobs we do?"

"I try not to, Ian. We're assigned a job, and we do it; we don't make policy."

"That doesn't make it right. I've had some serious thoughts on the matter of late. It's as you say, we have no say in policy, but should we do what we do without question."

"You could always resign if it bothers you that much."

"I don't think that would ever be an option for me."

"Perhaps not; you're far too valuable a man, a value that's still being developed into its full potential." There was a short silence before Ian's melancholy tones delved even deeper into cynicism.

"I wonder what death and destruction our next assignment will cause."

"You have no control over it, so just do your job and try not to think about it. Understandably, you feel empty and down, returning to Zurich after such a great Christmas. If you get too depressed, just try thinking of your wife and other good things associated with your life."

* * *

Pete was absent, so Ian utilized this opportunity to address minor daily routines accumulated over the holidays. This menial work was usually directed towards Ingrid. When Lord Simpson ordered Ian's presence was needed immediately in his office, Ian's pottering ceased immediately.

"I have work for you of a highly sensitive nature." The order sounded ominous, but Lord Simpson wasn't a man to say no to.

"You can rest assured project confidentiality will be safe with me, Sir." Although Ian knew this was not a request. Lord Simpson expected nothing less of him, so Ian's words were treated as no more than idle lip service.

"Quite. This is work Peterson usually handles, but he's unavailable at present, so I'm entrusting you with the job, although it's well out of your work scope. The growing drug trade in South America, Columbia, to be precise, is made up of many small warring factions. Control would be less complicated if our dealings were channelled through one organization. First off, this would minimize disruptions caused by constant infighting. I'd like you to go there and orchestrate an end to these petty vendettas. You'll probably need a small strike force to accomplish this mission. Robert will organize and train them to job readiness once you've formulated your strategy. I'll leave you this brief giving you insight as to whom the major players are. It's an in-depth brief containing details of suppliers, distributors, lieutenants, soldiers, etcetera. Plus, there's are enormous amounts of relevant information. I'm sure you'll find it invaluable to successfully complete this assignment. I need not stress that this document must never leave this building." The brief was pushed across the desk to Ian. As he reached for it, Lord Simpson disappeared through the back door like a thief in the night.

Ian needed to talk to someone, and who better than Robert. He found Robert whiling away time constructing paper airplanes in his own office. As he entered, he made a quick evasive manoeuvre avoiding a Kamikaze attack by one on its maiden voyage.

"Glad to see you have your nose to the grindstone and keeping on top of things. So, you must be right up to scratch with our next assignment." Ian's sarcasm was delivered with a broad grin.

"There's been nothing on the grapevine, so I assume it's going to be very hush-hush."

"This one's on a need-to-know basis, so I'll enlighten you on all material directly concerning the execution of a successful mission. You'll have to know practically every detail anyway. I don't think you'd be able to fulfill all your objectives on this one if you didn't know all the facts. It seems we're going into the drug trade to improve their organizational skills." Robert showed a discerning expression as he dissected Ian's statement.

"I was under the impression it's been well organized for a long time." Another paper plane was launched.

"Apparently not well enough to appease company policy. We should go over this brief together. I'll need all the help you can give me on this one; I'm totally out of my depth. I'm used to dealing with businessmen and governments, not gangsters."

"I've always found it hard to tell the difference myself. Governments, gangsters usually are motivated by the same thing, money, so there's our cornerstone for this project. Moneywise, you'll be holding all the trump cards, so I see no problems there."

It was a long night of intrigue, bouncing around ideas, formulating procedures, then subjecting all final decisions to memory. A giant chess game had been set in motion, its goals, to control drug interests in South America. The board game's location they were about to play on was Columbia. Moves and counter moves were meticulously moiled over: Evaluating every deviation to guarantee the inevitable checkmate to Ian. With plans approved, it was time for the two of them to brush up on Spanish. At best, Ian's knowledge of the language was mediocre, so it was no easy task learning drug trade terminology. Robert gave him a crash course on slang and profanities for better insight into conversations with the criminal element. The campaign could now move forward to the next phase.

Robert's task: select a team, arrange for the acquisition of arms and equipment, then coordinate training. He outlined his training program for Ian's final approval, although it was a mere formality.

"People we'll be dealing with all have significant well-armed gangs. Their operating philosophy is might is right. We need them to understand we're the right ones. They must be forced to accept we're not just another gang to be dealt with in their usual manner. As you suggested, it would be beneficial for us to imply this is a covert U.S. operation. I'm proposing three helicopter gunships and two supply choppers with appropriate flight crews. Two dozen well-trained ground troops should be sufficient; special forces experience preferably. It should be easy to set up headquarters in an isolated area. That way, we'd be able to avoid the authority's attention and keep a tight rein on security. I'll need about three weeks to assemble and train the right people.

As you know, the brief contains names of high-ranking U.S. military personal with authority to issue requisition orders for equipment, and materials, which we will need. Once my helicopter crews are assembled, I'll arrange delivery of equipment and supplies."

"I imagine the people you intend to work with will be familiar to you for this operation."

"It's not work for amateurs, Ian. Mistakes in this line of work usually cause fatalities at best, with the worst-case scenarios being unthinkable."

A ranch in Texas was chosen as their training ground. Headquarters were set up in an isolated desert valley. The dry arid conditions were a far cry from Columbia's, but Robert was more interested in forming a well-trained, cohesive team capable of working and thinking as one. Ian's somewhat pampered lifestyle had ill-prepared him for boot camp tactics Robert applied unilaterally. Never realizing when he approved this training program, it would also apply to him. Insisting Ian participate fully to condition himself for the mission, no favours were given. Ian tried pulling rank several times. He soon learnt the hard way of Robert's philosophy on might is right. Definitely not a time in life for Kodak moments. He was expected to equal or better any other solder in the unit. Robert was a hard taskmaster and a strict disciplinarian. This was a side of him Ian had never encountered but came to respect. Besides the twenty-four men Robert selected as assault troops, there was a dozen more support staff. This group consisted of a supply Sargent, ground crew, and catering.

Tex arrived a week into training, on orders from Lord Simpson's to assist Robert. As a high-ranking member of Lord Simpson's security team, he'd be acting as second in command. It was an unforeseen turn of events, but Robert weathered the change as a willow bends to the wind. He was under no illusions as to the motives behind Tex's arrival. Ian knew Tex would be a pipeline straight to Lord Simpson's office.

Like Robert, his features gave the impression he wore a permanent grin, although his smile was more like a condescending smirk. Robert's worldly eye observed transparency in his Vernier. It reviled a vacant space where a soul should reside. He assessed this as a dangerous attribution for someone in the business of manipulation and control. A firm believer in keeping his friends close, but enemies closer, Robert worked a twist into this concept. Robert assigned Tex the critical job of reconnaissance. This job kept him away from the main body but left him obligated to divulge all knowledge he'd accumulated.

Two weeks into training, Tex was dispatched to Columbia, ahead of the main force. Once there, his objectives were to establish a base and reconfirm the locations of all significant players.

Training complete, they were packed and ready to move out. Tex had arranged the rendezvous in Columbia. Helicopter crews had plotted their courses utilizing military basses. This had been set up with signed CIA authorization codes that had been supplied in Ian's brief. The men under Robert's command were given limited information regarding their mission's goal. They asked nothing -other than the extent of their duties- and were told no more. Army discipline had instilled the ability to blindly follow orders without question, and a hefty paycheck guaranteed this. All had served in one army or another at some time, most in special forces. Everyone to a man was a seasoned mercenary.

Ian heeded Robert's advice remaining tight-lipped about who he was and where he came from. They were left to draw their own conclusions, pegging him probably as the controller of a CIA covert mission.

That evening Robert addressed the men with an operations pep talk.

"This," he paused to check out the room, emphasizing his authority. "Is to refresh your memories. For all intents and purposes, we are a U.S. Army special forces unit on a training exercise. If you are questioned at any time by a superior officer well on a military base, you will refer him to me. Are you all clear on this order?" His glare searched out every man in the room. This whole operation relies on complete secrecy travelling too, and from our mission. If there are questions or doubts, now is the time to speak." One man raised his hand. "Yes." The man stood to attention.

"Sir, when we reach our destination, if a situation develops, are we sanctioned to use lethal force."

"If lethal force is used, we'll have probably failed in our primary objective. Our job is to act as a deterrent, not a combat unit. However, should the need arise, and you deem it necessary, each man must use his own judgment at that point? Remember, we're part of a well-planned military operation and must act accordingly at all times. Now I suggest we all turn in for an early night. Tomorrow, there will be an early start to the day."

Three days had been allotted to reach their destination in Columbia. A military base in Panama was their last stopover; it was an early evening arrival. Robert headed straight for the base commander's office to report in, accompanied by Ian. Ushered into his office, Robert was surprised to be greeted by a familiar face. After a quick salute, the man came from behind his desk to shake Robert's hand with the intensity reserved only for old friends. Ian's look begged the question, who is this person?

"Robert, you old son of a gun. I thought you'd retired, but then, they never really retire you intelligence types, do they." Robert breathed a quiet sigh of relief.

"It's an unexpected pleasure to see you here, George; it's been so many years, and your right, officially, I am retired. So, I need your discretion on this one if you know what I mean." He tapped the side of his nose with his finger and winked. He then turned to Ian. "Ian, this old reprobate is George." They shook hands. "George and I were classmates at officer training college. He got me into more trouble than I care to remember. Although there were plenty of good times and fond memories. We must have been two of the most unruly cadets ever to attend West Point without getting expelled."

"Came dam close, though, didn't we?"

"Perhaps it was as well for both our careers we lost touch after acquiring our commissions." They both found those possibilities amusing.

"Yes, perhaps your right. I've been able to keep tabs on you over the years, through a few of our old classmates, like Chesty Burgeon. He made general last year you know."

"Old Chester was always one to exploit every angle."

"What do you say we go to the officers club and make this a real reunion. I'm sure we both have a lot of catching up to do."

"We'll have to check back on our men first, but we will see you there in, say, half an hour."

"That sounds fine; half an hour it is then." Robert and Ian gave a salute and left the office. Making their way back to the barracks, Robert put his hand on Ian's shoulder and said with a smile, "don't let him get us drunk, will you? He was always a mischievous guy, with a flair for making things spin out of control."

"We're grown men, not young virgins about to be seduced. Give me a break."

"Well, don't say you weren't warned. Who do you think taught me the trick I pulled on you at Bloody Joseph's palace."

"In that case, I'll watch your back."

"I thought you'd see it my way. Seriously though, he is a good friend, but I don't think we should plan our return this way."

"I agree, that wouldn't be a good strategy."

Robert called the men to order at the quarters assigned them. Posting a guard at the door, he gave strict instructions to allow no one entry, or exit, without his permission.

George was readily found, holding court to many of his officers seated around a large table. Heralding them to the table, he introduced them to his staff one by one. Pulling up a chair for Robert next to himself, Ian was invited to sit close by. Drinks were then offered.

"I'll have a bottled beer George if you're buying." Ian thought a tamper-proof bottle to be the right choice, having experienced some of George's teachings firsthand.

"I'll have the same, George." He ordered drinks and turned his attention to Robert. Ian paid particular attention to their conversation, avoiding engagement in other friendly banter.

"So what's all this about? I heard you'd retired to Seattle."

"Semi-retired George, I was reactivated to train units for special missions. I think I'm considered too old to be actively used in the field. They just require my brains, not my brawn. I assume that the units I train are kept finely tuned for covert operations, rescue missions, homeland security, and such. I've been relegated to a training officer, so I'm not actively involved with operations. Although such units' whereabouts are always classified, so gentlemen, I trust I can rely on your discretion. Now enough about me, what about yourself, George. How did you end up running a place like this?"

"The backwaters suit me; neither of us was social climbers, were we? Although I married a woman who was from what might be considered the upper crust. We had two daughters before she left me for a sales executive. He was prepared to climb on or over anyone to reach his goals. I got my divorce; he got his intro to the big league."

'I'm sorry to hear things haven't turned out for you as well as they could have."

"Life goes on, Robert, and I'm not unhappy with my lot in life. At least no one ever complains about my obsession with golf. I have no ties; my time is my own. Even my love life wasn't as active when I was married. A toast Robert (to the single life.") They clinked bottles and sipped beer. There was an underlying sadness to George. He was no longer the fun-loving prankster Robert had known and described. A few beers later, and their obligations to politeness fulfilled, they made a strategic withdraw to barracks.

At first light, the unit moved out, heading for their rendezvous with Tex. He'd chosen an abandoned open cast mining operation near a river. There was enough open ground to land the helicopters and old buildings that could accommodate a base camp. He'd also arranged for fuel and supplies to be left where they could be retrieved by helicopter. When setting up camp had been attended to, Robert and Ian consulted with Tex to bring them up to speed on the latest developments.

"Our information is still sound; as you're aware, there are six areas, each controlled by one or two groups. There have been no major conflicts between them in the last few weeks. Although that could all change overnight, they're more interested in fighting each other than co-operating. It would be easy to move in on any one group but to bring them all together, impossible."

"Then we will go with the plan Ian, and I formulated. We'll kidnap the head of each group and bring them here by force if necessary. As you say, Tex, it'll be easy to move in on them one at a time, so that's exactly what we'll do.

"I'd kinda figured you'd be pulling something of that nature, Robert, so I've photographed the layout of each gang's stronghold."

"Good, I was hoping to hear you'd kept yourself busy. We'll lay out a battle plan and get started as soon as possible with the first groups. "Stockades were built with high standards of security for the distinguished guests they anticipated accommodating.

The troops were poised and ready to move out under the cover of darkness. This would give them an increased element of surprise. It would also make it easier to keep their own whereabouts secret. The people they were about to kidnap would be more relaxed in the early hour of the morning. They would never anticipate an assault of the magnitude about to overwhelm them.

Three helicopters slipped out under cover of darkness to their assigned targets. It was decided Ian should stay at headquarters with the ground crews. At the first stronghold, helicopters swooped in quickly, assessing it as one of the more vulnerable targets. Using tier gas as an assault tool, the area was then flood lite. Spotlights, noise, and confusion overwhelmed any resisters, forcing them to lay down their arms without shots being fired. One helicopter landed, and Gerry, the ground troop squad leader, cordially extended an invitation, at gunpoint, for the head honcho to accompany them.

Using similar tactics stronghold, number two fell to Robert's strategic genius. In their third extraction, location dictated stealth should be applied. Helicopter disembarkations were executed beyond earshot, and an assault party of ten men moved in on foot. It was an arduous trek, having to scurry along a rugged narrow, exposed road to reach their objective. The estate seemed quiet; there were no guards or dogs, just an efficient security alarm system at the perimeter. It was quickly disabled. Inaccessibility and its well-fortified building had given its occupants a false sense of security. The assault team took nothing for granted after gaining access through an upper floor window. After disabling the inside alarms, exits and hallways were secured before Robert and two more men moved in. Making their way to the master bedroom, they slipped quietly inside. Their quarry was sleeping like a baby. A cloth was smothered with chloroform, then placed near his face. The same procedure was used on the woman in bed beside him. Robert whispered to Gerry.

"They looked so peaceful laying there; it would have been a pity to wake them. Don't you think?" With a grin, he threw his unconscious quarry over his shoulder and whisked him away like a thief hauling swag. Once outside, Robert dumped him unceremoniously onto the ground. He was then gagged, secured to a stretcher, and carried back to the rendezvous. It was time for the teams to split up. Prisoners were shipped aboard one chopper and flown back to base, while two remaining helicopters were dispatched to their fourth and final objective for the night.

This objective wouldn't be the pushover the previous operations had proved to be. Information told them its guards had a reputation for alertness. The plan was, neutralize security before presenting their boss his invitation to join them. The team was again dropped off well away from this fortified estate. They were now fighting time; the sun would be up shortly. However, this had been factored into the plan. Fatigue on guards would be most prevalent at this hour. This would maximize, their would-be victim's vulnerability.

This stronghold was a jungle fortress, boasting a high perimeter wall. Three of the team moved in, pausing briefly below to the wall; well, constant cover was maintained by the remaining team members. A rifle was taken in a firm grip between two men to be used as a steppingstone. Stepping on this improvised ladder rung, the third man was about to play pat a cake with the wall to steady himself. Like weightlifters performing an overhead press, he was elevated as far as they could reach. Grasping the top, he cautiously pulled himself up, all the while checking to see he'd not been observed. Maintaining a low profile by laying along the parapet, he waved in his troops. The two weightlifters were deployed outside to act as cover for a hasty retreat. Three men were deployed to cover each guard. Group one, using automatics with silencers, moved on to the back patio of the house. As shafts of sunlight greeted the morning sky, simultaneously, the compound floodlights were turned off.

Guards were slow and lethargic in this shadowy nether light. This gave Robert's team that planned edge. A lone guard rounding a corner was quickly made aware of his predicament by a simple greeting from the business end of Gerry's automatic. He was gestured into silence by his captor, touching fingers to lips. Bound, gagged and placed in a secluded spot, he would now be able to take that well-earned rest he'd been so looking forward to. After subduing the first guard, the task became more straightforward as the guard's numbers dwindled. Worries of alarms being raised by outside guards diminished; entering the house was easily facilitated by a captured guard playing Judas goat. A gun to the back of his head ensured full cooperation. Once inside, it was an easy job to secure the premises. This was made easy because most occupants were still sleeping. The head honcho was then invited to partake in festivities arranged for many more low-life guests at H.Q. Now the occupants and guards were secured, it was time for Robert to radio in the choppers. Landing one at a time gave provision for the one still air-born to render cover for the team.

Once at H.Q., there was time for some R. and R. before the final sorties, scheduled for that evening.

However, the best-laid plans of mice, and even skilled tacticians, often go awry. The last stronghold turned out to be an almost empty nest: just two henchmen occupied its main lounge. Neither of these two was under any illusion resistance to this seasoned assault group would be anything but futile. They surrendered immediately. Although this didn't mean they were about to co-operate. Robert figured some gentle persuasion might be in order. So the older of the two compatriots was then escorted to an adjacent room by Robert and Tex. The younger one was strategically detained within a muffled earshot of the proceedings. Inside this confined area, Tex forcibly persuaded their captive to sit. Defiantly spitting into Tex's face, he tried to rise from his chair, well-yelling obscenities in Spanish. This outburst provoked a swift collision between Tex's strong fist and compatriot's less rugged nose. Robert, who was standing behind the victim, quickly taped his mouth shut. This was for compatriot's own well-being, knowing Tex didn't share his ethical code. He then indicated Tex should kick and punch the back of a large soft chair; well, he gave out blood-curdling screams. A river of blood streaming from the compatriot's nose had now pooled in his lap.

Robert thought it time to assess the effects their staged show had instilled in the younger captive. Smearing compatriot's blood around with his hands, he encouraged Tex to cut compatriot's clothing, making more copious tears around the groin area. Using Spanish, Robert softly whispered into his ear.

"Unless you'd like these cuts a little deeper, I suggest you play dead when I go through that door." Robert opened it wide for a brief instant in time before stepping through. His hands were now dripping blood. This deliberate act allowed their younger captive a fleeting glimpse of his companion. It was apparent stress had taken its toll as he visibly shook with fear. On the pretense of a toilet break, Robert entered the room and spoke to a team member.

"Where's the bathroom? I need to get this off my hands; apparently, he's a bleeder." Gerry pointed.

"First door left, Sir, but when did you get so fussy about a little blood on your hands?"

"Mind your tongue, or there could be some of yours on them also." When out of their captive's view, he smiled and winked at Gerry. Knowing they shared that same wry sense of humour. Using this same guise of anger, Robert turned his attention to their detainee. "Do you speak English?" He seized the man with both hands pulling him nose to nose. Robert then proceeded to slowly wipe the blood from his hands into his captive audience's shirt.

"Yes, I speak English." There was no attempt to disguise voice tremors. Robert called out to Tex.

"Try not to kill this one; remember, he's the only one we have left." Grabbing the younger man by his collar, he dragged him towards their improvised interrogation room.

"Please, no, I'll tell you what you wish to know." Robert quickly pushed him back into the chair.

"Where's your boss? When's he due back?" Robert still feigned rage as he growled into his face. The young would-be thug's bladder was as weak as his fortitude.

"He's gone to visit his mother. She lives a few towns away. He is due to return around noon tomorrow. He's with friends; they're travelling in three four-wheel-drive vehicles." Robert's voice returned back to its usual tone.

"There now, that was quite painless, wasn't it? All you had to do was tell me what I needed to know." He then escorted him to the room where his companion was waiting. They were then and tied together.

"I take it you heard what went down, Tex. We're fortunate this place is only accessible by that one mountain road, so I'd say we've got them." Robert took a pencil and paper to begin drawing up a battle plan. His ambush was starting to materialize. "That road only accommodates one vehicle as I remember, Tex. Isolating one vehicle from a convoy should be an easy matter."

"I agree; let's take a chopper to select our best spot. We can repel down if necessary." Some men were mustered aboard one helicopter, leaving the other group to guard prisoners and maintain security.

Preference was given to one of several close locations they'd reconnoitred. Disembarking, they set about laying the groundwork for their planned ambush. The stretch of trail chosen was so narrow it barely accommodated two vehicles. This location would serve Robert's scenario reasonably well. However, his tactics demanded the road be narrower. By engineering a small slide, he envisioned achieving this effect. Such a diversion would undoubtedly channel the lead vehicle's attempt to avoid this manufactured obstacle to navigate dangerously close to the road's precarious outer edge. In conjunction with the slide, they would undermine its outer edge. This was purposely done so it wouldn't stand a vehicle's weight. This was Robert's plan for dispensing the lead S.U.V. If the outcome worked as planned, it would leave enough room for the following vehicle to maneuver through. This would be after removing some debris. When this second vehicle was safely around, this engineered obstacle a second slide would block access to any other escorts. Making it seem accidental would hopefully maintain their planned element of surprise.

The four men undermining the roadside had finished their task, and the rockslide was beginning to look authentic. The only job left was ascending the bluff above and prearranging a second slid. Several large rocks were found and manhandled to the edge of a ridge. Robert surveyed the area, mulling over any possible pitfalls in his mind, making sure no stone had been left unturned in this well-orchestrated scenario. He then turned to Tex.

"I assume that should do the job, don't you think? I'd like you to stay here with a few men and make sure everything runs according to plan. We'll need someone to start this second slide and get out without being seen. We'll pick you later at the rendezvous on our way out. I'll take the remaining men back to prepare our reception party."

Reaching the compound, Robert ordered the helicopters moved from sight. The main body took up their positions inside, leaving three for outside coverage. The inside deployment focused on the entrance hall. Seeking relaxation, as best able, they settled in for the anticipated long wait.

Sometime later, Tex radioed in an update. Robert was handed the radio to receive the call.

"The first vehicle's gone into the ravine as planned, with the third vehicle stopping to assist. The second vehicle, transporting the head honcho, is proceeding on alone. There's no need to start the second slid at this point, so we're holding our position. We'll use that delaying tactic only if necessary."

"Excellent, as soon as we've wrapped up our end, I'll arrange a pickup for you. Over and out." Robert hand off the radio. "It looks like our company will be arriving in about five minutes, so let's give them a homecoming to remember."

Even in a crowd, a silent solitude afforded minds time for exploration. Dwelling on trivialities made seconds pass like hours. Everyone sweated profusely as tension mounted: Perhaps this was from the humidity, or maybe it was caused by the anticipation of how the forthcoming events would unfold. It was somewhat of a relief when the vehicle finally arrived. Tension eased as professionals with a job to do, gave total concentration to the task at hand.

The four occupants of vehicle entered the house, arguing and swearing profusely. Oblivious to their predicament, the last man closed the door. This heralded the perfect opportunity to spring the trap. The team slowly and quietly emerged from their concealed positions. They were like ghosts emerging from the woodwork. Assault rifles were pointed at this astonished group of villains, inspiring faces to mirror the fear they were obviously experiencing. Taken totally by surprise, disarming these villains became little more than a formality.

Robert checked the photograph of Carlos he'd been given and then looked at the prisoners in disbelief. He shook his head, then whispered to Gerry.

"How the hell do I tell them apart? They looked like peas from the same pod. There must be an excessive amount of inbreeding in these parts." Robert had used Gerry's street-smart wit, with the blood on the hands' scenario earlier. Perhaps he could come through for him a second time.

"Carlos! I've got a question for you, the men with you, would they like a Catholic burial?" Gerry raised his rifle.

"You don't have to kill them all, except maybe that fool who walked us into this mess." Robert wore a broad grin; Gerry had lived up to expectations.

"Not to worry, we'll leave you to discipline your own rabble. Right now, we're taking you for a job interview; if you accept, you could be back in a day or two."

"And if I don't accept your proposal?" Robert's grin became almost sadistic as he gave a quick glance skyward.

"I'm sure one of our helicopters," pausing, biting his lip, he glanced skyward once more before continuing, "will be only too pleased to drop you off here sooner. If that's what you'd prefer." Two team members manhandled Carlos to his waiting ride while the remaining assault group members executed a strategic withdraw. Once safely airborne, one helicopter was dispatched to pick up Tex, and his crew, while the other containing Carlos, and Robert, flew straight to base camp.

These mob bosses may have been forcibly assembled, but close proximity only served to fan flames of feudal grudges. From their own stockades, they snarled and spat at each other like caged animals. It was now Ian's unenviable task to somehow bring this group of aggressive warring gangsters together in a collective unity.

Ian set his diplomacy in motion with an invitation to supper. There was reluctance at first, but a day of meagre rations made empty belies compromises quick. A table had been set under an awning, surrounded by mosquito netting. Ian's hope was that men with full stomachs would be somewhat less aggressive and more amiable to suggestion. It was more an elaborate feast than a meal. Ian commenced with informal dialogue as soon as they were all settled.

"Gentlemen, I must apologize for the way you were brought here. However, I deemed it necessary. I couldn't imagine you all sitting at this table of your own free will. Your first question, I'm sure, will be, why have I brought you here. My answer to that is simple: money. I am going to make you rich beyond your wildest dreams." One gangster stood up, surveying the table with arms outstretched.

"Everyone here is already rich." Ian agreed but never allowed the conversation to interrupt eating. He then encouraged the spokesman to sit and sample more of the many dishes. Relaxation was his strategy to discourage adopting aggressive attitudes towards negotiations. Anticipating the spokesman's assertiveness, he posed the question.

"If you have enough money, why are you not retired and enjoying life?" Carlos gestured towards the first spokesman.

"My friend is correct: we are all rich," he hesitated before adding, "but one can never have too much wealth." This was the breakthrough Ian had hoped for; knowing greed had prevailed, it was now just a matter of greasing palms.

"I'm glad you see my point of view. This brings me back to my first statement, which was, I will make you rich beyond your wildest dreams." Carlos savoured one of the many delicacies but didn't let a full mouth impair his speech.

"And what is in this for you, my friend?"

"That's easily explained. Product control, from cultivation to marketing. Market Stability; will ensure this goal." Another man spoke up.

"I have many buyers; why do I need you?"

"You do; it's as simple as that. After this meeting, no drugs will enter the United States without our say. We're fully aware of your connections, and believe me, they'll be playing our game or sitting on the sidelines." Ian passed out a list containing drug corridors and contact names. "I can close doors or transfer individuals for none compliance to a place too despicable to even imagine. With the States being the major importer of your product, noncompliance would create an insurmountable business problem. Please don't underestimate the power I wheeled. The people that join us now will become more powerful. Through our help, any new upstarts can quickly be eliminated, and their operations absorbed. As easy as it was to bring you here, it would have been much easier to have destroyed your activities with a few rockets from our gunships. One thing I demand from you is co-operation amongst yourselves. Disrupting scheduled through petty feuding will not be tolerated. There's enough profit here for everyone. I've laid out a set of laws for you to study and follow. These laws will dictate your operations from here on." Carlos looked at the document distributed to each man.

"If there is a feud, how would it be handled."

"As you see in the documents before you, you will hold weekly meetings. Together all such problems will be resolved by a majority decision. If you can not run your affairs in a business-like manner, I will replace you with someone who can. I guaranty by following this plan, at year's end you will have doubled profits. If this does not occur, I promise to subsidize any shortfall from our own profits from this endeavour. I will now leave you gentlemen to iron out your differences at this first of many meetings I've convened on your behalf. When you've formed a workable cartel, you will be taken back to your homes and not before."

Ian went looking for Robert and found him lying on a cot, resting. He propped himself up on an elbow.

"Well, that was quick. There must be a lot of dead bodies in there."

"It seemed to go better than expected. Without some unforeseen upset, I think we can wrap the whole thing up by day's end."

"That's good. I'd like to be out of here as soon as possible."

"I agree. Start making necessary arrangements to break camp. We may be able to fly out tonight."

"I'll get right on it."

"I'd appreciate that I'll inform our guests if they reach an accord; they could be ready to leave in an hour."

He walked back to the meeting. Taking his chair at the table's head, he called Tex over.

"Well, gentlemen," he paused for a moment, allowing time to survey each individual at the table. "I hope you understand accepting the agreement I've laid out before you will be regarded as a binding contract. I have no time for anyone who puts self-interest before those of this cartel. We will be moving out within the hour; I trust you will have everything finalized by then.

The gentleman standing beside me is Tex Williams. Tex will be chairing your weekly meetings for the next month or so. I expect only favourable reports. If we were forced to return, I would not look favourably at the situation. Does everyone understand?" A few said yes, proudly, to maintain dignity. The rest with bent heads ate humble pie with mumbled yeses.

Ian left the meeting to pack his belongings, leaving Tex to acquaint himself with the group. He soon exerted his authority as boss of bosses. It was time to dispatch two helicopters with their not-so-precious human cargo. The somewhat subdued bosses were delivered back to their strongholds without incident.

After making one last discreet stopover for fuel, the mission's departure was shrouded in darkness, enabling their low flying helicopters to exit the country without incident. Morning's first light danced across Golf waters below them. The plan was to island-hop until they reached Cuba's Guantanamo for a rest stop. Setting down at the base, Robert immediately reported to the base commander. Again, presenting orders supplied in Ian's brief and reiterating the story of a training mission. They were assigned quarters. He felt smug, knowing they had encountered no problems and was complacent enough to allow the men mess-hall privileges for breakfast. It was a busy place, even though they'd arrived early. Robert's orders were clear, keep to yourselves, and speak only if spoken to. As a body, they left the mess hall when breakfast was finished. The maintenance crew topped off helicopter fuel tanks, and they were on their way without incident. Heading back out over the Gulf, their first landfall was Florida. On arrival in the United States, arrangements were made to leave the helicopters and equipment at a designated U.S. army base. A warehouse containing cloths and alternative transportation had been laid on. It also served as pay off station, from where the team would disperse. Ian and Robert took the first available flight to London; fortunately, the departure time was within the hour.

As the aircraft gained altitude, they both felt it was an appropriate time to relax over drinks. This resent sense of relaxation was a sensation Ian had missed since this operation started. Although always in control, alertness, he considered, was an essential element throughout any mission. Being a perfectionist, constant concerns of plans going awry was continuously in his thoughts. Any mishap he'd view as an inferior scenario, but that was behind him now.

"I was about to tell you to cheer up, but it looks as though you just have." Robert raised his glass and chinked Ian's. "Cheers to the completion of another successful mission."

"Cheers, Robert, you don't know how sweet it'll be to savour this drink."

"Oh, I think I can have a good guess." The stewardess passed by, and Robert ordered another bourbon. Unlike Ian, his first savouring was done in one quick swallow. His second drink was rolled around in the glass, and its clarity admired before sipping. Now seemed a good time to sit back and analyze their success.

"It was good to see all the plans we made in Zurich unfold so neatly." Robert was more flippant with his analysis of the operation.

"Yes, and nobody had to die, did they." This observation was accompanied by his usual grin.

"Although Without those fake orders, supplied in my Zurich brief, the mission would never have got off the ground."

"I'm beginning to question the fact they were fake orders." There was a look of surprise on Ian's face.

"How do you mean, not fake."

"Well, it was a little too neat and tidy, don't you think? Does anyone really know who runs special operations? The military always seems to be in the dark about them, and governments deny they exist. Who authorized those orders, and why were they never questioned? Tex was a referral from Lord Simpson's team that I was obliged to use. He was a good man, too good. The information he came up with in just a week should have taken a month. The brief we received seemed common knowledge to him, and he corrected me three times when I misquoted something from the summary. The first time I misquoted something was an accident: He corrected me before I could correct my mistake. On two other occasions, I did the same thing purposely. Without realization, again, he corrected me. As I said, do we know who controls covert operations throughout the world and whose agenda they adhere to? Activities like this one take place worldwide, yet all agencies deign any knowledge of them. Why was it so easy to requisition helicopters and equipment? Someone some were must have checked our orders. If our orders were checked, who in the Pentagon verified them."

"Good point Robert. Perhaps there are some things better left unsaid at this point in time. Through the company, my department controls banking systems around the world. Who's to say our security department doesn't also manage intelligence networks worldwide."

"Scary thought: it would certainly answer many questions. In the interest of our own safety, I think we should terminate this conversation for the present. We're in far too public a place."

"I agree it's too scary to think about when you put it that way." The subject was dropped and left to mental speculation; neither Ian nor Robert mentioned it again during the flight.

CHAPTER 22

Ian makes an enemy.

Clearing Heathrow's arrival terminal, Ian's first thought was to phone Barbara. The thought of her hearing voice soon increased the feelings he was experiencing tenfold. The mere sound of her velvety soft tones was music to this lonely traveller's ears. His connecting flight would be departing soon, making their brief conversation intensely emotional.

"It's been hell not seeing you these past weeks, and I'm not relishing the thought of prolonging that situation. Unfortunately, as you know, I'm required to submit my report to Zurich before this assignment's completed. I should be home to see you immediately after it's been compiled and presented. Rest assured; I'll be burning the midnight oil to be with you. I can't wait to put my arms around you, hold you close, kiss you, and make love to you. I love you so much it hurts." Overwhelmed with pent-up emotion and resent stress, a tier welled in his eye.

"I understand darling, I share those same feelings for you. The bedroom's been a lonely place without you. However, I've occupied my time by keeping busy. There's been so much happening since you've been away. Completely immersing myself in work's been a great distraction. I'll tell you all about it when I see you. Please just come home soon. I'll be counting down the hours until your here."

"I love you, Barbara, and I will be home soon."

"Get that work finished, my darling; I miss you. I need you." Pressing his lips to the mouthpiece, he fantasized it as being her lips; he gave a tender kiss.

"I'd better hang up; Robert's looking at his watch. It must be time to leave to make our connecting flight." He gently stroked the receiver's back after hanging up, symbolizing a caress to her locks. Drying the watery eye, he then joined Robert.

Motivated by the compulsion to leave this place, unpacking was not a priority, so he arrived at his office with bags in hand. Toiling like a man on a mission, well voiding himself of distractions, words required to compile his report flowed from his pen. Personal desires determining every minute was a relevant factor. However, his blurring site finally demanded some well-earned rest was required.

Intending only a short nap before returning to complete and submit the report, his plan was thwarted by fatigue. Awaking late in the afternoon, he realized the time he'd gained had been reclaimed by human frailty. Desperation spurred his return, hoping Lord Simpson or Pete would be working late. Ingrid had already departed, along with most other office personnel. It became a frantic race to finalize his report. With fingers crossed, he headed for Pete's office. Hearing what seemed to be a child crying from inside, he banged hard on the door. The response he got was unexpected. It flew open, and a young girl of about twelve came running out, almost balling Ian over as she ran past.

Pete was sitting behind his desk in a state of disarray and trying to look nonchalant, shuffling paperwork. A notion ran through Ian's mind that this was probably the company's hold over Pete. Perhaps there was some blackmailing axe dangling over everyone's head that worked here. He'd sampled company policy regarding employee recruitment firsthand. Entrapment, and coercion, were the methods used to secure his own company affiliation. However, it was impossible for Ian to perceive empathy for Pete's dark side. He threw his report on the desk, well glaring in sheer contempt.

"Here's the damned report you've been waiting for. I'm going home for a few days."

"When will you be back, Ian?" There was again a vain attempt to act nonchalant, feigning nothing untoward had taken place.

"When I dam well feel up to it, and not before." His statement was emphasized with vocal anger. He slammed the door hard as he made his exit. Front desk security was non-cooperative regarding Ian's concerns for the young girl's well-being. Rushing outside in a vain attempt to trace her steps proved futile. She'd vanished; perhaps a waiting car, Ian could only speculate.

Walking a little way towards the apartment in solitude allowed his anger to subside before completing the journey by cab. Instructing the cab driver to wait, he picked up his unpacked bags and continued on to the airport. This incident had upset him deeply. Taking the first available flight plan from Zurich that would eventually deliver him to England, he boarded an aircraft. Being an indirect flight, it would be a more extended trip than usual. In this depressed state of mind, it didn't seem to matter. His main concern was distancing himself from an organization that encouraged corruption and exploited everything and everyone it touched.

Changing aircraft in Holland, he continued on to England. Hiring a car at London airport proved the best option for continuing his journey. Embracing the solitude well-driving afforded him time to contemplate this job that had sent him on a downward spiral from decency. The world he was entering was a far cry from the one left behind in Zurich; he kept telling himself over and over. He knew, in his heart, this wasn't true. What happens in Zurich affects everyone in some way or another. This was not a good line of thought, beating himself up over things beyond his control, but melancholia affects everyone at some time or another.

He climbed the stairs with a heavy heart and quietly slipped under the covers beside Barbara without disturbing her. Laying quietly in bed, his mind was still moving at ninety miles an hour. It was hard to block thoughts of what had happened in Pete's office. The drug trade he'd stabilized; there was no way of knowing how many young lives that would destroy. It was a sleepless night for Ian: There was so much soul searching. These thoughts filled his restless night. Feelings of helplessness compounded his dilemma.

A restless night finally gave way to several hours of deep sleep. The following morning he was greeted by a smiling face and a gentle kiss on the cheek. A tray of toast, boiled eggs, and coffee was accompanied by the morning paper placed on the bed. Setting it on the bed beside him, Barbara then plumped up his pillows.

"Well, sleeping beauty, you were quiet when you snuck in last night." He stretched over, put an arm around her, and kissed her. She responded by putting her arms around his neck and prolonging the kiss.

"Now, I can fully appreciate what I've been missing." He caressed her breasts. "Get back in bed with me. We can spend the whole morning here. We have everything we need, food, coffee, and each other." His mood had changed; he had something to smile about; now, his Barbara was close. All was well in his world again. She smiled and gave him another kiss.

"Enjoy your breakfast Casanova, I have a busy day ahead of me. I'm off down to my office now. Come see me when you're ready." He gave a pout, well emphasizing his disappointment with a loud sigh as she left the room. Finishing a leisurely breakfast in bed, he glanced through the paper before showering and throwing on some causal clothes to go downstairs.

Popping his head around her office door, he just gave a little wave, seeing she was busy on the phone. Putting her hand over the mouthpiece, she called him as he was about to leave.

"I'll be with you in about five." She continued with her phone call. He whispered so as not to interrupt her conversation.

"I'll be in the lounge." Picking up her coffee cup, he gestured if she'd like a refill. She nodded, yes. The kitchen percolator contained a fresh brew. He filled the cups continued towards the lounge with coffees in hand. Choosing his favourite chair near the window, he settled in, awaiting her company.

Bubbling over with enthusiasm, she waltzed in a few minutes later.

"I've so much to tell you. I hardly know where to begin." Perching on the footstool of Ian's chair, she cuddled her knees in her arms. "I've booked a Stateside tour for Ann. Her record's topping the American charts, and we're releasing it here this week. Her first engagement starts tomorrow, so she has already left. I've hired a backup group over there to accompany her. The tour promoter really wanted The Blue Boys, but that was out of the question with their schedule; they're starting to be noticed. Tony's finished his musical, so he's back on the road, and as I said, doing very well. Avebury's got another single in our charts, so they're fully booked and getting top billing. There's also a television pop music show interested in them, so I'm in the middle of negotiating a guest appearance. This is what we've all worked so hard for.

A deal has been set for the actor Richard Wilson to record that song of Tony's we talked about. He grasped the chance at making a recording with both hands. It seems he's auditioning for a show where singing's required, so he's eager to prove he can carry the roll. I've arranged for him to be here next week. Tony will be spending time with us supervising that little project. He'll be Richard's singing coach; that's all part of their deal.

I haven't made much headway, finding a producer interested enough to stag the musicale. From your club associate, whose name you gave me, I've been able to make lots of contacts. Some people have shown interest, but not as an immediate project. It seems they all have prior commitments. I'll just have to keep on trying. I'm sure something will give; it's just going to take time." She paused to sip her coffee and gazes out the window.

"My, you really have been busy since I've been away. Are you going to have any free time today?"

"Afraid not."

"Then I'll take you out for supper this evening. We'll go to a good restaurant, and dress for the occasion.

There's an abundance of excellent restaurants in Bristol. I'm sure I can get us a table at one of them. If you'd like to make it a real evening out and maybe catch a show, I'll find out what's playing in town."

"That sounds great. You've just given me the incentive to get back to my office and finish that workload on my desk before evening." She gave him a kiss on the cheek before leaving.

Alone, Ian's thoughts again turned to Zurich, and how in his haste to leave, he'd given Robert no consideration. Being totally in the dark regarding circumstances that had brought him home this quickly, contacting Robert became a priority. The phone was almost in his grasp when it rang; it was Robert.

"Ian, I'm at Bristol airport. Is there a problem?"

"I'm sorry it was a personal issue with Pete. I'll explain when I see you."

"I was worried when I couldn't find you first thing this morning. Then I talked to Pete, and he said you'd gone home. I knew the last assignment bothered you, so I thought I should come straight here."

"I'm glad you did. I was about to pick up the phone and call you when you rang. Wait where you are; I'll be there to pick you up in twenty minutes."

Ian stopped by Barbara's office to tell her he was leaving before going to the garage to take the old X.K. 120 for a spin. The day was bright but cold; for comfort, the soft top was up. The old Jag was still an exhilarating car to drive. Its mint condition made it an eye-catcher, whenever Ian drove it. Watery sun rays penetrating hedgerows highlighted odd patches of frost that lingered on branches, enhancing the airport run's enjoyment. It gave him pleasure putting the old jalopy through her paces along narrow country lanes.

The lone figure standing just inside the main terminal was the unmistakable form of Robert. Driving to the front doors, he parked close to where Robert stood. Jumping out, he hurried to assist with baggage.

"I'm glad you took the initiative and followed me here."

"I didn't have time to phone and let you know I was coming; I barely made the flight. Now, these personal issues, have you sorted them out?" There was still a tone of concern in Robert's voice.

"I'm fine, but there are problems that need venting, and perhaps you're the only sounding board capable of relating to complexities created by our work's true nature. I'm sure you realize I could never fully discuss company intricacies with Barbara."

"I understand what you're saying. Most of the work we do isn't typically another day at the office, is it? By the way, where are we going? This isn't the way home."

"Barbara's busy in her office, so I thought we could spend the afternoon at Weston-Super-Mare."

"Weston-Super-Mare." The words spilled from his mouth in disbelief, accompanied by a look that said, you're having me on.

"It's a seaside resort."

"There's actually a town with a name like that. Only the English could come up with a moniker that far out. I've still got to see it too, believe it." Ian gave a pondered look that seemed to relate to what Robert had said. He'd never really analyzed the name before.

"It's really quite a nice place; you'll see. The name is derived from William the Concorer's time. It means a west town, superior or above, Lamar, French for sea." He parked opposite the beach swimming pool. "Let's take a stroll on the promenade. I think I'll find it easier to unburden myself on you as we walk."

Leaving the car, they headed northwards; words still eluded him. The assumption that he'd feel more at ease walking was wrong. Robert said nothing, allowing Ian time to speak when he was comfortable to do so. Slowly, cautiously, Ian broke his silence.

"Robert! Robert! Robert! what have I gotten us into." He paused, seemingly lacking the courage to make eye contact. "I've grown to hate myself and what I seem capable of doing. I can't imagine what you assess my moral standards to be. Banking's a harsh industry, but that's business, and I've never had a problem with that. Now I take direction from sociopaths without question. My work scope of late encompasses business practices even unscrupulous people would probably deem unethical. Arranging questionable loans for corrupt governments and condoning dubious repayment arraignments. Wars we've started for-profit or retaliation for opposing company policy. Soliciting financial aid from rich countries in the guise of third world development: Knowing that assistance will be converted to cash for armament purchases. As if all this isn't enough, I now find myself a controller of drug cartels to increase profits. I left the office yesterday evening, unable to cope with what I had just seen. I knew there was nothing I could do about it, but neither could I just accept nor condone it." Robert's immediate concern was Ian's depressed mood.

"What did you see last night that upset you so much you just had to leave."

"I stumbled upon a situation yesterday evening confirming my mind that good old Pete, Mister nice guy Pete, is a pedophile. It wasn't only the incident last night; that just tipped the scales."

"I knew about that, Ian. Didn't it occur to you that it was strange you should be chosen to host the summit and not your boss Pete?"

"I never really thought about it. I'm surprised you knew all about it, though."

"There are many things I make it my business to know. I consider it part of my job description." Ian's following words sounded like the request from a desperate man.

"Is it possible you could somehow get me out of this? Fake my death, set me up with a new identity, or something of that nature."

"What have they got on you, Ian, what's their hold over you, and how did you allow yourself to get into this situation in the first place?"

"Greed and stupidity, it was that simple. I thought I was smart, buying stock with insider knowledge. They were smarter, setting me up for a fall that would have ruined my carrier and sent me to prison for years."

"Then, you were guilty of what you were accused of."

"No, but I couldn't prove that. It was all tied in with insider trading, which I was involved with. The company had me over a barrel, and their lucrative offer seemed fair and legitimate. They also made it impossible for me to decline, considering the alternative consequences. They proved their power was also capable of wiping my slate clean. As we know, they're capable of manipulating and corrupting justice. Since then, I've found myself sinking deeper and deeper into a bottomless quagmire. I'd give anything for the chance at a new start, no matter what it might take."

"I'm pleased you finally made the decision to tell me what happened. I've been aware of your predicament for some time. And I know a lot more about the company than you can imagine. Do you recall that London flight how you speculated about the company's security? You surmised perhaps it controlled world intelligence organizations in much the way your department controls banks. It was an accurate assumption; that's why you're so valuable to the company. Your organizational skill, combined with an ability to see the big picture, makes you a valuable commodity to them."

"It's not flattering, finding my skills to be regarded as a prized commodity in such a destructive organization. So, can you help me? I can no longer stomach participating in the death and destruction I see all around me."

"I don't know, Ian. As you say, you're in a situation there seems to be no way out of. There may be another choice, but It wouldn't be what you had in mind."

"How do you mean another choice? Please explain and let me be the judge."

"It's a long story. I can best explain it this way, the company's black, and black's in control."

"I can understand that things look very black to me right now, but how does this affect my situation."

"Black's one end of the spectrum, white being the other, with a whole array of collars in between."

"So, you're telling me there's an organization opposing the company?"

"Correct."

"You're also inferring you're a member of this organization, am I correct?"

"Yes, now the question is, are you willing to join us?" Now, more focused and calm, Ian was quick with his decision.

"If you're genuinely opposed to what I've seen company policy inflicts on the world, I think I'd be ashamed of myself if I didn't join you. Although I'd like to know a bit more about it before committing myself totally."

"It's quite simple, Ian. There's a network of people in government, military, and other world organizations, fighting company policy any way they can."

"Is there the remotest possibility we could bring the company down?"

"I'd like to believe so, but this would mean you keep doing exactly what you're doing right now. That situation might not change for years, if ever."

"Then what difference would it make who I work for if a change is not forthcoming?"

"In some respects, none, but our objectives completely differ from company goals; look at the big picture Ian, tell me what you see."

"Regarding my work, things are being organized much more efficiently, giving company heads hands-on control. Yes, I see what you're getting at, take power from the top, take over their organization. Caesar is dead, long live, Caesar."

"Right first time, I knew you'd catch on. The situation today is, no one knows who's working for good or bad, except for the top people playing this game. So what could be simpler than replacing senior people? It really is chaotic out there right now, and that makes the company particularly hard to fight. They use our people; we use theirs, sometimes never really knowing who's fighting who. We may often be doing precisely what company policy determines without realizing it. You, and I, are the closest our organization has ever come to infiltrate the company's top echelon."

"Has the company ever managed to infiltrate your organization?"

"Yes, long, long, ago. It had a devastating effect on us, completely crippling our organization for a millennial."

"But you rebuilt, and now you're poised to stage a comeback, I hope?"

"With your help, this could be the strongest we've been in a very long time. Have you ever met the company head, Ian?"

"No, I only heard his name recently, Luk Desate. Before that, I was under the impression Lord Simpson headed up the company, and like all companies, it was run by a board of directors."

"In another place and time, Lord Simpson would have been an excellent obedient little Nazi. He's not a leader, just a ruthless person who enjoys power. His skills are intimidation, deceit, and cruelty. As you said, he's a sociopath. This is the reason he needs you. Your ability to formulate plans and perform specific tasks are skills he lacks. You round out his team nicely."

"What do you know of Desate, yourself, Robert?"

"This is one part of the story; you may have a hard time believing."

"Try me. I think I'm open to anything right now."

"Do you believe in god Ian?"

"Well, I don't go to church regularly if that is what you mean."

"No, that's not what I mean. I mean, do you believe in a supreme being?"

"I believe there's someone or something that's connected to everyone. Whether it be a collective good that dwells inside our soul or a higher being that oversees everything, I'm unsure. I can't define God, but I suppose I believe in him. Why are you asking such a strange question, and what's possible connection could there be between religion and Desate?"

"If you believe in God, it's easier for you to believe in the devil. From what you've seen of the world we're involved with; you must surely think it's the devil's domain."

"The thought had occurred to me. Pete's even made remarks implying something of that nature."

"Then you'd agree, the devil does seem to hold control of the world in his hand.

"Well, if you put it that way, yes. Then start thinking of Luk Desate as the devil. Is that so hard to do? Because that's exactly who he is."

"You mean metaphorically speaking."

"No, I mean, he is Satan. Forget what religion has taught us. Forget other hocus pocus stuff you've heard. He's always used cheap tricks to scare the masses, and myth and legend have clouded truth over time. Most of his methods can be duplicated by top illusionists today. He did those illusions first, with a world of naive people as his audience. He's created and nurtured this elaborate hoax over time to perpetuate this illusion about himself. He works within the same parameters as we do, fear, intimidation, greed; he uses them all. An expert in seduction, and love, he'll also use these emotions in his arsenal to achieve his own ends. There are many things he's mastered that we stand on the threshold of discovering. Immortality is just another of those things. He's also encrusted his body with some form of a fibrous shell that seems to make him invulnerable. I believe he can cast off this shell at will, like a shake shedding its skin. He's then seen as a handsome young man. He then undergoes metamorphose and changes back into the fiendish looking being, which to me, is the mirror of his true inner self. I'm sure one day science will explain this phenomenon, and we will acquire this power. For now, we must accept the fact that his skills in biology are far superior to ours. Perhaps as far as our own abilities are above apes. If you find it hard to accept this explanation, I suggest you think of it in any way you feel comfortable with Ian.

Somehow, we must strip Desate of his power. First, we must find where his empire's seat of power's situated. Through you, we already know where his main relay post is." The solution seemed clear to Ian.

"Couldn't we hit him, and hit him hard, by wiping out the offices where I work. Without that, how would he be able to control anything."

"There are several reasons for not taking that approach. For instance, Desate may have an alternative backup post; this would set back any recent gains. It could also destroy the world's industrial economy by sending commerce into a tailspin. We could be causing more chaos than there is today. Every nation relies on world banking to regulate currencies and trade. Imagine what would happen if there were no controlling body; total confusion would prevail. The monetary system of every country in the world might collapse. Millions of people would die, and who is to say Desate would not again come out on top. Both his people and our people would be in a race to restructure, and we couldn't guaranty a win."

"I understand. There is one more thing I would like to ask, why did you divulge all this information to me; how did you know you could trust me?"

"We know you much better than you think, Ian. You have always been on our side. When we were infiltrated many years ago, we vastly improved our screening methods. We only use people that we have worked with before or are certain they are loyal to our cause."

"I've never worked with you in the past. Am I the exception to that rule?"

"It'll all be apparent to you one day, but that may not be for a long time yet."

"So, what happens now? Who am I to report to?"

"You do nothing and report to no one. You just keep on doing what you are doing. That is the hardest part of what we do. A time will come when you know what must be done. Then, and only then, will we set plans into motion to accomplish our goals? Now, will you be able to go back to Zurich and do your job without question, the same as before?"

"I'm sure I can; knowing there is a light at the end of that dark tunnel, however faint it might be."

"You'll have to be wary of Pete. You've made a dangerous enemy there. He's known for his vindictiveness. He's a person who sees nothing wrong in what he does and doesn't like being judged by others. He may even try to bring you down, in one way or another."

"Any advice on what I should do to protect myself from him would be appreciated."

"If I knew what he might do, I'd stop him. In the circles we move, there are no laws; we make our own. As long as you're an asset to the company, all he'll be able to do is make things difficult for you. If you make mistakes, he may have you killed. By the same respect, if he makes mistakes, he then becomes expendable, and you could kill him." Ian looked at Robert in shock, hardly believing what he'd just heard.

"Your talking of murder, like it's nothing more than just another work chore."

"You asked for my advice, and I gave it. It may seem harsh to you right now, but your outlook may change with time. I just don't want the morals you were brought up to believe in jeopardizing your life. In the business we're in, you can not really on the rule of law as protection. We're all above that type of law; your diplomatic passport alone guarantees that. I suggest you dwell on what we've discussed. It's a lot to digest in one sitting." Nonchalantly he then changed the subject as if the conversation had never taken place.

"You're right; this is a beautiful place. We must have been walking along this promenade for nearly an hour." Ian glanced at his watch.

"Fifty-five minutes, to be precise. I never realized the time had passed that quickly. We really should be walking back to the car. I promised Barbara, I'd take her out for supper this evening. I hope you won't mind us leaving you to find your own entertainment this evening."

"Not at all. Perhaps I'll try an evening at the local. I'm sure I'll find someone there willing to play a game of darts with me."

A drizzling rain had now blanketed the area. Picking up pace from the slow stroll they used, when immersed in conversation, had enabled a quicker return to the car.

There was little need to talk well driving home. The radio played a selection of soft music, which included a song Barbara had written for Ann. They nodded at each other knowingly and smiled as Ian turned up the volume.

CHAPTER 23

Robert requires medical attention.

The sound of voices in the hallway brought Barbara from her office. Robert was met with a hug. In turn, she was greeted by Robert's usual bear-hugging lift and kiss on the cheek. This was done in his typical gentle manner before setting her down.

"It's good to see you, Robert. I hope you've been well entertained this afternoon."

"Ian drove me to Weston-Super-Mare, and we went for an afternoon stroll on the promenade. Unfortunately, rain set in after about an hour, but it was time to come home anyway by then.

So, I hear you're being wined and dined this evening."

"We'll cancel that; now your here."

"Please don't alter your arraignments on my account; I've made my own plans for the evening. I plan to go pub crawling and taking in some of the local colour." Ian then picked up the phone.

"If that's settled, I'd better book a table, or we'll be spending an evening at the pub with Robert."

Robert picked up his bags and retired to his room. Barbara returned to her office to tidy up her desk. She left Ian to sort out their evening's itinerary.

Before leaving, Ian stopped by Robert's room. He tapped lightly on the door, it opened, and a blurry-eyed Robert was confronted by a hand dangling a set of keys in his face.

"Take the Jag this evening. You'll not get a taxi in this area tonight." A large hand gently accepted the entrustment of Ian's prize possession. A sense of Deja-vu came over Robert, rekindling memories of his innocent teenage years. He revisited feelings felt when first entrusted by his father with the family car keys in that brief instant.

"The Jag, I'm honoured. I know what the car means to you, so it'll be in safe hands with me." Ian smiled.

"I sure it will. Enjoy yourself tonight, and don't let the locals hustle you at darts."

Leaving Robert, he joined Barbara, who had been waiting in her car. The rain had let up but not the wind. Clouds, silhouetted by bright moonlight, streaked silently across the sky. Their shadows whisked across the landscape like spectres from some horror movie.

"So, where are you taking me this evening, or is it a secret?" He glanced at her, gave a slight smile, and affectionately squeezed her hand.

"No secret, I've booked a table at a restaurant for later this evening, but first I am taking you to the theatre. The Merchant of Venice is playing at The Old Vic. I hope you like Shakespeare?"

"H'm Shakespeare, that should prove interesting. I'm sure I will. Have we been to the restaurant you mentioned before?"

"No, it's in one of those trendy back streets, across the center near the Christmas steps. Supposedly it's first-class; very upscale."

"Sound very swanky. I think I like it already." Placing her hands on her knees, she gave a very coy, prim, and proper pose.

"OK, I get the message. We don't have to put on airs and graces there. We just relax and enjoy it." She gave a girlish giggle.

Entering the city on the elevated south approach road took them across Bedminster Down. Their route, bordered by vast stretches of open parkland that sloped gently down into the city before gradually accelerating into a sharp drop. The city below became obstructed from view at this point. This higher area offered a perfect high vantage point for an unobstructed northwest view of the Avon Gorge. Lights lacing the old suspension bridge, straddling the dark gorge, seemed reminiscent of a pearl necklace above a woman's black vee neck dress. Housing lights sparkled on that dark night as they illuminated the northern cliff face. Built into the lower cliff face bordering the river, these houses twinkled on the otherwise dark precipice like jewels set in some elaborate broach. The river's path could be easily traced by street lighting closely following its banks. Ian pulled over and stopped the car to admire this vista.

"I find it very relaxing, sitting quietly to appreciate this view before us." The tone of her voice indicated drowsiness as she snuggled down into her seat.

"I thought you might; that's why I stopped. It'll give us time to unwind from a hectic day before continuing on." Sitting in silence and holding hands, they took full advantage of this respite together. Momentarily mesmerized, it took willpower to forcibly rejoin reality. Such treasured moments captured in time endure in memory long after the event's passing.

Parking in Queens Square, The Old Vic was just a short walk away in King Street. King Street hadn't changed much over the last few centuries. This cobbled stone thoroughfare so rich in history accommodated many businesses, such as old pubs and inns. Its eastern end dock, in times past, played a prominent role as a gateway to the world. Bristol, in that era, was a thriving port system. The city center was but a short walk from King street's opposite end. It would take only a tiny stretch of the imagination to step back in time and picture old sailing ships docked at the quay. It would have been a place where taverns, frequented by merchants, mariners, and adventures, searched for work and trade. Press gangs also roamed this street that probably inspired one pub's tongue-in-cheek name [The Navel Volunteers]. In this era, the rowdiness of bars full of people seeking entertainment perpetuated that vibrancy of old Bristol. Barbara found the atmosphere intoxicating.

"I love it here. We must do a pub crawl of the area one night with the gang."

"We'll do that. The day we were married, we spent our first night together in The Unicorn Hotel near the center, close to this street's far end. I"ll always treasure the memory of that night." That statement rated him an intimate, soft kiss on the cheek.

Intrigued by the look of one old building near the docks, she pointed. "That old building looks interesting. I bet you'll be able to give me the rundown on it."

"I'm not that bad, am I? I can't help being it. I've always been a mind of useless information. Sometimes I feel compelled to spew garbage without thinking. I'd never wished to bore you with it."

"I'm sorry, I didn't mean it to come out sounding catty. I only asked because I find the things you say interesting, and you are a fascinating mind of information."

"Well then, seeing as you've asked, that's the Llandoger Trouwe tavern. It's reputed to be where Daniel Defoe met Andrew Selkirk to chronicle his adventures and turn them into the novel (Robinson Crusoe). It could also be the inspiration for The Admiral Benbow inn or the Spy-Glass Inn, mentioned in Treasure Island. Stevenson was also reputed to have spent some time there. History lesson over Barbara, we've reached the theatre."

"One last question, the name Llandoger Trouwe."

"Now I'm boring me also. OK, a Trouwe is some kind of sailing barge. I'm assuming it was called Llandoger because there is a small town in Wales with that name, and there was an association between the two. That's speculation on my part. However, the dock there." He pointed at the end of the street. "Is called the Welsh Back because ship from Wales unloaded their cargo there."

The theatre's warm atmosphere set the stage for an evening of rich experiences. Such an atmosphere was easily accommodated in this beautiful old theatre. Its ornate plasterwork, plush drapes, and old but comfortable seating provided the perfect backdrop for Shakespeare's play. It would have been visible to a blind man as the final curtain fell that she'd enjoyed the show.

"I had no idea a Shakespeare play would be so funny. I really enjoyed it. It was hilarious when sweeping Porsche up in his arms; the hero tripped well, running up the stairs."

"That was hilarious, but the trip was a trip and not part of the show."

"Well, there was some good improvisation then."

"It was, wasn't it. I can only hope we will enjoy the restaurant experience as much as you seemed to have enjoyed the show. We can walk to the restaurant from here. It'll only take about five minutes."

The food, service, and decor all lived up to the standards Ian had been given to believe it would be. Sitting back in his chair and sipping coffee, his thoughts momentarily turned to Robert.

"I wonder if Robert made any new friends, playing darts this evening."

"He should find himself a girlfriend. He's much too nice a man to be spending all his time alone."

"I'm sorry I spoke; now you'll probably make it a project to try to marry him off if he's around here much longer. I hear you had a hand in getting Tony, and Ann, together. They'll be calling you Dolly Leavy if you're not careful." His baiting struck the raw nerve he'd been aiming for. She pretended to take umbrage, and lifting her nose high in the air, indicated she was above such contemptuous remarks.

"Ann merely asked me about Tony, and I just gave her some good advice." This quick retort was calculated to validate her intervention.

"Right, and who's been merely asking your advice about Robert." She was back on the ropes.

"Well, no one yet, but I'm working on it." He portrayed a frown of disapproval.

"I see, then once you've selected someone you've deemed appropriate, you'll give this advice only when they've been prompted to ask for it. Is that the way it works?" Round one to Ian.

"You make it sound so cold and calculated." She gave a giggle. "But your so right; you men don't have a chance." She looked very smug with that reply.

"What say you, I settle the bill, then we go straight home and discuss your plans for Robert with Robert. I'm sure he'd be more than interested." Her jaw dropped.

"You can't be serious. You'll embarrass everyone." Tiers of laughter started to roll down his cheeks.

"I had you going there for the moment, didn't I. You should have seen your face for that split second. You thought I was serious." She knew she'd cottoned on to his tease just a tad late.

"And you have the nerve to frown at me."

"Well, there you are, planning the poor fellow's life for him, and he's completely unaware of the trap you're planning on luring him into."

"I suppose you're right, Ian, but I'm sure there must be someone out there who's right for him."

"Then don't you think you should let him find that person for himself."

"But it's in a woman's nature to try to help these things along." The devilish grin on her face mirrored her intentions, making it clear there was no headway to be made in this debate. He graciously conceded to her last words.

"Thank you for a beautiful evening. I've really enjoyed myself. The last four weeks, when you were away, seemed so empty. Evenings like this more than compensate for those times we must spend apart." Embracing his arm in a tight squeeze, she snuggled to him as they walked. Her overtures became more seductive when shrouded in the car's privacy. A waiting bed offered far too distant a promise for urges she'd aroused in him. Seclusion found in a quiet country lay-by rendered uncontrollable stimulation of spontaneous lovemaking desires. He'd barely stopped when she started unveiling his body, well caressing him with her hands and lips, and overwhelming him with her seductive powers. Licking her way up his body, his shirt and tie were quickly discarded. As her lips reached his, Ian's hands cupped her breasts before sliding down to massage her thighs. The bench seat was pushed back as he lowered her head into the driving seat. Easing himself onto her, slowly, gently, his hands stroked every curve and sensuous spot on her body. As he touched each portion, he loosened the clothing, easing each garment slowly from her body. His gentle pushes gave way to more vigorous, more frequent thrusts. Feeling the heat now generating deep inside, she responded by pushing herself onto him harder. Synchronizing their movements, she intended to make his gift the prisoner of her body. Going as hard and deep as he possibly could, she felt a fountain of warmth ooze from his body. He lay still, exhausted, but she was not about to give up that part of him he had so freely given. Rolling over to reverse positions, she was now on top and in control. As their hips Gyrated, her beautifully shaped breasts captured his attention as they rolled slightly in synchronicity. Cupping them in his hands to showcase their beauty, his massaging flowed with the rhythm of her body. Holding his arms, she threw back her head in ecstasy as this electrifying experience controlled her very essence. Held hostage by the pinnacle of euphoric pleasure rendered her motionless until the natural high of the experience dissipated with exhaustion.

* * *

The following morning, sauntering into the kitchen, she was greeted by Brenda's offer of fresh coffee.

"Would you also like breakfast this morning?"

"Ian should be down soon. I think toast and marmalade would be fine for both of us." He joined her, unshaven and with a bad hair day. The smell of musk about him she usually found pleasurable, but this was overkill.

"Couldn't you have washed and dressed before coming down?"

"I didn't think breakfast was going to be formal."

"Formal, you look positively primeval, go back upstairs, and don't come down until your presentable. What must Brenda think? I'm sure Robert wouldn't be seen parading down here in that state."

"Where is Robert, by the way? Has he not been down yet?"

"We've not seen hide nor hair of him, so don't try changing the subject. Just get yourself back upstairs, and don't come back down until you're appropriately dressed. A more respectable-looking Ian appeared some ten minutes later.

"Is Robert still a no-show? Perhaps someone had a beer or two too many last night."

"Or perhaps he met a lady friend, and he's not home yet." Shaking his head, well rolling his eyes, and tut-tutting, before she'd finished, telegraphed the fact he'd anticipated such a comment. Airing his thoughts in a light heart-ed retort came easy.

"I half expected you to be still on that kick. Just couldn't resist the opportunity for a comment of that nature, could you? Brenda expressed her support for the female point of view.

" Barbara could well be right, you know, after all, Robert is a very attractive man, in his own way."

"In his own way, what's that supposed to mean. Do you think of him as some poor sap who needs a helping hand to get a date? I think women are all tared with the same brush. They see a single man and immediately think he be happier if they can get him married off." Unwittingly he'd invited Brenda into the verbal sparring arena, and she wasn't about to allow Ian the last say.

"Any more off your cheek, and you'll be making your own toast." Barbara made it quite clear where her loyalties lay.

"That's telling the male chauvinist pig." A flow of uncontrolled giggling followed. He could only muster a sheepish look in reply.

Barely able to keep abreast of Barbara's verbal assaults, it wasn't a well-thought-out scenario to enter into a war of wit with two women.

Envisioning himself being completely overwhelmed if this skirmish continued, he decided retreat was the better part of valour. Picking up the morning paper coffee and toast, he prepared to make his exit.

"I see I'm going to be outnumbered here until Robert comes down anyway. I'll be in the lounge, where I can read my paper in peace."

"It's time for me to pop along to my office to start the day's grind also. See you at lunch, my love."

An hour or more had passed, with no sign of Robert prompting a knock at his door by Ian. There was no response. He was then brought scurrying back downstairs by the phone ringing. Answering the call, he was relieved to hear Robert's voice.

"Ian, I've been in an accident, but I'm OK. Although, there's some damage to the Jag." Ian detected disorientation in Robert's tones.

"I'm not worried about the Jag; my main concern is, are you alright. Where are you phoning from anyway? And where did you spend the night?"

"I'm in The Bristol Royal Infirmary."

Realizing he was beginning to sound like a concerned parent, he toned down his aggression.

"The infirmary, then obviously you're not alright. People aren't take taken to the hospital because they're alright."

"It's just a slight concussion. I hit my head on the windshield."

"So that's it, that's all that's wrong with you."

"Well, yes, except for the broken arm."

"Broken arm, and?"

"Some bruising around the ribs and face."

"So that's what you call being alright. I'll be right there to see you."

"There's no visiting until two-thirty, and I'm told they're strict about that. Believe me, you don't want to mess with the sergeant major who passes herself off as a matron." His sense of humour put Ian more at ease.

"I'll be there at two-thirty. Is there anything you need?"

"From what I've seen and heard, I think I'll be needing food."

"I tend to agree with that statement. English hospitals aren't exactly known for their cuisine. I'll see what I can rustle up for you in the kitchen."

"Thanks, I'd appreciate that. The jag is in a lay-by on the road to Winford. Perhaps you can arrange to have it towed to a garage for repairs." Ian's curiosity was now getting the better of him.

"Is there much damage? Is it towable, and how did it happen anyway?"

"I was driving to The Prince of Waterloo, and a cow strayed onto the road. There was no chance of stopping, so I swerved across the road to avoid it but instead hit that side's hedgerow. I think there's more damage to the hedge than the car."

"Seems to me you're lucky you weren't killed. Get some rest, and we can talk later when I visit."

"You must admit, you still sound a little groggy. I'll see you later." Putting the phone down, he went to Barbara's office to commiserate with her. Trying the casual approach, as not to alarm her, he popped his head around the door.

"No wonder the stop out didn't come home last night; silly buggers put himself in hospital. It's nothing serious, but he obviously can't be trusted out alone. I'm going in to visit him this afternoon. Do you want to tag along?" A worried look came to her face.

"If it's not serious, what's he doing in the hospital? What's happened?"

"He pranged the Jag but says he's okay. He has a broken arm. I'm sure they won't keep him in long for that."

"Of course, I'll come in with you. What time's visiting? And what do you mean, shouldn't he be allowed out on his own? I thought he was supposed to be your bodyguard. That say's a lot for your confidence in the job he does for you."

"Just a figure of speech." He gave a little chuckle. "Two thirty's visiting, and we should be there prompt; apparently, visiting hours are quite strict."

"I'll finish this thing I'm working on and go get myself ready. The rest of this stuff can wait until we return."

City parking, being at a premium, made for a ten-minute walk to the hospital. Barbara took this opportunity to brighten Robert's bedside by shopping for flowers. Together, armed with gifts for the wounded, they arrived at the hospital. Placed in a large ward with some twenty beds, it was no easy task picking him out from the crowd. Blackened eyes, and swollen cheeks, made him hardly recognizable. Being the only one with an arm in a cast did help with identification. Barbara placed the flowers on the bed and gave him a hug and kiss.

"I just knew you weren't to be trusted out on your own last night." She turned to Ian and smiled as if to invite comments. Looking bemused and recalling how he'd been chastised for saying practically the same thing, he then smiled quietly to himself. Perceiving a trap had been baited; he thought he rather play soccer with a hornet's nest as the ball than touch that one. Instead, he quietly placed his goody bag on the bedside table.

"You'll find a plowman's lunch in there and a few beers to quench the pallet."

"Thanks to both of you."

"Barbara's under the impression you need a woman to look after you, Robert." Wearing a broad grin, Ian thought it safe to be smug. He should have realized a remark like that couldn't pass unanswered.

"Well, I'm sure there's plenty of nurses here that would enjoy the company of a single man like Robert."

"Robert's been in the hospital one night, and already you're planning his social calendar to include nurses." Robert couldn't contain his laughter.

"Come on, you two, stop making me laugh; my ribs are hurting. The more I laugh, the worst the pain becomes." She reached out and held his hand.

"I'm sorry, we were just trying to cheer you up. After all, you may not be home for a day or two."

"I believe someone mentioned two or three days." Ian viewed the ward.

"We must see about getting you a private room."

"I'm fine here, honestly. I find the other men in the ward to be good company. I'm sure a private room would be dull, with no one to talk to all day. The ones who can walk visit with men who are confined to their beds. It's all amicable, the ward's not so different from an army barracks, and I'm used to that lifestyle."

"You're comfort is all that's matters." She reached out and gave his hand a reassuring squeeze.

A passing nurse stopped to look at Barbara as if she recognized her.

"Excuse me, but aren't you Barbara Shaw."

"Why, yes." Momentarily Barbara was taken back at being recognized by someone she couldn't recall.

"My name's Linda. I was at the New year's dance where your band played. Perhaps you remember. I was dancing with a friend of yours, and at twelve o'clock I came over for a new year's kiss. I never did get his name, and we were lost in the crowd at the end. He seemed to be such a nice man. I wonder if you would pass on my address to him if I wrote it down." Barbara's face beamed as she gave Ian that smug look he knew so well. This glance didn't need words to convey her message. Is this being asked or what?

"I can do better than that. Linda, I'd like you to meet Robert;

Robert, this is Linda. Now you've both been appropriately introduced; Ian and I will leave. This will give you a chance to get acquainted properly." She grabbed Ian by the hand and pulled him towards the door.

"There now, wasn't that easy, and you were there to hear, I was asked." All he could do was shake his head and roll his eyes in disbelief.

"See you tomorrow, Robert, so try to say out of mischief until then, and remember, If there's anything you need, I'm only a phone call away." Tugging his hand harder, she hustled him out.

"This town visit allows me to pick up some specialty food items not available at local stores." Caught up in a feeding frenzy of shopping, she seemed utterly oblivious to the numerous amounts of provisions she had lain upon him with. Only when items started to fall from his grasp did she realize he wasn't the beast-of-burden she'd imagined. Helping as best she could with some of the load, they headed for the car. It was not an easy process, walking and talking with such a heavy load. Being a woman, she'd been well-schooled in this procedure.

"Will you still have to leave tomorrow, now that Robert's in the hospital?"

"I'll have to be out of here by tomorrow evening. I've no idea what my next assignment might be. Hopefully, it'll be work that can be done mostly at home. I wouldn't want a foreign assignment without having Robert along. Although I'm just going to have to accept the fact, he'll be out of action for a while, I suppose."

Forgetting the reason for the big shopping spree for specialty foods, he needed a prompt. "We've bought a lot of party goodies. Who are you trying to impress, and do you think we'll get around to using it all?"

"I have that actor friend of Tony's, Richard Wilson, plus Tony's band showing up to stay shortly. Richard will probably bring a girlfriend, so there will be lots of entertaining to do."

"Ah, I'd forgotten all about that. Being so caught up in my own little world, It completely slipped my mind you're doing all that entertaining."

There was some reassurance that people would be at home to keep her company while he was away. He knew she was a people person who craved the company of friends.

"It's always fun having Tony around. You can guaranty there will never be a dull moment. I imagine he's already planning practical jokes to play on Richard. I think he has as much fun doing the planning as playing the pranks themselves. I can't imagine him ever growing up; he's just a big kid at heart."

Over time subtle changes in Ian's persona, helped by her influence, were now so deeply entrenched they'd become second nature to him. Changes for the good included outwardly displaying the person he really was and discarding that cold, calculating image he'd fostered in past times. One such change, the poker face that had been his stock and trade, had given way to facial gestures as explicit as words from a well-written book. The endorsement of a smile, and nod, was only a fraction of the story his face was telling her.

"You can say that again; we've all been on the wrong end of his practical jokes, haven't we?

How's his big romance with Ann doing, by the way?" Not wanting it to sound gossipy and unable to keep a lid on juicy information, her logic was Ian's inquiry had dragged it out of her.

"I could have sold tickets to the big goodbye scene when she left for America. There were so many tears, we considered calling out the water company to control flooding. They've phoned each other so much there's talk of laying another transatlantic cable to handle the extra traffic." The colourful commentary produced the laugh it was intended to.

"So, it's still hot and heavy."

"Hot enough to scorch their pants off."

"By the way, any luck finding someone willing to put up money for Tony's show."

"No, it's all quite complicated; once I've found a backer, there will be the next problem, finding a theatre."

"Have you been able to work out a rough estimate for the cost of the project?"

"Having no experience in that field, I've relied on rough estimates given to me by people in the industry. Start-up costs are high, and the financial risk is significant. However, financial rewards from such a successful show are enormous."

"Ever considered forming a company to finance the project yourself. I imagine you could list it on the stock market and sell shares. Why not start by relying on friends for financial support, and when it's off the ground, go public with the company."

"That's a great idea. Avebury and Ann will be making enough money to be looking for some kind of investment to shelter them from the taxman. The royalties from my own work are starting to mount up. Tony will mortgage his soul to get his baby off the ground."

"I'd contribute, and I'm sure Robert would throw in a few of his American bucks."

"I wish you could be here when Tony arrives to explain your idea. I've been working on this thing for weeks, and you've shown me the solutions been right under my nose." The passion that stirred in Ian for this project was an emotion long lost in his own career.

"I'd like to be a little more than an investor. I'd like to be fully involved in the project. If I leave for the airport as soon, we arrive home, perhaps I can get a flight and pick up my assignment today. If I can work at home, it may be possible to be back early tomorrow, if everything goes to plan. There's a lot of ifs in play here, but I'll phone Pete to find out how cooperative he'll be to my request." Heeding Robert's advice, he would bite his tongue and try to carry on as if nothing had happened.

First things first, he confirmed travel arraignments before phoning Pete. Pete was surprisingly cordial. He even did some rescheduling to ensure Ian's next assignment would be a favourable one. His latest project in place, he was on his way to Zurich.

He gently tapped Pete's office door, with his index finger knuckle, in an almost submissive manner. This was a prelude to how he intended to conduct himself in what he hoped would be a brief meeting.

"Come in." The voice sounded calm and friendly. This was unlike their last meeting. Ian was cordial but cold as he pulled up a seat in front of Pete's desk. An air of uneasiness loomed over the room. It belied Pete's outward portrayal of friendliness. Ian felt he was sitting on a powder keg, and Pete was callously playing with matches. Producing a bottle from his desk drawer and pouring himself a drink, he offered up the bottle to Ian with a wiggle of the wrist. It seemed entirely out of character to see Pete with a drink in his hand, especially at a meeting. What Ian found even more unsettling were Pete's friendly overtures. If Pet was looking to bury the hatchet, Ian felt it would somehow be maneuvered towards his head and buried there. Sensing some kind of setup, he figured to sidestep the offer.

"No thanks, Pete, I have a lot to do, and I'd like to be doing it with a clear head." Pete grabbed another glass.

"Come on, join me. I'll pour you one." Ian, again, graciously refused.

"Pete! The last thing I need right now is a drink, honestly. I'd like to get this meeting concluded as quickly as possible. There's an early flight tomorrow, and I'd like to be on it."

"Some other time then perhaps."

"That would be my pleasure." Pete wasn't the only one able to conceal his hand. Although Pete's sleight of hand was apparently much better. Ian missed the small package he'd been palming and the way it was slipped back into a pocket. Perhaps this would be for some future use.

Pete handed him the assignment brief. "Everything you need to know is in this brief. This one's pretty self-explanatory, so I won't keep you any longer. If you have any questions, get in touch with me through the office. I may not be here, but I'll arrange to have your messages forwarded to me."

"That sounds fine, Pete." He opened the brief and quickly glanced through it. "As you say, fairly straightforward, so I'll bid you good night." Ian's relaxed and casual look was a hard image to maintain, well trying to exit the offices with all the urgency of a man leaving a building engulfed in a three-alarm blaze.

"Good night, Ian."

CHAPTER 24

Barbara meets a whirlwind

The airport terminal had become a familiar place for Barbara. She even had her own preferred place to stand. A place to observe the coming and going of world travellers. A place where her imagination could concoct underlying stories behind each trip being made. Time could be whittled away fabricating such tales. These were not idle times for Barbara, whose fantasies had always been a basis for her creative talents. Some people like to work nine to five, then switch off that part of their existence to immerse themselves in their social lives. For others, creativity flows when the mood takes them. This phenomenon for Barbara would never change. However, the sight of Ian's face always stirred such strong emotions as to void all fantasies.

"You must be worn out from your travels; what time did you leave this morning? It must have been early?"

He found it more pleasurable to hold and kiss her than immediately answer her bombardment of questions. He drew back and held her hands. Breathing deeply, he took in her familiar fragrance, allowing himself to be immersed in the essence of her being.

"Now, to answer your questions. I'm feeling fine. I had an early night and awoke to feel quite refreshed. I was even able to make a start on my assignment in flight. Coffee's kept me wired, so right now, I'm all bright-eyed and bushy tailed. Perhaps you'd like me to drive home? You're probably more tired than you thought I'd be."

"I'm fine, although I am hungry. How about you take me out for breakfast? I could murder eggs and bacon about now."

"Good idea. I've not eaten since yesterday."

A small roadside cafe gave an invite hard to resist. Picking up the Buffy-style breakfast, they found a table and settled in to enjoy. Ian finished breakfast first. His hand then reached across in a reassuring touch. This action prompted her to stop eating as their eyes met.

"I think I love you more today than the day I married you, if that is at all possible." Placing her fork on the table, she caressed his hand.

"For someone who professed he never knew how to express his feelings, you've certainly learned the art of saying, and doing, the right things to impress a woman. It's those little things that keep strengthening the deep emotions I'll always hold for you."

Mesmerized by the eyes that were a gateway to his inner being. She was aroused by an affectionate squeeze of her hand. "That does it; I'm taking you right home. You're a keeper."

Arriving home, the mood was broken by a phone call from Robert, requesting a pickup. "I've been discharged earlier than expected. I'd appreciate it if you brought me a change of clothes. The clothes I have here are blood-stained.

"Not a problem. I'll be there within the hour." His newfound love interest had inspired him to become a little more than just presentable.

"Oh, don't forget my hairbrush and scissors. I need to trim my beard. Cologne, I'll need my cologne too."

"You're coming home, not going to the prom. Now is there anything else you might need for this wondrous journey?"

"I think that's everything I'll need, except for the blue shirt. Yes, I think I'll look good in blue."

"Cloths, including the blue shirt, hairbrush, scissors, and cologne, I've got it. I'm on my way." Hanging up the phone, he felt her hand touch his shoulder.

"I take it that was Robert telling you he's coming home." As he turned, her hand slid seductively down his arm clasping his hand. He grasped her other hand and pulled it to his chest. He then stroked her hair as he spoke softly.

"Yes, that was Robert. Sounds to me he's been smitten by the love bug." She gave a quirky grin, feeling confident she engineered some of that scenario. Planting a kiss on her forehead, he stepped back to quell his passion.

"I'll have Brenda prepare lunch for when you return. Robert will probably be hungry."

"Expect us in a couple of hours." He kissed her again before leaving.

The ward was a more familiar place this time around. His focus was on Robert, who was impatiently sitting on his bed. Beckoning frantically to Ian, he reached out to grab his clothes. Dropping them unceremoniously on the bed, he foraged through the pile, making a quick mental check.

"It's good to see you too, Robert, and I think you'll find everything you asked for there.

"Sorry, Ian, hi. It's just that I'll be so glad to get out of these hospital clothes. It feels so undignified to be walking around with the back of your gown open, especially when there are ladies present."

"The only ladies on the ward are nurses Robert, and I'm sure they're accustomed to that sort of thing."

"That doesn't make me feel any more comfortable about it." Scooping up his clothes, he scurried off to the washroom to change. It wasn't long before the door quietly slipped ajar, and Robert's face peered through.

"Pist, pist." Instinct made Ian check around to see if it was really him being summoned. "Can you give me a hand? I'm having problems dressing with only one hand." Ian felt more than a little embarrassed at this suggestion.

"You want me to come into the bathroom with you and zip up your pants."

"Yes, Ian! I'm asking you to zip them up, not zip them down." This was becoming more embarrassing by the minute for Ian. There had to be a way to sidestep this issue.

"Perhaps I can get a nurse to help you dress."

"I don't want a woman in here dressing me. Do you realize how humiliated that would make me feel?"

"Because you have no problem with a man dressing you, don't mean I have no qualms with it." Ian's prayers were answered with Linda's timely arrival.

"I hear you're leaving us today, Robert, so I've come to see you off." His head was now protruding a little further out of the door. Ian saw his chance, "Robert's having problems dressing, Linda."

"Yes, I am. I'll be with you soon. I'm trying to get dressed right now, so if you can, just give me a minute. I'm pleased you came by Linda. You've saved me the trouble of looking for you before I leave. It's awkward with my arm in a cast, so I was asking Ian for some assistance." Ian was gazing off into space, trying hard at distancing himself from this plan.

"That's what nurses are for, and I'm here now."

"That's fine, Linda. I think I'll be able to manage." Robert's worst nightmare was starting to materialize.

"Don't be silly." She pushed her way in, practically balling him over as she brushed past, forcing him back and slamming the door behind herself. The words, "I'll have you dressed in no time," boomed from the room. This was accompanied by some faint whimpering from Robert.

Five minutes later, Robert emerged, smartly dressed, with hair and beard neatly groomed.

"You look smart, Robert. It must have been hot in that washroom though your face is quite flushed." This subtle ribbing, spoken loudly, was designed to prolong Robert's embarrassment. He was quickly becoming a primary source of entertainment in the ward's otherwise mundane daily routines. Some patients were bidding him good-by, with knowing winks and grins, well others cheered. These subtleties turn to loud whistles and catcalls as Linda gave him a parting kiss. She seemed to take as much pleasure as Ian in exploiting Robert's self-consciousness. So as not to add insult to injury, she whispered her following words softly in his ear.

"I'll pick you up at seven-thirty this evening then, as arranged."

"Seven-thirty." He whispered back with the smile of a man who had just won a lottery. Ian picked up his bag.

"Come on, Romeo, let's get you home. Barbara should have lunch ready when we arrive." Slowly dragging himself away from Linda, he hurried to join Ian, who had now reached the corridor.

"Lunch sounds good to me about now. Have you ever tried the thick salty porridge they pass off as breakfast? Believe me, not what I'd recommend, and the tea was even less palatable. It was strong enough to bend the stirring spoon."

The drive home presented Ian an opportunity to vent concerns regarding Pete's over-friendliness.

"Don't trust him for a moment, Ian. He'll work every angle known to discredit or demoralize you. That's the nature of the man."

"My thoughts exactly. I felt uneasy in Pet's presence; I'm sure, as you'd say, he's trying to set me up for a fall."

"I'm glad you feel that way; it'll make you cautious around him. I'm sure your work in Columbia weakened Peterson's position in the organization. Up to that point, he was in complete control of all drug operations, legal and illegal."

"I must admit I was puzzled when Lord Simpson gave me that assignment. Even when passing me the brief, he mentioned this should have been a Peterson job. His explanation being, he was otherwise occupied." Robert's assumption was astute and to the point.

"I have a feeling Peterson was in rehabilitation. I think he'd been sampling the product. That's pure speculation, but perhaps his drug addiction got the better of him for a while there. I'm also sure he uses drugs to entice young girls into doing things they wouldn't normally do." A light bulb went on in Ian's head.

"Things are starting to make sense if that's correct. I thought it callous when you said that if he got in my way, kill him. You must hate him as much as I for what he does to young children."

"There are many people with bad things to their credit; remember, hate has a way of consuming you. See them for what they are and try to comprehend where they're coming from. It's a good thing to remember hate can always be used against you. Hatred, greed, lust, all these emotions are Satan's tools. Don't ever give them a foothold in your thoughts. In this business, try to do what has to be done without emotion; do it because it needs to be done."

"Love's also a strong emotion."

"Love is probably the strongest of all emotions. If you portray true love and compassion towards any being, it's usually returned with a positive reaction. Even if it's not, you'll always be a richer person for having love and understanding in your heart. That's a lesson worth remembering." The conversation ended, leaving Ian a cornucopia of mind food to devour.

Barbara's smiling face welcomed them at the front door, and a hearty country lunch greeted them in the kitchen. The aroma of freshly baked bread, ham on the bone, assorted cheeses, chutney, pickles, and nut-brown ale, had Robert drooling like a baby. Sitting himself down, he tackled the job of appeasing his appetite. It took him a minute or so before coming up for air as he inhaled the bounty of food set before him.

"You have no idea just how good this all tastes to me right now."

"I think I have a pretty good idea by the way you seem to be savouring every mouthful. Did you have a chance to talk to Linda? I'm sure there's chemistry between the two of you." It was a chance Ian had been waiting for to fire up some gossip.

"Robert has a hot date with her this evening." This new opportunity to satisfy Ian's sadistic pleasure with Robert's squeamish attitude towards his personal feelings was something he intended to milk to the max.

"It's not a hot date; it's just two friends going out for an evening together."

"Don't be so modest. Linda's already seen you naked in the washroom, so she's fully aware of your physical attributions." There was no sympathy coming from Barbara after all; this was payback time for past harassment's she'd endured from Robert regarding her own love life.

"So, she's seen you in the buff before your first date, and she's still hot to trot. I'm impressed." Robert's red face mirrored a man about to have a coronary.

"It was all Ian's fault. If you had just done as I asked, that would never have happened." She couldn't contain her laughter, seeing him floundering around, well trying to float this poor excuse of an explanation.

"So, explain to me, what did Ian have to do with all of this?"

"If he'd just have done as I asked and helped me dress instead of debating the issue, Linda wouldn't have stepped in." Ian figured the ribbing had run its course. So with a smirk on his face, he decided to let Robert off the hook. Ian changed the subject.

"Tony will be here tomorrow. Barbara and I've been discussing forming a consortium to produce Tony's musical as a stage show. I thought you might be interested in joining the venture."

"That sounds like an interesting proposition. Who else would be involved?" Barbara took over.

"The principal people involved would be friends to start the project. We would then go public and sell shares like any other business." Robert, aware of their Midas' touch for business, was susceptible to a commitment.

"I hear that sort of investment is risky, but with you two at the helm, I think it'll be a good investment. So yes, you can count me in."

"I must warn you, Robert; it all depends on the show being a success. Show business is a very fickle mistress; there are no guarantees regarding the audience's likes or dislikes."

"I understand that Barbara, but I still trust your business sense to make it work. You can count me in on the deal."

"Have you mentioned it to Tony yet?" Ian asked Barbara.

"No, I'd like to tell him tomorrow when he arrives, but that leaves no time to contact everyone else who I'd like involved in the project. Before breaking the news, I want all my ducks in a row, so I'm planning a dinner party for that evening and springing it on him then. Until then, I'd like to keep it hush, hush, and away from Tony's ears."

"Just what kind of dinner party did you have in mind, Barbara?"

"Oh, just a small intimate thing for guests that are visiting, and you can entertain over drinks in the lounge after, Ian."

"That doesn't sound too stressful. Now, as much as I'd like to stay and chat, I should get back to work; I have a lot to catch up on. If anyone wants me, I'll be in my office."

"You're not the only one in that frame of mind. I also have a workload that's not getting any smaller; well I'm just sitting around here. Contacting people regarding this new project's high on my priority list."

"The hospital routine started at six-thirty this morning, so I think I'll go take a nap for an hour or two. Unlike you two, my time's my own right now." He departed for his room.

Their day of labour completed the early evening found everyone gravitating towards the lounge. There was a tray of tea, cakes, and biscuits set on the coffee table. Robert was spruced up and awaiting his date.

"You're looking extremely smart and dapper this evening Robert."

"Thanks, Barbara."

"I'm sure Linda will be equally impressed. Where are you planning on taking her, if I may be so bold to ask?"

"I'm not sure; it's more like where's she's taking me. Her family has an anniversary party this evening, so we'll be going there." Ian spoke.

"Well, be sure to have a good time, and don't be in bed too late." There was a punch on the arm from Barbara for that comment. Robert just gave a little snicker.

"I'm sure there won't be a dull moment if the rest of her family is anything like her. Linda's an outgoing sort and fun to be around. That's my impression of her to date."

The conversation was interrupted by a knock on the front door. Barbara responded. She returned with Linda in tow.

"Linda, this is my husband, Ian. You probably remember meeting him several times at the hospital." They both said hello.

"Would you care to join our little tea party?"

"Thank you for the offer, but we really should be on our way. We're going to a party, and I wouldn't want to be late." Robert finished his tea and stood up from his chair.

Ready when you are, Linda." The two of them bid goodbye and left. At the front door, Ian couldn't resist a final ribbing.

"Now, don't keep him out too late; you know what his curfew time is." An uninhabited Linda laughed well, firing off her quick rebuttal.

"You can rely on me to get him absolutely staggering drunk and taking total advantage of him on the drive home." Robert, embarrassed with this leg-pulling, quickly took refuge in the car. Ian and Barbara went back into the house to spend a quiet evening together.

The following afternoon Richard Wilson arrived with a young lady friend whom he introduced as Pamela. Shortly after, Tony showed up with his band. Tony's group commenced readying the studio, well Barbara showed Richard, and his girlfriend, to their rooms;

before giving them a tour of the house. Richard, then joined Tony for rehearsals. Barbara, and Pamela, joined Robert in the lounge. Having difficulty reading his newspaper well wearing his cast, he'd resorted to spreading it over the coffee table.

"Robert, this is Pamela, Pamela, Robert, our American cousin." He stood up and greeted her with an awkward handshake and a smile; she reciprocated.

"I've invited Linda over for supper this evening. I hope that's alright?"

"If you hadn't invited her, I would have made you phone her right now." Robert laughed, directing his reply towards Pamela.

"You see how I'm treated here. Barbara thinks of everyone here as her children, she mothers every one of us." Barbara wasn't about to let a pun like that go unchallenged, even if it was in the form of a compliment.

"Cheeky blighter, you can make yourself useful by entertaining Pamela for me. I'm going to prepare dinner for everyone." Robert never had time to reply before Pamela interrupted.

"Can I help you in the kitchen, Barbara?" This took Barbara by surprise. Pamela did not seem the sort of girl who would be of much help in a kitchen. She looked every bit like a model with her waif-like figure, long painted fingernails, short tight skirt, and blond immaculately styled hair. Barbara's thoughts were Pamela would be more at home on some fashion show runway than performing kitchen chores.

"I'd appreciate any help at this time, Pamela. There are lots of things to do, and I think I'd enjoy your company right now." Reaching the kitchen, Pamela was handed an apron. "There are vegetables to be prepared and salad to be made. Which would you prefer to do?" Pamela had already made her choice before replying by selecting a potato.

"I'll start with vegetables if you that's alright, Barbara. I come from a large family, and my brothers have enormous appetites. Mum feels their tummies up on spuds. As a result of that, mum made sure I knew how to peal fast and efficiently. Waste not want not is her motto. We never seem to have that much money, so every little bit counts when you're hard pushed to make ends meet."

By the time she'd finished talking, she'd filled a saucepan with water to deposit that first peeled potato. Barbara just looked in amazement, thinking (this girl is a one-man army). Barbara readied the oven roast well-making conversation with Pamela.

"Where did you meet Richard, if you don't mind me asking Pamela?"

"I met him through work, but he invited me down here after we ran into each other in a nightclub a week or so ago. He's hoping to get me into bed, no doubt. He's a nice enough man, but I wasn't brought up that way. And I've made that quite clear to him."

"So, you've been, heeding your mum's advice, have you, Pamela? I was half expecting Richard to show up with some floozy, but I must say that you are a pleasant surprise.

"Why, thank you, Barbara. Why don't you call me Pam? Everyone does. Introducing me as Pamela was just Richard's formal flamboyancy.

I've been looking forward to this weekend in the country. I knew there would be lots of other people here. Richard introduced me to Tony, and Tony told me there would be no hanky-panky going on here. He also said you'd see to that. He thinks highly of you, you know."

"Tony, and I, have been close all our lives, Pam. Do you know any of the other members of the band Tony used to be with?"

"What band was he in?"

"Avebury, have you heard of them?" Pam's eyes lit up.

"I love that group. I saw them several times before they became famous. I thought Tony's face looked familiar. Do you know the lead singer, Jim Evens?"

"Yes, I know them all; they're friends of mine. Jim's on tour; that is why he can't be here this evening."

"I'd love to meet him. Is he as nice as he seems to be?"

"He's a nice boy. I'm sure you'll like him when you meet him, Pam." Caught up in conversation, Barbara hadn't noticed Pam's latest achievements until it was handed to her. After finishing the vegetables, she'd move on to and complete making a sauce.

"I've made up this glaze for your roast, Barbara. It'll help seal in flavours well cooking. Have you prepared Yorkshire pudding batter yet?" Barbara, still in awe at Pam's kitchen abilities, shook her head in embarrassment.

"I've never had much luck making Yorkshire pudding."

"We must have Yorkshire pudding with roast beef Barbara. That would be like having fish without chips or peaches without cream. It's quite easy to make. Please, allow me to show you."

"Believe me, I'd appreciate the benefit of your expertise." With what seemed to be her usual efficiency, Pam demonstrated to Barbara the finer points of making Yorkshire pudding, well continuing their conversation. Finally, she removed her apron.

"I think we can safely leave things for three-quarters of an hour or so, Barbara."

"Thanks for your help, Pam. I would have been here all afternoon, working my fingers to the bone, if you hadn't have pitched in." She wiped off her hands. "Would you like a glass of wine? I think we both deserve one."

"Yes, please. A glass of wine would be appreciated about now."

"Red or white."

"A chardonnay if you have one." The cork was popped on a chilled bottle, and glasses were filled.

"Let's take our wine along to the studio and see how the boys are doing."

Pam showed more than a passing interest in the sound equipment as they entered the studio through the control booth.

"This is a top-of-the-line setup you have here, Barbara." Her fingers affectionately flitted over the controls like a musician caressing a finely tuned instrument.

"The best money could buy. You seem familiar with this type of equipment, Pam?"

"I am; my dad installs all kinds of electronics, and when he's busy, I've helped out. I've helped him balance systems exactly like this one."

Tony beckoned them into the studio.

"How's it coming along, Tony."

"It's going like a house on fire, Barbs. We're far enough along to start some preliminary recording, checks. We really need someone in the control booth right now."

At that precise moment, Barbara heard the phone ring.

"I'm expecting an important call, Tony; I have to get that." Leaving the room, there was casual confidence in her voice as she called back to him. "I'm sure Pam will work the control booth for you if you ask her nicely."

"But Barbs, I need someone that knows what they're doing. You know how frustrating it can be having to run in and out of the control booth."

"Trust me, Tony, you'll be fine." Barbara exited the room, smiling. Fully confident, the whirlwind she'd entrusted the control room to would be a pleasant surprise for Tony.

Picking up the phone, Ann's familiar voice greeted her.

"Barbara, I just received your message; it sounded urgent."

"Nothing serious, Ann, but I would like a quick decision from you. We're forming a company to back Tony's show. I'm breaking the news to him this evening as a surprise. Do you want to invest in the company? There is a risk, but it could also be a good investment for all of us."

"If it's for Tony and you, of course, I'm in. I'll do whatever I can."

"That was the answer I was expecting. Thank you, Ann. I'm heading back to the studio right now to join Tony and the gang. I'll give them your regards."

She rejoined Pam in the control room. "How's everything going, Pam."

"Just perfect, Barbara. Tony's been teaching Richard the scales prior too. Now he's tapped a few bars of a song to playback so they can check their progress. This all seems like lots of fun. Who usually plays sound engineer for you?"

"No one, in particular, Pam; myself sometimes, or Tony when he's here, but it's getting to a point I need someone permanently. It's nice having you here right now. It gives me the opportunity of tending to other needs without pressure; for instance, checking dinner's progress right now." Touching Pam's shoulder, she made the last comment before leaving for the kitchen. "Show them what your worth, girl, and have fun."

Checking detail twice, ensuring everything was shipshape, she'd allotted this period as personal grooming time. Her assumption was, there would probably be little time later when final preparations would require her constant supervision. Ian had finished work for the day. On entering the bedroom, she found him catching forty winks. The peaceful aura surrounding him was one she didn't wish to impose on. Readying herself as quietly as possible, Barbara slipped back down to the lounge. Snuggling into a favourite chair, she felt at peace with the world: A feeling enriched by the serenity of her picture-perfect lake view. Robert was still quietly reading his paper, well passing the occasional comment in an almost hallowed voice tone. A half-hour or so had passed before Ian came down to join them. Deigned the privilege of a relaxing talk, he was immediately pressed into service.

"Ian, be a darling and tell everyone dinner will be ready in fifteen."

"Will do."

"Supper should be ready about now, so I'll be setting everything up in the dining room." Intending to ask her if there was anything else he could help with, the doorbell interrupted his inquiry. Robert's paper was pushed to the floor as he moved to his feet with extreme speed and agility for an invalid. Heading Ian off at the pass, like a man possessed, he made a mad dash for the door.

"Leave it to me, Ian. It's probably Linda." Ian graciously stepped aside, content to wait and greet Robert's guest after she entered the house.

The group started trickling into the dining room as Barbara finished her supper table display. There was some polite jostling before everyone was comfortably settled. Barbara then tapped the table with a serving spoon, come gavel. There were a few whispers; she tapped again.

"Before we start dinner, there's a quick announcement I'd like to make. Ian, would you please open the champagne." Removing the champagne from the ice bucket, he readied himself for the appropriate moment before popping the cork. "We're forming a company to produce Tony's musical." The cork made a resounding pop. He then filled everyone's glass.

"Now, if you'd all like to raise your glasses, I'd like to propose a toast to our new venture." Holding her glass high, she continued. "To the show, Tony's named, Awake, Awake; may it be a successful venture for everyone." Then as a body, the words, 'To the show' were shouted before sipping champagne. Glasses were then set on the table. Tiers started welling in Tony's eyes as he walked around the table to embrace Barbara.

"Thank you, Barbs, thank you so much for finding the way to make this happen." Tiers of emotion flowed freely down his cheeks.

"Ian also deserves a lot of credit. It was his idea that got this ball rolling." Ian also received a back-patting hug. Show talk dominated dinner conversation. Barbara was constantly bombarded with questions designed to glean every ounce of information possible regarding the project.

Dinner concluded with a sherry trifle dessert; made by Brenda the previous day. As the last empty dish was pushed aside, Ian rose to his feet.

"I suggest we retire to the lounge for coffee and liqueurs."

Tony gravitated to a favoured position, the piano stool. His hands, drawn to the keys, glided fluidly across the ivories. The audience was treated to an evening of compositions created for his musical. Appreciation for this evening's private concert was unanimous.

Brenda had cleared the dining room's evening's aftermath, setting the stage for breakfast. Everyone arrived at the predetermined time. Sitting opposite Pam and still impressed by her previous day's control room performance, Tony knew he'd be begging if that was what it would take to enlist her skills once more.

" Pam, you have the control booth magic. I'd like to utilize it again for a few hours today.

I'll make sure you'll be well compensated for your time."

"I had so much fun yesterday; I'd love to. I would have never dreamed of being involved in the record production industry this weekend." Barbara gave a cynical glance toward Pam.

"Don't be so eager, girl, at least until you know how much you'll be paid. Make sure they really do make it worth your while." Barbara directed her next words towards Tony. "And don't try palming her off with a pub supper."

"Would it be fair if they pay me, scale, then take me out for supper this evening?" Barbara's wink, accompanied by a thumb approval gesture, indicated her endorsement. Tony was quick to fake some cringing and wincing.

"You drive a hard bargain, girl; you have me over a barrel, so I must capitulate. I'll wine and dine Richard and you this evening at a little country pub I know. That should fulfill all my obligations." He winked at Barbara. She smirked, having surmised where Tony intended to take them: And pranks that would be played there. There was little doubt

Richard would be the primary target for these particle jokes. Turning her attention to Ian, who seemed oblivious to everything except his breakfast, she waved a hand in front of his face.

"Earth to Ian. It seems I have the day off. Can you give work a miss also?"

"I don't see why not. We could drive across Exmoor. I've never taken you there."

"I read Lorna Doon when I was a young girl, and the setting for that story was Exmoor. I've always wanted to visit the places mentioned in that novel to experience its authenticity for myself."

"If you're familiar with the book, I'm sure you'll not be disappointed with the rugged beauty of Exmoor. Towns and villages on the moor also have a unique character to them. I'll get the map, and we can plan our route."

Their little excursion took them south towards Bridgewater before turning west. The next place of interest on their trip was Dunster with its picturesque castle. The Castle was easily viewed from the roadside. The coastal town of Minehead was only a short drive. Passing through Minehead and weaving between the coast and countryside, Porlock town was their next port of call. Porlock heralded itself as the gateway to Exmoor. This was now Lorna Doon's country. Porlock, worthy of a more extended visit, was reduced to a short respite as time was a factor. They pressed on. The car laboured under the challenge of the infamous Porlock hill.

The hill's challenge was met and conquered. Exmoor's rolling hills beckoned them forward. The Bristol Channel, the broad body of dark blue water off to their right, contrasted sharply with lush moorland colours. Moorland melded with the coastline with an accumulation of numerous small, secluded coves and bays. They were isolated in most parts by steep hills or cliffs. The bleakness of this winter day couldn't be masked by a clear blue sky: Winter's watery sunshine gave inadequate suppression to the moor's wild foreboding nature. Their chosen route continued across exposed moorland for several miles. It then dropped steeply into a valley that narrowed as it edged towards the coast. Descending through a dense hoar oak tree forest, it followed the Lyn River valley's south bank. This peaceful valley showed a sharp contrast to moorland's bleakness by providing an almost womb-like comfort. This road eventually delivered them to their primary destination, Lynmouth.

"Our plans were to stop in Lynmouth, so we should find parking. You'll enjoy Lynmouth. It's your kind of place. It's small with interesting shops to browse through." Ian saw shopping as a necessary chore, not enjoyment.

"You know my pleasures well, don't you, my darling?" The smile lighting up her face was the tariff he'd happily accept.

Lynmouth village was nestled atop sturdy sea walls surrounding its small harbour. This wall also provided more than adequate protection from the Atlantic Ocean compacting into the Bristol channel's funnel. This body of water, accompanied by prevailing winds, often spawn gales. Northeastern faced escarpments on the village's southwest side sustained abundant vegetation. Both hamlet and greenery were sheltered from these severe weather conditions by the shelter given by the cliffs.

The community now relied heavily on tourism and sport fishing for its livelihood. The snug, narrow entranced little harbour once accommodated a small fishing fleet. The only boats the harbour host these days were brightly coloured pleasure craft. Parking lots near the upper village's riverside church offered visitors a leisurely walk along a gently graded road to the harbour. This road bypassed the lower village after bridging an adjoining river's arm. This arm tumbled down its rocky bed from the moor high above. The hi-way united the upper and lower village with a junction spur to the lower elevation. The main road then continued its path south. The narrow bridge also afforded an excellent vantage point for a harbour and river view before accessing the lower village's dead-end junction road. High river containment walls blended inconspicuously into the harbour abutments at this point. The two river's waters now united flow seaward through the harbour's seaward entrance. Commerce on the river's southwestern bank centred around tourism, with its northeastern side catering almost exclusively to hotels, guest houses, and residential properties that peered through small forest clearings in the surrounding hills. The steep terrain ensured the village's size remained small.

Entering the lower community, its access road split to utilize its widest point to the fullest by forming an elliptical island containing stores and restaurants. Other establishments on the south side of this Island's Road backed up to the cliff face. This inside street made sheltered shopping comfortable in harsh weather. Cliff face's encroachment then forced the two roads reunification before continuing on to the harbour mouth. It then made a sharp left turn under windward cliffs for a short distance before dead-ending at a bluff.

Browsing through stores, Barbara eventually found one specializing in leather goods that aroused her curiosity. Rummaging through the overcrowded racks, she sampled many of the garment's quality through sight and touch.

"I wouldn't have expected low prices like these in a tourist spot. Ian, these leather goods are a bargain." Slipping a jacket from the rack, she held it to her body and postured with it before a mirror. "I'd pay nearly double this price for a warm sheepskin jacket of this quality in London."

"If you like it that much, I'll buy it for you." This promise earned a kiss on the cheek.

Her own coat was quickly discarded for a proper sheepskin jacket fitting. There was an ulterior motive behind Ian's generosity. He knew it would probably quench her shopping appetite.

"You really are a sweety. I love you." He received another kiss on the cheek.

Walking from the store, she proudly toted the bag containing her new jacket. Continuing their walk, they happened on a hydraulic rock railway scaling the cliff wall near the end of the road. A wall plaque explained its operation. A ballast tank, when at the clifftop, would be filled with water. When a counterbalance equaling slightly more than the laded bottom tram was reached, the ballast tank was allowed to descend. Its cable attachment ran through a top secured pulley system; the cable's other end was connected to the bottom tram. As the counterbalance tank descended, the tram ascended. Once the counterweight had reached the bottom, the tank's water weight could be adjusted by draining or increasing water capacity; thus reversing this process. Deciding a tram excursion would be an enjoyable experience, they entered its car.

The village of Lynton stood atop the cliff. With a quick stop for tea and Sandwiches, a brief village exploration seemed in order before making the return trip.

Barbara could not return to the car without at least one more store browsing experience. Ian could not be coerced into more shopping, instead electing to read through second-hand books set on a rack out front. Rejoining him, now entirely shopped out, they strolled back to the car. Leaving the village on a continuous route south, a steep hill beyond the bridge gave Lynton's primary arterial access, which they'd visited by tram.

"This isn't the way we came. Are you planning another stop before we head for home?" He pondered over his words before answering.

"When you were in that last store, I spent my time glancing through a book on local places of interest. The Lorna Doon story popped up quite frequently. Apparently, some story episodes were written around natural areas. The church where Lorna and John Rid were supposedly married actually exists, and it's not far from here."

"I remember that part of the book. It was the climax of the story. It was Orr church if I remember correctly."

"Your memory serves you well, darling. According to the book I was reading, Orr village is only a short trip from here. I thought you might find the church visit interesting."

"Yes, I would, and you say it's not far from here?"

"According to the book, it's quite close." As Lynton dropped from the rear mirror view, moorland again took dominance. A different landscape aspect now presented itself. Pastureland supporting grazing animals, with weathered stone walls marking field boundaries, indicated farming.

A neat white painted cast iron road sign, with black razed lettering, pointed the direction to Orr down a narrow country lane. The lane ended abruptly at a tee junction. A small church, on the junction's opposite side, stood Orr's church. Its gray stone lichen adorned walls and moss ladened weathered slate roofing stood as a solitary greeter to Orr. Orr's main village was a short distance left. It looked almost as bleak as the moor itself. The churches unspoiled by time appearance gave the distinct impression it could be expecting that famous wedding soon.

Parking a stone's throw away, they walked until reaching its small, blackened oak beam side porch and door, displaying its original black wrought iron hardware. The church's weathered exterior exhibited centuries of extreme weather exposure. The heavy oak door still gave adequate protection to its interior from the outside elements. This untreated weathering befitted the unique structures qualities.

"It's much smaller than I imagined it to be, Ian. It's so old yet so beautiful. I hope we can go inside." He tried the Gothic iron latch, it opened, and he pushed the door ajar. The pointed-arched top still gave an illusion of inadequate headroom. Ian's reaction was to stoop on entering.

"It's precisely how I imagined it to be. It would take no great stretch of the imagination to picture Lorna, and John, kneeling at that very altar. Can't you just see it, Ian? It's so quaint and old. It has a charm all of its own. I'm so glad you brought me here." His arm gave her a reassuring squeeze.

"Never having a church wedding, how nice it would be to come back here one day to reaffirm our vows in a church ceremony."

"You're such a romantic, Ian. I love you." Turning wheels of thought produced a puzzled look on her face. "Do you think that would be possible?"

"Anything's possible."

"Then, perhaps someday."

Snuggling into his arm gave her comfort as they walked back to the car. An alternate route took them off the moor and onto the main road for a homeward heading. Leaving her neither land experience behind, the conversation turned to more mundane business talk.

"I'm becoming really bogged down by paperwork. It's become practically impossible to juggle office business and my other commitments. Setting up a company for Tony's show will be a full-time job in itself. I've made up my mind. I'm hiring some help."

"Have you anyone in mind."

"No, but I know the type of person I'm looking for. Someone experienced and able to take control of situations, plus work independently. It would be a bonus if they had a good aptitude for the control booth. I'd be more than willing to train the right person. They would also have to be proficient in coordinating schedules and possess good people skills."

"That sounds like a pretty tall order to me."

"You're right. It'll be hard enough finding someone to suit my needs and practically impossible to find someone local to fit the bill."

"I have a suggestion. There's a large basement area still unused. Perhaps Rodger's uncle, who renovated the house, could transform it into a suite. The job could then be advertised with its own accommodation."

"You really do get some good ideas; I'll speak to Roger about it."

The evening had arrived when reaching familiar Chew valley landmarks.

"If you feel up to it, we could go for a drink."

"Let's try to hook up with Tony and the gang. I think I know where we can find them."

"I was hoping you might say that. I'm in the party mood."

Richard made himself an easy target to spot with his flamboyant personality, even in a crowded pub. Barbara joined the group, seating herself next to Pam. Ian went to the bar for drinks. Tony was in fine form, leaving his seat to greet Ian with the offer of drinks.

"It's good to see the two of you this evening. So where did your little outing take you."

"Lynmouth and Exmoor. I wouldn't want to steal any of Barbara's thunder by telling you more." Tony just grinned as he glanced at the table.

"Shopping again, no doubt. That girl could find a shop on the moon." He could see her flaunting the new acquisition she'd slipped on before entering the pub. She was odiously bending Pam's ear with every shopping detail. Ian placed their drinks on the table.

"Tony paid for this round." She razed her glass to him.

"Cheers, Tony."

"Your welcome, Barb's. Now I have a favour to ask, would it be all right if Pam stayed on a few more days to help in the control booth. She's much better in there than you or I." Barbara's nodding head and knowing facial expressions said it all.

"Why doesn't that surprise me. I'd appreciate all the help she can give us right now, and we will pay her for her time.'" Pam seemed pleased with the news.

"I'd better phone mum to tell her I'll be stopping on here for a few more days."

"She won't mind you being here, will she, Pam?"

"No, just as long as she knows where I'm staying, and it was you who asked me. I think she's secretly looking forward to the day she and dad can have the house to themselves when we kids leave home for good. We've only a small house with two bathrooms. I share my bedroom with two sisters." She was more than pleased when my eldest brother married."

"What about your work Pam, will they not mind you taking time off."

"I'm between jobs at present. Last week, I worked for a solicitor who retired, so I lost my job, but he paid me a good separation bonus. That's where I initially met Richard. He handled all of Richard's legal work."

"What type of work did you do there, Pam."

"Oh, bookkeeping, typing, arranging, his schedule, that sort of thing."

"I'm looking for an assistant Pam. Would you consider working for me?" You seem to have all the qualifications I'm looking for in an assistant, and I'd be more than pleased to at least match your previous salary."

"I'd like to say yes, but this is a long way from home, and I have nowhere to stay in this area."

"You'd be able to stay in the room you're in right now until we can arrange a basement suite for you. There would be no rent charge, so you should be much better off financially." Pam felt like she'd just won the lottery.

"Now I've really got something to tell mum. I know I'm going to enjoy working with you and everyone." She then leaned over and whispered, for Barbara's ears only.

"Now, I really will get to meet Jim Evens, won't I?"

"That you will, Pam."

Two independent conversations had been in progress. The men talking sports had given little time for other distractions to this point. At an appropriate time, Barbara interrupted.

"Pam's agreed to work for me full time, as my assistant. I'd like to buy a round of drinks to celebrate." She passed Ian a five-pound note. "Be a sweety and do the honours, please." He plucked the fiver from her hand as he winked at the group.

"It's amazing how things seem to work out for you. Only today, you told me you need an assistant, and this evening you have one. I really think you're involved in a lot of clandestine planning. It would be too much of a coincidence for things to happen the way they do for you by chance."

"Part of any good business practice is making your own luck. You should know that Ian." He shook his head with a bemused look.

"Come on, Richard, you can give me a hand with the drinks. I take it you've already had Richard buy drinks at the bar, Tony." A fact check that Richard was aware of welded countertop coins. Tony gave a knowing grin as the two of them trotted off to the bar.

Barbara now had Tony and Pam's undivided attention.

"I've done very little song writing lately, and I need to get back to that, and you'll have the studio help you've so desperately needed. I'm sure you will fit right in with our little group Pam, so this will work well for everyone.

Obviously, there will be things you'll be needing from your home, Pam."

"My clothes, and a few small personal items, that's about it."

"I'll drive you home to pick them up. It'll give me a chance to meet your Parents at that time."

"That's nice of you, Barbara. Mum's mind will be at ease meeting the person I'll be working for and knowing where I'll be living."

Ian and Richard returned with drinks, and the remaining evening was spent talking.

First impressions meant a great deal to Barbara, and she'd liked Pam from the start. As they became more intimately acquainted, she perceived the beginning of a firm friendship.

CHAPTER 25

Pete demoralizes Ian.

With the central office lights now dimmed, Ian was left burning the midnight oil once more in what he assumed would be an empty Zurich office block, except for security. A gruelling self-imposed regimented schedule, well away from home, had become his accepted solitary existence. Other than the constant lonely sound of conditioned air flowing through ducks, the office had a deadly silence about it. Ingrid's voice startled him; he'd not heard her at his door.

"I'm about to leave, Mr. Shaw. Is there anything you need before I go? Someone's made a fresh pot of coffee in the outer office. I could fetch a cup if you'd like."

"Not right now, thank you. I'll probably get myself a cup later. There's nothing else I need, Ingrid. Have a good evening, and I'll see you tomorrow."

"Good night Mr. Shaw." She slipped away as silently as she'd arrived.

Fifteen minutes had passed when he thought he heard sounds coming from the outer office. Venturing out, Ian checked for the source of this disturbance. The entire main office seemed empty. Checking Pete's office, he confirmed that it was also unoccupied. Shrugging his shoulders, he passed it off as possibly being a security guard on his rounds.

This interlude from work presented an opportunity to pour a coffee. Returning to his desk, he resumed work, well sipping his coffee spasmodically. Its taste was unlike the regular office coffee blends he'd become accustomed to. Feeling drowsy, he decided standing up and walking around might reinvigorate him slightly. He was startled again by what he perceived to be girlish laughter emanating from the outer office. His immediate thoughts were Pete had smuggled young girls in for his personal sexual indulgences. Moving towards the outer office to reinvestigate, his legs seemed wobbly and quite unstable. Stumbling into his desk like a drunken man, he fell to the floor. Driven by desperation, he tried crawling for help, but his strength eluded him. Blurred vision accompanying this weakness gave distorted images of two scantily dressed young girls in his now open doorway. As they approached, he reached out for help. One girl slipped her panties off and sat astride his chest, with her knees pinning his shoulders. With blurred vision, he turned his focus towards the timid-looking other girl standing beside him. The girl pinning him down told her to disrobe and sit on Ian's legs behind her.

"I can't do this Mandy, it's not right." Mandy kept insisting until she was coerced into compliance. Mandy was definitely the madam in charge and was not about to take no for an answer.

"Yes, you can. Just do as I say. It'll be easy. Just remember I need to get this done for uncle Pete; I promised him, and you owe me." Reluctantly, as if blindly following orderers, she obeyed Mandy's instructions and unzipped Ian's pants. Mandy then turned and fondled Ian. He was able to control himself with the thoughts of Barbara. His senses became aware of Mandy's Vaginal odours. Still astride his chest, she turned back and moistened his lips with her body fluids as she slowly rubbed herself against his mouth. He Still did not waver. She turned again to perform oral sex on him. This seduction continued for what seemed an eternity until, finally, base body functions overrode morality, and an erection ensued. He felt her coaxing his penis between the second girl's legs, well offering her encouragement through subtly woven coercions. Feeling himself entering the young girl's body, his erection began to waver. Mandy again stimulated Ian, well coaxing the young girl into lowering herself onto him. Now fully aroused sexually, through Mandy's continual stimulation, he'd been seduced into participation. As his groin heaved upwards in orgasm, flashes from a camera illuminated the room. Even his befuddled brain deduced Pete had finally compromised him in this unguarded moment. This scenario had never occurred to Ian, but he felt it should have. If Robert were here, this would have never happened. He would not have allowed Ian to fall victim to such a juvenile scheme. He would have anticipated Pete's every move.

Mandy, and her young friend, vanished as quickly as they'd arrived, leaving Ian wallowing helplessly on the floor. It was several hours before he'd recover sufficiently to arrange transportation home. Laying alone in his apartment bed, shame and guilt consumed him. The sexual assault bothered him, but what he found harder to accept was near the end of the seduction, he'd become, in his mind, a willing participant. He thought of Barbara and wept, in the belief, he had somehow been unfaithful to her. He must tell her, but how would she understand, would she forgive him, could he ever forgive himself? Could things ever be the same between them again? So many questions with no answers. He'd never had cause to doubt his marriage by betrayal before. Could it stand what had just happened? Could he expect things to ever be the same?

Early next morning, returning to his office full of anger and confusion, he was confronted by photographs graphically depicting the previous evening's activities taped across his desk. Slowly, methodically, he took his gun from the desk drawer. After checking it over thoroughly, he clenched it with a firm grip. Now more mechanical than methodical, he found himself at Pet's office door. Ian's emotion erupted into a fit of rage. Kicking in the office door, he'd caught Pete entirely off guard. He was mulling through the pictures taken that previous evening. Ian leaped onto Pete's desk, knees first. Pete tried to smile. Ian's hand went for the throat, and as his grip tightened, Pet's mouth opened, gasping for air. Ian seized this opportunity, forcing his gun barrel down an open throat until stopping at his own hand. Frantic gagging and death throw rattles emanated from deep within Pet's chest ensued as Ian's finger started to squeeze the trigger. He then recalled Robert's words. *'Don't let hate or anger consume you; these things can be used against you. They do not enhance you as a person in any way. They only serve to diminish you as a human being.'*

"I should kill you for what you did, you son of a bitch but this must be your lucky day. Now's not your time." Relaxing his grip, he slowly removed the gun barrel from Pete's throat. A blood-covered fore site was wiped clean in Pete's shirt. Collecting the photographs, negatives, and camera, he calmly exited the office, relishing the look of terror etched into Pete's face. Gagging, well periodically spurting blood upon his desk, Pete was incapable of mounting any form of retaliation.

Ingrid's arrival at her workstation coincided with Ian's return from his little foray. Projecting a calm demeanour to subdued close surface anger, he spoke. "I'll be at home working next week. You know where I can be reached if I am needed."

"Yes, Mr. Shaw, of course." Her intuition sensed Ian's turmoil. "Is there something else I can help you with, Mr. Shaw?" No words passed his lips as the pain, written boldly across his face, cried out for a compassionate shoulder to cry on. However, she perceived it would not be hers.

"Do you need me to work on anything other than my regular work? Well, you're away?" A confused reply came from a voice now filled with remorse.

"No, yes," there was a short silence well-regaining composure. "I'll lay it out for you before I leave."

Closing his office door, he stood as if in a trance, viewing the photographs still displayed across his desk. Rage determined the contents of his hand be dashed upon the floor. A sweep from an angrier arm ensured that the offending desktop collage followed. This burst of undisciplined emotion sufficed to vent some pent-up frustrations, allowing him to regain better composure. Logic now dictated no one should witness these portraits of disgrace. One by one, items were meticulously gathered and subjected to a fiery wastebin as uncontrolled tiers rolled down sad cheeks. Remorseful tiers echoed pain that emanated from that episode of shame.

Before leaving the office, he instructed Ingrid to book him the first available flight to England. A quick apartment stopover was required to pack some clothes. An airport wait seemed preferable to lingering anywhere else at that moment. Alone in the hustle and bustle of a crowd provided focused distractions. It diverted his thoughts from the more relevant task ahead.

Eventually, arriving at Bristol airport, he chose a taxi home, not wishing to unburden himself on Barbara in the car. He knew she would sense something was wrong the minute she laid eyes on him. This crisis needed to be dealt with in the privacy of their own home.

Reaching the house, he left his bag in the hall and went straight to her office; a quick knock on the door before entering caught Barbara totally off guard.

"Well, this is a pleasant surprise. I wasn't expecting to see you so soon."

"Barbara," his pause, and the forlorn look on his face told her he was the bearer of bad- tidings. "Could we go to our bedroom where we can talk in private without interruption?" Her expression changed to sombre, anticipating the magnitude of what he was about to say. Without a word, she rose from behind her desk and solemnly followed him.

Once in the bedroom, he sat on the bed. He patted the spot next to him as an invite to her. She sat down and clasped his hands in hers. As they made eye contact, words he so meticulously rehearsed in his mind were swept aside as a quickly mumbled sentence poured from his lips.

"I've been drugged and molested." At first, the shock of this statement overwhelmed her. Compassion then poured from her as she wrapped her arms around him. Tiers so strenuously held back now flowed freely as he told her the whole story. His story included everything. It started when he had found Pete with the young girl until he had been drugged and raped. Her embrace eased, then she pulled away crying. Unable to touch him, she stood up to regain composure.

"We're both victims here, Ian, and I am not going to let this evil little man destroy us. I'm going to make some phone calls. We need professional counselling."

"Do you really think that's necessary?"

"Yes, it is. I'm not about to allow this incident to fester and destroy our relationship." Incapable of making rational decisions at that moment, he put his faith in her more than capable hands.

"I'm sure your right. I'll do all it takes to come to terms with this mess and put it behind us." Barbara left the room and returned ten minutes later. "Pam's driving us to Bath. We're leaving right now." Her eyes were red from the tears that were now pouring down her cheeks freely.

"There's no reason to bother Pam; I can drive."

"Ian! Neither one of us is fit to be behind the wheel of a car right now."

"Of course, your right: I wasn't thinking."

"We have an appointment with a man who specializes in trauma. He did say there is no quick fix, but that we've done the right thing, seeking help immediately."

The following weeks were filled with frequent visits to Bath for therapy. I took time to re-establish the relationship that had cemented the close bond between them, but time and love have a way of healing open wounds such as these.

Unbeknown to Ian, his health had been monitored closely by Lord Simpson, and when he deemed him fit, he was summoned back to Zurich. Unsure of the reception awaiting him, it was a hesitant Ian who found himself knocking on Lord Simpson's office door.

"Come in." Ian tried to show a brave face as he walked through the door. "I've been expecting you, have a seat." Lord Simpson did not make eye contact; instead, he pointed to a chair with his pen's back end. Ian took this as a good sign. To be stared down by Lord Simpson was usually a prelude to the unleashing of his wrath. At this point, Lord Simpson had barely taken his eyes off work on his desk. Putting down his pen, he leaned back in his chair. "So, will you be able to put this Peterson affair behind you?"

"I wasn't aware you knew so much about it, Sir."

"There's little that goes on here without my knowledge."

"Then you will understand, Sir, that I can no longer work for that man and perform my duties to the best of my ability."

"I understand that Ian. I don't know why you didn't shoot him when you had the chance. No one would have blamed you for that. Compromising the companies efficiency to that extent makes the person responsible expendable. We've been less than satisfied with Peterson's performance of late. So as of now, Peterson is no longer your boss. You'll receive your assignments directly from me. You can regard this as a promotion of sorts. We feel you're now ready to be entrusted with more responsibility. Your work has achieved a standard we're more than satisfied with. As you know, you were scouted and thoroughly assessed before your integration into the company."

"As you say, I'm aware of that, and I am satisfied with this new arrangement Lord Simpson. I know I'll be able to live up to Mr. Desate's expectations, under your guidance, of course."

"I'm pleased you're satisfied, Ian, Mr. Desate thinks highly of you, and no one wants to upset Mr. Desate."

"Lord Simpson, am I to continue with the work I've been assigned, or is there another project you wish me to undertake?"

"You're now in total control of all current work, and I will expect you to bring that to a satisfactory conclusion. There will then be several important assignments requiring your attention, but none of them are priorities at this point in time. When they do need your attention, I'll have the briefs delivered to your office. You can then deal with them as you see fit."

"If there's nothing more, Sir, I'll return to my office." Lord Simpson's eyes returned to the paperwork on his desk. His pen dismissed Ian with a gesturing wave.

CHAPTER 26

Songs were written, and pranks were played

Broken melodies coming from the lounge told Pam Barbara was composing at the piano. Knowing the importance of not disturbing an artist's mood, Pam waited until there was a period of silence before pouring two coffees and joining Barbara. Her timing couldn't have been better. She found Barbara sitting back from the keyboard, stretching entwined fingers backwards on outstretched arms.

"I thought you might like to take a coffee break." Placing one coffee on the piano in front of Barbara, she snuggled her own cup close with both hands. Peaking over the cup's brim at Barbara, she sipped her hot beverage slowly.

"I'd appreciate your company right now, and this coffee wouldn't go amiss." She slid to one side of the piano stool to make room for Pam. Without the need for words, Pam sat down beside her. Sensing Barbara's melancholia, she felt obliged to comment.

"The way you feel, shouldn't you take some time off rather than trying to work through it."

"It's good to express yourself when emotions are running high; you must let those feelings pour into your work. Life is not all sunshine and roses, you know. That's why some sad songs are called the blues. Artistes often overflow with creativity in life's low points."

"I never equated blues music as coming from real hardship and sadness before. I've always looked upon it as music and no more. Can you tell me, is there a story relating to what you've written?"

"Well, I'll let it be interpreted as the loss of a lover, but that's not it. It actually relates to quite a different episode in my life. I lost my parents in a car accident when I was in my early teens. I've always tried to forget that dark period until now. Thoughts and emotions I once suppressed have now been allowed to re-emerge. I am now confident of laying that sad era in my life to rest. Tapping into my present emotions and using them to recreate how I felt back then, I've been able to write about it for the first time. I think I'm finally strong enough to face that awful time in my life and give it closure."

"That's very brave of you baring your soul in a song."

"That's how most artists archive their best works."

"May I read the words? I've heard you perfecting the melody on the piano. I found it haunting. It really moved me." Barbara handed Pam the song sheet.

"This is exciting for me. Imagine being the first person to read the words of a hit song." Barbara was flattered.

"I never said it was going to be a hit song." Pam's enthusiasm was not that easily quelled.

"If the words are as good as the melody, I'm sure it'll be a hit." This brought a smile to Barbara's face.

"Flattering the boss will get you everywhere, Pam." Pam read the lyrics in a soft voice to emulate a soulful rendition of a favourite poem.

WILL THE SUN SHINE FOR ME TOMORROW

Happiness once filled my heart, and love was all around me. A light from deep inside would seem to shine about me. Now, storm clouds gather overhead to darken every day. Can that inner light shine through and brighten up my way?

Will the sun shine for me tomorrow? Will there be a brighter day? A love once strong now leaves me hollow. Will I ever find a way to fill my heart with love again for me; what's there to follow? Will the sun shine for me again, will there be a bright tomorrow?

Can blue skies break the hold of these dark clouds that surround me? It's the place I hide my pain and the sorrows that surround me. Can light then pour on through and brighten up my way, or must I live my life through dreams of yesterday?

Will the sun shine for me tomorrow? Will there be a brighter day? A love once strong now leaves me hollow will I ever find a way to fill my heart with love again for me; what's there to follow? Will the sun shine for me again, will there be a bright tomorrow?

My friends tell me, be strong, they say I'm a survivor, they tell me life goes on and time's the greatest healer. I know what they say is true, but still, I have this sorrow, so once more I ask myself, will there be a bright tomorrow.

Will the sun shine for me tomorrow? Will there be a brighter day? A love once strong now leaves me hollow; will I ever find a way to fill my heart with love again for me; what's there to follow? Will the sun shine for me again? Will there be a bright tomorrow?

I now know faith will guide my way to happiness from sorrow. These dark clouds will slowly drift away, so brighter days may follow. Until those days return, I will bear my sorrow. The Sun Will Shine for Me Again----- but not tomorrow.

"How sad. If you hadn't told me what the song was about, I would have thought it was the end of a relationship. What will you name the song? (*Will the sun shine for me tomorrow,*) after those recurring words."

"I like that suggestion, Pam; that's exactly what I'll call it. Now I need to work. Ann will be here in a few days, and I need more material for her to record. Thank you for the coffee and your company. It was much appreciated."

Collecting the coffee cups, Pam slipped away as inconspicuously as she had arrived. Barbara toyed with the keys, and a new melody started to take form. This time the song was more upbeat.

Tony was about to seek Pam out but was saved the search by their chance hallway meeting.

"I'd like to make an attempt at a master tape for Richard's record. He's as ready as he'll ever be, and I think we can give him a marketable sound."

"Sounds great; just give me a minute to get set up."

As evening approached, the lounge became the gathering place. Everyone was trying to respect Barbara's space until Tony noticed she was beginning to look tired.

"Why not call it a day Barbs, you'll wear yourself out if you work much longer."

"I desperately need one more song. It's so near yet so far." Tony gently bummed her over on the stool as he sat down beside her.

"Make way, Barbs, and let's hear what you've got."

"It's not so much what I've got. It's this theme begging to take form."

"Tell me about it."

"The story's about a young woman who falls deeply in love with a young man. At some point in the relationship, she discovers that she is the illegitimate daughter of his long-deceased father. This information comes to light when shown an old family photo album of this young man's family. Her own mother had a photo of this young man's father. She was told this same man was her father. Her birth was a secret, until now, only his father and her mother had knowledge of. A secret well kept from other family members. Now knowing she's forbidden fruit, the turmoil is causing catastrophic repercussions in her life."

"I get the drift." He scribbled down a few lines, and as Barbara mused over them, her fingers rolled out a few bars. After making a nip here and a tuck there, a workable song started to emerge. The tension caused by pressure and frustration had left her face. The block she'd experienced lifted like the removal of a heavyweight. Penning a few more lines of the story, Tony quickly converted them into poetry to accompany her melody. "This is the result of our collaboration, Barb's."

He then read the words out loud as she played the piano softly.

MY SECRET

On a tree that bears forbidden fruit, a bitter harvest grows. The thought to sample such a dish surely poor judgment shows: But, oh that apple's taste I yearn for Oh so much. Each time you walk into the room, I tremble for your touch.

There's a secret deep inside my heart no one must ever know. I keep my secret to myself and never let it show. To do so would bring hurt to those I love around me. So, I keep my secret to myself and never let it show.

I've tried to leave this place, but there are ties that bind me. Each time I try to leave, another snare entwines me. I fear that if I stay, the truth would soon be known. This secret that I bear is too hard to bear alone.

There's a secret deep inside my heart no one must ever know. I keep my secret to myself and never let it show. To do so would bring hurt to those I love around me. So, I keep my secret to myself and never let it show.

This love pent up inside is driving me insane, growing stronger the day I still manage to contain. You're always Oh so close, and yet so far away, you rule my every thought confuse my waking day.

There's a secret deep inside my heart no one must ever know. I keep my secret to myself and never let it show. To do so would bring hurt to those I love around me. So, I keep my secret to myself and never let it show.

I now know I must leave this place and start my life anew. Perhaps someday I'll again find love; there's little else for me to do. Please don't think bad of me for leaving in this way. There's far too much at risk should I decide to stay.

There's a secret deep inside my heart no one must ever know. I keep my secret to myself and never let it show. To do so would bring hurt to those I love around me. So, I keep my secret to myself and never let it show. Oh no, no, no. Never, never let it show, Ohoooooo no, no, no.

"This is the first time we've ever written anything together, Tony. I love it. It is a little long, though. We'd have to drop a verse or two to record." However, in its extended form, it'll make an excellent stage performance."

"Yes, and it turned out rather well, even if I do say so myself." The lull in the sound of composition allowed Richard's flamboyant persona to capture the room's focus.

"Let's spend the evening in one of these beautiful country pubs you have around here." Standing up from the piano stool, Tony locked the fingers of both hands together well stretching out his arms.

"Sounds like a good idea Richard. I could use a snack. I'm feeling a little peckish right now." The suggestion was unanimously accepted, although Barbara seemed a little hesitant. This prompted Pam to walk over to her and put her hands on Barbara's shoulders from behind in a massaging motion.

"It'll do you good to come with us, Barbara, and I'd appreciate your company. You know when men get together, their conversation usually gravitates to sport, cars, or politics; not necessarily in that order."

"You've talked me into it. I'll get my jacket and purse." Hearing the word pub seemed to make Robert magically appear.

"Have you any idea which pub you might be going to," he said as he entered the room. "I'm seeing Linda this evening, and we might like to catch up with all of you later." Richard made a grand sweeping gesture with his hand as if making a speech from the footlights.

"We shall drink and dine at that picturesque pub overlooking the lake."

"Do you mean the pub we had Sunday lunch at?" Tony was seeking some clarity from a man who very often spoke in metaphors.

"The very one, my good fellow." Tony then deciphered the message for Robert's ears.

"That's the Blue Bowl, Robert." Robert's acknowledgment was no more than a nod and knowing grin, but those gestures were all that was needed to convey his thoughts on Richard's performance.

Arriving ahead of the pub's evening supper crowd, table choices were extensive. A large corner table was chosen to foot their bill. After the ritual of ordering and devouring food was accomplished, Tony's attention turned to Richard; the setup had begun.

"I once knew a man with nerves so steady he could balance a full pint of beer on each outstretched hand. Holding his hands out in front of him, he would appoint someone to place two full glasses of beer on the backs of his fingers. He would then hold that position without spilling a drop of beer."

Barbara rolled her eyes at Pam and whispered, "here we go," as Richard stretched out his hands to verify their steadiness.

"That sounds an easy task for a man like myself who's graced with nerves of steel." Tony backed off a little but then allowed Richard to goad him into a bet. "I'll wager the sum of one pound I can match that feat."

"You're probably just waiting for the chance to call me chicken. I suppose I'll have to match your bet to save face." The wager was made, and the fish was nibbling at a baited hook. Tony was sniggering to himself as he scurried off to buy the two full pints of beer required. A poker face replaced that jubilant expression on his return. "There we go, two full glasses of beer; note no spillage as yet." Richard had a smile on his face as Tony carefully placed the glasses on the table. Richard's outstretched arms were as steady as a rock with the aid of his palms resting firmly on the table.

"You may place the glasses on the backs of my hands now, Tony." Indignation poured from Tony's mouth, as reluctantly, he complied. That quick jerk of the line had hooked the fish. Richard, the unsuspecting flounder, beamed with confidence at the thought of outwitting Tony.

"There was no stipulation in the wager; it could not be performed in this manner, so this fulfills my successful obligation. I'm balancing two glasses on the backs of my fingers without spillage. I believe the sum mentioned was one pound." Tony smiled at the girls. Taking a one-pound note from his wallet, he placed it on the table in front of Richard without saying a word. Richard now realized his predicament, being unable to pick up his ill-gotten gains. "Would you mind removing the glasses now, my good fellow?"

"I will, for a price, Richard. It will cost you one pound ten shillings." The mark was now semi-aware of the sting. Unable to stand and reach the glasses with his mouth or move his hands without spilling the contents, he opted for a reckless move.

"Stand back everyone, I'm about to pull my hands away very quickly." Tony quickly intervened.

"If you spill the beer, Richard, remember you lose the bet, and you will be out one pound. If I remove the glasses for you, you get to keep the pound on the table."

"Yes, but then you'll expect me to pay you one pound ten for that service."

"Correct, but think about it, my way, you only lose ten shillings." Richard, conceding a no-win situation and capitulated to Tony's terms. As the money changed hands, it was apparent Tony was not the only winner. One man's loss is often the gain of others. Richard's ten shillings had bankrolled some exciting entertainment for the group. Their appreciation was shown with side-splitting laughter and cheeks rolling with tiers. Barbara, barely able to contain herself, was not above giving some sarcastic advice.

"Let this be a lesson for you, Richard; don't tangle with the master of particle jokes."

Robert and Linda's arrival interrupted any more cheap shots at Richard.

"It looks like we've arrived just in time by the smiles on everyone's faces." Barbara spilled the beans.

"Tony's just caught Richard with his beer balancing joke. Linda's curiosity was engaged.

"What joke is that? Robert."

"Believe me, Linda, it's better not to ask." Richard hadn't learned a thing, jumping straight in feet first; his deflated ego needed a boost. Perhaps if he could humiliate someone else, he would achieve this much-needed ego boost.

"Please, allow me to explain, Linda." He quickly shuffled the two pints into position before requesting she put her outstretched hands over them. After explaining the game's ground rules, he offered her the identical wager Tony made him. This was done in the guise of making it more interesting. Convinced, he'd found a mark as gullible as himself made him smug and over-confident. Laying back, he eased his chair's front legs from the floor and rested its back against the wall. Linda performed the task in the same manner as Richard had. Conceding defeat, he then repeated the previous offer made to him. However, he was quick to point out all the pros and cons of the arraignment. Linda, who had never sat down, put her own spin on the game. Slowly pushing the table towards him, on a smooth carpet with her legs, she'd trapped him in his seat; by way of the precarious position, he had chosen to sit. Everyone else was able to move aside. Sliding her hands to the table's far side, glasses still balanced, Richard was now her captive.

"Stop, you're going to spill those drinks all over me."

"Then take them off my hands," she said softly, with a cute smile, well wiggling her hands just enough to disturb the liquid. Her message to Richard had been clearly transmitted.

"If I do that, I'll lose the bet."

"It would be less costly than your cleaning bill, and you wouldn't have the discomfort of sitting in wet clothing for the rest of the evening." Reluctantly he removed the glasses from Linda's hands, only to be the object of more ridicule. Barbara patted his shoulder with a consoling hand.

"I did warn you to leave practical joking to professional pranksters. I don't think you're cut out to be a con man, Richard."

Barbara eased back towards Pam, whose hand-cupped mouth made it apparent she intended some word for Barbara's ears only.

"This beats the hell out of most evenings I've spent in pubs. You get fed up with listening to the same rhetoric night after night." They both had a little giggle.

"There's never a dull moment with Tony around, Pam. He's on a high at present, knowing Ann will be here the day after tomorrow."

"I'm looking forward to meeting her, especially after hearing her singing on the radio."

"You'll like Ann. I'm sure the two of you will get on like a house on fire."

As evening drifted towards its climax, Barbara's busy day took its toll on her party spirit.

"I think I'll be calling it a day. I'm tired, and I would like to phone Ian before he goes to bed." Pam picked up her purse.

"I'll come home with you, Barbara. I could do with an early night myself." Pam then leaned over and kissed Richard on the cheek. "You don't mind, do you, Richard."

"Not at all, you sweet young thing. If you were to stay, I'd probably only end up humiliating myself in front of you again." Tony picked up the empty glasses.

"Don't take it to heart, Richard, come on, I'll spot you your round of beers."

"I'd appreciate that Tony, I'm fast running out of money with all the bets I'm losing."

CHAPTER 27

Ann gets a lesson in book-keeping.

Meeting Ian's flights were pleasant brakes now factored into her work schedule. The driving and the waits for those fond reunions were relaxing respites in her otherwise busy days. On this occasion, their work commitments deprived them of each other's company upon reaching home. It wasn't until late evening they were again able to enjoy each other's company.

Recording work had been completed on Richard's project. This saw his departure that afternoon: And the troops had scattered, leaving them an empty house for the evening. The lounge was chosen as a place to relax and unwind. Sitting at the piano, Barbara played and sang, for Ian's enjoyment, as he sat quietly in his favourite chair. Her repertoire included material recently composed for Ann. Finishing her recital, she joined him and draped her body across his. The close proximity of her warmth turned his constant burning flame for her into a raging furnace. Standing upright, well cradling her in his arms, he whisked her off to their bedroom. Laying her gently onto the bed, her clothes were removed in massaging motions by his sensitive hands.

Straddling her body, he then slowly disrobed, revealing his well-sculpted physique. Watching, in a mesmerized state, she could feel her whole body quivering uncontrollably in anticipation. Reaching out her hand, she stroked the part of his body he'd reserved solely for her pleasure, and with fingers used as sensitive tools, she created music for a different rhapsody, the one of love. Legs moved to accommodate each other as he lowered himself onto her. His fingers then rippled over her body like a harpist caressing string producing harmonies of wonder. After gently guiding him to the place of unification, she pulsated with a rhythm orchestrated by the flow of life as he entered her body. All the while, his lips had been accompanying this concerto with subtle enhancements. Their hearts pounding like tympani's, beating faster and ever more quickly, forcing this unsustainable intense rhythm to momentarily falter. After a short pause, they returned to a subdued level of lovemaking, which accommodated appreciation for the performance's full beauty. Slowly at first, they accelerated to the Plateau previously reached, accompanied by thunderous moans and screams of a decibel intensity equaling the 1812 overtures canon fire accompaniment. Sleep then overtook their entangled, by love, bodies.

In a sparsely occupied train station platform, Tony and Barbara awaited Ann's arrival the following day. The train had barely halted as Ann leaped from her carriage with tiers of joy rolling down her cheeks. Throwing herself at Tony, she smothered him with kisses. He, in turn, reciprocated the treatment. Barbara waited patiently for this passionate reunion to simmer off the boil before giving Ann her own warm welcome.

After collecting Ann's luggage, they proceeded to the car. Barbara walked ahead, figuring to give love's young dreamers the space she'd appreciate having if it was one of her own reunions. Reaching the car, Tony and Ann snuggled into the back seat together while Barbara played the chauffeur's discreet role.

Dropping them at the front door, she garaged the car. Tony helped Ann carry her luggage to her allotted room before joining Barbara in the lounge, where small talk ensued.

"Now you've settled in, tell us all about your trip."

"I have no idea where to start. I had a fantastic time. I was treated like royalty. I was chauffeured here, there, and everywhere. It's amazing how the other half lives, and the shopping was fantastic. I found things so reasonably priced, I've practically bought myself an entirely new wardrobe. Needless to say, I've also bought gifts for everyone, but that'll have to wait until I've unpacked. Jeff sends his regards and hopes your writing lots more songs for him to use."

"Speaking of new material, I have some new songs for you to record, on your stay here Ann. I've also hired an assistant to help with the workload. I've invited her to join us; I'm sure the two of you will hit it off just fine." Pam arrived several minutes later, and Barbara made the introductions.

"I have Pam hard at work starting up our new company at present, but when you record, you'll find her indispensable in control booth duties. She'll also be handling a lot of your day-to-day needs, like travel arraignments and such." The two girls then talked extensively, finding much common ground and shared interests. Tony and Barbara were relegated to audience status. As their conversation subsided, Barbara considered it time business should be attended to.

"If you're up to it, Ann, I'd like you and me to have a business meeting. We can go to my office and review your tour's gross figures and expenditures."

Ann sat down and tried to make herself comfortable in Barbara's office. A room best described as spik and span, to the point of being sterile. A set place for everything and everything in its place. An exception was her desktop of organized clutter. It was apparent Barbara had no part in cleaning, a service probably allotted to Brenda.

"I've some of the financial figures in from your tour Ann." It mystified Ann that Barbara could instantly put her hands on any scrap of paper she deemed relevant.

"I don't understand that sort of thing, Barbara; I'll just leave that to you. I know I can trust you to cater to my best interests." Barbara was all business in her reply.

"I appreciate your confidence in me, but I insist my people understand what's happening in regard to their fancies. I'll walk you through it very slowly, so you understand. If there's anything your unsure of, please don't be afraid to speak up." The next hour or so was spent explaining the basics of bookkeeping relating to Ann's tour. "I think we've covered as much as I can explain to you in this short time. The more times we do this, the easier it'll be for you to understand. By year-end, when your financial statement has been prepared, it'll not be just a page of meaningless figures to you. You'll have followed it through your monthly statements. Now to the music side of our business. As you may recoil, when you were on tour, I suggested you spend any downtime song writing. Did you have any success with that?"

"I have tried using the formula you laid out. Tapping into my experiences and letting my feelings control the pen, but I've not had much success, I'm afraid."

"May I see your work."

"Of course, I'll get it for you right now." Barbara got up from her chair.

"Bring it to the lounge. I'll meet you there." Barbara was sitting at the lounge's piano playing when Ann walked in.

"Come sit beside me, Ann, and let me hear your work." Ann sat down and began to play as Barbara hummed along. This gave her a feel for the melody. "That's lovely, Ann; I like It."

"Read the Lyrics Barbara, you'll see they don't do the melody justice." Barbara scanned the lyrics.

"I agree; the words need work. I suggest that you choose someone to assist you in this area at this point in your career. Perhaps one day, you will develop a talent for lyrics, or maybe not. However, many song writing duos have achieved a highly successful lifelong career together. You have an ability for music, but to ensure that talent serves you well, in my opinion, you must use your own material. Perhaps I could start you in that direction by collaborating with you on an album. I believe albums are the future in this industry, rather than singles. I'm sure this will be a step in the right direction for your career. I've already written several songs to begin this project.

It surprised me when I worked with Tony to find how easy it was to write with him. I'm confident we would have the same success. I know he'd also be willing to work with you on the album. His arraignments are second to none."

"I consider myself lucky to have met you, Barbara. My career propelled itself forward on the first day I let you take the helm. You gave it that particular interest only a genuinely passionate person about work and music could provide. When I auditioned for Avebury, I was sure it would be my last kick at the can, and I didn't know where to go from there. Look at me today; I've money in the bank and a bright future ahead of me in this short time. I'd like to take this opportunity to say thank you again for being more than just my manager, but someone I also consider my best friend."

"My philosophy is, we get out of life what we put into it, Ann."

Composing at the piano until late evening, creative juices that had previously flowed in abundance were experiencing drought.

"Enough for today, Ann; we'll start fresh tomorrow. I think I'll go see what Ian's been doing all day. He's probably as hungry as I am."

"I'm going to lay down for a while, Barbara. I think jet lag's starting to take its toll."

"I'll page you when supper's ready."

Tracking down Ian to his study, she found him completely engrossed in his work, with no perception of time.

"Are you ready for supper?" He checked the clock.

"I am, but I'd like to finish up here first. That should only take me half an hour tops." Hugging the door's edge, she smiled at him in a caring way.

"I'll go to the kitchen and see what I can rustle up. It should have something ready by the time you get there." She met Pam in the hallway, heading in the same direction.

"Everyone's hungry, and I volunteered for kitchen duty."

"That's precisely where I am heading, Pam. Were there any special requests for supper? I could do with some fresh ideas."

"No, so let's make something quick and simple."

"I'm all for the simple life. It sounds like a good plan to me. Any suggestions?"

"Toad in the hole would be good if we can find some sausages." Barbara had reached the fridge.

"We have lots of sausages, now how do we make it, Pam?" With her usual kitchen proficiency, Pam had preparations already well underway. Barbara was given a running commentary on events as they unfolded.

"I've placed a large baking dish containing a quarter-inch of oil into a high oven to heat. Now I'll carry on making the Yorkshire pudding batter. Two parts eggs, two parts milk, one part flour. When the oil's hot, we pour in the batter, then add the sausages." Barbara was then given the instructions to make a dark, thick gravy, bring it to boil and set it to simmer. "Now we open that bottle of chilled white wine I saw in the fridge."

"I didn't realize white wine was an ingredient of toad in the hole."

"It's an essential ingredient in kitchen work. We kick back our heals and enjoy drinking it; as we sit and wait for the oven to do its work." Barbara started to laugh as Pam poured the drinks.

"Oh, Pam, you're so bad sometimes. But a glass of wine would hit that particular spot right about now." They clinked their glasses in some kind of triumphant ritual. Sitting, sipping wine, they whittled away the time with talk while supper cooked.

"Do you intend to see Richard again, Pam?"

"He said he'd give me a call, but in a week or so, I think he'll have forgotten who I am. I don't think he's the sort of man it would be such a good idea to get attached to. I know he's a lot older than me, but I found him immature in many ways. Can you understand what I'm saying, Barbara?" Barbara's head was buried in the fridge as she retrieved the second bottle of wine. Her reply was not that clear to Pam's ears.

"Oh, completely. I went out with him once myself." Now Pam started to laugh.

"Did you just say what I thought you said? Oh, I find that's so funny; you dated Richard?"

They were well into the second bottle when Robert walked into the kitchen. This stopped their conversation, but not the laughter.

"What are you two girls giggling about, or dare I ask?" Barbara stopped laughing only long enough to reply. The wine was having its effect.

"Nothing important, Robert, just having a good time drinking our wine." Robert's nostrils detected sweet oven fragrances wafting through the air.

"Something smells good. What are you girls baking?" Pam razed her glass in an unsteady manner, then spied through it at Robert with one eye.

"We're preparing toade in the holee." Robert chuckled at her inebriated reply.

"Perhaps I should cork the remainder of this bottle until you two have eaten something."

Ian walked into the kitchen, rubbing his hands and smiling.

"I see you've set the timer, so I suggest Ian, and I, handle it from here on. Sit yourself down, Ian, and I'll grab us a couple of beers from the fridge." Perhaps you girls should move to the dining room. Ian and I will bring supper in when it's ready." Barbara was in better shape than Pam, but only just.

"Dam right, us girls have done our share." You boys can start by confirming Tony's band will be joining us for supper, then the table will need setting."

"I hope there's enough food for everyone, Pam?"

"The answer to that's simple; don't let people serve themselves, allocate portions." Her voice still had a slur to it, but her logic made sense. "Robert, you and Ian can play butler, dish up servings in the kitchen, and bring everyone proportionately filled plates."

She pointed to fruit adorning the side cabinet. "Place that large bowl of fresh fruit on the table for dessert."

Ian returned with Tony and the band.

"Five more beers and nine for supper."

The men were still savouring their beer when the oven timer started ringing. Ian and Robert were ordered to attend their allotted duties. Ian's was to slice and place the pie portions on the plates, and Robert then smothered them with an ample amount of gravy. Then meals were ferried to the table.

Finishing super, Robert sat back in his chair with the look of a contented man. Giving himself a belly rub of satisfaction, he then sipped the remainder of his beer.

"I was always given to understand English food to be bland and poorly cooked, but since I've been here, I've sampled some of the finest tasting food in the world." Barbara pointed to Pam.

"We have Pam to thank for this meal; she's our kitchen wizard. Although I can accept part of that compliment, for the many meals you've eaten in this house.

This particular social event evolved into a card game that saw unlucky players leave the table one by one as evening drew to its close. This left only diehards and winners vying for that final winning draw of cards.

CHAPTER 28

Mission successful.

A ringing phone in Ian's study heralded the type of message he always received with some reluctance. He, and Robert, had been summoned to Zurich immediately by Lord Simpson. Urgencies dictated Ian be given a brief outline of their separate assignments. He was also informed of possible dangers on the route there, prompting an immediate meeting with Robert in his study.

"You're to accompany me to Zurich under tight security, from where, after my briefing, I will proceed on alone to Southeast Asia."

"Why am I not going with you, Ian? It's my job to supervise your security."

"You're needed in Zurich on more essential matters, apparently. It seems the company's been severely compromised in Asia. My assignment will be a field investigation. Lord Simpson's men, in Zurich, work closely with Peterson, who controls this area, so he'd prefer someone else discreetly investigate that end."

"I don't like the way this is going down, Ian. Experiencing past your vulnerability to Peterson's Machiavellian ways proved a harsh learned lesson. Someone must always be there to watch your back. I'll screen a suitable replacement when we reach Zurich." Is there any other information you have to work with?"

"Only that one of our units controlling an area under Peterson's jurisdiction has been wiped out. I'm sure we'll learn more after reaching Zurich."

* * *

Ian and Robert entered Lord Simpson's office, experiencing the usual cold spinal shiver that always seemed to accompany a greeting from him.

"Gentlemen, please be seated. There will be no reference briefs for these assignments. Our entire system must be considered compromised, and therefore off-limits. Your duties could quickly be neutralized if discovered. The whole company may have been exposed to this unforeseen vulnerability, and no one should be considered trustworthy at this point in time. Indeed, our own safety could well be in jeopardy.

The situation is this, Peterson set up drug trade control in Southeast Asia under the command of a Vietnamese General. His pipeline then funnels cargo to our western associates. The General's either lost control of his own organization through incompetence or, more seriously, our organization has been corrupted. This would put the companies entire command structure at risk.

Drug gangs in Cambodia, and Laos, were permitted to become much too powerful, which may have bred disloyalty. Peterson should have foreseen this situation long ago, but now it's gotten out of hand. It's also possible the gangs have found other markets for their drug and are using that money to buy unsanctioned arms from China. I realize this is not in your work scope, Ian, but we have been impressed with your past capabilities. There are far too many unknowns in this equation, and I'm sure if anyone can solve this problem for us, it's you." Ian looked to affirm the scope of his authority.

"I'm assuming these gangs control regions outside the jurisdiction of this Vietnamese general, but not outside the bounds of my authority?"

"Your operation is covert and knows no boundaries. The flow of merchandise must be funnelled back to the border and under General Nugen's jurisdiction. He can then take back control and responsibility. He's the man you'll be meeting. He's been instructed to give you his full cooperation. I'd like you to assess him and his entire operation and report your findings directly to me."

Lord Simpson's cold, lifeless eyes focused on Robert. "I would like you to investigate office security to ensure one of our own people has not gone into business for himself. With your arm still in a cast, you wouldn't be effective as a field operative anyway.

Ian, you can pick two men from a security team working in Africa until last week to assist you. There should be no connection to our present situation with that team. I'll arrange for them to be at your office for interviews when you're ready. When you've made your selection brief them yourself on what's required of them. All documentation regarding authority, I will attend to personally. I've arranged a private flight to Germany for you. From there, you will use American air force transportation."

"In that case, Sir, I'd appreciate you sending those men to my office immediately. I'd like Robert to assist me with interviews before he starts his own assignment."

Two men were whittled from the team and called in for a briefing. Both were solidly built, clean-cut, and reflecting other desirable character traits sought after in security operatives. Robert had sensed a ruthlessness in one, Dick Preston. His well-trimmed mustache and cold, detached attitude told Robert's discerning eye; he would be a man that would execute any order given him without conscience. A man perhaps needed for work others of conscience would have qualms executing. The other man, who was soft-spoken, with a French accent, introduced himself as Dominic Allen. Knowing Dom from previous assignments, Robert deemed him trustworthy. His allotted appointment would be Ian's personal bodyguard. Leaving Ian in this man's capable hands gave Robert an adequate assurance for Ian's safety.

"As you're aware, I'll be directing this operation. All you need to know at present is we'll be leaving for Southeast Asia tomorrow. It's a jungle assignment under the guise of American military advisers. Draw the appropriate uniforms from supplies. As soon as you have been kitted out, I would like you to meet me back here. This is an extremely sensitive mission, so I expect complete discretion from both of you. That's an order." Dominic stood to attention.

"Permission to speak, sir."

"By all means, and you may both drop the formalities in private, call me Ian."

"I was in Vietnam for a few years, and I'm familiar with its customs. I'm assuming that's our destination." Ian was impressed with the man's deduction, perceiving him more intelligent than most other operatives. However, this was not a question he wished to confirm or deny, so he diverted the conversation with his own question.

"Your accent sounds French, Dominic, but your last name Allen. Is that not English?"

"If formalities are put aside, please call me Dom, and yes, my surname is English. I had an English grandfather."

"Well, Dom, a man with some knowledge of Southeast Asia, will be a definite asset. No doubt, you have some understanding of Asian dialects."

"A little." Ian turned his attention to Preston.

" Dick, as an American, you're the obvious choice to coordinate the team of American advisers we'll be using on this mission. I will remain in the background. All orders will be given to their senior officer, who will answer directly to you. You, in turn, will be directly subordinate to me."

Returning with his full kit to Ian's office, Ian made a statement. "We'll be leaving as soon as your ready, gentlemen. I've just stepped up the schedule."

* * *

Two days later, they'd arrived in Vietnam, under the guise of American intelligence officers. Ian first met with an American Colonel, who commanded military advisers in the specific sector their operation was expected to unfold. After a formal salute, the Colonel was given sealed orders. Orders, commanding him to provide Ian with full cooperation. This was an astute man, a man familiar with military politics. The power exerted by a person carrying such orders, orders he perceived to be drafted by the Pentagon, was far-reaching. Such a man could quickly bury a promising career in some military backwater posting. He was not about to jeopardize his own future by the slightest perception of noncompliance.

Ian allowed him time to absorb the information and then outlined the requirements to ensure his mission's success. All the equipment, transportation, and men he had requested were assembled. His following orders were, that they beheld in reserve for his exclusive use. Ian then made arrangements for Dom, and himself, to be flown by helicopter to meet with General Nugen, the Vietnamese General he'd come to interview. Dick was left in reserve to deploy men and equipment as Ian saw fit.

Ian felt full of confidence as he and Dom landed in the small riverside clearing housing General Nugen's fortified jungle H.Q. The General had an officer greet Ian's helicopter on arrival. The reception was cordial as he introduced himself as General Nugen's adjutant.

"The General's been expecting you. If you would be as good as to follow me, I will escort you to him." Following the officer into General Nugen's tent, Ian ordered Don to stand guard outside. After introducing Ian, to Nugen, the adjutant took his leave. Ian's instinct told him to control the conversation and establish authority.

"As you realize, we're dissatisfied with regional instability. Have you an explanation for what's happening here?" Ian was not looking for lame excuses, and neither did he get one.

"I take full responsibility for disruption in our operations here. I intend to rectify that problem swiftly. Someone in my organization has successfully diverted our trade elsewhere. I discovered the man responsible for this problem just days ago. Before I could apprehend him, he fled to Laos. Since then, I've had a team working full time tracing his movements. I believe we now have him, and his operatives base located."

Ian mimicked Lord Simpson's detached mannerisms, and voice patterns, in an attempt to command authority and respect through fear. A method, in Ian's opinion, that usually left brave men quaking in their boots. His imitation of that cold dead glare paled when compared to the original one, but it was good enough to intimidate General Nugen as he stared him down.

"These people disrupting our operation must be made to understand, this is not a profitable venture for them. The man who betrayed your confidence, was he a man you personally recruited?" Ian had asked a pertinent question, as Nugen was to reveal in his reply.

"No, He was one of Mr. Peterson's men."

"Well, General, the situation seems to have changed. You're now placing responsibility on Peterson's shoulders." The General, a confident, aggressive man, had his next reply honed to that end.

"This is my operation, and I will deal with the problems in my own way. However, I do need time to achieve my goals."

"I am also working on an agenda, and my tight schedule dictates every minute I save is a crucial one. I suggest we work together to form a plan of action."

"Mr. Shaw, I can't just go into Laos with a show of force and not expect severe repercussions. If that were possible, I would have done so."

"But I can. Jurisdictions and their boundaries mean nothing to me. I will have the appropriate people notified of our impending action. Then it will be made clear that there will be no objections from any countries claiming intrusion of their sovereignty.

What's required from you is the location this man can be found at and someone to identify him." The General smiled.

"I'm starting to like you, Ian. you're a man of action, not words." Ian then summoned Dom.

"Contact Preston and give him the coordinates the general's aid will supply you with. You can then tell him to make ready for an extraction mission. "

"I didn't realize you had troops at your disposal."

"And I didn't know if you were trustworthy, General. I'm not a man who's prepared to take chances. You will, of course, accompany us on the raid."

"Naturally, Mr. Shaw, it'll be a pleasure to get the man that betrayed me in my gun sight."

Ian had no enthusiasm for such cavalier action. He was also not about to let Nugen, or any other man, dispose of a vital link in the insurrection chain he was charged to investigate. Recalling Robert's words enforced that determination (Keep playing the game, Ian). Only by continuing this charade would someday, he hoped, make the world be a better place to live.

As Nugen boarded Ian's helicopter, Ian gave him a stern warning.

"Remember, we need this man alive. We must be able to extract every ounce of relevant information he possesses. When we are through with him, and only then can you do with him as you wish. Once his organization has been realigned, control will then be your responsibility. I will then accept no more excuses."

"I'm not a man given to excuses. In the future, I will not be pressured into using anyone who is not of my own choosing."

Evading border patrols, their flight into Laos was uneventful. The helicopters landed Ian's group in a small clearing well away from their intended destination. Nugen's scouts, who tracked the suspect, could also supply coordinates for this secluded location. Ensuring their presence would not be detected was vital to this planned hit-and-run operation. Stealth would also enable the strike force's reconnaissance to confirm where the man that betrayed Nugen was holed up. They could then be confident of this operation's success before committing to their attack.

Dick deployed the men into two sections, one to the fare left and the other to the right. Each flank's fire would converge to the drug gang's camp's front and center from different angles. Only after a long quiet wait was Nugen himself able to positively identify their quarry. A scheme hatched for his capture started to unfold. Dick took two men. Slithering like snakes, they reached the camp's far side. Dick calculated their position to be in a dead spot beyond the two diagonal firing lines created by both friendly groups. It was close to their prime target. They dug in, and sufficient cover was established. The main body's officer, aware of their exact location, gave the order to open fire. Mortar bombs were fired onto the camp's closet's perimeter, leaving a far side escape route, where Dick was positioned. Bodies were running at him from all directions, looking for close, safe cover. The sporadic return of gunfire further increased the chaos. Two marksmen were assigned to lay down fire to funnel their intended victim's retreat towards Dick's specific location. This chosen location was where they would spring their second ambush. Unaware of the game plan revolved around him, he ran straight into Dick's men at full gallop. Dick merely reached out a hand from where he lay to grab a fleeing foot to bring down his quarry. One of Dick's men was not so sensitive in the apprehension. A hit in the face with his rifle's butt end ensured no resistance from the detainee. Dick signalled his situation to the officer commanding before starting their retreat.

They manhandled their prize through the carnival of confusion. Sniper cover fire continued until they rejoined the main force. The attack was brought to as abrupt an end as its initiation. The marks for this blitzkrieg sting were still moving around in a state of chaos. They were utterly incapable of mounting a counterattack. When they realized what had or had not hit them, the entire team reached the helicopter rendezvous and flew out.

CHAPTER 29

Heartbreak and disaster.

General Nugen's camp had the same look of order about it as on their first arrival. Ian ordered a meeting with Dick, and Nugen, immediately on landing. This meeting was designed to leave no doubt about who would be in charge when Ian made his departure.

"Mr. Preston will be in complete control of the interrogation, and he is to have no interference from anyone. Mr. Preston will then deliver the sensitive information gleaned from our guest personally.

He will then return here, and oversee your operation, until he, and only he, decides things are running smoothly again.

"Dick, I no longer see a need for my presence, so I'll be leaving immediately."

"I'll ensure your orders are followed to the letter, Ian."

Generals Nugen's aid, who first greeted Ian, came hurrying over at that moment, waving a piece of paper in his hand.

"Mr. Shaw, I have a message for you marked urgent. It has just arrived." Ian was handed the paper. Turning slowly, he walked away for privacy. Its Contents to him seemed incomprehensible, like something out of a bad dream. It read, 'Your wife had been hospitalized after collapsing and has been diagnosed with an inoperable brain tumour.'

Stunned by this information, he re-read the paragraph for confirmation. There was no mistake. He had not misread the massage. He read on. 'We hold little hope of any possible change in this condition.'

Completely unaware of the fact the paper had slipped from his grasp, his head drooped as he silently walked away to be alone. He'd known sadness in his life before, but somehow this time, it bore a sense of hopelessness. He walked into a tent, sat down, and cried. All he could think of was Barbara and how much he loved her and missed her. The thought of life without her, for him was not worth contemplating. His thoughts now turned to see her, perhaps for the last time. Pulling himself together, he mustered up the courage and went back outside. Ian could see Dom walking towards him with the letter in his hand. Dom had noticed Ian's lack of awareness as he'd walked away and the sadness that hung over him like a dark cloud. Concerned over Ian's distraught state, Dom had picked up the letter. This ensured a message he perceived to have had such a profound impact on Ian would not be read by curious eyes.

"I thought you might not want to lose this."

"Thank you, Dom. I hadn't realized I'd dropped it." Fighting hard to control his emotions, he fumbled with the letter, placing it from one pocket to another. He dare not make eye contact, feeling tears welling up inside. He dropped his head as he unloaded his grief on Dom. "My wife has been taken seriously ill, with little chance of recovery."

I'm so sorry seems such inadequate words right now, but I genuinely am sorry, Ian." Ian had chosen Dom because he was a man of deeds rather than words. So it was no surprise he reacted quickly to the situation. "I'll get in touch with the airbase and have a plane waiting for us when we arrive. Perhaps I should tell them to take us straight to England." Ian, still in a half-daze, nodded.

"England, yes, England, as soon as possible, please, Dom."

"I'll make the arrangements and meet you at the helicopter."

As Dom and Ian were climbing into their transportation to the American airbase, Nugen's aid again came running over, waving another message. He handed it to Ian. The helicopter took off. Ian could not bring himself to read this message immediately. His reason being he could not stand more bad news at this time. When he finally did read this latest update, it was more devastating than his worst nightmare.

It read, 'Your wife passed away without regaining consciousness.' My condolences for your loss, Lord Simpson.'

Ian stood up and walked to the helicopter's door. He stood there looking down at the jungle below for what seemed like an eternity. His mind still numbed by his resent shock. It was not so much Ian was thinking of jumping, but his legs suddenly felt weak. His willpower was ebbing. He could see no point in his life without her. As his legs slowly buckled under him, he was jarred violently backwards. Gunfire was ripping the cockpit to shreds around them.

He came too, lying face down on the ground. Dazed from a blow he'd somehow taken to the head; he slowly rose to his feet. The helicopter's burning wreckage was the only site not obscured by dense jungle. He staggered slowly towards the wreck to look for other survivors. There were bodies inside. Before he reached them, an irruption from exploding fuel tanks engulfed the helicopter in flames. Anyone still inside would now be beyond his help. Intense heat forced him back. Experiencing total desperation and hopelessness, he fell to his knees with negative thoughts flooding his mind. 'Why did I survive? I have nothing left worth living for. Why me.' Tears rolled down his cheeks as he drew his automatic and placed its mussel in his mouth. His hand shook as his finger quivered on the trigger. A friendly hand reached over his shoulder from behind, clasping the gun firmly. He looked around to see Dom looking down at him. His presence shocked Ian, as he seemed to have appeared from nowhere. Dom's experienced iron grip had frozen the gun's firing action. Twisting the weapon slowly from Ian's hand, he rendered it harmless. There was no resistance from Ian as he slowly rose to his feet.

Dom was stood uneasily on one leg; his other leg looked in bad shape. A makeshift tourniquet was helping ebb its blood flow. His soft, calm voice instilled an air of confidence in Ian, despite their predicament.

"We can both get through this if we work together." Ian realized Dom would not last long on his own. Placing Dom's needs above his own personal grief gave him a new focus in life. Their immediate safety in this place was precarious at best.

"Trust me, Dom, I'll get us out of here." Now in a more stable frame of mind, he took back his gun and returned it to its holster.

"I managed to gather a few things together before I was forced to leave the chopper." Dom pointed to a small rucksack, "we'll need that when we leave." Ian picked up the bag and handed it to Dom. Placing Dom's arm around his shoulder, together they staggered away from the crash site in a predetermined direction. They moved slowly but with resolve for several hours until fatigue forced them to rest and take some refreshment. Ian also used this rest period to tend to Dom's leg as best he could.

The rucksack contained a first aid kit, which Ian utilized to redress Dom's wounds. Although still feeling tired, they decided they'd rested long enough and should try to press on. Ian again took Dom's arm over his shoulder and helped him to his feet. They started walking. Considering themselves lucky at this point to have evaded detection, they assumed the enemy hadn't thought it worthwhile looking for survivors.

Emerging from the jungle, the cultivated land stretching out in front of them offered little cover. Taking advantage of the field's ditches, they continued on until a village came into view.

"The villagers may not be friendly Ian; we should wait here until nightfall." Ian lowered Dom to the ground where he could rest. Foraging through the rucksack, Dom retrieved a map and compass. They scrutinized an area map to confirm their position with little else to pass the time; it was a way to stop boredom from setting in.

"If our estimations are correct, there should be a road on the village's far side. Five miles down that road should be a Vietnamese military post with American advisers."

Looking up from their map, they spotted several villagers walking through the fields towards them. Ian drew his automatic. Dom eased

Ian's gun mussel downwards with a tempering hand.

"Steady, Ian, it may be all right. Let me talk to them first." With Ian's help, he rose to his feet. After speaking a few Vietnamese words, the villagers replied, and Dom continued the conversation in French. Turning to Ian, he expressed his view of their situation.

"I think it's going to be all right. They say they'll help us." Several villagers assembled a makeshift stretcher to transport Dom to their village. Ian cautiously brought up the rear. Dom was carried to a small church, where he was made comfortable. With this first opportunity for relaxation since the crash, the adrenalin he'd been high on had started to deplete. Pain and stress were now taking their toll. With only one jab of morphine left to offer relief, Ian gave Dom the option for its use. He chose to try and tough it out until the morning, knowing it would be essential for the last leg of their journey.

"It'll be night soon and unsafe for travel. The villagers say we can spend the night here. They will bring food and water later."

"Tell them, thank you, Dom. We understand the risk they're taking sheltering us." The message was translated into French and passed on.

The thought ran through Ian's mind about how much longer Dom could continue without proper medical attention. Time was becoming crucial in this equation, but little could be done about this downtime. Ian was determined to maximize this rest period and conserve energy for the next day's ordeal. Trying to keep morale high was also a priority. He made a personal resolution to carry Dom out over his shoulder the whole five miles if necessary.

"We may as well make ourselves comfortable Dom, something tells me we're in for a long night. Although I don't recommend, we do the campfire song thing."

Distant sounds, like those of a helicopter, broke the uneasy silence engulfing them. Ian's spirits rose as he moved towards the main door to assess the situation. Before he could open the door, the sound of gunfire erupted from what he perceived to be the jungle's perimeter.

He slowly opened the door to see if he could confirm his suspicions. The shooting indeed was coming from the field's edge. A pitched battle ensued, as the gunship, laid waste to the jungle foliage. The ground fire silenced, the copter's sound faded back into obscurity as it moved away. It never returned to the area Ian was observing. Returning to the small vestry where Dom lay, his hopes for an early rescue had been dashed. Resigning himself to the fact their only option was a night full of tension in this sanctuary, he again settled down. Barely an hour had passed when the sound of an opening door once more sent Ian's adrenalin into overdrive. Gun in hand, he peered from their hiding place to see who had entered the church. Three women were walking towards their humble abode, carrying food and water. He returned his gun to its holster. Entering the room, the water and food were set down for them. Dom spoke to the women in French. One of the young women replied, and a conversation ensued. Dom acted as interpreter, relaying their conversation to Ian.

"This young woman worked as a nurse in this mission. The priest in charge was murdered, and it's been abandoned since then. She said she would like to examine my leg to see if there is anything she could do. I said I'd appreciate her help." After carefully removing dressings, she cleaned his wounds. She then sutured the lacerations. It was time for that last shot of morpheme. Sweat poured profusely from Dom's brow as she worked. He grimaced and continuously talked as a detraction from his pain.

"She said you did an excellent job of dressing my wounds, and that's helped control any infection. Apparently, she thinks you'd make a good nurse if you ever wanted to change your profession." He forced out a laugh.

Fresh dressings had been brought to complete the job, along with some pain killers, which he saved for later. "She said I'm incredibly fortunate there's doesn't seem to be any infection, considering my leg's in such bad shape. It also desperately needs hospital treatment. Hay, but we knew that, didn't we." He again forced out a laugh. She spoke to

Dom for the last time before joining the other two women in prayer at the altar. A moment of serenity engulfed the church. They then moved graciously back down the aisle to slip quietly out the front door.

"I think they threw a prayer in there for us, Ian. She said we should be safe here for the night. I told them we probably won't see them again, as we'll be leaving early tomorrow morning. I again thanked them for their help."

They then ate the food and drank some water. The remaining water was used to top up the canteen.

"Try to get some sleep. I'll stand watch for the remainder of the night. I think I'm too wired to sleep anyway." Dom, weakened by his wounds, and dosed up with morpheme, soon drifted off into an uneasy sleep.

In the solitude of his surroundings, thoughts of Barbara flooded his mind. It was inconceivable to imagine life without her. She was his life. It was a way of life that had now ended. His every sense was spent mourning Barbara that night. Sunrise brought little comfort, but there were goals he'd set and resolutions to fulfill.

Dom was barely conscious as Ian eased him over his shoulder in a fireman's carry. Keeping as low a profile as possible, he headed for the road. Once there, he chose the roadside's ditch cover to continue the trek. Fortunately for him, it must have been a dry season. He walked for several hours, although it seemed much longer. Stopping for a rest, he laid Dom down onto the roadside bank.

Once more, the sound of a helicopter raised his sprites. Climbing from the ditch and looking skywards, he waved frantically at the small silhouette. Instinct told him he'd been spotted as the helicopter arced in the sky. After heading directly for their position, it settled down close by. After making sure Dom was first onboard, Ian then climbed in himself. In Ian's distraught state of mind, the take-off seemed to coincide with their safe landing at the American air force base. Medics rushed Dom to surgery. Ian's task again became apparent, and would not be completed, until Dom had regained consciousness in the recovery room.

Life once more became aimless. Having fulfilled recent obligations, he kept himself active trying to track down Robert. It was nighttime in Zurich, and the office was all but closed. Ian settled for leaving a message for Robert with night security. It stated, 'Robert, I feel it imperative to fly directly to England under the present circumstances.' It also went on to request, Robert joins him there. He had thought Robert might already be there but had not been able to raise anyone to confirm this. Ian then arranged his own transportation before going back to see if Dom was out of surgery. It was several hours before Dom regained consciousness. Ian was then allowed a visit.

"They tell me you're a fortunate man. The doctors only just managed to save that leg."

"I hear the field care I received probably saved my life."

"I think you can thank the young nurse for that, my friend." He placed his hand on Dom's shoulder.

"Don't make light of your part in all of this. You're the main reason I've made it into this bed safe and sound."

"I only did what anyone would have done under the circumstances. I must leave for England in thirty minutes, Dom, but I'll be back in Zurich soon after. When you are well enough, come and see me there." The intensity of their handshake echoed the bond that had formed between the two men.

CHAPTER 30
Something to live for.

The early morning's cold gray hours greeted him as he stepped from the plane. A greeting that well-matched his inner feelings. There was an air of detachment about him. He was devoid of passion, going through all the motions of life without having any of its meaning.

A taxi boarded at the airport was now delivering him to the house, once a home's driveway, in past times, his safe haven of joy. He quietly walked through the front door, knowing there would be no warm welcome, no loving embrace awaiting him, just emptiness. Barbara was not there. Being in this house alone was not an experience he relished. Ian went upstairs to a cold lonely bedroom and entered with apprehension. He knew all the happy memories that room had held for him; today could only make him sad. The bed had not been made, clothes were scattered about the room, it was as if Barbara was still there. Sitting on the bed, contemplating arraignment that would need his attention, he heard muffled sounds of what he perceived was someone throwing up in the bathroom's toilet startled him.

"Who's there! Dam it! who's there!" Grief was now venting itself in anger. There was a garbled reply from a female voice. Ian was already on his way towards the bathroom. Pushing open the door, he saw a woman that looked like Barbara with her head in the toilet.

"What the hell's going on here?" To his amazement and joy a person seldom experiences in a lifetime, Barbara looked up at him from where she was kneeling. Her pale white face was wet from the tears flowing from her eyes as she looked at Ian and smiled. Her tiers were now tears of joy.

"I think I'm pregnant. Well, don't just stand there looking like you've seen a ghost; say something. Aren't you happy at the prospects of being a dad?" There was a long pause; he was in shock. Words failed him as he placed his hands on her shoulders. He then helped her to her feet, and putting his arms around her, he held her in a tight embrace. It was his turn to cry. Wiping away the tiers, he was now able to utter a soft watery whisper.

"Please tell me I'm not dreaming, and if I am, don't ever wake me." His reaction overwhelmed her.

"I wasn't sure how you were going to take the news. I thought you'd be happy, but I didn't expect this much emotion."

"I'll explain everything to you later after I've talked to Robert." He held onto her tightly until finally, she had to ask to be released. Still riding an emotional roller coaster, Ian eventually let her out of sight long enough to wash, shave, and change his clothes. Reality slowly prevailed.

"Have you seen a doctor yet?"

"I have an appointment this afternoon."

"I'll come with you. If that's OK?"

"Of course, it's OK. I wasn't expecting to go without you, now your home." Looking in the mirror, he put the finishing touches on his appearance. His lust for life was returning, along with a healthy appetite.

"First thing first. I must go to my office and try to contact Robert. Why don't you go to the kitchen and start breakfast? I'm starving. I'll join you there as soon as I can."

This time, he contacted a puzzled Robert, who was as much in the dark regarding Ian's situation as Ian himself. Having little or no information on Ian's recent whereabouts didn't help matters either.

"Where are you, Ian? Why aren't you here? and that message you left for me, it made no sense whatsoever."

"It would seem many things are making no sense at present. For me, it started with the messages I received from Lord Simpson." Robert's tones turned sombre.

"Ian, Lord Simpson's been dead for several days. I can tell you no more than that over the phone. Things became pretty hairy here following that episode. It's settled down now, but you should be here. We were expecting you to return directly after your mission. Dick Preston sent a communique in which he mentioned you had left. Then you seemed to have dropped off the face of the planet. What possessed you to go to England, and why did you seem to think I might already be there?"

"You obviously have no idea of the recent happenings in Vietnam regarding Dom and me. This, along with many other things, we'll discuss in private when we meet. Those messages allegedly sent by Lord Simpson, I now realize, were fabrications of someone's overactive imagination. This whole affair makes no sense whatsoever. I'll be on a flight to Zurich this evening. We can talk more about this early tomorrow morning."

Ian left his study to join Barbara in the kitchen.

"You look quite shaken. Are you all right, Ian?"

"It would seem I've been the focus of Someone's mind games. It'll take a while for me to sort out what's been happening of late. So, I'd rather not discuss any details with you until I know the whole story. Robert will fill me in on what he knows when I see him. I must leave for Zurich this evening, and I'll be away at least several days."

"Will you still be able to visit the doctor with me this afternoon?"

"Yes, if you drop me at the airport on your way home."

Moving past days' experiences to the back burner, today, he determined it was for living life to the fullest. Enjoying her company over a leisurely breakfast was a start to this day's philosophy.

"I'll be swamped this morning. Having to go to the doctor this afternoon will put me behind with work." He reached his hand across the table affectionately, covering her hand. Work did not enter into the strategy Ian had planned for recharging his psyche.

"Let's forget about work for a while. There are more important things in life for us right now. I want to spend as much time as possible with you today. I just want to indulge myself in the scent of your body and the presents of your being."

"My! How can I refuse a proposal like that; of course, I'll spend the morning with you if it means that much to you. It's plain to see there's something still bothering you, and I wouldn't want you alone harbouring negative thoughts."

"I'd enjoy a long walk together, somewhere cheerful to reflect the way we fill. Weston comes to mind. We could walk the promenade; plus, the exercise will be just what the doctor will order for you. Ian grind at that quip.

Now that you're a successful businesswoman, surely, there's no need to spend so much time at your desk. Be the boss delegate."

"What makes me a successful businesswoman is a hands-on treatment. Although I miss our walks, and you're right, I don't get out as often as I should. Weston, it is then. I've not been there for a while. Pam can hold the fort today; just give me a minute to let her know I won't be here." Ian called to her as she left the kitchen.

"I'll fetch our jackets and my overnight bag; meet you at the car."

The chilly, overcast morning was not quite what he had envisioned as they drove to the coast, but today he was full of optimism.

"I think the weather will brighten up."

"I hope so. It does look brighter to the south." Parking the car near the winter gardens, they walked to the promenade. She pointed north.

"Let's walk towards Anchor Head." Old memories sparked his imagination.

"Do you remember the first time we walked this way? Avebury was the opening act for The Bones, and I said I'd never heard of them." She laughed and tucked her arms around Ian's arm.

"You know who they are now, don't you."

"I now know most of the famous English band personally, thanks to you. You're quite the backstage celebrity, you know." She laughed and gave his arm a squeeze. "When are you going to make a record yourself? Everyone who's using your songs is having great success on the charts. People we've never met, Stateside, are in their charts courtesy of your writing talents."

"I'm so busy, I don't think I'd have time to fit something like that into my schedule. It's not just studio time; it would mean touring, concerts, interviews, you know the scenario." He knew a snow job when he heard one.

"I think you're still a little nervous about being in front of an audience, aren't you?" She gave him a shocked look as if he had just thrown her the ultimate insult. Her glare then turned to a giggle.

"You're so right; it bloody terrifies me."

"You were fantastic at the new year's dance. You had no problems there, and you enjoyed yourself."

"I never thought about being nervous at that time. I was just helping Ann out, and we were all there for a good time."

"Then you should always think of it as having a good time. If you weren't having a good time, why would you want to do it?"

"Perhaps one day I'll write a song I'll not want anyone but myself to sing."

"Tony told me, some of those beautiful songs you sang for me, you've kept." A smile lit up her face as she looked into his eyes.

"They were written for you, like love letters. They're too personal to be read or sung by anyone else."

"Then you do have songs that you wouldn't want anyone else to sing."

"Yes, but as you say, if it isn't fun, don't do it." His retort was in a light-hearted vein.

"That's a cop-out, and you know it." They bathed in the glow of their happiness.

"Let's go back to the pier. We could walk out to the end and sit quietly looking out to sea, over a coffee."

"That sounds enjoyable."

The Heavens were parting, allowing bright sunlight the opportunity of painting an otherwise dull gray sky into a canvas of dazzling silvers and blue. The sea was not to be excluded from nature's celebration, reflecting its own sparkling dance of light from the fast-flowing waters of the Bristol Channel.

Walking to the pier's end, they sat at a restaurant's outside table, a table Ian quickly furnished with two coffees.

"We've never talked about children, have we, Ian?"

"I couldn't be happier about the situation darling. I'm looking forward to being a dad." He took hold of her hand.

"I'm happy to. Would you prefer a boy or a girl?" He teased her with his reply.

"I wasn't aware we had that choice." Her face sparkled with an inner glow that was so much more than just a smile. "I'm not worried about what sex the baby is. I'll just pray for it to be healthy." He gave her hand a reassuring squeeze.

Barbara's focus centred on what she deemed to be efficient planning. This all seemed a little premature for Ian, who was still adjusting to the happy thoughts of parenthood.

"We'll have to consider names."

"Barbara, shouldn't we wait until we hear what the doctor has to say before getting our hopes up."

"Going to see the doctor is nothing more than a formality. I know."

She was straight back into nesting mode. "We'll have to start by planning a nursery." Ian tried to get into the spirit of things.

"The bedroom opposite ours is the obvious choice, don't you think?"

"My thoughts exactly." Finishing their coffee, Barbara pulled her coat collar up around her ears. "Let's walk back to the car. I'm starting to feel a little chilly after sitting here for a while."

Walking back to the car, with his head high in the clouds, Ian felt ten feet tall. In contrast, Barbara's feet were planted firmly on the ground. The morning spent with her was the exact therapy needed to alleviate the trauma incurred in recent days.

"If we drive straight to Bristol from here, we'll be early for your doctor's appointment. Perhaps you'd like to use that time for window shopping."

"That sounds fine by me. I'd like to check out maternity clothing, and I've always wanted an excuse to shop for baby clothes. Some of the things they have in the stores are just so cute."

"I'd more envisioned checking out cribs, baby carriages, and such like." Shopping being Barbara's favourite recreational pastime, she was fully aware that what was a pleasure for her was sheer boredom for him. Taking this into consideration, she fully intended to try to accommodate his interests also. This courtesy went out of the window after a reassuring doctor's visit. Elated with her results, she'd forgotten promises made regarding Ian's feelings. The gloves were off, and a shopping frenzy ensued, depleting any time remaining before Ian's airport trip. Shopping had now put Ian in a better frame of mind for his inevitable departure.

CHAPTER 31

Ian sits at the devils left hand

While reading a newspaper, Robert's laid-back way of passing the time was sitting in Ian's office, with feet upon his desk. This was something Ian mused over on his arrival. They immediately started a discussion regarding past happenings and future concerns. Outlining the contents of messages he allegedly received from Lord Simpson. Ian then gave Robert his conjecture on what was to him was a meaningless scenario.

"I can only think of one person with a mind warped enough to engineer such a senseless scheme, Robert, and that would be Peterson."

"I totally agree; it had to be Peterson. This makes things so much clearer now. I understand why you went straight to England: And thinking that I might already be there. Those fabrications must have devastated you."

"You can't begin to imagine. What would be Peterson's motive to do such a thing? What would be the point; where's the gain?"

"Perhaps to shed some light on his motives, you should first know what happened here. Peterson somehow discovered the reason for your assignment to assess the Vietnam situation. A situation he was totally responsible for, we've since found out. This information was obtained from the man you'd apprehended in Laos. Apparently, Peterson was in collusion with this cohort of his, skimming money from the system. This was probably in an effort by Peterson to form his own little Empire. Had he'd been successful, I'm sure he would have expanded into other company interests. Only his accomplices overstepped the mark by finding another distributor for the product, thus making the situation visible. That's when things got out of hand for Peterson. Fearing the company's wrath, his makeshift plan was to move first. He went into Lord Simpson's office and shot him. Illusions of grandeur then took over as he tried to establish total company control. At this period, he probably sent those messages hoping to distract you in some way. Perhaps as part of some overall strategy that went awry. Or maybe it was just the inept planning of a deranged and desperate man. We may never know. Peterson was fully aware that Mr. Desate would have relied on you to handle the situation on your return. However, Mr. Desate, in person, apparently showed up in Lord Simpson's office. Peterson was hold-up there in wait. The noise of automatic weapons fire was deafening throughout the building. Everyone was ducking or running for cover. Peterson came running out with an assault rifle in his hands and a look of fear on his face like I've seldom seen before. He left the building and hasn't been seen since."

"So, you finally got to see Desate, Robert."

"No such luck, he used the office's back door. After Peterson had left, Mr. Desate phoned from the office and asked to speak to me. He instructed me not to enter immediately but wait and give him time to remove Lord Simpson's body. When we finally entered, Mr. Desate had left, along with the body."

"Then Peterson's the only person alive, know to us, that has ever seen Luk Desate."

"It would seem so, Ian. My guess would be Peterson thought he could take over the company by disposing of Desate, as he did Lord Simpson. His plan: Wait in ambush for Desate to show up. It could have worked, but you know what I believe, Ian."

"Yes, you believe Luk Desate is the devil himself.

"Although I'm still baffled why Peterson would send a message saying Barbara was dead. Surely there could have been fake orders issued or some other devious plot he could have set in motion."

"Perhaps, but what he did in itself was quite ingenious, giving it a second thought. News of that nature would have had you so distraught it would have been impossible for you to reason. You were lucky you weren't in a situation where you might have done something reckless."

"I did contemplate something irrational, Robert, but Dom's intervention and curbed any foolish decisions. You chose him well."

"Sound like he was the best choice for your bodyguard then. I'm glad you had him along."

Ian pondered his fate for a moment and how it could change the scenario's outcome before turning his attention back to matters at hand.

"I wonder who Desate will choose as a go-between, now Lord Simpson's dead."

"I'm sure there will be someone waiting in the wings. As I've said before, job requirements only entail relaying information with authority."

The phone rang, and an apprehensive Ian answered it. The voice on the other end was that of a soft-spoken man. Introducing himself as Luk Desate, he requested Ian's presence in Lord Simpson's office immediately. Putting down the phone, he looked at Robert, who sensed an element of fear radiating about Ian.

"I'm to meet with Mr. Desate in Lord Simpson's office. We'll talk more after that meeting." Robert's following words were chosen to bolster the inner courage in Ian that few men possess.

"Show him that confident manner of yours, Ian. Remember, he holds you in high regard."

Ian left his office and went straight to Lord Simpson's old office. He nervously knocked at the door. The same voice he'd heard on the phone answered.

"Come in, Ian, and shut the door behind you if you would be so kind. Ian entered the room. To Ian's surprise, he saw a handsome young man sitting behind Lord Simpson's desk. This was not Ian's perception of Desate he'd expected. His eyes were then drawn like magnets to walls and furniture. All were riddled with the bullet hole he expected to see. Feeling embarrassed knowing he was being observed doing this, he still could not distract himself. So many bullet holes, so much damage; it was inconceivable anyone could have survived such a battle unscathed. The sound of Desate's voice brought Ian's focus back in line. "It's good to finally meet you face to face: Although the circumstances necessitating this meeting are unfortunate. As you see, the room is, to say the least, a little untidy, but please sit down, Ian, and make yourself comfortable. We must get this room repaired as soon as possible. For now, there are more urgent things at hand. Strictly for an interim period, I would like you to take your orders directly from me. You will relay those orders through the appropriate channels and report all company business straight back to me. I hope to have a replacement for Lord Simpson shortly, but until that time, I will expect you to run the company."

"You've entrusted me with great responsibility. I will do my best not to disappoint you."

"I'm sure you won't, Ian." Ian's paranoia interpreted this as more a threat than a vote of confidence.

"The file cabinets in this room contain all necessary information needed, and they will be updated daily." Desate then pointed to the blue-coloured desk phone. "You may reach me on that line at any time. Phone me only in an emergence. Handle all other day-to-day business yourself." Desate then opened a desk drawer, took out a key, and handed it to Ian. "You'll need a door key to gain access to this office and file the cabinets. Always make sure the door is locked. It's imperative, no one, but you are allowed into this room."

"Does it also unlock the door behind you?"

"I'm the only one allowed access to that door. It will always be bolted from the far side." Desate then handed Ian a brief. "Read this to fully understand the workings of our operations, and I will expect you to follow all stipulated protocols to the letter. You have a busy time ahead of you until Lord Simpson's replacement arrives. Have you any questions, Ian."

"No, Mr. Desate."

"Good, then you are dismissed."

Ian glanced down to secure the brief firmly in his grip before leaving. Desate left in that very instant of distraction, so quickly and quietly, it was hard for Ian to now imagine him ever being there. Ian looked at the key closely before using it to lock the door on leaving. It was crafted much like a piece of fine jewelry. It was unlike any key he'd ever seen before.

Ian found Robert anxiously awaiting when walking into his own office.

"How did the meeting with Desate go, Ian?"

"I've been placed in charge until a replacement for Lord Simpson is found."

"This means you'll be spending more time in Zurich than you'd like."

"It'll only be until a replacement arrives, Robert, and that can't be too soon for me." Robert's curiosity finally got the better of him.

"So what is Desate like, Ian."

"He's young, soft-spoken, not at all what I would have imagined, but there was something sinister about him. And you saw the mess that room was in, Robert."

"Yes, I did."

"How anyone could have survived gunfire that intense is nothing short of miraculous."

"It's beyond belief. Peterson must have used several clips of ammunition in there. It must have scared the hell out of him that so much firepower had no effect on Desate. He probably beat his hasty retreat after running out of ammunition."

Robert looked at his watch and rose to his feet. "I have to leave now Ian. I have a flight to catch. I'll talk to you later."

"Are you going to England, Robert?"

"Yes, if you don't mind, Ian. I would like to see Linda, and there's not too much I can do around here with my arm still in a cast."

"I may need you back here within a day or so. I have a brief to familiarize myself with, and when I find out the extent of my duties, I may want to offload some of them on you. It'll be your expertise I'll be needing, not your arm. I'd also better let you in on a little secret before you leave. Barbara and I are expecting an addition to the family." Robert's face beamed with pleasure.

"Congratulation Ian. Son of a gun." He shook his head, well smiling as though in disbelief. Ian smiled back. Robert then grabbed his hand and shook it vigorously.

"Hard to believe, isn't it? We're going to be parents."

"I'm sure it's a situation you'll quickly adjust to. I'm sure you'll make great parents." He opened the door to leave and turned. "I'll give you a call tomorrow."

On his way to catch his flight, Robert stopped at a toy store and bought the most gigantic Teddy bear he could find.

Ian then phoned Barbara under the pretext of telling her of Robert's plans. The actual motive was to check on her condition. His call was intercepted by a mischievous-minded Pam.

"Is Barbara available, Pam?"

"No! She's not! She's in the bathroom, throwing up." Ian could hear giggling. "What have you done to that poor girl Ian? I suppose congratulations are in order, somewhere along the line."

"Thank you, Pam," Ian replied in a somewhat sobering tone. His voice then lightened up. "If she's not available, would you please take a message? Tell her it may be a while before I can get back home, but to expect Robert. Could you also tell him to give me a call when it's convenient?"

"I can do that for you, Ian, but be warned, the way she's feeling right now, your name will still be Mudd. It's going to take more than a little sweet talk to charm your way back into her good books." He heard another round of giggling.

"Thank you for that insight, Pam." He hung up the phone.

CHAPTER 32

Fish and chip go with what?

Material developed in studio sessions that had kept Tony and Ann busy all morning still eluded their quest for perfection. "I really like it, but it's kind of blah. It needs some humph. Perhaps the rhythm should be pepped up slightly. I don't know; what do you think, Tony?"

One of Tony's band interjected with an opinion.

"Perhaps we should double track the vocals."

Barbara entered the studio, sparking thoughts in Tony's creative process.

"Just the person I need. Ann and I are having a discussion about a song we're rehearsing. Bill there, suggested double-tracking the vocals. I think he's got something. But seeing you here, I'm now thinking duet." Barbara walked over to the piano, where Tony was seated. Sitting beside him, she immersed herself in the song by humming a few bars. Tony then started to accompany her softly on the piano.

"Let's give it a try Tony, I'll sing back up for Ann. We should get Pam in here first to tape what we're doing."

Pam soon had everything set for a first try. A first attempt turned into a second, a third, and so on. Finally, the feeling of perfection that had eluded them came into view. The next take was the holy grail they had been searching for all this time; it was a rap. Barbara was about to leave the studio when Tony waylaid her.

"Before you go Barb's, perhaps you'd allow us to record those songs you wrote. The ones you seem to cherish so dearly." He grinned and waved copes she'd left lying around the studio.

"How about it, Barbara?" Ann beckoned her to sit back on a stool in front of the mike.

"You'd want me to sing them. I thought Tony meant for you to record them." She looked at Tony, he shook his head. Shy embarrassment took its hold on her. They highlight your personality, not mine. Those songs personify you, and only you. My singing couldn't possibly do them justice." Those words from a songstress she admired were the only push she needed to make a hasty commitment in the spur of the moment.

"OK, I will, If you will sing backup Ann?"

"I never thought you'd ask. It would be my pleasure."

It only took a few dry runs before the right arrangement had taken shape, and four songs were taped. After listening to the playback, Tony went into the control booth and spoke to Pam.

"There are a few more things I'd like to try with the orchestration." Explaining his concept, he then insisted on redoing the four songs again. Ann was ecstatic over Barbara's last performances, and a hug around the shoulder was her way of venting her emotions.

"That sounded great; it's got to be your best work yet."

"I am rather pleased with it myself."

Tony again went into the control booth to join Pam. This time to make duplicate tapes of the work that had been done that day. Barbara and Ann were in mind to moisten their vocal cords.

"Let's go to the kitchen for a tea break. Tea in the kitchen when you're ready, everyone." She shouted as they left the studio. On their way to the kitchen, Barbara was overcome by a compelling urge. "I must go to the store; there's something I need to buy. Go ahead and get the tea going. I'll be as quick as I can." This request surprised Ann.

"Yes, of course, I will." Barbara returned some fifteen minutes later, her cheeks bulging.

"What are you eating, Barbara!" Barbara's reply was garbled due to a full mouth.

"Wine gums Ann." Pulling a whole carton from a shopping bag, she placed them in the cupboard.

"Barbara, are you pregnant? You are, aren't you?" She gave Ann a startled look. Her secret was out. This left no time to wallow in personal satisfaction when creating the perfect time to make the big announcement to everyone.

"Did someone tell you, or does it show?" Ann started to laugh.

"You made it fairly obvious; the way you were stuffing those wine gums down your throat, something was up. Buying a whole carton of them gave the game away. You must have had a real craving." Seeing the funny side of her erratic behaviour, she joined the laughter.

"I always thought people exaggerated craving stories. It wasn't until you pointed it out did I realized what I was doing." Ann hugged her and kissed her on the cheek.

"I'm so happy for you. You must tell me all about it. When is the baby due? Do you want a boy or a girl? Have you picked a name yet?" The bombardment of questions was interrupted by people drifting into the kitchen for a tea break. Ann had no sooner started to serve when there was a loud knock at the front door. Pam answered it. Robert was standing there, bag in hand, and giant teddy bear tucked underarm. She hustled him into the kitchen, making sure he had no time to put down his belongings. Steering him to center stage, she left him there posing with a big silly grin on his face and the giant Teddy Bear displayed for all to see. Tiers of laughter rolled down Ann's face.

"Well, everyone knows now, Barbara." She was the center of attraction for the next few minutes. Tony hurried to the phone, laughing, and giggling like a little girl.

"I've got to tell Avebury about this."

On Tony's return, the commotion had subsided, and appetites had driven two or three of them to scan the fridge.

"So, who's hungry?" There were a few raised hands and a few verbal replies.

"How do fish and chips sound to everyone?" Barbara leads a chorus of conformation.

"Fish, and chips, sounds good, Tony, and get some ice cream for dessert."

"Are you sure about the ice cream Barb's?" He had a little chuckle to himself. "I think I'd better make it a small block unless anyone else would like some." There was a lot of head shaking and grimacing.

Ann finished her tea and rinsed her cup off in the sink.

"I'll grab my jacket and come with you, Tony."

"I was hoping you would, Ann."

It was an hour before they returned. Tony placed his neatly wrapped newspaper package at the center of the table.

"Inside, the outer wrapping portions are individually wrapped. There's one for each of you, so don't fight over them. Just help yourselves." Pam set the table with plates and cutlery. Barbara, oblivious to anyone else's needs but her own, put herself out a large portion of ice cream, sampling a spoonful. She seated herself at the table. Spreading her fish and chips on a platter, the group was then astounded by her eating antics. Periodically, she would stop eating her fish and chips to take a nibble of ice cream. Being wrapped up in her own little world made her unaware she'd become a focal point of attention. To prolong this source of entertainment, no one made a sound. Looking up to speak to Pam, Barbara was embarrassed to notice everyone's eyes on her. She then became fully aware that one hand was holding a fork, bearing fish and her other hand a spoon containing ice cream. Pam's burst of laughter shattered the silence.

"I can't see anyone letting you forget this moment in a hurry."

"I can't help it, Pam. You should try it before you criticize. It does kind of go together." Even she could see the absurdity in this reasoning. It was a spur-of-the-moment attempt to justify this irrational eating behaviour.

"I think we're just going to have to take your word for that, Barb's." Tony always had a way with words that seemed to bring out more than just a few snickers. The ribbing had run its course, and after supper, they withdrew to the lounge. Their evening was spent in much the same way as many other evenings, talking and entertaining themselves. For Barbara, such evenings were becoming monotonous, being deprived of the person's company she needed most.

A week had passed since Ian had been home. Feeling lonely and withdrawn, she made the decision. It was her turn to commute. If a few hours stolen here and there from Ian's busy schedule was all that she could have, then that would have to be sufficient. These stolen moments continued for the next six weeks. In all of this time, Ian had not set foot in England. This would undoubtedly make all future homecomings all the more pleasurable.

CHAPTER 33

John needs more information.

"They walked to where Barbara had parked her car. Ian's steps were lightened by the fact her arm was firmly entwined in his. Fetcher trailed behind, transporting their luggage. There seemed to be no need for words between them. Fetcher, however, mumbled colourful comments concerning local happenings of late. Breaking their silence only to give brief replies to Fetcher. The warm, comforting feel of Ian's homecoming conveyed a message louder than any spoken word.

Ian was now sensing fatigued in her steps. "Would you like me to drive home, darling?"

"If you would, please." Reaching the car, Fetcher loaded Ian's luggage. Ian gave him his customary tip before helping Barbara into the car. They talked as he drove.

"All this travelling must be taking its toll on you. How are you feeling? You seem quite fatigued."

"I'm glad the morning sickness seems to have died down, but I do seem to be constantly tired, and I don't know if that's normal or not."

"I imagine that's probably normal, but you should mention it to your doctor on your next visit."

"I will. I'm just glad that you'll be home for a while."

"Hopefully, Lord Simpson's replacement will be taking over soon. Since taking temporary charge, I've implemented a few changes, changes that will benefit us. Hopefully, then I'll be spending more time at home when devoting my time exclusively to company banking affairs once more."

"Having you home, more often, would suit me just fine."

"It's been my aim since starting this job to work more from home and limit my time in Zurich. Perhaps, I also won't have to make so many business trips as in the past. Most of my future trips you should be able to accompany me on; that's if you're not too busy."

"Business is booming. I'm pleased to say." She gave his knee an affectionate rub with her hand. "Although I think I can always find time for you." He placed his hand on hers and smiled.

"Tell me, how's that project of Tony's, involving ourselves and the gang, progressing."

"Just another part of my booming business, but we still have to find a theatre." Wheels in Ian's mind started spinning as he searched for solutions.

"I wonder if we could find a vacant cinema to suit our needs, lease it, and renovate it for live theatre. Heaven knows there seems to be enough of them going out of business these days."

"Ian, that's brilliant. You do come up with some great ideas. Most of the ones closing down are being turned into bingo halls or stores. I don't see why we couldn't convert one for live theatre. You've just given me a lot more work to do; you know that?" She leaned across the car, smiled, then kissed him on the cheek. "I love you so much. The theatre would have to be in London, of course. It would be useless staging a show like that outside of central London." Although excited, she was quiet in thought, mulling over options to be considered, and plans that would need formulating before coming to fruition.

"I wonder if we'll find Robert at home."

"He may be, but he does spend a lot of time with Linda. He's also bought a rowboat and all the equipment needed for lake fishing. I'm sure He's looking forward to taking you out and teaching you how to fish. With John's new posting in England, I'm expecting him home any time, so he could also be there when we arrive."

"I wonder how John feels about the prospects of being an uncle."

"I think he's as excited as I am, but you know John, he keeps his feeling to himself and doesn't say much." They pulled up to the front door, and Ian unloaded the luggage. Barbara went inside while Ian garaged the car. Walking back to the house, he was greeted by John, who had already gathered up the bags, and taken them inside. There were some vigorous handshaking and shoulder slapping, accompanied by verbal Congratulations. The commotion stirred Robert from his cozy seat in the lounge, where he'd been indulging himself in the pleasures of reading morning papers. Ian spoke as he entered the lobby.

"Good afternoon, Robert, So Barbara's tells me you've bought yourself a rowboat."

"I see it's hard to keep a secret around here. But yes, It's a real classic, all wood, beautifully constructed. It's the perfect little vessel for a day of fly fishing on the lake. It's moored at the garden's new jetty right now. When you've got a mind, we'll go check it out."

"I'll definitely work it into my schedule." John was a little more eager than Ian.

"I've unpacked and settled in, so my afternoon's free, and right now seems as good a time as any for me, Robert." Barbara saw an opportunity for a nap.

"Why don't you change into some casual clothes and join them, Ian. Take the boat out for a row: exercise, and fresh air, will do you a world of good. Besides, I can see you're all dying to give it a go. I'm going for a lie down; I'm feeling quite tired."

"That said, I think it fair to say we'd all enjoy a quiet afternoon, in one form or another."

Robert embellished the attributes of fishing to Ian as they made their way down to the dock. Boarding the boat, Robert assigned seating positions. He then tried to impress his passengers by relating his naval architecture knowledge as they cast off.

"The boat's clinker-built: This means overlapping planking, as opposed to a flat smooth planking design. This gives slightly more stability from rolling; each plank's overlapping ridge provided water resistance to boat roll. This makes for better stability when casting." Robert apparently shared a family trait for irrelevant boring information with Ian: Although perhaps not to the same degree. Ian's mind is a sponge for this type of trivia. " Life jackets stowed front and back." He pointed. "Right, now let's enjoy an hour or so on the lake." Ian relaxed in the back; well, Robert tested his arms, pulling ores with John. The little craft glided smoothly towards the lake's center, barely making a ripple in the water. Ian trailed his fingers in the wake.

Peaceful out here, isn't it?" Robert gave a hard pull on his ore and grunted.

"That's why I'm glad power boats aren't allowed. That would ruin the lake's tranquillity, don't you think?"

"I agree." Ian's lay-back feelings soon deserted him as business thoughts encroached on this pure pleasure they were sharing.

"By the way, Robert, I must meet with you in my office soon. There are some important confidential things to discuss." John seemed to show more interest in the statement than Robert.

"There's nothing you can tell me that would be inappropriate for John's ear's; he's with us."

"Well, that was kept hush, hush, I had no idea."

"We thought it best to keep you in the dark. You see, Ian, you're the first of our organization to get this close to Desate. For security reasons, it was decided the less you knew, the better. Now tell us what you have learned." Ian perceived, through this conversation, John somehow outranked Robert.

"As you probably know, I gave Robert total control of security, hoping that would provide us with better company networking knowledge. Unfortunately, this did not circumvent the system. He still receives information as I do; via prepared briefs filed in Lord Simpson's office. I'm the only one with a key to that office, apart from Desate, that is. I had Robert duplicate it." Robert then furnished some informative information regarding the key.

"It's no ordinary key, and it was almost impossible to duplicate. Precisely cut diamonds aline the edge. We're not sure whether this reflects some sort of light that activates the lock's mechanism or just for a precise fit. Finally, we turned to a jeweller to produce the copy we now have. One of Ian's latest tasks has been to try our key, to make sure it works."

"I did that. It works fine. As you know, there's a back door to that office. It doesn't seem to have a keyed lock. I was told it's bolted on the far side. This door was used by Lord Simpson and now by Desate. It must be the same door files are delivered through. Both Robert, and I have checked the building thoroughly, and we can't find another exit to what must be a large room behind this door. It's an area some thirty feet by fifty feet and extends from the ground floor to the roof. At the top, it seems to encompass the whole upper floor." John pushed for more information by prompting Ian.

"Is there roof access?"

"Not as far as we could tell, and the only roof access is by stairwells. This information Robert is aware of. We're assuming this area is a mechanical room for elevators, air conditioning, and such." Robert made a comment.

"I find it strange because most mechanical rooms occupy space above elevators, not beside them."

"Then the two of you must get back there and find that access; you've done well." John paused in thought for a moment. "Speculation, suppose Desate has a complex deep underground. That could be a place intelligence information worldwide is utilized. That would also explain the need for an extensive mechanical system to support such a complex." Ian handed John a paper from his pocket.

"I've made a list of people I believe help supply that information to the complex. I was able to do this by recording the names of generals, ministers, dictators, and operatives, who authorize covert operations word wide, and tender sealed briefs through me. I've theorized this information is the basis to formulate activities such as Robert, and I, have been involved in from time to time. Now you have me wondering why Desate has his headquarters so deep underground. It's not like anyone's likely to invade Switzerland." Robert laughed at Ian's pun.

"You've got that right, but It's probably been there for eons. In the event of war, past or present, Desate's complex would be safe. It would be more impregnable than any castle and even capable of withstanding a nuclear attack in today's world. I suspect he maneuvered Switzerland into the position it holds, giving even more security to his operations. The complex has gone undetected until now. Placing it in where we hypothesized it could be would prove to be strategically sound."

Ian was brainstorming. "If theories we've surmised are accurate, I think there's a flaw in its invulnerability." John's ears pricked up, being an admirer of Ian's past strategies that had been related to him through Robert.

"And what flaw might that be, Ian."

"Robert said the complex could probably stand a direct hit from a nuclear bomb."

"I believe he did."

"Now consider If we could deliver a nuclear bomb into the complex, it could be completely obliterated on detonation, leaving everything above safe."

"By God, you may be right; I'll get people working on a feasibility study immediately. We'd need to know at what depth the underground complex lies and strata formations above it. It would be imperative to know the exact layout and size to ensure it would be one hundred percent successful."

"When are we due back in Zurich, Ian?"

"A week, so we can't start searching for access before that time. I wouldn't want to raze any suspicions by arriving back early."

"I agree with Ian. This is something we can take very slowly. Time's on our side now."

John then placed a hand on Robert's shoulder to steady himself, as he indicated to Ian, with an inviting sweep of the hand, to take his place at the ore. "Speaking of time, we should be heading home; Barbara will be expecting us back about now." Although the late afternoon air was crisp, Ian managed to work up a sweat on the return trip.

"I'm sure I'll regret this exercise tomorrow. I've been using muscles in ways they're ill unaccustomed to." Reaching the jetty, they moored the boat. Ian left the two of them exchanging fishing stores, well covering the small craft with its tarp.

The house seemed quiet and lifeless as Ian searched the ground floor for Barbara. He then tried the bedroom and found her still sleeping there. On waking her gently from a deep sleep, he thought it strange that she seemed groggy and almost incoherent.

"I really don't feel too good." He placed a hand on her forehead.

"Perhaps I should call the doctor Barbara." She tried to sit up in bed, and Ian noticed a large amount of blood on the sheet. "I'm not waiting for the doctor. I'm calling an ambulance myself. You're going straight to the hospital."

After his first priority calling an ambulance was done, he went to the garden to alert Robert and John. When that was done, he returned to Barbara. He stayed by her side until the ambulance arrived.

The ambulance attendant's whisking her on board. A distraught Ian trailing behind. Robert and John followed in a car. The drive to the hospital, in Ian's mind, took forever. Although in reality, barely twenty minutes had passed since his phone call, and the emergency entrance was in sight. Barbara was rushed into surgery well Ian was steered towards a waiting room. It wasn't long before Robert and John showed up. John, to relieve stress slightly, suggested he should fetch three coffees. Robert waited with Ian, offering moral support. Ian felt a familiar fear welling up inside. The all too familiar fear he'd so recently faced down. The feeling of helplessness aggravated any attempt to subdue this emotion. Barely noticing John's return, he stared compulsively at the surgery door. John placed a coffee in his hand, then set a reassuring hand on a very tense shoulder. There was little said in the next while. The doctor finally emerged from surgery. Looking towards the three of them sitting in nervous anticipation, he called for Ian by name.

"Mr. Shaw." Ian rose to his feet to identify himself.

"Yes, I'm Ian Shaw."

"Ian, I'm pleased to tell you your wife is fine." Ian felt the mussels in his body relax at this news.

"The baby! what about the baby?"

"I'm sorry, there was nothing we could do. The fetus had aborted." He sank back down into his chair, face in hands, confused by mixed emotions. Allowing himself time to absorb the news, he then looked up at the doctor.

"When will I be able to see my wife."

"She's sedated at present. You'll be able to look in on her as soon as she's moved onto the ward. Although I'd prefer you didn't disturb her because what she needs right now is rest."

"Yes, I understand. Thank you, doctor." Ian then turned to Robert and John. "I'm going to stay here for a while."

"Of course, Ian, we understand." Robert pondered, thinking Ian probably needed some space right now. However, he still felt obligated to offer companionship. "Would you prefer John and I stay here with you?"

"I appreciate your offer, but there's really nothing you two can do here right now. You may as well leave and get some supper. I'll be fine here by myself."

"Just phone when you need a ride home, Ian. I'll come right over to pick you up."

It was several days before Barbara was allowed home from the hospital. Understandably she was in an extremely depressed and vulnerable condition, as was Ian. Ian did all that was humanly possible to help ease the empty feeling that hung over them like a dark cloud. There was little more to do than to allow time to heal this significant loss that had darkened all future plans that should have been joyous ones.

After a short time, Ian encouraged Tony to involve her in song writing, hoping to occupy her time constructively.

Ann used Barbara's life experience to inspire her first song. Without outside help, Ann thought it to be something to be proud of. An accomplishment she'd nerve been able to achieve before. Ann titled the song (The love I never knew), which was perhaps inappropriate to air at that time. Although she regarded it as her best work to date, she decided to keep it under wraps until the hurt had eased.

CHAPTER 34

Spy and report.

It had been prearranged by Ian and Robert to work later than usual on their first day back in Zurich. This would enable a thorough check of the top floor's office space in secret by avoiding office personnel's prying eyes. Robert met up with Ian in his office, from where they casually made their way to separate stairwells. Proceeding independently to the top floor office, they again joined forces. Solid concrete stairway walls eliminated these areas from hiding the salute after remote access. Their search then centred on the uppermost floor's office space.

Silently, methodically, they moved from office to office, looking for anything unusual. With no leads forthcoming, Ian was becoming convinced they were searching the wrong area. Figuring they'd drawn a blank, he was sure other alternatives would now have to be considered. Robert was not about to give up so easily. Beckoning Ian to the center core's far side, which housed elevators, and washrooms, Robert drew his attention to the washroom doors.

"There's a large space between these washroom doors. Wouldn't you agree? let's give the insides a thorough check."

Each door housed a vestibule containing two more doors. One door in each was designated as a washroom door. In the men's entrance, another door was labelled, Janitor. The extra ladies' door displayed an electrical room nameplate.

"This room's probably the place we're looking for." Playing a hunch, Robert placed their duplicate key to Lord Simpson's old office into the lock. "I'm betting this is a master key for the whole building." Turning the key in the lock, he opened the door with a look that said I told you so. A flick of a light switch reviled a small room displaying numerous electrical fuse boxes. Robert's discerning eye spotted scuff marks on the floor, as a door might possibly make. Meticulously he scrutinized this wall. The lone fuse box attached to this wall was locked. Placing his key into the lock, he pulled down on its breaker handle, and a concealed door swung open, revealing a stairway to an upper landing. There was an exit door on this upper landing; his key also matched this lock. Gingerly he opened it, making sure the area was clear before entering. Before he threw a light switch close at hand, he noticed a security camera above his head. "Quickly, Ian, your jacket." After covering the camera securely, he threw the switch, which illuminated the whole area. A platform before them provided access to a series of maintenance catwalks. Stairways and walkways below lead to the elusive room they'd been searching for. A Massive cable drum, with machinery surrounding it on multi-levels, filled most of its upper portion. They were standing at the uppermost level, where air conditioning machinery also took up a significant section.

Robert took a small camera from his pocket and started taking snapshots from every conceivable angle.

"By gauging drum size and cable thickness, we should be able to calculate the approximate service elevator shaft's depth. We must go down to the ground floor and take a few more shots. That should wrap up this evening's little reconnaissance trip." On their way down, Robert made brief stops, photographing things he deemed to contain relevant information. He became intrigued by the elevator's surrounding cage that extended upwards to Lord Simpson's office floor. The cage itself opened up onto what he perceived to be an upper floor elevator door's vestibule. Surmising, this must be the room that the entry in Lord Simpson's old office led to. He took many more pictures of this area.

The cage also accommodated a raising gate on its backside. Ground-level access could be used for supplies from the outside if there was a door to a loading dock. For Robert, this meant one thing, there had to be a lower back door to this area providing ground-level access. A clear path from the steel gate terminated at a blank outside wall. The open shaft indicated the elevator itself was on a lower level. Reaching the floor, Robert's fascination with the shaft drew him to its edge for a closer look and collected more pictures.

"This shaft has an iron staircase on one side, with its own access door through the cage Ian." He tried his key in the lock. The grin on his face told Ian it was a match. We'll go down there and see if we can access the lower areas on our next visit. I feel if there's a locked door at the bottom, our key will open it. I've photographed enough information, for now, so I suggest we make a strategic withdraw."

Ian scurried up and along the catwalks well ahead of Robert, who had paused to take a few more close-up shots of the pathway's blank wall termination point. Retrieving Ian's jacket after switching off the lights was Robert's last task.

He then returned to his office. Ian secured the brief he'd been working on before they both left the building. They headed for Ian's apartment and spent the remaining evening hours rehashing their recent foray over beer and pizza.

Ingrid's enthusiastic voiced greeting was accompanied by the message he'd been anticipating.

"Good morning Mr. Shaw. I've been informed we have a new boss. You have a meeting with him at nine this morning." Ian looked and waited, expecting to hear the remainder of a message he deemed incomplete. Ingrid gazed back with a vacant look, apparently thinking there was little else in the way of information to be offered. Ian gave a sympathetic smile, paving the way for his next question.

"And his name, woman, did he not mention his name?"

"Oh yes, let me think, he introduced himself as Barkley, Lord Barkley, that's it. He said he'd be moving into Lord Simpson's old office and taking control of the company." She looked at the clock on the wall.

"It's nine right now, so you're late." It was her turn to smile as Ian quickly set his briefcase down and hurried to the office he'd always felt uncomfortable visiting. A soft tap on the door summoned the response from within.

"Is that Ian."

"Yes, Sir, it is."

"Enter, enter, quickly, please." This was not the sombre greeting Ian was accustomed to. He thought it sounded almost paranoid, perhaps not surprising considering the demise of this office's last occupant. Inside he was greeted by a gnomish-looking little man. He stood up from behind his desk with an outstretched hand. Ian's hand accepted the greeting. "I am Lord Barkley. Please sit down and make yourself comfortable." Scrutinizing Ian with a series of piercing glances, the man seemed incapable of maintaining a steady focus. This almost detached, doddering attitude spilled into every aspect of his personality.

Ian surmised that all information regarding himself in this first meeting with Lord Barkley was methodically being storied to Barkley's memory despite this facade. This perception led Ian to believe this man was a more complex individual than the one he portrayed.

"Ian, I've heard a lot of good things about you."

"I'm pleased to hear that, sir, and I look forward to maintaining the same working relationship with you as I enjoyed with your predecessor." Dropping his head, he glanced up at Ian from beneath his brow. Ian's interpretation of this gesture was shallow flattery had no meaning to this person.

"I'll be relying heavily on your support overseeing all of our interests. We have several new operation executives in China, the middle east, and Russia. There will also be a replacement needed for Peterson, and this job has already fallen on your shoulders. You will collect all assignments from me and distribute them as you see fit. This promotion will require you to spend more time here than perhaps you had planned. However, I'm sure your organizational skills will accommodate an expansion of your English workload capabilities. A task simplified by the exclusive personal use of an aircraft. A little promotion bonus that will ease your commute time." Ian's enthusiastic reply echoed his thoughts regarding this bonus.

"With an aircraft at my disposal, I could practically commute to work every day. Rest assured; I fully appreciated this gesture." Lord Barkley gave no sign of emotion regarding Ian's elated statement but simply replied with a demand.

"I now require my office key back." He held out a hand. Ian fumbled with the key, which he was wearing around his neck on a gold chain, like an expensive piece of jewelry.

"Of course." Having become accustomed to wearing it, he reluctantly passed it over. It also signified he was relinquishing his badge office. Lord Barkley then passed several large files to Ian.

"Familiarize yourself with these before distributing them to your subordinates." A quick handshake from Lord Barkley told Ian the meeting had concluded.

Two days later Ian, and Robert, were on their way to England in more luxury than even Ian had become accustomed to. The necessity for schedules to revolve around flight availability no longer existed. Sleeping quarters, lounge, dining area, bar, and even an office, were now at his fingertips on this private jet. Having John waiting to collect them at Bristol airport to chauffeur them home was the icing on the cake for this first trip.

Robert gave John a detailed account of their little foray to the upper floor, emphasizing what he thought it had achieved on their drive home. Robert then passed John the roll of film.

"A picture being worth a thousand words, this little roll of film, should revile a wealth of information. Most interesting will be what we can learn regarding the mechanical room. We'll just have to wait until it's developed."

"I'll get our people working on it immediately. You've done well. Until this film has been analyzed, and we've gleaned as much from it as possible, I suggest we sit tight. I see little point embarking on any further reconnaissance missions until we're able to fully utilize the information you've recently collected." He then carefully selected a pocket in which to stow the film safely. John then patted his pocket several times to reassure himself the film roll really was there. He then directed the conversation abruptly to a lighter subject. It was as though their previous conversation had never taken place. It was perhaps his way of inferring this information was top secret.

CHAPTER 35
More information required

Flying on cloud nine, Ian headed for Barbara's office, assuming he would find her there working. His knuckle's gentle rapped the door, announcing his arrival, before peering inside. The glow on her face lit up the room on seeing him.

"How are you feeling today, my darling?"

"All the better for seeing you. It always makes my day knowing you've arrived home safely." She stood up and moved towards him with outstretched arms for an embrace. The embrace evolved into a passionate kiss. His hands started to explore her body as his foot gently pushed the door closed. Pulling back, she gazed into his eyes. His hands slipped to her waist, and his fingers started to work their magic towards her backside. Before he could reach her legs, her hands brought his arms abruptly back to her waist.

"I've arranged a meeting with Tony in the studio shortly. Apparently, there are a few things he needs to discuss. I don't anticipate it taking long, so after that, I'm all yours to do with as you will." The last part of the sentence was emphasized with seductive overtones.

"I'll tag along to the studio if that's alright with you. After all, when you've finished there, I wouldn't want to miss out on any time I've been allotted; to do with you as I will." He gave a dirty little chuckle as he patted her rear.

Tony, engrossed in his work, didn't notice them at first. Not wishing to distract his creative aspirations, they decided to wait quietly in the control booth. Finally acknowledging their presence, he stood up at the piano and beckoned them into the studio.

"I've something I'd like you to listen to. I've just finished daubing the new album of your songs, Barb's."

"Album of my songs." There was more than a bit of surprise in her voice.

"Yes, your songs. The songs you've been singing in the studio and allowing me to tape. I've put them together with some excellent orchestrations to form an album. I hope you approve, the material's great. I'd like you to listen to what I've come up with. Make yourselves comfortable, and I'll pop into the control booth and set things up. I think we can better appreciate it sat in comfort out here." He trotted off to the control booth to start the tape. Body mannerisms, combined with his enthusiasm, made it apparent he was very proud of this work. Setting up the playback, he rejoined them in the studio to sit back and listen.

Tony had little tolerance for interruptions and talk throughout this presentation. It was a completely different attitude that followed its completion as he begged for comments.

"Well, what do you think? I need your input, people." Ian's first remark was a sarcastic pun at Tony.

"Oh, I'm allowed comment, am I." Tony grind, realizing he'd been so controlling regarding this project. "I'm overwhelmed. I really am. It sounds fantastic; you've both done an incredible job." Barbara was modest, praising Tony's effort over her own immense contribution.

"I think you've done an excellent job, Tony. This tape is a true embodiment of your production talents."

"Then you approve of what I've done with your music, Barb's."

"Of course, I approve, Tony." She reached out from where she sat, put an arm around his shoulder, and gave him a reassuring hug. "How could anyone be disappointed with those wonderful arraignments. I'm also grateful for the time you've invested in this project on my behalf." Tony was now overwhelmed by enthusiasm.

"We can't just let this tape sit; it's too good for that. Jeff would jump at the chance to handle it. Barb's, what do you say?" Ian saw potential in this business opportunity that perhaps Tony hadn't foreseen.

"This might be good for you right now, Barbara. Now, perhaps you can enlighten this layman; would it be too much of a challenge to weave some of Tony's songs into this album? I know there are songs from his show explicitly written for a female singer. Think of the exposure this could create for that project. The public would have already been familiarized with the show's music even before it opened. The song your actor friend did is doing quite well, I hear."

"Ian's right, Tony. Let me put some of your work into the album, then you can release it with my blessing."

"I'd never considered that possibility, but yes, that would be great. We can at least work two more songs into an album. It won't take much to reorganize. You could record them whenever you feel ready."

Barbara walked over to a guitar set on a stand in the corner. Picking it up and walking to a stool in front of the microphone, she seated herself before starting to strum.

"Tony, would you fetch copies of those songs. I'd like to see which ones I like best for my style." Tony returned minutes later and presented her with the requested song sheets. She thumbed through them, strumming, and humming, to the ones that took her fancy. Ian remained seated on the settee, watching quietly. Eventually, she focused on three she felt best suited to. "I feel comfortable with these, Tony." She showed him her selections." I'd like to give them a whirl and try to inject my own slant into the melodies."

"I'll get things set in the control booth, so you'll be able to hear a playback. That should give you a better idea of where you want to go with this."

This wasn't turning out to be the short meeting she'd predicted it would be. It took several hours before achieving the perfect interpretation her creative expressions had been searching for. On what was supposedly the day's final playback, she gave Tony two thumbs up. He came out of the control booth to speak.

"I'd like to try it a little different next time, Barb's. Let's try it with piano accompaniment, giving less guitar emphasis." Barbara acknowledged with a knowing nod. "I'll call Pam to take over the control booth." Several more rehearsals followed before deciding to make a finale tape. "I'll tweak this around a little until I think it's ready to send off to Jeff. Now, what say you we take a well-earned break." Ian, who had passed way beyond boredom, agreed.

"Sounds like a good idea to me. I feel tired just sitting here watching the three of you work."

Pam's suggestion of coffee and sandwiches in the kitchen became a unanimous decision. After finishing the sandwiches, a final coffee was poured before retiring to the lounge to sit back and relax in comfort. Ian's small talk turned to their new pet project

"Have you had any luck locating a theatre that could suit our purposes? Well, I've been away?"

"I think I may have found something of interest. I'm going to have a look at it next week. If you're in England at that time, perhaps we might stay at your London apartment for a few days. We've not spent time in London lately; it could be fun."

"I'd like that. We could make like tourists, do a show, shop, you know make it a mini holiday."

Tony grasped his empty coffee cup. "Working vacations may be O.K. for some people, but others have real work to do, so it's back to the grindstone for me. Are you coming, Pam."

"I'm with you, boss man. Lead the way." Before returning to the studio directly, she totted all the remaining dirty cups to the kitchen.

A London visit stirred nostalgic thoughts as they snuggled together in front of the hearth's radiant red embers. Soft stereo music added ambiance to this romantic setting, not too different from that not-so-distant day when they first fell in love.

The following week their London dream visit materialized. Abandoning the car at Ian's apartment, they utilized London's transportation system. Barbara's intent was to spend time doing some serious shopping. Ian's mindset revolved around sightseeing, and long walks, to reacquaint himself with parks he loved. This made for some heated opinions to be aired. Barbara assigned him to carry shopping bags, but he insisted they walk to familiarize himself with beauty spots he had long forgotten. However, he flatly refused to do any more of Barbara's chores to give some much-needed leverage until his choices were considered. The day became a saw-off for both parties, mainly walking in silence until early afternoon. A light lunch and the promise of an afternoon's shopping eased tensions by making Barbara exceptionally happy. Walking and shopping made for a far too tiring a day, so there was little remorse when Ian hailed a cab for their return trip to the apartment. It was relaxing sitting back, isolated from the hustle and bustle of public transportation. This made a pleasant, sealed with an affectionate kiss, finale, to what they had to begrudgingly concede, was still an enjoyable day's excursion.

"I've made plans for this evening, so be sure you're well-rested before we spend our night on the town."

"And what have you planned for this evening, something that doesn't include walking, I hope." She gave a little snigger at this teasing.

"I would suggest you should bring your dancing shoes. If you don't want to walk, I'll make sure you won't have to, starting now." He swept her up in his arms and carried her to the bedroom.

Laying her on the bed, his hands glided smoothly, confidently, over her body. Every curve of her familiar form held nothing but pleasant memories for him. As soothing hands Carried her into ecstasy, cloths were slowly, gently peeled away. His tongue lapped at her breasts, a prelude to the suckling from his lips. She reached down, giving encouragement to his already strong urges. Bearing the part of his body she'd come to regard as her own exclusive domain for pleasure, she stimulated it with her hand. Maneuvering her body towards it and guiding it past his magical fingers, a slow thrust from his hips produced all the momentum necessary. Relaxed bodies indulged themselves in the moment's pleasure before kissing. Stimulated by his tight embrace, her body raised to press closer to his, encouraging him to thrust ever deeper. Letting out a half whimper, a half sigh of painful pleasure, she wrapped her legs around his body. In unison, they seethed, accommodating each other's fantasies. Finally, exhausted, he pinned her shoulders to the bed to limit their exertions. Throwing his head back slowly in ecstasy facilitated a desperately needed respite. Breathing deeply, he looked down to admire her beauty as she reached out to caress his body. With newfound invigoration, their grand finale was achieved in the highest plane of euphoria.

It was late evening, and Ian's continuing plan to give her a holiday break to remember now centred on visiting some of the more exclusive nightclubs in London's West End. Generous tips to appreciative doormen ensured quick passage through long lineups. It was a night for fun and enjoyment, and money flowed like water to fulfill this dream. Their dancing matched their high-spirited mood. As the last club visited emptied, they found themselves alone on the dance floor. This determined their own departure.

Outside and on empty sidewalks seemed a deflating finish to such a sensational night on the town. They strolled slowly towards a taxi stand, with Barbara snugging into Ian as they walked.

"I've had a wonderful evening, Ian. This is the first time we've enjoyed a whole night out in a long time, and I don't want it to end."

"I have an idea to round off the perfect night on the town. The markets will be busy soon, taking deliveries and setting up shop for a new day. Let's take a cab to Covent Garden's flower market and have breakfast in one of the cafes that cater to the market's workers."

"I like the sounds of that idea."

Stepping from their cab, wet shinny cobblestones glistened under the street lighting, and market stalls drenched in illumination welcomed them to Covent Garden. This place was already a beehive of activity. A melody of voices, blended with the clatter of delivery carts unloading fresh blooms, were busily ushering in another business day. Some stall owners had already set up most of their displays. Vying for potential customer attention, each stall strived for the most eye-catching arrangements.

A small cafe, commanding a complete market view, caught their eye. Its brightly painted exterior design helped complement mother nature's abundant wealth of displayed colour.

"I like the look of this place; let's try for window seating so we can view the market as we dine."

The first wave of clientele had just departed the café. This fact was made evident by the frantic table clearing process now underway to accommodate the next sitting. Window tables had been cleared first. This offered them their preferred choice of seating. After settling in, Barbara glanced out the window.

"I love your breakfast idea, flowers, people; this such a vibrant place to be."

The waitress stopped her cleaning duties to take their order. Without a word said after ordering, Ian stood up and went back outside to a nearby stall. Barbara watched him as he spoke to the lady working there. Money then changed hands, and attention was drawn to Barbara's location. Ian's smiling face then returned to the table.

"What have you been up to."

"You'll just have to wait and see."

Only minutes had passed before the flower lady entered the café: She approached their table, carrying a beautiful flower arrangement in her hands. It was then set for display at the center of the table. Ian thanked the woman and passed her a tip as she left. Barbara reached across the table and touched his hand.

"Thank you, Ian, that was so thoughtful of you and so romantic." Ian acknowledged her appreciation with a smile. He then expressed his love in words.

"I think you're worth all the attention I can lavish on you. You're as beautiful as any of these blooms. You're the perfect English rose. Without you, the reason for living would not be the same for me. You've taught me how shallow my life was, chasing wealth, power, and self-indulgence. These things have little or no meaning without true inner peace and happiness. My Life has become so much fuller merely from the privilege of knowing you and loving you." Standing up and reaching across the table, she placed her hands on his shoulders and kissed him.

"I'm sure you realize that sentiment's as true for me as it is for you."

The coalition of reds, blues, and grays, low in the morning sky, heralded the start of a new day. Shafts of light from this heavenly graphic display also severed to glorify the blaze of colour emanating from numerous flower arraignments. This Victorian-styled market was now transformed from just a place of business to a place of unique beauty. What better way could there be to round off a perfect night than by enjoying breakfast in such a picturesque setting?

Reaching the main road, Ian hailed a cab that returned them to the apartment. The remaining morning was used to recoup before their afternoon business meeting with a Realtor at the theatre for lease.

* * *

First impressions were not good. The place seemed quite dilapidated from its outside appearance. Exterior woodwork, with prevalent dull peeling paint, highlighted signs of extreme water damage. Plastered columns that once stood like proud sentinels were no longer able to project that image of grandeur. They now depreciated pitting and erosion from inclement weather. Neglect had reduced this once noble palace of entertainment into a sad reflection of its former splendour. On its plus side were the location and the fact that it was huge: They favoured large. The Realtor greeted them on arrival and escorted them inside. Inside appearances were no better than its outside. Inadequate temporary lighting and the chill of a vacant building could hardly be described as favourable viewing conditions. Barbara had a look of disappointment on her face as she spoke to the Realtor.

"Not exactly what I had in mind." The Realtor was sympathetic but upbeat and intent on making a deal.

"The theatre would need a complete renovation, but that could be a plus from what you've outlined in your requirements. The owner would be responsible for any structural repair. And I'm sure a deal could be struck in the lease agreement to accommodate tenant improvements." Barbara looked at Ian for input, but his noncommittal look told her he wished their options to remain open. She made her call.

"I'll need my contractor to inspect the premises as soon as possible. I'd like his input, on restoration costs, with an eye to cosmetic changes that will work for us. Then I'll talk it over with our investors and come back with our decision.

"I'm always available to assist your contractors with his assessment, so when ever's convenient for him will be fine with me."

The main excuse for this junket concluded; they were off to enjoy the day. Driving westward out of the city, Windsor became their preferred destination. Parking near the River Thames, they found pleasure walking its adjacent footpath. The Queen's standard, wafting in the breeze atop the castle, indicated Her Majesty was in residence. This pleasant late spring afternoon induced numerous paying passengers aboard the many pleasure craft plying the river at this point. Even crowded boats of tourists could not depreciate the river's casual lay-back feeling. A leisurely cruise on this placid stretch of river was a far different experience than the expanse in its busier working areas from Greenwich to Westminster.

Trees displaying delicate green foliage were upstaged by others, presenting an added attraction of blossoms. Their sweet smells intertwined with those of freshly mown grass were appreciated by Ian as he indulged himself in long deep breaths.

"How different this is from the hustle and bustle of London. We could be a thousand miles away, and yet we're so near, Barbara."

"True, but for me, it still doesn't compare to our valley in the Mendip Hills." Ian showed appreciation for this sentiment by giving her an affectionate hug around the shoulder.

"I agree. There really is no place like home, is there?" Arm in arm, they walked, and walked, with this lazy spring evening dictating their pace.

* * *

A brief apartment rest over; supplied sufficient time to rejuvenate before their theatre outing. The hit musical chosen exhibited a similar flair to Tony's planned staging. Perhaps there were things to be learned from this evening's performance. The success of Tony's open night might possibly depend on attention to fine details. Afterward, at the restaurant chosen to round out their evening, marketing techniques dominated supper conversation.

On returning to the apartment, a night of more lovemaking overrode any necessity for sleeping. As his hands roamed her body, vigorous acts of love produced sweat from her, which became a sweet fragrance to his senses. This aphrodisiac made him indulge her body with unending gratifications, as his seemingly endless energy spurred them both to multiple orgasms. The strength needed to produce such a night's fond memories contributed to the lacklustre chore of baggage packing late the following morning.

* * *

As expected, Robert and John greet them on arrival home. Stowing fishing tackle away under Robert's meticulously scrutiny, John, the unwilling lackey, was more than willing to forego this position favouring the welcome committee supervisor. Ian knew there would be deeper motives behind this cordial reception. An analysis of Robert's film would undoubtedly be forthcoming. It was sure to be accompanied by possible applications for information gained.

Robert made pleasant small talk as John gave Barbara her customary hug and kiss. "Well, how was London, and did you have a good time?" As John placed his sister back down on her feet, she turned to Robert and kissed him on the cheek before answering.

"It was great; the best few days we've had in a long while. Although we do have misgivings regarding the theatre, we're considering renting. On the upside, it's located in an excellent spot, and the lease is favourable. Its main setback is it's dilapidated. I'm having a contractor look at it and supply me with renovation options and costs."

"I'm still hoping it'll work out for us. I think it fair to say we're all excited about this venture." John took her bags.

"Let me give you a hand upstairs with these." As Ian retrieved his bag, Robert whispered in his ear.

"When you come back down, John and I need to talk with you. Perhaps in the privacy of your study, or even better, over a round of golf."

"A round of golf might be preferable."

"I thought that would be the case."

Entering the bedroom, Barbara dove onto the bed. "Please don't disturb me for a while. I'm bushed." Ian just laughed.

"Not so young anymore, ha. You know age is creeping up when you can't stand the pace anymore." She hurled a pillow at him as he made a hasty retreat to the sound of giggling.

"Come on, John, I can see I've worn out my welcome here. Robert's suggested a round of golf." The car was quickly reloaded with golfing equipment and all the correct attire, then driven to Ian's local club.

It wasn't until the privacy of a secluded seventh fairway that John felt safe speaking freely as Ian took up position behind his ball. Robert stood to his right, well John paced too and fro, on Ian's left. Ian lowered his club, realizing John's agitation was caused by his need for conversation.

"We've learned all we can from the film, and now it's time to enter the complex."

"What sort of information were you able to gain from the film? It was just a room with machinery in it." Robert answered the question.

"You'd be amazed by the amount of information we were able to retrieve about security measures regarding the elevator. The complex's approximate depths have been calculated from elevator cable drum size. Machinery power controls, alarm systems in areas we'd require accessing have also been located. If our calculations prove correct, it's deep enough to utilize a nuclear device in its destruction, with minimal impact at ground level. It would be preferable for the device's delivery to use the elevator itself. We need a feasibility study on this possibility. An in-depth analysis could also provide valuable information regarding shaft decommission before detonation. The successful confinement of blast and debris beneath the ground would eliminate surface damage."

"This all sounds fine in theory, but how would we be able to achieve this shaft decommissioning you speak of." John elaborated on Robert's scenario.

"A team would set demolition charges at intervals down the shaft. Detonating the bottom charges first in a cascading sequence upwards until the top-most charge is detonated. This should total collapse the shaft, isolating the complex from ground level. Regarding the nuclear device, we plan for its blast to be beyond the elevator doors and into the complex itself, which could then be detonated safely. We still need to know the complex's size and if there's more than one level. Also, we must be sure the elevator shaft is its only access. This reconnaissance must be done without raising suspicion; a tipped hand would provoke increased security. What we plan to do will be extremely difficult. If Desate had the slightest inclination of anything amiss, it would render our plans useless." The thought of entering the complex made Ian very nervous.

"How could we hope to check out an area filled with people without being discovered. It would be foolish to assume security would be lax at the bottom entrance." Robert tried to bolster Ian's confidence by acting casual and diverting the conversation.

"Take your shot, Ian, and try to keep it on the fairway this time. It would be desirable to walk and talk together rather than have you scouting the ruff for your ball." Robert then laughed at his pun, fully aware of Ian's prowess at golf. A feigned scowl from Ian told Robert he would be eating those words. Even with this light-hearted distraction, Robert could see the task John had set for them weighed heavily on Ian's mind. With this foremost in thought, he decided the sooner this foray was underway, the better. This would lessen Ian's time of concern. "I think the reconnaissance should take place at the earliest opportunity. What say you, John?"

"I agree. Any information you gather will be vital in training a strike team. There's also the task of acquiring a bomb or bombs. And coordinating the delivery of the ordinance to the site. As to your concerns Ian, that's what recognizance is all about, alleviating such problems. Scenarios must be planned with sound knowledge gleaned from reliable intelligence information, which is best acquired firsthand. I'm sure you'll find it no different than any past company assignment. Robert's responsibilities will be to assure the success of this mission and your safety. Our experts have manufactured some specialized equipment they hope will accommodate your needs to help facilitate any problems you may encounter. These specialty devices will be waiting for you at a prearranged drop spot in Zurich. It'll be just like those James Bond novels you like to read, Ian, including all the fancy gadgets." Ian showed a brave face by giving a little chuckle.

"Surely, it'll be no easy task securing nuclear weapons." Driving his ball, John replied as Ian's eyes followed it towards the green.

"Easier than you think, with our security clearances Ian. Now I suggest we concentrate on this game; remember that the loser pays the bar tab for food and drinks. That's if someone can keep their score correctly, and we can finish this game before nightfall." He shot a glance at Robert and grind.

The Prince of Waterloo staff were tending the early evening work crowd as they entered. As Ian kept referring to him, Robert (the loser) was first at the bar to order three pints of bitter and food. Mike, Ian's realtor, sitting on a barstool at the opposite end, called to Ian.

"I hear your wife is putting more work, my brother's way, Ian."

"That could be the case, Mike. If everything works out, it'll be quite a significant renovation job. Tom's submitting sketches of his ideas for the theatre, along with an estimate by early next week, all being well."

"Word has it, Barbara's going big time and staging a London musical."

"She's managing the project for a consortium, Mike. Being the front person involves doing most of the leg work and acquiring most of the headaches. It's really Tony's baby; it's his music and storyline. I imagine he'll be overseeing the production end. The way he fusses over every minute detail, I'm already calling him (The opera's Phantom Bishop). I can imagine him spying on everything going on throughout the production." Mike repeated Ian's phrase.

"The opera's Phantom Bishop! how do you mean?"

"Oh, nothing to do with any saintly ways he might claim to aspire to. You just know him as Tony. His sire name's Bishop." Mike gave a quirky grin that indicated he now understood this inside joke.

"All sounds very interesting, Ian. We'll have to arrange a charter bus to take us local folk to see the show when it airs."

Robert turned from the bar presenting two beers to his thirsty companions. "I overheard that ideal, and I think it's a good one. We could probably fill several buses with people we know." Robert, the loser, was again satirically reminded of his obligation to foot the bill for the food they were about to order.

Engrossed in tall tales, well-appeasing appetites, thoughts of an early evening did not cross their minds. A few more pallet cleansing ales steered a course for the evening's natural progression. Only when the stories became embellished to the point of absurdity did they concede that perhaps they'd all had enough to drink. Now seemed as good as any to consider returning home. It was also a case of not overindulging themselves before driving.

Immersing himself in work for the remainder of that week helped keep Ian's mind off the daunting task ahead. Robert and John repeatedly went over every detail they'd learned about the complex. It was deemed essential to eliminate any surface complications that could arise: Realizing there would be enough unknown challenges lurking below.

CHAPTER 36

Entering Purgatory.

With Ian's new promotion, his tight reins had been slackened somewhat. This allowed him considerable leeway in determining the pace of company projects. Ian was no longer required to continuously report to a superior. His next scheduled briefing had been arranged for late that afternoon.

With time on his hands, he decided to track down Robert and run an idea past him that could possibly take advantage of this later meeting than usual. Today Robert wasn't an easy man to find, having locked himself away in his secret basement storage room. Only after Ian had identified himself by name did the door cautiously open. Dragged quickly inside by a giant hand, the door was again tightly secured behind him. It was apparent by broken packaging strewn about the room Robert had already assembled equipment required for their evening's clandestine operation. Ian assumed he'd interrupted Robert's self-orientation of gadgetry spread out before them.

"Playing with your new toys, I see." Robert's caution bordered on paranoia.

"Keep your voice down, Ian. I've been extremely cautious about keeping this equipment under tight security. It would be unfortunate to have some bright spark put two and two together."

"Your right; point taken. Perhaps we should go out for an early lunch that way we can talk more freely. I have an idea I believe is worth your consideration."

"Just as soon as I can stow these things safely away from prying eyes, we can leave. Then I'll be all ears." As soon as they'd left the building, Ian started to outline his plan.

"A situation has arisen that we may be able to exploit. I have a meeting with Lord Barkley late this afternoon. I've been contemplating our chances of riding the elevator roof down to the complex."

"I suppose it's possible, but how would you get from his office to the mechanical room in time. He'll probably take the elevator down immediately after you leave?"

"I don't think he always leaves immediately after meetings, so the worst that could happen is we miss our ride. If you're there waiting for me, I don't see a problem. I'll be wearing appropriate footwear and clothing, so I shouldn't hold you up."

"That might work. I'll make sure everything's ready at the elevator before your meeting. Then I'll come back and wait for you at the Mechanical room door."

"Now we have that planned; how about grabbing a Sandwich, and coffee, before returning to the office."

Lord Barkley was exercising his usual paranoia as Ian taped at his door. Only when Lord Barkley was satisfied Ian was at the door did he unlock it and allow him in. A quick glance up and down, the corridor followed before the door was secured behind them. Ian then gave a brief presentation regarding various projects' well-submitting folders containing the appropriate paperwork. As their meeting concluded, Lord Barkley scooped up the reports and escorted Ian to the door. As Lord Barkley opened the door, Ian saw a chance to gain a little more time. Ian Distracted Lord Barkley, who was preoccupied with door security, by engaging him in a handshake. An intentional accident scattered the report's in Lord Barkley's grasp across the floor. Apologizing for his clumsiness, Ian started to scoop up these same papers. Lord Barkley's instincts to secure the door was something Ian was counting on.

"I'll see to this, Ian, as soon as I've locked the door behind you." Ian dropped the papers back to the floor.

"If you're sure, Sire. Again, I must apologize for my clumsiness."

"Yes, yes." Ian was hustled through the door, and it was slammed behind him. Losing no time, he ran the stairs to meet up with Robert. Together, with extreme hast, they made their way to the elevator. Robert quietly climbed on top of the cab, and Ian handed him up the bag of tricks before starting his own cab top climb. He'd barely made a firm climbing hold as it began its downward journey. Robert's large hand locked firmly around Ian's wrist. It started to accelerate rapidly. A quick glance into the dark abyss below gave Ian's tense limbs ample encouragement to re-establish their purpose and propel his body onto the roof.

Robert donned a set of goggles. He then issued Ian with another pair from his bag of goodies. He indicated Ian should put them on. The darkness was now transformed into an eerie green sub-light. Specks of light twinkling like stars in a dark night sky bled through from the interior of the elevator.

It seemed an eternity then passed in this strange eerie darkness. Ian became aware of the gentle intermittent whisper in his ear, created by blood pulsing through veins. Elevators guide rails rollers purred put rhythmic accompaniment to this strange melodious surging sound. The elevator's speed reduced gradually before it finally came to rest. Only after the elevator door had opened to release its occupant, then close again, did Robert use his flashlight. The contrast from intense darkness was disorientating for a brief instant as goggles were discarded. The torch was shone around the shaft to scan their surroundings. To one side, the iron staircase terminated several feet from a door. Above them, it spiralled up the dark elevator shaft into obscurity.

Robert took a small tube from his pack and snapped it before throwing it to the ground below. Glowing like a lantern, it provided all the light required for safe cab top disembarkation.

Robert brushed the dust from a handrail with his finger, then whispered to Ian. "It doesn't look like anyone's been here in a long time." Ian acknowledged with a nod. As they moved towards the door, Robert took a small box from his equipment bag. He attached a flexible flattened snake-like tape to it. What appeared to be a transparent strip sealing its end proved to be a micro lens. As he stroked a small roller on top of the box, the tape moved up, down, and sideways. This was all done at his thumbs command. The flick of a switch illuminated a view screen on its back.

"It works like a periscope Ian. It'll enable us to see around corners, or in this case, behind doors. First, let's neutralize the door's alarm system with my key." Then, placing a small pry bar under the heavy door, he indicated Ian should apply weight to it. Ian then gently did as Robert asked. Securing it with a wedge, he then fed his periscope devise through the door's bottom gap. He, and Ian, then viewed images transmitted from its panoramic lens as he scanned to and fro. They saw a room with a security guard sitting at a desk, with his back to the door, viewing surveillance monitors. The elevator doors were to his left, with double glass doors to his right. These doors opened into a large office area, surrounded by numerous smaller offices on its outside walls.

"How can we go any farther without being detected," Ian whispered.

"This is the fun part, where we wait and watch, Ian." Fifteen minutes passed before the guard even moved. Robert used this time to assemble what resembled a fishing rod. At the touch of a switch, it extended or contracted. He then attached a small cylinder with a nozzle to its end. Ian held vigil. Robert supplied masks to don. "Now we're ready," he whispered.

Standing to stretch his limbs, the guard then settled back down to continue his monitoring duties. It seemed apparent boredom had created a certain laxness in his concentration. Capitalizing on this situation, Robert quietly opened the door. Reaching around with his rod, he telescoped it out over the guard's head. The press of another button released a downward puff of gas. Ian felt a cold trickle of sweat run down his back. Well, Robert, on the other hand, seemed to be experiencing a high from the ordeal. The man slumped forward onto his desk. Moving quickly, they set him back in his chair.

"What's in that cylinder, Robert?"

"Some kind of knockout gas would be my guess." He gave a chuckle. "When he wakes, he'll think he dropped off to sleep. We have about two hours before he comes too. Let's utilize these surveillance monitors to scan outside before we make our next move."

The main office had cleared considerably and was now dimly lit. Each workstation and office still in use were relying on desktop illumination for working comfort.

Inconspicuously, they slipped through the double glass doors after accessing their surroundings. A sea of workstations, separated by low partitioning, stretched out before them. Stealthily they made their way through this maze of cubicles and hid in empty ones when someone approached. They then moved on whenever the coast was clear. Robert took pictures of anything, and everything, with the same camera that accommodated the periscope device. Office fronts were constructed mainly of glass, the lower portion frosted, with a clear upper band. This made it relatively easy to photograph the rooms from outside without the risk of entering them.

They were caught off guard by two people who passed close by. Keeping their heads down and acting as if they were deep in conversation seemed an appropriate tactic to avoid a face, to face, contact. The two people continued by without giving them a second glance.

"That was close, Robert. It almost looked like they were in some kind of trance."

"Perhaps they were tired. It's probably the start of a rest period down here, Ian. That would explain why this office is quite empty."

"Let's move on to the next section. This place is starting to give me the creeps. The sooner we're finished and out of here, the better, as far as I'm concerned."

The subsequent division contained what they assumed to be living quarters: Libraries, lounges, and recreation areas sprawling across this main floor's closest side. There were kitchens, and dining rooms, situated at its far end. Noise emanating from this direction indicated group Activity. The far side was a maze of walkways containing shopping precincts, theatres, and numerous other leisure areas. This area was also crowded. Galleries, many stores high, overlooked this common area. This communal focal point was of sufficient size and diversity to supply ample cover if the need arose.

Ascending a stairway and exploring the lower galleries, they concluded these areas were designated as private accommodation. Higher floors seemed to be allocated to maintenance shops with storage and supply warehousing. More well-equipped maintenance shops stood adjacent to the generating facilities and a water treatment center. This plant received water pumped from a stream that ran throughout the precinct below. Adjacent to this area, they viewed walk-in freezers containing meats, vegetables, and dairy products. Many other coolers had vast quantities of food. There were also ample supply storage rooms for sundry items.

One work area housed equipment, the likes of which neither of them had ever seen before. Their conclusion, it was for reprocessing air because of its ducting system connections. Robert took many photographers for others to assess. This self-contained city could function independently for a considerable amount of time.

From these balconies, a vantage point, a complete floor plan view of below was available. Robert's camera clicked rapidly, prioritizing the maze of walkways in the precinct they'd not chanced to enter.

"This place must comfortably accommodate thousands of people, Ian. It's enormous, and there's enough food down here to feed an army for years."

"But how do they restock the stores? Is there another way down?"

"Well, we've not found any other way up or down than the one we know of. So, it's my guess; the elevator is also used for fright. After all,

It's rather large for the exclusive use of personnel."

"But how could supplies be delivered to the elevator? Certainly not through Lord Simpson's old office.

"We'll let someone else figure that one out. Perhaps the film in this camera can shed light on that mystery."

They returned towards the elevator by way of a full circle. Keeping to the far side, they avoided the central maze of walkways. A sizeable polished-faced quarts wall, with a massive ornate door carved from similar stone, was the only unusual feature on this perimeter walkway. The door's intricate carvings were designed to enhance the effect of this quarts structure. Deep red and orange translucent colours reminded Ian of smouldering embers cradling an intense blaze. Surmising quarters protected by this door hewn from a solid rock was for a person of importance. They investigated further.

"This must be where Desate resides, Ian. I'd like to check inside, but that probably wouldn't be the wisest thing to do." The mere thought of what Robert had just said sent chills down Ian's spine. Ian was aware of Robert's bravado, sometimes overriding his better judgment. Ian then put a listening device, supped by Robert, to the wall. Ian pulled away quickly, alerting Robert to what Ian heard had disturbed him immensely. "What's wrong?"

"Those sounds; they're like grunts, and snorts, from some great beast." He placed the listening device back to the wall. "Robert! it's getting closer." Lowering the listening device, he stared at Robert with a cold, detached look. "What now?"

"We leave, Ian: We leave quickly!" Their hasty retreat was accompanied by the sound of the heavy door opening behind them. This produced an overwhelming urge in both of them to find a dark hole to crawl into. Robert quickly checked an enclosed area they were passing with his periscope. "It's empty. Inside quickly." Ian needed no coaxing to go through that door. He was inside like a flash after pushing a slower, more curious Robert through first. As Ian closed their door, a low heavy thud indicated what he perceived to be the door to Desate's quarter's closing simultaneously. Its noise reverberated throughout their bodies like an earth tremor. Only seconds passed before the office's frosted glass darkened as a large shadow clouded its light. Through frosted glass windows, a shadowy head cast an image best compared to that of a bison.

"What the hell was that Robert?"

"That's Luk Desate in his natural form Ian. He is the devil. I have already told you that." This once alien concept was now confirmed by these recent events. Ian paled with fear.

When the coast was clear, they ventured out and continued on until they'd explored the perimeter's entirety. At the elevator vestibule, a discerning eye could see the guard was still passed out at his desk. Quivering with anticipation, Ian's thoughts were centred on getting out of this place as quickly as possible. They were so close to what Ian considered the relative safety of a dark empty shaft. He waited anxiously for Robert to finalize preparations for their surface climb through the darkness.

At that moment, an office door opened not too far from where they were. Both Ian and Robert gazed in amazement as lord Simpson emerged.

"You told me he was dead, Robert."

"He was. I saw the body myself." His camera was out for a last fleeting snapshot of this phenomenon.

Lord Simpson had that same glazed look in his eyes as the two people they'd encountered in the office area earlier. His body still bore scars of the bullet wounds Robert had described. After visiting several workstations and distributing paperwork to empty desks, he returned from whence he came.

In shock or total amazement, Robert opened the door with his key. The two of them slipped quietly into the stairwell's dark comfort.

"How do you explain that one?" Ian whispered.

"Even our doctors under certain conditions can grow tissue, skin, for instance. Apparently, Desate can do that and so much more today. This does not make these achievements miracles. I predict one day; our scientists will be able to achieve similar accomplishments.

"Robert exchanged his handheld flashlight, for one attached to a head harness, then handed Ian another headlight from his bag.

"I'm glad we're finally ready to make our long trek upwards."

"I guess we are. Now we've come this far, please let's take care not to trip any alarms or draw undue attention to ourselves on the way out." This was emphasized to temper Ian's enthusiasm in exiting this place with an overconfident attitude.

The walk up the iron staircase took them many hours, with Robert utilizing rest stops to record shaft conditions. Reaching the mechanical room made burning leg muscles a tolerable tariff. Packing all equipment into two large briefcases, left for that purpose, they took one each. After removing a lens cap from the valence cameral Robert had placed on before the mission, they left the dark mechanical room.

Together made their way back to Ian's office. Reaching there without incident gave them the satisfaction of knowing the operation had been a success. Tension and stress related to this expedition were now relished as victories and memories. A weight now lifted from Ian's shoulders was giving him a high from the ordeal.

"That key really made it so much easier for us, didn't it." Robert sat himself down in a chair before answering.

"I'd venture to say what we did would have been impossible if not for that key, Ian. The key, as I told you, was just about impossible to duplicate. Without unlimited resources available for our reproduction, the amount of information gathered without it would have been minuscule in comparison. I never did tell you the key's price tag."

"How much money are we talking about, Robert."

"Millions, upon millions, of dollars." Ian's astonished look was accompanied by a whistle that echoed his surprise.

"As I said before, it wasn't just an ordinary key. As you know, its edges are set with diamonds. We surmise this will make precise tumbler contact by reflecting a light source inside the lock. This enables access to control code for alarm systems. That's why we had no trouble bypassing alarms." Ian bit his lower lip and acknowledged with knowing nods.

"When do you think we'll be ready to mount an attack, capable of obliterating the Devil's domain?"

"You're jumping way too far ahead. We haven't even evaluated our freshly acquired information yet. There will be untold assessments and multiple scenarios to consider before planning a decisive strike. Of all people, you must understand the enormous amount of planning to be done before attempting an assault on such an impregnable complex.

When all this is done, and not before, arrangements will then be set in motion for a bomb delivery. As for the time frame, It could take weeks or even months."

"I was hoping for a quicker conclusion."

"Time is on our side, and we can't afford mistakes by trying to move too fast. The slightest mishap could give rise to suspicion. If that should happen, Desate casts a large shadow. Just the hint of a plot would be sufficient to invoke mass executions."

"Then, there would be no way of getting the people out of the complex before we destroy it."

"No, but my thought is, all the people down there are like Lord Simpson. They've already died once and were brought back to serve Desate. What better way to keep a willing workforce, in such a place, than by offering them immortality? I think we've just visited purgatory. Their other option was probably hell."

"If that's true, do you think we can destroy what's down there?"

"I believe we can erase everything down there, except for perhaps

Luk Desate himself. His quarters looked impregnable to me. To smash his organization and imprison him in that place would be a significant victory for us. It would be a long time before the Devil could raise his ugly head again."

"I hope you're right; I sincerely hope your right, Robert."

Robert bagged up his equipment with garbage and disposed of it after leaving the building. Ian worked into the morning's early hours to complete his Zurich assignments. The following day they both left for England. This Zurich visit's main objective was not company work, and their fundamental mission had been fulfilled. Ian had his plane land in London, where he was to meet Barbara. Robert continued on to meet with John.

CHAPTER 37

Tom feels uneasy

Ian tracked Barbara to the theatre she'd leased. Glancing up from drawings she'd been pondering over, Ian's image, silhouetted in the gloom of temporary lighting, gave her cause to smile. His welcomed sight induced her to forgo all other immediate commitments. First, he was allotted his usual kiss before being handled on a grand tour. As she took him through the theatre, the emphasis was given to the recent improvement. Ian's admiration for the artistic concepts worked into the design was summed up in one word.

"Impressive! I can't believe so much has been accomplished in such a short time. The theatre starting to reclaim its former glory. You're doing such a fantastic job. I like the idea of the lounge bar in the foyer. The upstairs dining room being tied into the show's theme, I think it really works well. Will it all be ready by the tentative date you've set?"

"We will, even if it takes working three shifts to meet the deadline. Tony's hired the key people he requires, and we're holding auditions tomorrow for cast members. Will you be here to watch auditions and the start of rehearsals?"

"That's my plan. I'll be in England for the next few weeks as luck would have it. Will the cast be able to rehearse with all this construction going on,"

"The construction crews finish the stage area. That was a priority. Rehearsals can begin immediately after cast selection has been completed." Tony appeared from beneath the stage and came over to say hello to Ian.

"Well, what do you think of our theatre now, Ian." There was a little more than just a smack of pride in his statement.

"I must say it a great improvement on the first time I saw the old place, Tony."

"When it's ready to open, it'll be one of London's most spectacular theatres. No expense has been spared on decor. I plan to dress staff in period costume; Saxon for women and Norman for men." "That sounds like a good marketing idea, Tony. I like it. Barbara's been showing me around the dining room upstairs; it has all the makings of a fine eatery."

"We plan to look at the restaurant as an independent business venture, with its own separate entrance. My main focus will be the show, the restaurant, and the bar, just added gravy on the dish. Speaking of food, we plan to serve fare befitting the period, all top quality, of course. There will be such things as venison, pheasant, salmon, trout, and of course, beef on the menu. I've engaged the services of an excellent chef to partner us in this venture. He has some fantastic ideas of his own on how meals should be presented. He's also researching period beverages, like mead, you know, wine made from honey, and various ales. We also plan serving food and drinks from pewter wear, in keeping with our theme."

"It sounds like I should be booking a table for the opening night now."

"It's already been booked for you. On the show's opening night, the restaurant will be open, to invited guests only. So, you see, I'm one jump ahead of you there." That brought a few sniggers.

"I should take my bags to the apartment and unpack. Will you join me, darling?"

"I'll be tied up here for a while. Why don't you drive the jag there? It's parked outback. I drove it up from Bristol for you. When you have unpacked and rested, you can pick me up here later. Perhaps we can all go out for supper together."

"That sounds like a good plan." She dropped the car keys into his hand. "I'll be back in a few hours."

Tony and Barbara were sitting nursing mugs of tea and talking with Tom, the contractor when Ian returned. As he pulled up a chair, the conversation died.

"Discussing the day's progress were we. Please don't let me interrupt you."

"Oh, I think it's been all hashed out fairly well."

"Perhaps you should consider joining us for supper, Tom?" Ian's inquiry was posed as more an invite than a question. Barbara chimed in.

"Come on, Tom, you don't want to have super alone, do you?"

"Well, when you put it that way, I'll be glad to take you up on your offer." Ian stood up and fished out his car keys.

"Now that's settled, has anyone any suggestions on where we should eat." Tony walked to the side stage and picked up the phone before turning to talk to the group.

"We must book a table at Oliver's restaurant. Oliver's my chef. He and his wife run their own restaurant." This made Ian curious.

"If he has his own restaurant, why would he want to work at our restaurant, Tony?"

"Ah, you see, Ian, he and I have an arrangement. It'll be his name over the restaurant door, and we have an amicable split of profits. I have an excellent chef with a vested interest. He has good exposure with a chance to promote his name. And He'll be expanding his business."

"That seems to be a sound business arrangement, Tony."

"I thought so, Ian."

The restaurant was everything Tony had touted it to be, at least in appearance. Plush, quiet, with the promise of an excellent dining experience. Its atmosphere portrayed it as a place where the clientele could expect to be pampered. If its food matched the establishment's ambiance, they were in for an enjoyable evening. They were first introduced to Oliver, who, in turn, introduced Jane, his wife. Ian noticing Jane as being rather muscular, glanced at Barbara, and seeing no one watching, showed a raised eyebrow to her; she, in turn, gave a knowing look Ian's way.

Oliver sat them at a table near his kitchen so he could supervise their meals personally. His wife, Jane, went back into the kitchen. In the confusion of seating, Ian took the opportunity to lean forward and whisper into Barbara's ear.

"Jane! a man in drag, right?"

"Let's just say I'm not going into the washroom at the same time to find out."

Oliver recommended several Italian dishes, from which they made their selections. He also suggested a Chianti accompany the meal. Oliver served all the meals personally. The presentation alone was enough to make the most discerning connoisseur's mouth water. Colourful displays, and aromas, were practically enough incentive to initiate a feeding frenzy.

Oliver fluttered around the table, attending to every minute detail. Tom soon became the recipient of excessive attention. He was hovered over as he was affectionately touched by caring hands. All this attention made Tom ill at ease, although he seemed oblivious to any underlying motives at this point in time.

Ian cleaned the corners of his lips with his napkin as Oliver started to clear empty platters from the table.

"My compliments to the chef, that was an excellent pasta dish. " Oliver gave a nodding bow.

"I'm pleased you enjoyed your main course. Now please allow me to bring you the dessert menus." Passing out menus, he recommended a different dessert to each person. It was apparent he wished the entire spectrum of his culinary delights to be sampled.

Choices were made, and desserts were served. Oliver then left for his kitchen. Ian's seat, facing directly towards an ajar kitchen door, felt unease seeing Oliver spying on Tom. His perception was seeing what was akin to a love-struck adolescent in awe of his idol. He looked away in embarrassment, feeling prolonging his gaze could be construed as voyeurism. Suddenly a loud crashing sound reverberated throughout the kitchen. Ian's attention was again drawn to where Oliver had been standing. Shards of crockery from plates apparently broken over Oliver's head were falling to the floor. Oliver's hands began comforting his aching head as the kitchen door closed, and the commotion continued. Neither Tony nor Tom, seated with their backs to the kitchen, was privy to this floor show's added attraction.

Although barely audible, the odd swear word could occasionally be heard echoing through the restaurant. This did bring some inquiring looks between Tony, Barbara, and Tom. Although perhaps through politeness, nothing was said. Minutes later, Oliver emerged from the kitchen. He tidied himself up, well keeping a weather eye over his shoulder. He then closed the kitchen door securely behind himself.

Barbara, unaware of what Ian had witnessed, made eye contact with Oliver as he approached. An uneasy silence fell over the table. Feeling obliged to alleviate this seemingly awkward situation, she blurted out a few hasty words. Her speech was slightly impaired by food. It was helped along with her fork, repeatedly stabbing towards her plate.

"This is very good, Oliver." Tension's eased as Tony smiled at her approval.

"I knew you'd enjoy the food here, Barbs. I'm sure a restaurant of this calibre in our theatre will be an asset." Ian also felt the chilled air warming as he offered comments.

"I agree." This started a conversation between the three other men, allowing Ian to relate previous happenings in Barbara's receptive ear. Her first reaction was a look of disbelief, which quickly turned to some discreet sniggering.

Tony fetched a chair for Oliver. Oliver, however, used this opportunity to take Tony's vacated seat next to Tom. This left Tony with little option other than using this added chair himself. With the new restaurant being the main topic of conversation, Oliver encouraged Tom's input as a blatant excuse to ease in ever closer. Tom nervously looked at his watch, clearly uncomfortable by this turn of events.

"My goodness, look at the time. We have an early day ahead of us tomorrow." He shot to his feet, hoping everyone would follow suit. Tony, unperturbed, continued with his self-indulging conversation that no one was really paying attention to. Ian grinned at Barbara as they made Tom stand and sweet it out for a while. They made him contemplate the thought of maybe having to sit back down. Their little inside joke over, they slowly started to clear the restaurant. Oliver escorted them to the front door to say goodnight.

A gentle caring hand swept over Tom's back as he bid them all farewell. Tom's embarrassing situation had gone entirely unnoticed by Tony, who was becoming more wrapped up in expressing his inner thoughts. Speaking with flamboyant self-esteem and intoxicated fluidity was giving Tony a severe case of verbal diarrhea. His babbling continued until they reached the cars.

"I did say the food here was good, didn't I." Was his final statement before anyone else was allowed a voice. Barbara giggled like a little schoolgirl as she spilled out a comment she knew would eventually be received as the joke it was intended to be.

"It was, but I enjoyed the improvised entertainment more." Completely oblivious as to what had been going on, Tony looked puzzled.

"Entertainment! what do you mean." Ian was a little more explicit.

"Don't you find something strange about Oliver and his wife, Jane?"

"Strange! in what way strange?"

"Tony, haven't you noticed? They're both men!" Tom put his face to Tony's, and palm slapped Tony's forehead. Tony clued in.

"Oliver's been making passes at me all night, or hadn't you noticed.

That's why I was acting uncomfortable when he was around. I felt like I was number three in a love triangle, in there." Tiers of laughter started rolling down Tony's cheeks.

"So, the commotion in the kitchen was a lovers quarrel over you, Tom. Tell me which one did you fancy then, Jane?" Tom's face went beetroot red before everyone burst into laughter.

"Oh my god," Tony exclaimed. "I can't have them fighting like that in our restaurant. That's not quite the image I'm aiming for." Ian, still laughing, tried to reassure Tony.

"I'm sure Jane will be running this restaurant, and Oliver will tend to ours."

"That was my understanding, so I do hope they honour that agreement." Revelling their sexual orientation in such a colourful manner had defiantly made for an unusual evening. On that note, they said goodnight, got into their separate vehicles and went their different ways.

Ian opened the apartment door and guided her slowly through well caressing her shoulders and kissing the back of her neck. This escalated to more intimate stroking of her body. Closing the door behind him, he was embraced by the tigress he'd aroused. She clasped her hands to the back of his neck and kissed him passionately. Slipping her hands under his jacket, she rolled it smoothly and quickly from his body. In turn, he gently caressed her breast and peeled her clothing away in much the same manner to bare her smooth, soft skin. Their clothing fell into piles around their feet as passions raged. Ian continuously paid homage to her body with his lips. He stimulated her emotions with his fingers as he moved behind her. His palms now pulled her lower body close, well his fingers continued to excite her. She braced herself with her hands as she was gently leaned forward towards the door. A sigh of pleasure accompanied the touch of his fingers as they encouraged the flow of lubricants, well gently parting her lips. She then felt that the desired part of his body slipping between his fingers to tantalize her. This part of his body, she found to be much more pleasurable than his fingers. It seemed to embody all his strength and vigour as its heat burned into her. She felt the pressure from his hips as their bodies united. Her hands pushed harder and harder, against the door, with the rhythm of his intensifying love.

A gentle tap, tap, to the door's knocker, startled them. The sighs were muted, and motions were frozen in time as they contemplated their predicament. Hearing nothing more from outside the door and confident they were alone once more, Ian continued with some hefty thrusts. Again, came the tap, tap, tap, from outside the door. Ian stopped the tapping stopped, he started, the tapping started. The varying pressures of her hands on the door had caused it to pulsate and vibrate the knocker. Passion gave way to laughter as the realization of what was happening sank in. Ian now fantasied, holding a fairground hammer; his goal, ring that pole top bell. Louder knocks, to him, represented higher marks on the pole's achievement indicator. These blows, in turn, were applauded by Barbara's moans. As the hammer pounded faster, the knocker's noise on the door increased. It became louder stronger, and with increased frequency until it was no longer synchronized to their rhythm. The final clatters from the door signified the bell had been indeed wrung. As they pulled apart, she turned to kiss him on the lips. After the embrace, they looked into each other eyes, then started to laugh.

"Are you thinking what I'm thinking, Barbara? What are we doing in the lobby? We could have done this in the comfort of our own bedroom."

"True, but this was much more romantic, don't you think?" Picking up their clothing, they made their way to bed.

Ian did his mandatory workload in the comfort of the apartment the following day. Barbara spent her time overseeing theatre renovations. When that was completed, she phoned Ian to say auditions were about to start. He made the trip to join her for these initial tryouts. The stage was set as he took a seat next to her, front row center. Tony was at the ivories on stage, going over music scores with the director and choreographer. The choreographer collected a chair from the side stage and sat close to the piano. The director came down to sit next to Ian. An introductory handshake was thrust out towards Ian.

"I'm Barry, and you must be Ian." Ian acknowledged, and after a cordial handshake, Barry took a seat. He then turned his attention towards the stage.

"Bring out the first victim," he bellowed. A young woman full of confidence strutted onto the stage. She gave a brief introductory speech before being invited to sing. Handing Tony a music score, he opened it on the piano. He played, and she sang. She completed a few verses when Tony suddenly stopped. He'd obviously been impressed with her talents because he handed her the lyrics and music to one of his songs. Although she undoubtedly had read Tony's intention in a much different way.

"I'd now like to hear you sing this song I've chosen." This seemed to upset her, and she glared at Tony

"I haven't rehearsed this."

"I'll make allowances for that." She opened up the song sheet aggressively and never relented on a glare that could have frozen mercury. Taking several minutes to read the words, she then hummed the melody to familiarize herself with it. She then snapped at Tony.

"I'm ready." Tony's then made the unforgivable mistake of starting to replay her music. This prompted her to walk over to the piano and snatch her piece from the rest. Loud sniggering from the small audience shattered the theatre's serene silence. Tony joined in by laughing at himself; again, through misinterpretation, this made her even angrier. After taking time to regain her composure, she continued on to finish her singing audition. Barry gave his seal of approval on her vocal talents by inviting the choreographer to put her through some dance routines.

Barry whispered to Barbara. "She has ample ability, and she's spirited. I like her for the part. I like her a lot."

Several more people appeared at the side stage, and one by one, they completed their auditions. More groups replaced the first round of hopefuls as auditions dragged on. This process continued for many hours. Finally, a shortlist of applicants had been selected. Barry was becoming agitated as fatigue set in.

"I think this would be an excellent time to take a break. We've reached a point where I believe everyone deserves a timeout."

OK, people, attention, please. Everyone here's worked hard and has made the first cut. Coffee, and sandwiches, have been laid out in the foyer. Use this brake well, because when you return, this will be when the real work begins. From this group, we'll be making our final selections, and for the lucky ones, the hard grind of rehearsals will be starting."

Refreshments were brought on stage for the executives. Sitting around eating and drinking coffee allowed them to compare notes. Barbara and Ian found it interesting to see how the actor's personalities were dissected and analyzed for various roles. Barry finished his coffee and clapped his hands.

"OK, people, back to work. Will someone inform the hopefuls?"

The second person to come back onto the stage was a shy young man with long black hair tied in a ponytail. Barry checked his notes before indicating he was ready. On his second audition, again, this young man showed the quality of his powerful voice. Decrying his shy demeanour, he portrayed commanding stage presents. Barbara Whispered to Ian.

"I think Barry's found his, Heroward." Then she couldn't resist adding her own little spin into the mix. "But he'll need a date with the dye bottle to be a believable, flaxen Saxon."

The laborious task of cast selection was finalized, leaving many hopes fulfilled, well others dashed. Barry assembled the successful candidates to congratulate them and arrange rehearsal schedules for the following day. Dismissing the cast, he then turned his attention to the choreographer Brian and also Tony.

"Their day may be over, but we have tomorrow to plan. Perhaps we should continue this conversation over coffee at my place?" Barbara could see no point in delaying their departure.

"You people toddle off and do your thing. Ian and I will tidy up around here before locking the place up for the night." With just the two of them left in the theatre, she voiced her thoughts more freely.

"I'm really enjoying this project. It's quite different from anything else I've ever been involved with."

"I wish my work gave me the same satisfaction. It used to, but not anymore. I now find myself more intrigued by your projects. By the way, when is Jeff supposed to release your record? That's got to be soon."

"Next week, all being well."

"You've taken on a large workload for yourself. Will you be able to manage?"

"Work is the therapy I need right now, and I've been grooming Pam to take over much of the administration, as you know. She'll make that happen, allowing me the opportunity to do other things I enjoy doing. A tour is in the cards, but I'll limit that to a minimum. It wouldn't be fair to burden Pam with the responsibility of running things alone for an extended period. If the tour does materialize, it will take place in the United States and Canada. Well, I'm there; it might be a good opportunity for you to join me and visit your old hometown."

"I'd like that very much. I could visit, Dom. When his leg was injured so severely, he was pensioned off by the company, and that's where he decided to settle. I never could bring myself to sell my parents' small farm, so it made sense to let him have the place. I thought it a fitting gift for saving my life. We keep in constant touch: by all accounts, he's getting the farm back into shape after years of neglect. It's given him a new focus on life. He's also found himself a love interest that sounds serious. It'll be good to see him again. Robert will also be able to visit his hometown, Seattle. Perhaps we can get some sea fishing in, around the gulf islands. You'll enjoy reacquainting yourself with the spectacular scenery, I'm sure."

"Before I forget, tomorrow we have tickets, along with Tony, for a show. Richard landed the part he was after, and we'll be his guests on opening night. The press will be there, so it could be an excellent opportunity to get some publicity for our own show. Richard's single record of a song from our show is in the top twenty charts. I'm sure Tony will be angling for any given opportunity to coral a press interview."

"So, we'll be along for moral support."

"Something like that, but there will be a party after the show for cast and friends."

The empty theatre was starting to chill, and with most of the lights out, it was rapidly losing its newfound charm. It was time to lock up and return to their cozy apartment.

The following day was a rerun of the previous day until late afternoon. Barbara returned early to prepare for the evening show. Arraignments had been made for limousine theatre service for Tony and themselves. A theatre lounge bar section was the location of a cocktail party for invited guests, held before the show's start. The lounge itself was crowded when they arrived. People jostled to and fro, exercising every skill required to be a successful social butterfly.

The lounge bar itself was elegant, and that had retained its Victorian charm. Slender marble columns rose from ornately carved large wooden bases. This type of wooden architecture was predominant throughout the lounge. Ornate cast iron tables and chairs were the dominant furniture, with silk-covered divans tastefully secluded by foliage in marble pots. Matching table tops blended with columns and planters. Painted walls showcased many paintings and photographs of artists and celebrities who had graced the theatre with their presents.

It was not hard for Tony to find an audience in this atmosphere. He soon became the bar's center of attraction, grooming his audience with outlandish tales.

"Know doubt one of his stories is about to lure some unsuspecting victim into being the butt end of a practical joke," she remarked to Ian as Tony beckoned them over. He was eager to promote Barbara to his new fan club, giving her a grandiose introduction. He also took the opportunity to satirically exalt press critics in the group. Hearing Tony's accolades, several press critics seized this given opportunity to engage her in conversation.

Barbara was then subtly grilled on her involvement in show business. Casually mentioning her upcoming record release in the United States, she quickly usurped Tony's pivotal role. Notebooks were out as camera flashes brought the room to focus on her. Several minutes of posing were required before she was able to work Tony back into the act. Capitalizing on this engineered opportunity, they then pitched their own show.

* * *

Richard's show's audience escalated its initial warm reception into rowdy accolades as the curtain rose for a second encore, marking it a hit in their eyes. The appreciation shown for Richards's performance was echoed with a boisterous standing ovation as he stepped forward for another personal bow.

Barbara, Ian, and Tony made their way backstage to meet with the cast. From there, revellers departed for a reception to celebrate, according to audience reaction, a successful opening night.

Richard came to Tony for what he knew would be an honest opinion.

"How was my singing."

"Your acting Richard, fantastic, great performance; sing a decent enough rendition, my honest assessment, adequate."

"Without your help, Tony, it would have been appalling. Let me get all of you a glass of champagne to celebrate the occasion." Richard summoned a waiter and ordered the best bubbly. Barbara echoed the audience's appreciation by showering Richard with her accolades for his performance.

"I think this has to be one of your best performances to date,

Richard. I can only hope our show will be as successful as your show seems to be."

"With Tony at the helm, how can you miss." He raised an open hand to Tony, who, in turn, hoisted his glass of champagne in acknowledgment. "Although, unfortunately, I'll not be able to attend opening night because I'll be performing here."

"Not to worry, Richard, I'll arrange for a limo to be waiting for you when you finish here. It will bring you straight to our opening night party after the show.

"I was hoping that might be the case. You know I'll not pass up a good celebration."

Parting carried on into morning's early hours, at which time even the heartier revellers had surrendered to fatigue.

There were no deadlines or commitments for the following day, so the activity's pace revolved around personal whims. A short theatre visit preceded their trip home to the Chew valley, where a quiet evening, curled in front of a cozy fire, rounded out their day.

The following morning Ian met with Robert at the breakfast table to discuss John's arrival that afternoon. Ian suggested a lake fishing expedition could provide the perfect opportunity for the three of them to talk freely.

After finishing breakfast, Ian went to his office; well, Robert had made himself busy pottering around the boat throughout the morning.

Soon after John arrived, he, and Ian, joined Robert at the boat. Rowing onto the lake, they cast their lines at a favoured spot. The conversation quickly gravitated to the trip's real purpose. John briefed them on new revelations gleaned from their reconnaissance.

"Some crucial facts went unresolved by the two of you, but fortunately not Robert's photography. One important issue: We've determined an entrance into the mechanical room from a door constructed to look like a wall. This door occupies the disguised mystery space between those two support columns on the lower level. It's built with counterbalance weights enabling it to lower into the floor. Its proximity coincides with the building's rear loading dock's outside location. With inside and outside shots, Robert's eye for detailed photographic building recognizance proved invaluable in determining this fact. Such access would undoubtedly be used for supply purposes. It could also provide access for us to deliver the necessary ordinance to destroy the complex.

However, Robert's camera has also detected a major stumbling block; blast doors can drop to seal off the bottom elevator security room in emergencies. This obstacle will have to be dealt with at the appropriate time.

Explosives to collapse the shaft will require a well-coordinated delivery procedure because of the sheer quantity required. It's been decided, the best plan will be to utilize the regular delivery schedule to the complex and exploit that window of opportunity. After manhandling the ordinance to the top of the elevator, we can attach the charges onto cables and lower them into the shaft. Steel cables that drop each side of the opening will support strings of munitions. Winches will be required to control paying out the wires, and as they run down, the shaft charges will be attached at needed intervals. The nuclear device can then be delivered by elevator to the security room. It can then be deployed into the main compound area, perhaps amongst regular supplies. The team responsible for this part of the operation can then bring down the blast door, ensuring it can not be reopened. Once all our groups have cleared the shaft area, it would then be collapsed by exploding the charges. They will be blown one level at a time, starting from the bottom upwards in a cascading effect. The bomb itself will then be detonated by the use of a time delay."

"Approximately how long before this plan becomes a reality?"

"Good question Ian. We'll need at least a month to assemble men and equipment for the operation. As I've emphasized so many times before, moving too fast could draw unwanted attention. Bringing teams together and training them to carry out the operation's different requirements will also take time. You'll both get plenty of notice before we're ready to make our move. Robert can make good use of this time checking delivery schedules, which, as I stated, could be crucial to the operation's success."

Cloak and dagger work taken care of, the three of them turned their full attention to catching trout for supper. The remainder of a pleasant afternoon was idled away lake fishing before returning home. Delivering their catch to the kitchen, each wished to play chef, with their own specific ideas on the best way to cook trout. Barbara finally took control of her kitchen and prepared supper her way.

Potatoes were peeled, quarter, lightly oiled, sprinkled with onion flakes and grated cheese, then roasted to a golden brown. Fresh asparagus was prepared in a steamer. Finally, the trout were pan-fried in butter until the skin was crisp. Placing them on oval platters, she added the other items with a creative flair for presentation. Feasting finished and clearing chores completed, they retired to the lounge. Coffee was served, and conversation flowed into the morning's early hours.

John's brief visit ended with an early morning departure, directly after breakfast. Ian dispatched Robert to Zurich under the guise of company business to do more reconnaissance.

Having completed his work for that day, he decided to take Barbara to Weston for an evening excursion. They walked the promenade before selecting a beach view restaurant with a patio for a light snack. When they had finished, the evening was still young enough to enjoy a stroll on the pier. Arm in arm, they walked and talked. Barbara never ever quizzed Ian about business, realizing the sensitivity of his work. She did, however, perceive John was now somehow involved, and this piqued her curiosity.

"May I ask, what's so important between Robert, and yourself, that involves John." Ian had been put on the spot by a question he'd rather not have to embellish with a lie.

"It's company business and something I'd rather not bother you with at this point in time. The fact that John's involved should make you feel confident that everything's kosher." Recognition from the archery sideshow barker, where Ian had once won her a Kewpie doll, was a welcomed distraction.

"Hay, Robin Hood! how about showing the people here how it's done." He held a bow and arrows in outstretched arms towards Ian. Ian smiled, shook his head, and with a low hand wave, signalled his decline. The offer of the bow and arrows was withdrawn. "Well, maybe next time then." As they walked on, the barker's sales pitch focused on more passers-by.

Reaching the pier's end, they paused to lean on the railing. Stars shone brightly in a clear night sky. Across the Bristol Channel, the Welsh coast's dark silhouette, dotted with twinkling lights, clearly defined itself from the channel's black glistening waters.

Barbara turned to Ian and placed her hands on his shoulders. Pulling herself up onto her toes, she kissed him on the cheek.

"I love you, Ian Shaw."

"You're the only thing in life that truly matters to me Barbara, you're the center of my universe." They embraced and kissed before slowly walking back to the promenade.

CHAPTER 38

A visit to the rodeo.

A week in Zurich preceded a flight to The United States to meet up with Barbara. Her tour had materialized earlier than expected. Replacing a performer incapacitated by a medical condition, she'd joined a production halfway through its road trip. Playing second billing, her first performance was in Seattle, Robert's hometown. After the show, he stayed on to visit, well she and Ian hired a car and travelled north to Vancouver, Canada.

Having the day to herself, before her evening performance, they visited Dom at Ian's parent's old Langley farm. Dom and his girlfriend were sitting on the front porch steps sipping refreshing drinks as they drove up. Dom looked every bit, the farmer on a lunch break from fieldwork. Dust-covered clothing and brow sweat mingled with dirt enforced this image. He rose from his seat and went to the car to greet them. Warm handshakes were followed by hugs and back slaps. Dom then introduced them to his fiancée Sue.

The four of them sat on the porch for a while to catch up on current events. Sue was surprised to learn Ian had once attended the same junior school she had. Realizing it was more than politeness that held Ian's interest in the neighbourhood, she felt free to relate local stories and events.

"There's a parade in Cloverdale today as a prelude to its Rodeo. It's one of the larger rodeos in North America. Do you remember the rodeo, Ian?"

"Now you've mentioned rodeo, it's brought memories of happy times flooding back. So yes, I do remember the rodeo and the parade."

The talk of a parade sparked Barbara's interest.

"I'd love to see a rodeo parade: I've seen them many times in the movies. I'd like to see one in real life."

"Then, perhaps we can all go. Does anyone know the parade's start time?" Sue replied.

"If we leave now, we should be there in plenty of time to catch the beginning. It'll only take fifteen minutes to get there from here."

"Will there be a chuckwagon race? I've always wanted to see a chuckwagon race live. Again, I've seen them so many times in western movies."

"There will, Barbara, but that race is usually run on the rodeo's last day, and not today; the first day."

"That's too bad, I'll be going back to the States the day after tomorrow to continue my tour, so I'll have to give it a miss this time."

"I'm sure there will be other times, Barbara. The midway will open soon after the parade has finished, and the rodeo will start shortly after that. I'm sure it's going to be a fun day. Now I suggest we stop talking about it and prepare ourselves to leave before it starts without us. Best follow my car, Ian. You're probably not sure of the way."

Small town Cloverdale offered ample parking in its side streets for the numerous vehicles that had delivered the crowds of spectators, now swelling the parade's route. Choosing a viewing spot nearer its start was determined easier than fighting crowds jostling near the parade's finish. Near the judging stand on Mainstreet, premium parade viewing areas had been staked out early by people with children to ensure an unobstructed viewpoint. This area was also close to the midway and rodeo ground's main entrance.

Shortly after selecting the best roadside space still available, a Cadillac convertible arrived on the scene. It carried the grand marshal: Seated on a gold-trimmed purple blanket spread over the trunk, above the back seat. He was accompanied by the local beauty queen and her princess. Accepting royalty's role for a day, they entertained the crowd, their subjects, with handwaves, well cruising slowly past. The car Itself was escorted by outriders on horseback. They held lance's skyward with their pennants fluttering in the breeze. Behind them came numerous other cars containing local dignitaries, most accompanied by pageant queens from other jurisdictions. They, in turn, were followed by parade participants competing for place-marks in their various categories. Marching bands with colour guards were first to take center stage to vie for the top spot in their particular group. These competitors had travelled from all over the Pacific Northwest to perform. Some had also journeyed from as far as California. As the first band struck up the music, its colour guard went into their skilful display of drills. These drills utilized a combination of rifles and flags. Each following group fiercely competed for the coveted first place ribbon in their specific category. This made for some spectacular performances.

As these presentations disappeared from view, a series of floats displaying creative themes promoting various interests and events were next to vie for crowd recognition. Coming from all over British Columbia and Washington State, their promotions were much diversified. The first float to pass displayed a small bandstand high upfront. A fiddler, come, caller, accompanied by a small band, occupied this area on the float. An ensemble of square dancers performed their routine on the small stage below. Following this first float was a team of eight mules pulling an old fashion coach. It was escorted by people dressed in pilgrim attire of the same period as the coach. The mule team was flanked by men holding lanterns on poles as if to light its way. This display represented The Sandman Inns, a hotel chain.

An old fire truck escorted by clowns on unicycles was next to start their show. The fire truck's water canons shot water high into the air as clowns began to throw firecrackers alongside. This immediately startled the mules and caused a stampede. Terror fueling their flight to nowhere drove them towards the square dancers' low-level float's dance floor. As the lead mules mounted the lower platform, they tripped and fell, scattering the terrified dancers. Mules harnessed behind press forward, steeping over the down animals. Ian rushed forward, grabbing what was now a lead mule by its bridle. Pulling its head down to its chest, he spoke softly to it as he blew gently into its nostrils to calm the poor creature down. Pushing on its flanks, Ian straightened the animal up. He then proceeded to back it off the lead mules underfoot. By now, others were helping, and Dom who's limp made him less agile, had also joined Ian. Once everything seemed under control, Ian and Dom quietly slipped back into the crowd and returned to where they'd been standing.

Sue grabbed Dom by the arm and kissed him on the cheek. "That's for you. As for you, Ian, you can take the boy out of the country, but you can't take the country out of the boy, can you? Working with livestock must have come back to you in a flash, how you handled that situation. And by the way, the two of you could easily get jobs as rodeo clowns." Ian looked at Dom and laughed.

"I'm not sure if that is a compliment or a putdown."

"I meant that in the most complimentary of ways. When you see the job those rodeo clowns do, you'll appreciate the courage those men display." Ian just laughed, knowing everyone knew his comment was satirical.

When the last float had passed, the four of them followed the procession towards the rodeo grounds to join the lines of patiently waiting people at the ticket wickets.

The hot-dog stand was their first stop. Set with food and drink, the bleachers were their next stop. The timing was perfect as they took their seats for the first event's immediate start. Sue was at one time a competitive barrel racer. In the course of that career, she had competed in many rodeos. Being familiar with most of the event's finer points, she could relate her knowledge as the show unfolded. Her comments made it so much more enjoyable for this small group of uninitiated spectators.

All too soon, early evening approached. Barbara's pending performance dictated her time to leave and become center stage in her own show. Biding farewell to Dom and Sue, they left them to enjoy an evening of rodeo entertainment.

Finishing her west coast engagements, Barbara's tour continued on to the Midwest. Ian joined Robert in Seattle the following day. Robert had received a message from Lord Barkley, which he relayed to Ian. Lord Barkley's communique informed Ian how Peterson had surfaced in South America. His presents had completely disrupted operations there. Ian reiterated his plan of action to Robert for just such an event.

"As you know, I've already made suggestions to Lord Barkley, anticipating something of this nature occurring." He gently shook the letter in a raised hand. "My position is, we put an end to his activities once and for all. You'll be in control of the fieldwork in this operation." This is the plan at my end. We put a bounty on his head and any underworld operative who helps him. It would be unwise for us to apprehend him, so we eliminate him by creating a false identity around him. This we can initiate by releasing stories through the international press. Stories that paint him as a bloodthirsty, murdering, drug dealing kingpin. Ironically that was a description not too far from the truth. If he wishes to remain in hiding, let's just make it worth his while. You can make it a full-time job as of now to track him down. He'll probably be using a diplomatic passport, so check out all embassies, then get the local police to check the hotels. That will help cut down on our search time. Once we find where he's staying, we'll arrange to have him arrested and prosecuted by local authorities. This should keep it off the world stage. A long sentence tucked away in an obscure backwater will end his career. We've already erased his birth records and other records relating to him, creating new ones. If the worst scenario arises, and we can't capture him, it will still leave him a poor man, in a poor country, with no one to turn to."

"Are there any alternative suggestions as to how I should handle it other than the ones you've already outlined?"

"As I said, it's your operation. We don't know Peterson's exact location. Tex has only been able to confirm that he's in his area. Peterson's smart, and he knows our operations well, too well to give himself unnecessary exposure."

"Your plan seems to be a sound one, Ian. You have a knack for coming up with ideas that shy away from the inevitable blood baths usually related to violent situations. I'll start the field operation in his last known location and get people there working on it as soon as possible."

Musing over the project, remorse in his voice echoed Ian's feelings. "I hate what's done in the name of company policy. We're no better than gangsters. In fact, we're the largest, most organized criminal gang in the world. I will be glad to see it all end." Robert's words again reaffirmed their commitment to that purpose.

"It is organized crime, and we're the undercover cops, who've infiltrated the mob, so until we're ready to move, we must play the game. Thanks to you that should be brought to a head soon; ready soon." Ian clenched his lips, slowly nodding acknowledgment.

"Make your plans for South America to oversee this operation, and I'll make sure you have all the necessary documentation for the job."

For two weeks, Robert's valuable time was wasted tracking Peterson's movements. As Ian had suspected, he had seemingly vanished from the face of the earth. The segment of the strategy that had stripped him of everything, hopefully, would now prove to be the most practical solution. An ice-cold trail, with no sign of a quick thaw, prompted Robert's return to Zurich.

CHAPTER 39

Opening night

Robert's arrival was impeccably timed for the social event about to take place by juggling his and Ian's schedules. Early that morning, Barbara phoned Ian explaining all prior arrangements regarding Tony's show's opening night. A bus had been laid on to bring valley friends and neighbours to London for Big night. Ushering in the prelude to hopefully successful opening night, favourable weather was determined to be a good omen by this party of travellers.

* * *

Arriving at the theatre, people were escorted to the lounge bar by ushers in Norman costumes. Umbrellas would not be required to shelter silk gowns, well dry sidewalks assured sparkling dress shoes would stay unsoiled for this auspicious occasion. Joining the multitude of other invited guests and media, the atmosphere was electric.

Opening night for Tony was full of anticipation; nervously, he mingled amongst his guests. Timidly working the room, it was plane this social gathering, before the show, was not his finest hour. Barbara, in contrast, was calm and controlling. She socialized well, juggling all last-minute behind the scenes decisions. Tony, freed from this stress, was intended to play the charming host. Not quite the scenario that was transpiring. Barbara made the decision to join him and give moral support. With Barbara at his side, any PR disasters that might have ensued had been alleviated. Just before the first act's curtain call, Ian escorted Barbara to their seats.

"Now it's my turn to feel nervous." She gave Ian's hand a squeeze. He reassured her with a few soft words.

"I'm sure it'll be a smash hit, and our audience's appreciation will echo that sentiment when the final curtain falls."

"I do hope you're right."

* * *

As a climactic storyline point was reached, the intermission curtain fell. This prompted the audience to drift into the foyer, and lounge bar, for a much-needed refreshment break. It was apparent from the crowd's reaction the success at this point was proving to be everything they dreamed it could be.

Tony had now regained his self-confidence. He expressed this attitude in his flamboyant mannerisms and speech.

"In my humble opinion, the show's second half contains our best work. So, with what seems to be a successful first half, I feel confident everyone should enjoy the entire show."

Robert razed his glass. "I'll drink to that." Their glittering Christos were held high, endorsing Robert's toast.

The second half curtain call ushered a hasty exit from the bar to experience all remaining acts in their entirety.

* * *

Standing ovations from an appreciative audience following the finale fuelled numerous curtain calls from a jubilant cast. Tony joined the ensemble on stage to bathe in this moment of glory. Introduced to the audience by the leading man, he received a resounding round of applause. Final curtain calls behind them, and greasepaint washed away; the cast mingled with invited lounge guests before the dining room banquet.

Oliver had catered an elaborate spread, and all seemed to be going well. 'Too well perhaps,' thought Barbara, 'things seldom go this smoothly.' She then noticed Jane appear from the kitchen to make her way to where Tom was sitting with his wife. Barbara gave Ian a nudge and discreetly pointed out Jane.

"This looks like some fun we could do without. I thought It was clearly understood; Jane's presence was not required this evening."

"Apparently not clearly enough, Ian." To their relief, Jane walked past where Tom was seated without incident. However, she then went to Tony's table instead. Tony was sitting next to Ann and, as usual, was the life and soul of the party. Jane stood beside Tony's chair and made a big production out of congratulating him. Jane then put her hands on Tony's shoulders and gave him a passionate kiss. Had someone captured for posterity the embarrassing look on Tony's face, it would have alone been worth the price of admission. Ann could hardly contain herself from bursting into laughter.

This little episode was followed by another commotion when Jane returned to the kitchen. Oliver's voice could be heard reverberating from inside, over the restaurant's musical backdrop and the steady drone of conversation. Although most of his language was indiscernible, his final words came through loud and clear.

"Bitch, whore, slut." This was accompanied by a chorus of crashing pots pans and breaking crockery. Tony saw relief at hand as the cavalry arrived. It was Richard, making his usual a grand entrance. Tony immediately stood up to applaud and cheer loudly, encouraging everyone at his table to join in. This proved to be a great noise diversion from the competing kitchen hostilities. As applause started to subside, so did the kitchen commotion, much to Tony's relief. Even the beautiful woman on Richard's arm, used as window dressing, was overwhelmed by his warm reception. In awe, she looked on in amazement. On the opening night of Richard's own hit show, he didn't command this kind of attention, even with his excellent personal performance. Rising to the occasion, he made sweeping bows of acknowledgement in a grand parade to his reserved table spot.

"What merits am I the recipient of to receive such an auspicious welcome, Tony?" He whispered as he was seated.

"It's a tale requiring more time than we have at present, so this story's best left until a more appropriate occasion." The banquet was then able to continue without incident.

As tables were being cleared, Tony suggested a relocation might be in order. Partying continued on in the lounge bar. Socializing for many jubilant revellers lasted into the morning's early hours. Pending revues from critiques in first addition papers; anxiously gave rise to mixed emotions in what had now become a waiting game. Early morning editions were hastily checked to ensure their reports were favourable. Tony then read the reviews loudly to a hushed audience. The words fresh, exciting, and innovative, with excellent melodies and lyrics, popped up in most readings. The talented cast was also credited with raising the show to its maximum potential. These favourable revues prompted Tony to leap onto his chair, waving the newspapers high in the air and shouting.

"We're a hit; we've done it. Let's drink to success. Champagne, we must have Champagne." His jubilation was easily measured by the speed his feet bounced up and down on his seat. Champagne was served, and he settled down to propose a toast. "To the cast, my gratitude, to our show's continuing success, and last but not least, to my bank account." With some laughter, glasses were raised, and the toast was met.

The reception's pinnacle was reached. Its high could no longer be sustained, and human nature and fatigue dictated its wined down. One by one at first, then in a block, people left to go their separate ways. It was also an opportune moment for Ian and Barbara to slip quietly away.

A nostalgic trip to the river was in Ian's mind as he gave the cab driver his instructions. Their destination, Westminster bridge, where he had taken her after their first encounter in Savel Row. Their cab came to a halt near the Thames embankment. Rejuvenated by a night of rest, the city was awakening from its sleep. Streets were flooding with a tide of people, almost mindlessly pursuing their separate repetitive paths in life. The river's gentle flow, combined with a lapping wash from boats whose crews had just started work, reinforced this perception of a day's lazy awakening.

"Do you recall the first time I brought you here?"

"Let's go to that same spot and immerse ourselves in that moment past, Ian."

"I'd enjoy that." He paid the cabby, and they walked down the embankment steps to gaze out over London's lifeblood.

"I remember that first day we met and came here like it was yesterday."

"As do I. I think I've come a long way as a person since then. Looking back now, I can see myself, at that point in life, chasing selfish ambitions for shallow reasons."

"I think you're a little hard on yourself, Ian. I could never see you as anything but a good decent man."

"I'm sure the person I am today has as much to do with your influence as anything else."

"You're underestimating your own integrity. It just takes time for some people to decide which path in life they wish to take. It's seldom anyone's choice but their own."

"I suspect your right as always, but I must give you credit for at least speeding the process along." She smiled and took his arm, and they walked for a while. Feeling so in tune with each other's thoughts, speech now seemed obsolete to convey emotions."

For most of London's population, the sandman had long since come and gone when the two of them decided it was time to find their own bed. Wishing to savour this time together, a certain sadness prevailed as they climbed into the taxi Ian held to take them home.

CHAPTER 40
The assault begins

John's much-anticipated orders had finally been received by Robert. Schedules had been approved, and the wheels of motion were rolling. All relevant information was then passed to Ian. He then rearranged his own and Robert's itineraries. This was done to ensure their presents in Zurich would coincide with that specific time.

* * *

Meeting Robert at the airport, they boarded Ian's private jet, and within hours had joined John at a prearranged rendezvous. They were introduced to specialists' teams before proceeding forward with their one and only briefing.

"I'll start with your part in this operation, Ian. Everyone else has been thoroughly schooled in their roles. They are now completely integrated into one efficient unit. Your effort, however, will be an individual one. And it will be a pivotal one at that. Using all the procedures taught to you by Robert, you should achieve undetected access for our teams. There will be just one variation, that being, instead of the lens cap Robert used to shield the security camera on your last reconnaissance, we have a much-improved innovation. It is a small box containing a projector that fits over the camera. When it's activated, it will create a scene of the elevator being loaded with supplies. This will leave us free from surveillance detection in our mission. There's a remote control to activate this device when required.

Robert, please pass Ian the key." John also gave Ian a blown-up photograph of the mechanical room's blank rear wall. " Please note the arrowed lock location that we believe will activate that well-hidden loading dock door. Robert will help you locate that door lock and set up the camera before leaving to continue his role in this mission. His next job will be to ensure loading dock surveillance cameras are dealt with similarly to the inside mechanical room one. He will also be responsible for neutralizing security before our arrival, and you open the door. He will be waiting for you on the loading dock outside when that's accomplished. Once we're in, your job is over. You can leave through the main entrance in the same manner as you arrived. We will all now set our watches to precisely the same time." He pointed to a clock behind him. "Trucks will deliver our equipment instead of their scheduled supplies, which will be intercepted and diverted. The time for the loading dock door opening will be two minutes before our seven-thirty arrival. Once we've cleared the loading dock, Robert, you can also leave. The rest will be up to the inside teams." Ian and Robert left John and his teams to organize their convoy.

A scheduled meeting with Lord Barkley was Ian's first obligation after entering the building. Attempting normality in what would be anything, but another ordinary day was proving difficult. Hours dragged by slowly. Unable to control his constant clock-watching didn't help matters. As evening approached, tension rapidly mounted, and mundane tasks became hard to accomplish through an inability to concentrate. Attempted forced focus couldn't block thoughts of his pending solitary key roll in this elaborate scheme to bring down this force of evil. His conscience reasoned success was worth any personal risk. Imagining the unthinkable price of failure still weighed heavily on his mind.

As seven-O-Clock approached, Ian met with Robert. Robert escorted him to the mechanical room. Once inside, doctoring the camera became their initial task before the door lock location was verified. Robert's segment of this part of the operation was completed. He left Ian to accomplish his continuing assignments.

A metallic-sounding coded knock from outside signalled Robert's schedule was running to plan. Slipping his key gently into the lock, Ian paused before making that crucial turn to activate its mechanism that would initiate the door's downward motion. Pulling himself tight to the wall, he drew his gun as a precautionary measure. He then turned the key. Robert stood facing the door's opposite end. Robert's position was close to the loading dock office.

Through the open door of the loading dock's office, Ian could see a security guard bound and gagged on its floor. As Robert greeted Ian, he turned slightly and slid the office door shut. In that very instant, another guard rounded the building's outer perimeter corner. Ian's position was obscured from this man's view. Robert's suspicious presence prompted the guard to immediately draw his weapon. Unaware of Ian's concealed position, this guard told Robert to put his hands in the air. His voice alerted Ian to Robert's predicament. As the guard came close, Ian slipped quietly from his hiding spot and stuck him over the head with his gun. The guard's weapon fell from his hand. On hitting the floor, the cocked weapon discharged itself. The bullet struck Robert in the leg, dropping him to the ground. As Ian ran to his aid, in anguish, Robert shouted an order directly at Ian.

"For god's sake, secure the guard first." He ran back and retrieved the guard's gun from where it had fallen. "There's a bag with rope and tape inside the office. Bind and gag him, then stick him in with the other one." Ian retrieved the tape and a first aid kit he'd found inside the office. Quickly taping the guard from head to toe, he dragged him out of sight. Then he turned his attention back to Robert to stop the bleeding and bind the wound.

"You'll have to stay and finish my job, Ian."

"I never did intend leaving before you anyway."

Little more than a minute had passed before the first truck backed into the loading bay. Ian went to the shaft. Using the key, he opened the rear gate and activated the control panel to summon the elevator. The mechanism above him was activated instantaneously by the mere touch of the button.

The first team wasted no time in going about their assigned tasks. The perimeter was now secured, and the explosives had already started to be unloaded. They were then stacked neatly around the elevator shaft. Being first out of the truck, John stood close by overseeing the operation as more vehicles arrived. He then took the time to look down at Robert.

"What the hell happened to you."

"An unexpected encounter with security, but Ian neutralized the situation like a pro. Well, except for the bit where he got me, shot." He grimiest out a bit of snigger. "Here, you had better take this remote now." John took it from Robert's hand, then gave Ian his orders.

"Both of you: Your jobs here are finished. I'd like you to take Robert out on the first empty truck. He needs medical attention, and pack those two security guards in the back also."

"I'll get him on board my aircraft and ship him to a military hospital in Germany. He can be properly looked after there, without any awkward question being asked."

"That sounds like a good plan, Ian." Ian then helped Robert into the truck. Before he could get in himself, he saw the elevator slowly coming into view. Its arrival was accompanied by deep throaty dog growls from within. John looked to his men. "They must have security with dogs in the elevator to oversee the supply shipments. Knives only men. We can't risk detonating the munitions in a firefight." John then called to Ian as he activated the security movie camera's box with the remote. "There's a compound bow behind the seat in the truck; bring it here." Ian grabbed the bow. There were several arrows mounted in a holder attached to it. Instinctively he removed an arrow and placed it in the ready position. As he moved closer to John, he'd started to pass it to him. Time had run out.

The elevator doors were opening. Seeing teams of men in the loading bay area, the security guards from the underground complex unleashed their dogs. Ian's reflexes were fast. His first arrow hit the lead animal's chest before it could clear the elevator. His second arrow caught another in mid-leap as it was going for the throat of a team leader. Two more dogs stood guard at the elevator doors as the complex's security personal tried desperately to close them amidst slashing blades. Team members from both sides were now engaged in fierce hand-to-hand combat.

John's team was becoming overwhelmed, being no match for the remaining two giant animals. Ian steadied his aim and picked off the two remaining dogs amidst the mayhem. Team members were then able to overpower the remaining security guards. John had a look of surprise on his face as he glanced towards Ian.

"This is the second time this evening you've surprised me by proving yourself a worthy combat member of this team." This praise seemed to go unnoticed by Ian, who had a puzzled look on his face.

"But how did they get in the elevator. I called it from here."

"Luck must be on our side. They must have activated the elevator at the same time as you. We must have surprised them as much as they surprised us."

"The size of those dogs, John; I've never seen anything like them. They were more the size of bears."

"You've heard of the hounds from hell know doubt. Well, I think we've just encountered them."

"I think I'd like to see this thing through to the finish now. I can give Robert the authorization to use my aircraft. I don't have to be there."

The team leader, who saw the imminent threat of a dog's jaws near his own throat, walked by. Overhearing Ian's request, he remembered only too well; it was Ian's second arrow that took that beast out.

"Don't let that man leave, sir. A marksman with a bow, like Ian, is too valuable an asset to stand down. It's much too crucial a time in this operation."

"If anyone has earned the right to stay, it would be you. And apparently, you're regarded as being invaluable. Send Robert off with one of the drivers. When that's done, restock your supply of arrows. Report back here, then find yourself a vantage point to stand guard." Ian smiled and gave John a salute.

"Yes, sire."

Crossbeams had been strategically placed to support mechanisms that would feed the cables carrying the explosives. They were all set to run down each side of the shaft. As each line was paid out, they were stopped simultaneously at precise intervals. The charges were attached at these regular intervals. This process continued until all the munition carriers had neared the shaft's base. John then approached Ian's vantage point.

"I hope no one's wandering why supplies are taking so long to be delivered. We must get a team down into the complex to place that bomb. It must be done before they realize what's happening. Only then can we seal those blast doors behind it. The bomb has been set in a tamper-proof casing. This should stop anyone from preventing its deactivation. So once we activate its timer, there's no turning back." The truck carrying the bomb reversed into the loading dock. Once unloaded, it was then slowly wheeled into the elevator, surrounded by a well-armed assault group. The key was passed to its leader, and John and Ian watched the elevator drop from sight. The remaining teams then began their withdraw. John was left with Ian and a small security force to cover the final retreat.

Silence rained as machinery noise was muted, signalling the assault group's arrival at hell's gate. The mission had reached a critical point. The smell of anxiety, created by nervous sweat, wafted around each and every person deployed at the shaft's opening. Tension mounted as the start of the elevator's machinery again signalled the cable's movement and heralding the cab's return. Weapons were trained on the elevator cab as it slowly came into view. The doors opened, and familiar faces emerged, to everyone's relief. The leader gave two thumbs up as anxiety turned to euphoria.

A final load of explosives was quickly pact into the elevator, and it was sent on its last trip down. Weighted blast screens were drawn over the shaft before the cab could reach the bottom.

John then gave the order to evacuate the building. John and Ian boarded the last truck out. Reaching the end of the building, travelling along the back service road, John ordered their vehicle to stop. Anticipating the inevitable explosions, he counted down seconds on his watch. The ground trembled as explosives in the shaft detonated. This sound was followed by the rumble of debris filling the now-empty hole. An ensuing plume erupted through the building's roof like a cannon blast. As it formed into a cloud, Ian caught a brief glimpse of what he perceived to be Desate's smoky image mingling in its haze.

"Did anyone see that?" The collective answer 'see what,' told Ian he was the only one to have witnessed the apparition. An unanticipated effect from this demolition was the ground opening up and swallowing the building's rear structure. The shaft's void had consumed its rock encasement and was now feeding on surface fill. A subsidence trench then spread down the back road towards them. Speeding forward, they anxiously watched the expanding chasm gaining on them inch by inch. As this subsidence slowly settled behind them, again, they felt safe to stop. A deep rumble akin to an earthquake shook the ground as chasm fill dropped further, engulfing more land.

"This one is going to take some explaining away."

"We have someone inside the authority responsible for inspecting such disasters. A story has already been formulated. A gas leak throughout the day had supposedly filled the whole basement, and that was why the explosion was so great. As for you, Ian, you will be summoned to view the damage. You must then undertake company restructuring. Your daily routines must not deviate from past habits. However, information on company policies and directions will come from our organization. Trust me, it will be for the good of mankind and not its exploitation for the purpose of power. Our ultimate goal is world unity under the jurisdiction of a freely elected government. It will include a strong global police force that will replace private armies."

"Your talking Utopia John, and I'll be proud to play a role in that dream."

CHAPTER 41

The age of Aquarius

Peace and love became life's passwords. War protests were winning over propaganda spread by corrupt regimes: A sense of well-being stifled hate that had promoted barriers between race and creed.

As months passed, Ian's workload grew extensively. He was now obliged to designate authority to hand-picked underlings to give himself some well-deserved personal time. A pet project he'd been dreaming of was now able to command some of his precious time. Secretly a plan was developing for Barbara's dream church wedding, where they could renew their vows. He'd always promised her the pomp and ceremony only the church could offer.

Shrouding it in secrecy until the last minute, with friends' help playing a crucial role in this surprise celebration of love and devotion. The church chosen for the wedding was the little church of Ore, on Exmoor. The church Barbara had fallen in love with on that memorable visit, the one she remembered being immortalized in Lorna Doon. The church: depicted in the book where John Rid and Lorna pledged their vows so many years before.

The morning of the day planned for the reaffirming of their promises, Pam drove Barbara to Lynmouth. Barbara was totally unaware of this well-conceived plot. The pretense for this day's outing was a girl's time-out, come shopping expedition. The weather played its part in the overall scheme of things by presenting mother nature in all her glory. Ann parked near the village's harbour for some shopping and browsing. Strolling its main street reacquainted Barbara with this picturesque little fishing village. Her attitude on this day was far too laid back to be lured into a full-blown shopping frenzy. So, Pam's casual suggestion was to explore the countryside. It was met by Barbara with a relaxed feeling of acceptance.

"The church at Ore, I've heard you mention it: I think it would be as good a destination as any for our drive. What do you think, Barbara?"

"We've got the whole day to ourselves, so why not. It's such a lovely day. Perhaps we can stop in the village and explore." Pam gave a little giggle.

"Oh, we'll definitely stop there." Pam wasn't the best con artist in town, so Barbara sensed something fishy afoot. Her intrigue heightened as awareness of minor annoyances emerged. Why on such a lovely day, with no one to please but themselves, was Pam so preoccupied with time. She kept checking her watch and asking questions relating to time.

"How long do you think it'll take us to drive to Ore." Then came other little clues to Pam's hidden agenda, as she was seemingly consumed by irrelevances. "Are you absolutely sure you know the way?" The clincher for Barbara came with Pam's subsequent request that sounded more like a plea.

"We really should leave now Barbara."

"I can see your mind's set on leaving here, Pam, so let's dam well drive to Ore. Please don't drive like there's a deadline to make; I'd like to enjoy the scenery." Pam was now preoccupied with her personal plan to get Barbara to the church on time. Unintentionally she let slip another give-away.

"I will be able to drive slowly if we leave now. We can't be there later than," Pam stopped in mid-sentence. There was a moment of silence as she racked her brain for a plausible cover story.

"Don't want to be there later than what, Pam? What's the big deal about time? Exactly what is going on?"

"Well, Barbara, you will have to know soon anyway. Ian has planned a surprise for you at Ore, and my job is to get you there on time."

"On-time, Pam? On-time for what?" Pam started to cry as she hugged Barbara around the neck and blurted out the surprise.

"Ian's arranged a church wedding for you and him at Ore." Barbara's hands pressured her cheeks.

"Oh my god, how can I possibly have a church wedding today? Look at me, I would need a complete makeover, not to mention a wedding dress and everything that goes along with it."

"Ian's seen to everything, don't worry. I'm taking you to a mobile dressing room that's been set up there. He's been very thorough at covering all the bases. Everything you need for the occasion will be on hand. He even has a dressmaker on hand for any alterations that may be needed." It was now Barbara's turn to reveal a secret.

"I'm sure the dress will have to be let out slightly. I wanted Ian to be the first to know when he came home. I suppose the cat will be out of the bag in the fitting room." Pam interrupted with another tearful hug.

"You're pregnant, aren't you? What fantastic news." She again threw her arms around Barbara and kissed her cheek. This can only make today all the more memorable for the two of you." Barbara laughed and threw in her own satirical comment.

"Well, at least I won't be the first pregnant bride to waltz down the aisle, will I?"

"You can be so bad at times, Barbara. Now I suggested we get started; after all, there's no excuse for me having you arrive late anymore.

As soon as they arrived, Barbara was ushered to her dressing room. She and Pam were

then joined by Ann. All three of them were then pampered with the complete spa treatment before dressing for the occasion. Preparations inside the trailer resembled a shark-feeding frenzy, with bodies hustling to and fro until every last detail had been attended to.

Peering through a window, she could see the last few guests filing into the church. All that was left now was for John to collect her and escort her there. John arrived outside the dressing room, and the door was opened for her. He presented his arm as she walked down the steps; bridesmaids, Ann, and Pam followed. The wedding train paraded to the church door.

The organist was then given the signal to start the wedding march. Right on queue, they started down the aisle. Ian stood waiting at the alter, with Robert at his side. He turned and smiled as she was walking towards him. He never let his gaze wander until they faced the minister. As the ceremony began, shafts of sunlight poured through the windows. This effect enhanced the magnificent flower display personifying the church's serenity. It made for the most picturesque of settings. As the minister completed the ceremony, Ian kissed Barbara.

The quiet opening of the church door behind them had gone unnoticed by the congregation. Peterson stepped into the aisle. Razing a rifle, he took aim and fired off one quick shot. The bullet hit Ian squarely in the back.

As he fled the church. Robert ran down the aisle in hot pursuit. His outstretched arms were an attempt to obscure Peterson's chance of another clear shot. Peterson ran back through the doorway, slamming it shut behind himself. This slowed Robert down just enough to give him the leeway needed to jump into a waiting car. The car sped away with Peterson's door half-open, giving Robert the opportunity of one quick, precise shot. It struck Peterson's hip. He then phoned the police to put out an alert. Robert knew in his mind, there would be little chance of an arrest. Peterson was not a man to have undertaken such a scheme without planning his own escape thoroughly. Robert returned to the church, where Ian lay bleeding profusely over the floor, cradled in Barbara's arms.

CHAPTER 42

The whole story is revealed.

It was an inappropriate moment the waiter had chosen to visit our table. His arrival at my side halted my interpretation of Ian's story at a crucial point. Distracted by his presence, I looked up at him. A quick glance back to Sylvia told me my story to this point had in no way eased the pain her face was now portraying. How could it? There was no meaning for her until the final piece of the puzzle was in place—that last connecting part explaining why we were bound so tightly together. The connection that also served to keep us so far apart. Her clenched fist, under an angry chin, ensure her tight lips stay firmly closed. This obvious hurt I'd hoped to ease somewhat in my final sentence was left hanging. I had been so close to sharing the explanation that remained unsaid.

Looking away from me, she was now staring out of the window towards Puget Sound. I was not pleased. Her pain was my pain.

"I asked not to be disturbed," I snapped at the waiter in anger.

"I apologize for interrupting you, Sir, but my shift is over, and I was hoping it would be convenient for you to settle your bill before I leave." Realizing it was the hurt I was also carrying that caused my reaction made me remorseful. I'd vented my aggression on an innocent party.

"I'm sorry, I hadn't realized how long we'd been sitting here. Yes, that would be quite alright." He set the bill before me. I reached for my wallet and settled my account.

Once again, we were alone. I sensed Silvia was stifling the pain from a wound she'd thought had long since healed. Instinctively I reach out to comfort her before quickly realizing the reaction this would

undoubtedly evoke. I pulled my hand back unnoticed.

As she turned back to face me, I could see her pain changing to anger. A hard slap to my face was, I'm sure, all part of her healing processes.

"What has this story you've told me to do with the fact that you never showed up to meet me in Hawaii. I tried to contact you for weeks after, but my calls were never returned, and the letters I wrote were returned unopened. When I had accumulated enough leave, I flew to England and tried to find you. You were not at your apartment. It was as though you'd fallen off the face of the earth. Then I read in the newspapers how the great Jason Shaw was performing live in New York. According to one article (with his new love interest), there was a photograph of the two of you, so I gave up the chase. I requested a transfer and was assigned to the naval base at Bremerton. I've now been told I've been selected to serve with an elite branch of the military. I was to meet the head of that branch here today. There was only one reason I didn't walk out of this restaurant when shown to your table. I was in shock at the sight of seeing you sitting here."

"The last six months have not been easy for me, ether Sylvia. When I learned of your meeting today, I upped the time to meet you first and explain everything. Let me finish the story, and you'll understand what I did at that time. I thought it was best for both of us." Again, she turned away from me as if she had no interest in what I had to say. "It would have been best had we never seen each other again, but destiny's about to change all that. So, for both our sakes, you must know the whole truth before you join the company."

"Why would you think I would want to work for the company after what you have told me about it."

"Thanks to Ian's legacy, things have changed there. We work for the good of humanity now, but the old foe's still as strong as ever. Now please let me continue the story.

Ingrid was very friendly with Peterson until she found out what he was really like. She then would have nothing to do with him. However, by then, it was too late. Peterson had already achieved his perverted goals. Unbeknown to Ingrid, he had got to Ingrid's young sister Monica. The sister she'd continued to raise after your grandparent died. It wasn't until I had planned to meet you in Hawaii that I learned the whole story. I had just prepared my last report before my holiday and taken it to Robert's office, he was not there. I placed the document on his desk. There was a folder lying there with your name on it. How could I have imagined the deviation it was about to reek on our lives: But how could I resist knowing why there was a company file on the woman I was about to ask to marry me."

Silvia looked at me as if in disbelief, as I saw the anger draining from her face. "It told your life story, Sylvia. The schools you attended, your marks, where you graduated, and some very personal things about you. It said who your friends were, the food you liked, clothing styles, and sizes. It included how you attended arts and theatrical school and then surprised your friends by applying to naval college. How you graduated with honours and went on to a successful career in the navy. It also mentioned you're involved in naval intelligence."

"I don't see where this is leading, Jason. You already knew most of this."

"I always thought about how much you looked like Monica Jordan, the film star."

"I didn't think there was a need to tell you about Monica at that time, and as you probably now know, she's mother's younger sister. My mother brought us up together.

Although Monica is thirteen years older than me, she's more like a sister than an aunt."

"Sylvia, this part of the story, is going to be a great shock for you, but I must tell it. When Ian's coffee was spiked by Peterson the night in the office, the young girl coerced into having sex with Ian was Monica. I had to tell you his life story, so you'd understand he was a good decent man, an honourable man. When Ingrid found out what had happened, she brought Monica to the States. After you were born, Ingrid raised you as her own, with company help. The three of you were always well cared for.

Sylvia, now do you understand why I did what I did, your Ian's daughter, my half-sister."

We looked at each other and cried as we took each other's hands.

"Oh, Jason, what have we done." I squeezed her hands tightly. It was the first time I'd felt comfortable enough to touch her since she came into the restaurant.

"We weren't to blame Sylvia. How were we to know." We sat looking at each other for what seemed to be an eternity. I finally spoke.

"I must leave before Robert arrives. It would be best he did not know we'd ever met. You will know Robert as your uncle Bob." It was not easy to leave her there, but she now understood why I had to go.

Leaving the restaurant, I could see Robert walking towards me through the crowded market. He did not see me as I waited to see him enter the restaurant.

Robert walked to where Sylvia was sitting and greeted her with a kiss on the cheek.

"I'm sure you didn't expect to see me here today, my dear." Let me order some food and coffee. Then hopefully, we will not be disturbed. I have a long story to tell you."

THE END

Epilogue

It had been many years since the old jag's wheels had rolled down Weston's beachfront boulevard. Coming to rest opposite the promenade in designated parking, an older but graced by time, Barbara emerged.

Walking the promenade northward, she passed the old Grand Pier, recently ravaged by fire. Its chard remains symbolically reflecting its former illustrious past. The Winter Gardens Pavilion renovated and well maintained, stirred fond memories, stimulating an artiste's need to physically express those emotions. Reaching into her pocket, she took out her tape recorder to document words an older memory has a habit of misplacing. In the solitude of that early autumn morning, her thoughts came slowly, but as they formulated into a song, she sang softly into its microphone.

(Cobwebs of time)

In this mixed-up chaotic world, I now regard to be my life, faced with confusion and inner strife. Drawn like a magnet to the solitude of our special place, with memories ghosting through that time can not erase.

Then a breeze swept through my mind to clear the cobwebs spun by time, sweet memories flowing through of our love when it was new, and I thought of you --yes–I thought of you. Rekindling embers long thought cold, as I thought of you --yes–I thought of you again, my love.

Through portals opened in this calmer mind, I see reflections of a world not so unkind. How could our romance ever end? You were my lover, my confidant, my friend.

Then a breeze swept through my mind to clear the cobwebs spun by time, sweet memories flowing through of our love when it was new, and I thought of you --yes–I thought of you. Rekindling embers long thought cold, as I thought of you --yes–I thought of you again, my love.

Fresh sea air fan embers deep inside, giving warmth to this poor heart cruel fate has left behind. Why were you taken? Why did you have to go/ One of life's many mysteries I will never ever know.

Then a breeze swept through my mind to clear the cobwebs spun by time, sweet memories flowing through of our love when it was new, and I thought of you --yes–I thought of you. Rekindling embers long thought cold, as I thought of you --yes-- I'll always remember you, my love.

Lucifer's Lair: The Devils Domain

Anthony John Hoare